THE IMAGE BEARERS

THE IMAGE BEARERS

ANNIKA GOODWIN

This book is dedicated to Shelly Kenney, who wrote her courageous story in the hearts of her children and friends.

We can't wait to see you again. Save a place for us around the throne!

Acknowledgments

Sincere thanks to

Jesus, the Love of my life. I cannot thank You enough for all You've done for me.

Matt—my patient, gentle, and loving husband and dearest friend. Your consistent pronouncements of faith in this project keep me on track.

Mom and Dad, for believing in me and encouraging me, from the *Artist and Author's Kit* you made for me when I was a little girl, to listening to my ramblings about current writings—and for being the most precious friends I could ever have.

Chris Kaempfer and Dr. Jim Thress, for their knowledge of medical emergency procedures and terminology.

All who helped with editing and revision: John and Jan Goodwin, Matt Smith, Connie Jones, Barbara Goodwin, Danny Burd, Vicki Curry, and Lee Gaar.

Savannah Clark, for her help with this project.

Those who offered encouragement at just the right moment: Gwen Stites, Susie Quiroz, Claudia Manning, John Schulte, Connie Jones, Dawn and Randy Cook, TJ Tyler, Carri-Ann Bard, Karla Morris, and Mike Troy.

1

Ira Owens removed his glasses and pressed his thumb and index finger gently against his eyelids. "Maybe I *should* get the vision implant," he mumbled to the grid-work of monitors in front of him as he attempted to rub the soreness from his eyes. "My eyelids feel like they're lined with sandpaper."

"I can't believe you're using those spectacles. You realize no one has worn anything like that for years. You're a walking anachronism, Ira," the woman at the station to his right commented. The images on the monitors in front of her flipped from one drone's visual feed to the next. "I don't see how your eyes can take it, seeing the readouts the old-tech way."

Ira glanced at his sole companion in the Mid-south Sector Drone Readout Room. She was leaning back in her ergonomically designed chair, eyes closed; but he could see them moving back and forth as if she were in REM sleep, watching the direct feed of the monitors to the chip in her brain. "Now that I have the chip, I don't even have to open my eyes to see everything that's going on. If I think something is suspicious, I can immediately take host in the drone and move it closer for a better look. No more flipping switches and using hand controls. The drone becomes an extension—"

"—of your body, yes, I know." Ira finished her sentence for her.

"I wish you wouldn't interrupt like that. What do you have against the new tech? I guess I can understand some people being hesitant about the chip, because it's such a huge life change, but to not even get 2nd Sight, when you work in a job requiring you to scan monitors with your eyes for hours on end—it just seems a little stubborn or paranoid, like maybe you're one of those conspiracy theory people."

"Vicey, you know one of the main reasons I got the job was because I *didn't* have 'Sight. They wanted something uncomplicated and unconnected to fall back on, in case the tech malfunctioned. And I think that's why they haven't pushed for me to get chipped, either. Nevermind that I was head of the class in programming tech interface. Nevermind that I was in the think tank with Dr. Jo-Mo. They—" The gangly man suddenly shoved his glasses firmly back up the bridge of his nose and leaned forward to peer into one of the monitors. "What is *that?* Vice, come look at this."

"You know I won't see it in time if I unhook, Ira. Just give me the link to your feed."

Ira typed a few commands into the key console, his eyes never leaving the monitor. His companion tensed and leaned forward, although the images she was seeing were streaming through her mind, rather than in front of her face. "Is that a person? That's a girl!" she exclaimed, answering her own question. "How did she get there, that far from the outer docks? That's miles and miles away from, from anywhere!" Vicey chewed on her lower lip. "Well, what are you waiting for? Take the drone in closer. Bring her in."

Ira smiled wonderingly at the screen. "Why don't we just watch her for a while, and see what she does? If she doesn't know she's being monitored, we might be able to get some answers just from observation."

"Again, the old-fashioned way. We could also just chip her and get all we need in a matter of minutes," Vicey said impatiently. "I'm calling it in."

"Very well," Ira said, with a hint of disappointment. "But I'll do it. It was in my region, after all." He sent the information to his immediate supervisor and continued his vigil at the screen. There was something different about this one —not just the clothes or the antiquated pack she carried. It was something about the way she interacted with her environment. Most of the Discards or the Un-hooked seemed completely at odds with their surroundings when they ventured into the Preserve. The Discards who had never transitioned from smart phones to Vista-Visor clutched their phones, holding them inches from their faces as they navigated through forests and abandoned towns. The Unhooked kept their visors on, eyes glued to the readout, unwilling or unable to comprehend the data being fed to their natural senses by their physical surroundings. They reminded

Ira of the old flatscreen movies about submarines traveling through the mysterious depths of the ocean. They were completely insulated from their environment. A few who had lost their visor or their mind—there wasn't much difference, after all—huddled on the ground and covered their eyes, overwhelmed by the emptiness and terrified of what could be hiding behind the nearest bush. But this girl seemed to be looking at everything around her as if she were an integral part of her surroundings rather than an intruder passing through in her own self-contained little world. She didn't seem to be afraid. She looked as if she were on a great adventure.

Ira frowned thoughtfully as he zoomed in on her face. She was talking to someone. So maybe she was connected, after all. But how had she escaped detection until now? His thoughts were interrupted by his supervisor's voice in his earpiece. "Do nothing for now. Simply observe and keep the link opened to my channel." Ira frowned again. This was, indeed, out of the ordinary.

Unless. . . "That must be it," he said to himself.

"What's that, Ira?" Vicey asked. "What did they say?"

"They don't want me to interfere. They just want me to watch."

"But why would they do that?" Vicey exclaimed, rising slightly out of her chair. "Oh, of course," she said softly, a sly smile curving her lips. "That girl must be part of the operatives program Jo-Mo started."

"To fish out isolationist outposts?" Ira asked. "That's what I was just thinking. But to be honest, I always thought that program was a little far-fetched. That a whole community could survive completely unhooked from the State is hard to imagine."

"Well, for whatever reason, Dr. Moses thinks it's possible. And I bet you next week's download that this girl is one of his spies."

Ira seemed to deflate a little as he settled down into his chair. Why was he so disappointed?

The girl's face broadened into a smile as she stopped suddenly to watch a small hawk swoop down and snatch a vole out of the grass in the road ditch. She had to be plugged in. That's why she looked so happy and at ease. She wasn't alone at all.

Ira focused his attention on the gear she was carrying. He was especially intrigued by the odd-shaped framework of her pack, which appeared to be a curved piece of wood attached to the side. A length of cord was stretched from one end to the other. What purpose could it serve? A place to tie up a bedroll, perhaps? Suddenly, the girl shrugged and hefted the weight of the pack into a different position. As she did so, the curved framework slipped down her arm. She caught it deftly, her fingers wrapped around it in a familiar way. It reminded Ira of the way a violinist would hold the neck of a violin, or the way a sculptor would hold a hammer or chisel. That wasn't part of the pack. It was a tool of some sort. "A bow, of course!" he exclaimed out loud, surprised at his own ignorance. To his credit, Ira had only seen bows in museums. He knew some people possessed private collections of similar artifacts, but such extravagance was generally frowned upon. What purpose could the outpost program have in giving its operatives a primitive weapon? Surely they must have some sort of modern self-protection hidden on their person, so why the clumsy antique? He rubbed the stubble on his chin thoughtfully. Maybe she wasn't using it as a weapon. He had seen a display in the Smithsonian in which indigenous peoples of the State used them to start a fire. But there were much easier ways. Perhaps it was an effort to blend in with isolationist outposts, if they even existed. It was certainly an elaborate ruse. It made Ira glad he wasn't part of that program— not that he would have qualified for it.

Ira shifted uncomfortably in his chair. The recruits he had seen for the special ops program were a different sort: terribly focused, frighteningly loyal to the State, chipped with the normal protocols removed so they could quickly accumulate all the skills necessary to perform their tasks. Their performance was always exemplary. The flawless execution of their missions, coupled with their unflinching faithfulness to the State, left other government employees uncomfortable in their presence. Ira remembered the time he and the rest of the surveillance teams were introduced to a special ops unit, called a *Pod*. The teams were allowed to watch some of the training exercises in which a Pod worked to solve a potentially life-threatening problem. The tests were conducted in a containment area so there was no real danger to the observers, but the threat to the Pod was real. What disturbed him most was not their emotionless response to surroundings, but their uncanny ability to coordinate their efforts to complete a task. There was no talking. It seemed they knew exactly what needed to be done simply by making eye contact. They didn't even appear to break a sweat, calmly and efficiently preventing the breach of a container filled with what was purported to be a poison gas. To demonstrate that the threat was real, a seven-month-old Unspoken was positioned on a platform in the center of the room. At the end of the test, the Pod members all donned respirators, and the gas was released into the containment area. At this point, Ira turned away. He had no desire to see the subject gasping for breath.

"Oh, wow, it really was real!" Vicey, standing beside him, whispered excitedly. "This whole time I was thinking it was just a mock exercise. They could have been killed!"

Ira kept his eyes averted. "Is it over?" he asked.

Vicey stopped gaping at the scene through the glass window and stared at him in consternation. "Ira, it was scheduled for exit anyway. It wasn't spoken for. That's what happens to the Unspokens. This is a better exit than some of them get, I guarantee you that. Which way would you rather go—poison gas, or to be on the menu for a tiger at the zoo? Or even worse, a boa constrictor? The tigers don't need live meat, but I think some of the boas won't eat unless their prey is alive."

"Vicey, will you shut up? I don't want to think about it," Ira said in a hoarse whisper. He was beginning to feel sick to his stomach.

But Vicey would not be deterred. "Look at it. You can tell it had something genetically wrong with it, anyway. Probably Discard parents with no implants to prevent birth defects or the like. No wonder no one came forward in the first six months with a D.I.N.! Who would want something like that? Who has the money to take care of it? Especially a Discard. They don't have the means."

"You're right, Vicey. This was an act of compassion. How could I have been so insensitive?" Ira said, his voice laced with caustic sarcasm.

Vicey smiled warmly, completely oblivious to the ingenuous intent of Ira's remark. "I'm glad you feel better about it now. See, it's all a matter of perspective," she said cheerfully.

Ira glanced at the motionless bundle on the platform as the surveillance team began filing out of the observation deck. Its hair peeked out from a gray fleece cap in little red ringlets. D.I.N. or not, he couldn't suppress the feeling that this was wrong. It was just another exit, and a humane one, at that. It was better than being snake food, as Vicey had mentioned. He supposed zoo animals had to eat *something*, and since it was illegal to use animals as a food source anymore—even for other animals—then planned exits for Unspokens as part of the zoos' nutritional programs were a good use of an otherwise wasted resource. But the exits weren't performed before the public during visiting hours, as some citizens were still squeamish about the idea. They knew it happened—Congress had voted it in, just as they had voted in the Declaration of Intent to Nurture Initiative.

Ira began to follow the others to the Meet and Greet area, and looked one last time through the window. He paused, causing a coworker to bump into him. "Sorry," he mumbled, and stepped out of line to view the scene below. One of the Pod members was picking up the Unspoken. Suddenly a voice was heard over the intercom.

"That's not necessary, Jayka. We'll send in a clean-up crew."

Pod member Jayka seemed to hesitate momentarily. She looked as if she were studying the tiny form. Ira thought he detected a flicker of something resembling emotion cross her face. "Jayka, report to decontamination. Your mission was executed successfully and is complete," the voice continued.

Ira winced as Jayka unceremoniously dropped the bundle back onto the platform with a *thunk* and turned to join the others. What he had mistaken for compassion must have been mere curiosity. "*What kind of people are these?*" he mused.

When he met them at the Meet and Greet, he was taken totally by surprise. They were definitely professional, but also warm and responsive as they mingled with the surveillance team.

Which is why the behavior of the girl he had just detected with his drone was not surprising anymore. They were trained—programmed—to be efficient and at ease in whatever environment they encountered. Ira frowned thoughtfully and leaned back in his chair. This should prove to be interesting surveillance in an otherwise mundane region. He kept watch on the other screens, but couldn't help focusing most of his attention on the lone Pod-Op. Suddenly, she dropped to her knees, her hands raised to the sky. What was she doing *now*?

2

Selah let the light of the spring morning bathe her face in warmth. The sun had finally melted the frost that formed during her escape from the valley. She knelt on the pavement to give a moment of thanks, closing her eyes so she wouldn't be distracted by her new surroundings. "I will love You, oh Lord, my strength," she said softly. "Thank You for Your hand of protection." She laughed to herself as her stomach growled loudly. "And thank You for Your provision," she added as she lowered her pack and took out a piece of the jerky that Addy had given her the day before.

So much had transpired in the last twenty-four hours. She had finally realized God was calling her to the mission field. Before she could tell anyone of her plan, her family had been advised by the elders of their community to lock up Selah for observation, fearing she was either mentally ill or possessed by an evil spirit. Somehow her parents had known beforehand that she was leaving and had prepared a knapsack with things she would need for her journey. God had orchestrated everything to help her escape, and Selah was grateful; but the minute she passed one of the community's boundary trees, she knew she might never be able to return.

Selah stopped chewing the mouthful of salty jerky and cocked her head to one side. Several times in the past half hour, she thought she had heard something —a slight humming noise—but when she looked around, nothing was there. It almost sounded like the distant, steady drone of cicadas when the rising heat of a mid-summer morning shoves aside the refreshing cool of night. But this was the wrong time of year for cicadas.

The humming had stopped again, making her think she was just imagining things. She stood up and shouldered the pack. The road stretched before her, scrawled with the ragged scribble of weeds that found cracks in its crumbling surface, disappearing over a faraway hill to the north. Selah sighed and resumed walking. She was tired but determined to make some headway to her destination.

"Wherever that is," she said to herself wryly. Selah shook her head, scolding herself for the negative comment. She had made up her mind not to be discouraged, even though she didn't know where she was going. If she would continue north, the direction from which the original founders of her community had come, she would eventually run into civilization. God was the one who had asked her to go. She was convinced that if she did what she could do, He would do what she could not. "Being confident of this very thing, that He which hath begun a good work in you will perform it until the day of Jesus Christ,"[1] she said to herself. Her friend Miss Genevieve had continually reminded her of the importance of quoting God's promises out loud. Thinking of the elderly lady made her smile. If only Genevieve could see her now. "Maybe she *can*," Selah wondered, and glanced skyward. Maybe Jesus allowed little glimpses from heaven, just to show people how the seeds they had planted in this life were bearing fruit.

And then she saw it—just barely. It was only for a fraction of a second when she had looked up, but she thought she saw the sun reflect off of something high above her. Selah froze. That was definitely *not* her imagination. Was it merely a plane, or was it one of the surveillance drones she had heard about? Should she attempt to hide, or should she jump up and down to get noticed? She stifled a laugh as a thought crossed her mind. What would Garrison have done? "He probably waved a red flag," she chuckled to herself. Garrison, being first to leave, had done so for far different reasons. Almost a year had passed since her friend had left the valley—his curious, adventurous nature too strong to be detained by a boundary marker and the repeated threats of what might be "out there." Where was he now? Had he been intercepted by a drone like the one that might be hovering somewhere overhead? If so, how had he been received? With suspicion, or with open arms?

---

[1] Philippians 1:6, KJV

She kept her eyes on the sky until she thought she saw it again. If it was a drone, it had surely spotted her by now. Selah grinned and waved. If God didn't want her to be seen, she would remain hidden, just as her community had been hidden for generations. If He did want her to be found, then she must trust that it was all part of His plan. She thought she heard the humming noise again, a little louder, and her heart began to beat faster. "For God has not given me a spirit of fear, but of power, love, and a sound mind,"[2] she said aloud. She looked down again at the old road and began walking resolutely forward. The humming sound faded, and though she looked for it frequently, she could no longer see the distant object overhead.

Miles away in the Mid-south Sector Drone Readout Room, Ira Owens laughed under his breath. This operative seemed cocky. Not only had she detected the drone, even in stealth mode, but she had waved at it to let him know she knew she was being watched. He wondered where she was going. Would she be successful in finding an isolationist community? It would be extremely difficult to hide anything from the drones, which is another reason Ira was skeptical of the existence of any pockets of resistance remaining. A few doomsday prepping groups had been easily discovered in the early days of the Great Consolidation. Much later, various cults had made unsuccessful attempts to leave, but the records showed nothing new had turned up in the last sixty years. Most people wanted the comfort of knowing they were being watched over and provided for. As the State settled into the role of the spiritual hub of humanism and the world's religions were blended into one all-encompassing, State-sponsored church that met its congregants' needs through implants, meaningful work placement, relationship coordination and the miraculous chip, the idea of leaving was viewed as the thought of a sociopath. Such behavior was rarely understood by the average citizen. It was certainly not tolerated by the State.

But if a few eccentric individuals wanted to be self-sufficient and live like they wanted to, was it really a threat? Ira grimaced. It *was* a threat, actually. It was a threat to everything the State stood for. Mother State couldn't hold itself

---

[2] See 2 Timothy 1:7

up as the answer to everyone's problems if private citizens found self-reliance was not only possible, but enjoyable. The current system would begin to crumble, starting with the Discards in the outer docks. Although they made a lot of noise about not being chipped and implanted by the State, Discards were still dependent on the government for food and medical supplies. And in a way, the State was dependent upon them. Those who considered them non-productive citizens were oblivious to the fact that they provided a buffer between society and anarchy. Discards, often sickly and seemingly without a purpose in modern society, were both pitied and abhorred. Citizens with a compassionate viewpoint donated to the Discard Outreach, sending emissaries of the State to recruit outer docks youth to a better way of life, but they rarely set foot there themselves. Discards were valuable to Mother State, simply because they pointed to how miserable you could be without her. To remove that example would leave disenchanted citizens room to wonder what it would be like without the government breathing down your neck.

Ira scowled and quickly rubbed his forehead as if to massage a headache. It wouldn't do to have the camera that monitored readout room employees revealing his inner feelings of distaste. He could be questioned later about his emotional state during the shift and might be given time off to recuperate from work-related stress. Ira did not want time off, and he didn't need a ladder-climbing supervisor jumping to conclusions about him and showing how proactive they could be. *Even the monitors have monitors,* Ira thought to himself. His eyes narrowed and he pretended to adjust his glasses as he focused on the Pod-Op once again. If he continued this line of thought, he would certainly have to work on his poker face.

He wondered how long the girl would continue on this road. For some reason he had expected Pod-Ops to spend most of their time sneaking through the woods on their mission to locate secret communes. This one had stuck to the road since he had spotted her. Maybe she had already covered a wilderness area she had been assigned and was on her way to another, and the road was the simplest means of getting there. It didn't seem a very efficient way to operate, when State-provided transportation could simply pick her up and drop her off near the next site. Perhaps the risk of being seen collaborating with the State was too great, if indeed she was adopting the persona of a disgruntled citizen looking for asylum or a wandering vagrant looking for a place to stay the night.

On the other hand, what if she had already discovered an outpost and was simply heading back to civilization to report her findings? What if the wave she had given him earlier was her signal that she was ready to come in from the field and he had misinterpreted it? That had been at least an hour ago. He wondered if he should report it. Ira sat back in his chair as he thought it over. She didn't need to give him a signal. She could simply make a report over a secure channel to whomever she was talking to every once in a while.

Ira turned the drone back down the road to the southwest—the direction from which she had come. There might be a way to find out if she had discovered something. He was certain that in his past surveillance, he had scanned every acre of this sector; but if she had found something in the woods near the point where he had spotted her on the road, maybe he could see it now that he could narrow his search. He brought the drone back to the correct coordinates and veered to the east, over a mass of bristly trees. This time of year, he should be able to see something if anything was there, because spring leaves hadn't yet emerged in their full growth to block his view. And there was always thermal scanning, which was reasonably accurate at being able to distinguish between humans and animals.

He brought the drone lower than he normally would have, trying to antici-pate the direction she would have traveled, and engaged the thermal scanning system. Immediately, he picked up an object below, and his pulse rate quick-ened. It was thirty feet off the ground. Suddenly it seemed to sail through the air and stop abruptly, still at least twenty-five feet above the forest floor. "Ira, you idiot," he said to himself. It was obviously a squirrel. He should have known by the small amount of heat it was generating.

Ira moved the drone on through the forest just above the tree line, down what seemed to be the rim of a valley. A creek below tumbled over the rocks in its bed, seemingly anxious to be on its way. It meandered through the valley, which was dispersed with old, overgrown fields and what appeared to have been an orchard at one time. A barn stood precariously at one end of the valley, its graying boards warped by sun, rain, and time. The corral that surrounded it was missing most of its rails and a few of its posts. This area didn't appear to have seen any human activity for over a hundred years. Thermal scanning revealed nothing throughout the wooded part of the valley except squirrels, a wild turkey doing some sort of ridiculous mating display for a few uninterested hens, and a healthy number of deer. The wildlife population of the valley seemed normal enough, although Ira was surprised not to see any mountain lions anywhere in the vicinity. They were fairly common in areas with an abundance of deer, and although secretive, were not impossible to locate with thermal imaging. But he was looking for people, after all, and had seen no sign of recent human activity whatsoever. He sighed, and a feeling of sadness settled over him as he maneuvered the drone back over the ridgeline to what was once U.S. Highway 63. If the girl had found an isolationist outpost, it certainly wasn't here. What would he have done if he *had* located it? It would have to be reported. The people would be evacuated and imprisoned and possibly executed, and the dream that they had of a different way of life would die with them. He was suddenly glad he had found nothing, and continued toward the girl's present location as she trekked north on Highway 63.

3

"Hey, Clucky! How's that fuzz ball doing?" Asha Merrit's blond curls cascaded down her shoulder as she bent over to toss a stale piece of cornbread into the isolation pen. The Black Australorp hen gingerly stepped out of her nesting box, wings lowered and feathers fluffed. Asha smiled slightly as she watched the extra set of tiny legs appear from under the hen's soft feathers, scrambling to keep up with mama. It was a little extra work to keep the pair separated from the rest of the flock; but Selah had insisted on it, knowing how brutal chickens could be to any member of the flock that was smaller and weaker.

Asha sighed deeply and rubbed her eyes. She had cried all night, praying desperately for her daughter's protection as she escaped the valley. Selah was on her own now, so Asha did the only thing she could still do as a mother—she interceded for her in prayer. Selah was safe from the community elders, since they would never follow her past the boundaries; but what awaited her back in the Old Country? Would she be successful in her attempts to spread the gospel, or would she be locked away forever and her message silenced? Asha imagined the awful things that might be done to make her reveal the location of the hidden community. Horrible scenarios began to unfold in her mind, and the bucket of grain she carried for the other hens clattered to the ground as she covered her face with her hands. "I cannot think this way," she whispered. "Father, she's in Your hands now." Asha didn't think she had any tears left to cry, but they began to flow down her cheeks again. Suddenly, an image began to take shape in her mind until its presence banished the darkness to the corners of her awareness. It was a fist, engulfed in flames. The skin on the hand didn't blister or melt in the heat, and it remained tightly clenched. As Asha was wondering where the thought had come from, the image of the fist changed. Asha could hear the sound of a howling wind which came and swirled about the hand, enveloping it in sheets of rain. The flame was extinguished, but after the rain came a barrage of hail that pelted the fist with larger and larger hailstones. The fist was immoveable. Hail the size of basketballs bounced off of it, but the hand was not broken, cut or bruised. Finally, the atmosphere around it changed to a calm that Asha could feel to the core of her being. As she watched, the fingers opened to reveal a tiny figure in the palm. Asha felt like she was right there with the figure—like she was small and the hand was gigantic. Then the figure turned and she could see it was Selah. She was perfectly fine—protected from the fire, the wind, and the hail by the giant hand. Asha laughed out loud and opened her eyes. What was it she had said right before she had seen the fist? "Father, she's in your hands now," Asha repeated. "Thank you, Lord," she said, closing her eyes and lifting her face to the sky.

Suddenly, she became aware of a soft humming noise. She opened her eyes and looked around. She thought she saw the flicker of a shadow pass over the ground. Clucky had stopped eating her cornbread and was giving warning clucks to her chick, tucking it back under her wings. Seconds later, the humming faded as quickly as it had begun. Asha blinked and wondered if it were an after-effect of the vision she had just had; but Clucky had heard it, too. The hen was looking toward the sky as if scanning it for a hawk. When no hawk appeared, she went back to her cornbread, pushing some of it toward the chick as she let it back out from under her wings.

Asha finished feeding the chickens and made her way to the barn. Jackson was milking Maggie. After their morning chores were complete, the couple was expected to appear at the community hall for "some answers." That's how Seth had phrased it. Asha wondered if it would be a repeat of last year's interrogation of Selah when Garrison left. *It didn't matter*, she realized, surprised by the boldness she felt. Selah was going to be alright, that much she knew from the vision.

When she reached the barn, she found Jackson leading Maggie to the stanchion with a makeshift halter. "You haven't started yet?" Asha was puzzled. Maggie never had to be led into the barn. Knowing she always got her grain during milking, she was usually waiting inside, stomping her hoof against the feed trough.

"Something spooked her," Jackson said, his eyebrows wrinkled into a quizzical expression. "What's strange is, I think I might have heard something overhead the same time she got spooked. But I never saw anything."

"Did it sound like a bunch of mosquitoes?" Asha asked.

"More like cicadas. And I only heard it for a second or two, but Maggie acted like she saw a ghost."

"I heard that humming noise, too. And Clucky acted scared at the same time I heard it. But you should have seen what I saw!" Asha bubbled over with excitement to tell him about the vision.

"You saw it? What was it?"

"No, I didn't see whatever made the noise. I had a vision. And I know now that Selah is going to be okay." Asha proceeded to tell Jackson what she had seen.

"He has her safe in the hollow of His hand," he said when she was finished, his eyes glistening.

When the milk pail was full and stored in the spring house, the two made their way to the community hall, with Asha clinging tightly to Jackson's arm. "We did the right thing, didn't we—even if no one here agrees with us?" she said. It was more of a statement than a question, because the image of Selah in God's hand had reassured her.

"Yes, we did." Jackson's eyes were on the road ahead, but he was remembering the dream he had a few weeks ago after he had received the baptism in the Holy Spirit. He hadn't understood it then, but now it made perfect sense.

The dream was so real that his emotions were close to the surface; and when he had awakened, his pillowslip had been wet with tears. In the dream, he was following Garrison down the path to the creek, pleading with him not to leave. "You don't want to do this, son. Come back with me. It's getting dark. Think of your parents, how they'll worry. Think of the rest of us you may be putting in danger by leaving." Garrison was laughing at him; and strangely enough, he was bouncing a basketball down the trail as he walked. Occasionally, he would dodge and dart away from an imaginary player, feigning his next move, then spinning in another direction. "Garrison, listen to me. You don't know what they may do to you once they find you. This isn't a game!" Jackson shouted. Garrison shot him a glance—and then shot him the ball. It hit Jackson's hands with such force that they were slammed against his midsection, and the wind was knocked out of him. He stumbled backwards and then looked up in time to see Garrison skirt around the roots of a boundary tree and disappear. Jackson took a step forward, and the tree grew in size. Its blackened "X" designating it as a boundary seemed to pulsate, vibrating in the growing darkness. *How is that possible?* Jackson wondered to himself. When he took a step toward the tree, the vibrating grew stronger and crescendoed to a deafening roar. Jackson dropped the ball, put his hands over his ears, and closed his eyes, trying in vain to shut out the noise that seemed to bounce his heart around in his ribcage. Suddenly, the noise stopped. He felt a tap on his shoulder. He opened his eyes.

"Hi, Daddy," Selah said. She was wearing a wide smile. There was something different about her, but he didn't recognize it immediately. As he was trying to figure out what was different, he realized she was walking down the trail in the same direction as Garrison. She was headed for the boundary tree.

"Selah, you can't go any closer to that boundary. The tree forbids it! I know this sounds crazy, but it's alive! It started making this sound, and I thought it would break my eardrums!" Selah looked in the direction of the tree, but she didn't seem to see it. She was looking beyond the tree at something he couldn't see. "What are you looking at, Selah?" he asked; and as he watched her, he realized what was different about her. She was glowing. A light was emanating from her that pushed at the shadows on the trail and threatened the approaching darkness of night.

"Don't you see it, Dad?" she asked. "It's dark over there. How are they going to see without any light?"

"Who are *they?* What do you mean?" Jackson watched his daughter carefully. She seemed so confident of what she was doing. A great peace settled over him, although he couldn't explain why. "Here," he said, and retrieved the ball from where it had rolled behind a scraggly clump of witch-hazel. "Take this with you." He handed her the ball, wondering why he was offering it to her and what good it could possibly do. As she stretched out her hands to receive it, the ball was suddenly a bag filled with items necessary for a journey. A book flopped out of the pack onto the ground. When Jackson picked it up to hand it to her, he saw it was a Bible. "I can't forget *that*," Selah said; and as she opened it, the night sky was flooded with a light as bright as the sun. Jackson had awakened to sunlight pouring through his window and assaulting his eyelids with its brightness.

Yes. They had made the right decision—it didn't matter how Seth and the others saw it. But Jackson was curious and not a little apprehensive about what would be done. Would they be locked up, as Seth and the members of the board had threatened to lock up Selah for observation? He wondered what he should tell them, but his mind kept coming back to a scripture in Luke in which Jesus was instructing his disciples what to do when they were taken prisoner and brought before the rulers of the day: "Settle it therefore in your minds, not to meditate beforehand how to answer; for I will give you a mouth and wisdom, which none of your adversaries will be able to withstand or contradict."[3]

"Lord, help us to speak the words You would have us to speak," Jackson prayed and squeezed Asha's hand in reassurance.

The community hall was just ahead. Seth's daughter, Sadie, and his son, Zack, were outside the front door with a few of the other youth. As Jackson and Asha walked up the steps, Sadie stepped timidly forward. "It's a closed meeting," she volunteered. "That's why we're not going in." Jackson stopped on the stairs and wondered what to say. "What I mean is, not everyone feels the way they do— the board, that is," Sadie continued.

Jackson felt Asha tense up beside him. "Sadie, you shouldn't tell that to any-one," she began. "Not yet, anyway," she added as Sadie's face fell. It had taken tremendous courage for the girl to reveal she didn't agree with her father. "It's just too dangerous right now."

"Don't you worry about us, Mrs. Merrit," Zack said in a low voice. "Don't think we all like being cooped up here. And now that we know it's possible to leave…"

"But we don't know what happened to them," Asha began, and then remembered her vision about Selah. She knew Selah was going to be okay, but that was

---

[3] Luke 21:14-15 RSV

because God had ordained her to leave and take the gospel with her. "The thing is, Selah didn't leave because she didn't like it here. She left because—" Asha's explanation was broken off as the door to the hall opened and Seth stepped out onto the porch.

"What are you kids doing here? You know this is a closed meeting," he said sternly. "Sadie, you're supposed to be home helping your mother. Zack, didn't I tell you to check on the heifers in the south pasture?" Seth's brows knit into a network of suspicion. "What have you all been talking about?"

Jackson came to their rescue. "I think they just wanted to let us know we don't need to be nervous about this meeting since we're all brothers and sisters in Christ." He smiled meaningfully at Seth, who narrowed his eyes.

"This is a closed meeting. No one but the board and the Merrits are attending," he said, and stopped as a loud, jovial voice was heard from within the building. "What? What is he doing here?" Seth asked as he turned to go back inside. Jackson glanced at Asha and grinned as they followed him into the hall. They knew that voice. It was Payton Hamby.

4

"Brother Seth! Come on back in. You folks must think I have some explaining to do. I know I said I was going on sabbatical—and I *am* taking time out to study and have a time of refreshing in the Lord—but I was just really surprised how much I already miss you all," Payton said merrily, clapping Riley Rosales on the back. Riley's eyes bugged out, and he stumbled forward at the rough display of affection; but his expression betrayed his delight and relief at having Payton at the meeting.

"What are you smiling about, Riley?" Seth growled. Riley cleared his throat and stared at the floorboards. Seth spun around to face Payton. "And what do you mean, you miss us? It's only been a day since you declared your sabbatical."

Jackson watched Seth in growing amazement. He was acting like a coon caught in a hen house, trying to decide whether to bolt or bite. It was fear, Jackson suddenly realized—but whether or not he was afraid for the safety of the community or at having his authority challenged, Jackson couldn't tell.

"Has it only been a day? It seems like longer." Payton scratched the back of his head as if it would stimulate his thinking process. "I guess it was just the idea of it all that made it seem more like a week. Anyway, after the big commotion that went on last night with Selah scootin' outta here, I thought you all might be holding a meeting this morning."

"How did you know Selah had left?" Seth asked suspiciously. His frown deepened. "Did you know about it beforehand?"

"No, indeed," Payton said honestly. "But I knew something was up when I heard the alarm being rung. And of course, Riley and Ethel came by our place last night to check if Selah might be there." He smiled gratefully at Riley. "I assume it's alright for me to be here, since I am still the acting pastor, even if I am on sabbatical. This is too important of an issue to ignore. I can't just stay in my hole and pretend nothing's wrong when folks are upset and parents are worried." He looked sympathetically at Jackson and Asha, who smiled slightly in return.

"If you assumed you would be welcome here, why did you sneak in the back door?" Seth accused.

"Sneak in? Well, I wasn't sneaking; but I didn't want to fight through that wad of young people on the porch," Payton explained. "The back door was easier, so I came in that way."

"You have an explanation for everything, don't you?" Seth said exasperatedly.

"It's easy to give the answers when you don't have anything to hide. Which is why I'd like to ask if we can open up this meeting to the entire community. There's much that needs to be said which wasn't generally known before Miss Genevieve passed away. It will shed a lot of light about the changes that are going on in our community, and I think the people need to hear it."

Something almost imperceptible had changed while Payton was talking. The air was charged with it—a sense of strength, power, and peace. It had blown softly into the room and settled on Payton as he spoke.

Jackson watched as the faces of the board members seemed to soften. They were still worried, but they seemed more inclined to listen to Brother Hamby than to dismiss him. Seth, however, seemed even more agitated. "That is the last thing that needs to happen!" Seth exclaimed.

"Actually," Clive Coffelt began, "I think it might be the right thing to do. Get everything out in the open."

"I agree. Maybe then we can understand just exactly what happened to start this whole thing," Joe Breedon broke in.

"It does seem wrong to keep the others in the dark, if Brother Hamby has some new information," Joan Ferrel added.

Seth stared at them, aghast. "We don't need to stir up a hornet's nest. We need to get this situation under control before it spreads to our children! I know mine were out on the porch just now, wanting to know what's going on, when I had told Sadie to help her mother and distinctly instructed Zack to check on the cows. This is how situations escalate. This is where it starts: rebellion."

"I don't reckon I would exactly call being curious an act of rebellion. I'm sure they meant to go help back at your place as soon as they found out what was going on," Riley said affably, then stopped short as Seth glowered at him.

"I'm not even sure why you're a member of this board," Seth said in a condescending tone, looking at Riley pointedly.

"I'll tell you why," Payton rose to Riley's defense. "He has the heart of a servant, and the spirit of a peacemaker: two traits which are very necessary when making decisions involving a flock of believers. Now, I'm not advocating we allow our children to ignore our instruction," at this, Payton looked at Seth and smiled gently, "but this situation concerns them, because it involves one—actually two—of their peers. And as your pastor, I'm advising the board that the entire community should be present for these proceedings."

"I'm not listening to anymore of this hogwash—" Seth began.

"Wouldn't you agree, Brother Beardsley, that one of the best ways to maintain calm and control in a situation is to understand it?" Payton interjected. "There's always more to people's actions than meets the eye. I'll be the first to admit I was hard on Selah after Garrison left, because I thought they were scheming together; and I thought I had to maintain control to protect this community. I found out later I was wrong about so many things. I was trying to squelch a rebellion that didn't even exist. I want to set the record straight about Genevieve, Selah, and Garrison. And if we don't, we may end up unintentionally *starting* a rebellion by causing a disconnect between ourselves and the younger generation."

Seth opened his mouth to say something, but Joan Ferrel raised her hand and quickly said, "All in favor of having an open meeting, say 'Aye.'"

Seth watched with pursed lips as the other board members all said, "Aye," in unison. Then he turned and quietly walked toward the front door.

"Brother Seth?" Clive Coffelt called out questioningly. "Are you going out to let folks know the meeting is open to everyone?"

Seth turned back to face the group, and the disgust was evident in his voice. "I most certainly am *not*. I hereby resign from the board and thereby wash my hands of this whole business. If you want to turn yourselves over to the State, go right ahead. As for me and my house, we will stay on our side of the valley.

Maybe the Lord will continue to preserve and protect us, even if the rest of the community wants to go against His will."

"Will you at least come to the town meeting?" Payton asked. "You are still a member of this community. You need to know, too."

"My family will not be in attendance," Seth began, but was interrupted by the sound of the bell being rung outside. The group in the hall froze for an instant, and then Seth's face grew red with rage. "It's those kids!" he bellowed, and was at the door in two giant strides.

"You kids have no business ringing that alarm! It's only for emergency situations," Seth yelled as he rushed down the steps toward a red-headed, freckle-faced boy who was frantically beating the community's makeshift bell with a piece of rebar.

"But it *is* an emergency!" cried the boy with all the authority an eight-year-old could muster. "Zack is hurt real bad! One of Mr. Breedon's bulls got in with your heifer, and Zack tried to get him out, an'—"

"That's a lie. There's no way Zack could have already made it all the way to the south pasture," Seth interrupted. "Some of the older kids put you up to this, didn't they, Logan? It's all right. You can tell me. They're the ones who're going to be in real trouble."

"They're already in real trouble! Zack is really hurt!" Logan was practically sobbing now, and a small crowd was gathering from every direction.

"We'll see about that," Seth said, but doubt had crept around the edge of his confidence. "Take us to him."

Joe Breedon, who had been listening from the porch, took the steps in one leap and headed toward the Beardsley place.

"Joe, I'm pretty sure this is all a story," Seth called after him. "I've got them in that far pasture..."

"No!" Logan said tearfully. "The bull got in with the open heifer you had sorted out in a pen right there by your barn. An' he got Zack down on the ground and he couldn't get away from 'im."

Seth's face turned ashen and he broke into a run, with Jackson close behind. Doc Stratton, who had arrived with his bag in hand in time to hear Logan's account, ran after them. Payton turned toward those who had gathered at the alarm bell. "Let's hold Zack up in prayer. His healing was paid for by the beating Jesus took for us.[4] We need to reach out in faith. If you have any doubt that God will heal Zack, please stay behind. We need to be in agreement and not doubt that what God said He would do, He will do," he urged, then turned down the road, praying audibly. Some of the crowd hesitated for a second, then resolves seemed to firm as their eyes met. As a unit, they followed their pastor, some of them running to keep up. Sounds of whispered prayers swept through the crowd like the varying currents in a river, individual voices surfacing in fervency as they continued toward the scene of the accident, unified in their purpose.

Seth and Jackson arrived at the corral in time to see Joe Breedon shooing the heifer out of the pen into the adjoining pasture. The bull followed, and Joe fastened the gate behind them. Sadie was kneeling down by Zack's crumpled form, applying pressure to a gash on his head with the wadded-up hem of her dress. Kiley, Seth's wife, was trying to clean cuts and scrapes with a wet cloth, her hands shaking. "Zack!" Seth cried hoarsely. "Zack!" He touched him tentatively, afraid to do more damage.

"Dad, I should've come—got help—before I tried to mess with—that bull," Zack said apologetically between gasps of pain.

Doc Stratton crawled through the corral fence and immediately began feeling the young man for broken bones and searching for any visible signs of internal injuries. "Well, Doc?" Seth asked weakly. Zack moaned again and then lost consciousness.

Doc Stratton sighed. "He definitely has a broken leg and arm, but what I'm more worried about is this," he said, indicating a bluish discoloration on Zack's abdomen. "You see the swelling here? He's been stomped, and there's no telling what kind of damage has been done to his liver. This is beyond my scope."

"There's nothing you can do? Absolutely nothing?" Kiley whispered desperately.

As Doc Stratton shook his head, Seth raised his head to the sky and yelled, "God! Save my boy! Save my Zack!"

---

[4] See 1 Peter 2:24

At that moment, Payton and the rest of the community arrived and began filing through the small gate on the side of the corral that faced the road. "How does it look, Doc?" Payton asked softly.

Doc Stratton's lips formed a thin line, and he shook his head quickly in reply. Payton glanced at Seth, who seemed frozen in fear, his mouth opened in a twisted gasp. "Brother Seth, Sister Kiley, we're all here in agreement," he said, his voice resonating with strength and calm. "We've been praying since we left the community hall, and we're going to pray now for Zack to receive his healing." At that, Payton reached his hand out to touch Zack's forehead.

Suddenly, Seth grabbed Payton's hand and jerked it away. "You keep away from my family!" he cried, his voice ragged with emotion.

Kiley's eyes were wide with shock. "What are you—why don't you want—"

"You don't know what's happened in the last half hour!" Seth whispered hoarsely.

"But God is our only hope!" Kiley cried desperately.

"Yes, He is! And that's why we're not going to allow this false teacher to pray for our boy!" Seth said loudly.

"False teacher?" Sadie exclaimed. "Just because you don't agree with him doesn't mean he's a false teacher."

"That's enough out of you," Seth reprimanded the girl.

"Oh, can you please just quit your arguing and pray for our *son!*" Kiley exclaimed, looking wildly from Seth to Payton.

"Brother Seth, our ancestors left the Old Country so we would be free to serve God as we want, so we could raise our children to know Jesus is the only Way," Payton said softly. "I know that you and I don't agree on everything, but I believe we agree on this: there is power in the name of Jesus. He is the Way, the Truth and the Life.[5] He said if we would ask, we would receive. He said if two or three agree together on anything we would ask, it would be done. Where two or three are gathered in His name, He is right there with them.[6] Now, as Zack's father, he is under your authority. If you would lead us in prayer, would you allow me to pray with you?"

---

[5] See John 14:6
[6] See Matthew 18:19-20

Seth looked at Payton, taken off guard. The expression on his face softened, and he nodded quietly. The crowd moved in closer as the two men huddled over Zack's still form. Kiley prayed silently, nearly overcome with emotion. Addy Hamby slipped through the crowd and put her arm around Kiley's shoulders, praying with her. "Oh, great God in heaven," Seth began his prayer in a stilted manner, but then his voice broke as the desperation of the situation set in. "You said You would be with us in trouble.[7] Well, Zack is in trouble! You are our only hope. We ask that You heal him, in the name of Jesus." Seth stopped abruptly, no longer able to speak.

"So be it, Lord. We have come together and agree in the name of Your Son, Jesus—the name that is above every name." Payton said simply and squeezed Seth's shoulder comfortingly.

"While he's unconscious, I'm going to try to set the broken bones," Doc Stratton said. "I'd prefer to do that right here, instead of risking more damage by moving him around. While I'm doing that, if someone can run back to my place for a stretcher, we can move him into the house afterward."

"I'll get it," Jackson offered, and took off running down the road.

Doc reached into his bag. "Okay, now, the first thing I need is—"

Suddenly, Sadie let out a little squeal. "What's going on with his arm?"

Seth, Kiley, Payton, and Sadie all watched as the muscles in Zack's broken arm twitched, and the arm itself moved slightly. "It's probably just the nerves," Payton tried to reassure her, but then all four of them jumped as Zack's broken leg, which was bent at an awkward angle, began moving back in place on its own.

"Look at his stomach!" Doc exclaimed in spite of himself. The swelling was going down before their eyes. Doc gingerly assessed the arm and then moved to the leg. "The bones have been set. In fact, I can find no sign of damage!" he said excitedly as he felt up and down the limbs. As he tried to assess Zack's abdomen, the young man woke up and cried out. "Hey, Doc! That tickles!"

Payton could contain himself no longer. He was up and his feet, jumping up and down in the corral. "Wooohooooo! Praise the name of Jesus! Praise Great God, Almighty! He is *Jehovah Rapha,* the God who Heals!"[8]

---

[7] See Psalm 91:15
[8] See Exodus 15:26

"Thank you, Jesus!" Kiley cried, tears streaming down her face.

Seth seemed dumbfounded as he sat back on his haunches. "Well, I'll be," he said slowly.

Sadie laughed and squeezed her brother around the neck.

"Stop it, Sadie, you're choking me!" Zack protested.

"Can you stand?" Doc asked timidly, and the men helped Zack to his feet.

"Hallelujah!" someone in the crowd shouted as they saw Zack get up off the ground, and the whole crowd erupted in cries of *"Praise God," "Thank you, Jesus,"* and *"Hallelujah!"*

Just then, Jackson trotted up, the rolled-up stretcher tucked under his arm. "What'd I miss?" he asked confusedly.

"Oh, Jackson! You just missed a miracle, that's all!" Asha cried, and pushed him to the front of the crowd where Zack could be seen walking around over the area where he had just been trampled.

Suddenly, the youth looked up and stomped the dirt that marked the scene of the accident, a smile spreading across his face. "Under my feet! Under my feet!" he chanted. It was the beginning of an old song which told of where God had placed the enemy. The crowd took up the chant with him.

In all the excitement, Joe approached Seth quietly and pulled him aside. "I'd like to dispose of that bull. I don't want to risk any more lives by having him around or even taking him back to my place to do it. Do you mind if I take care of it right here?" he asked. "He's probably tough and not very tasty, but the meat is all yours if you want it."

Seth nodded. "That would be fine. But really, if Zack had handled things differently, this all could have been avoided. You don't need to give us the meat."

"I want to. Everyone knows that bull is meaner than a snake. He comes from a long line of cantankerous bulls. I should've killed him long before something like this happened. I'd be glad to let you have my best heifer, too—not that it makes up for it," Joe said soberly.

"No, sir. You keep your heifer," Seth replied.

"I'll go get the gun," Joe said as he turned to walk back to his house. The Breedons were the keeper of the community's only firearm. Joe's great grandfather had donated *his* grandfather's 308 Winchester to the Stavesville Historical Farm where he worked when the Federal Firearm Buy-back Plan negated the special historical permit allowing him to have it in his home. When they left the Old Country, John Breedon had "un-donated it," as he liked to say, along with several boxes of ammo, a reloading press, and all the other equipment and supplies needed to reload bullets.

In a matter of minutes, Zack was helping butcher the bull that had nearly killed him. Seth insisted on giving the meat away to anyone who wanted some. Almost every family ended up taking a portion, even if they didn't really need it at the time. "It just seems like we're taking away the spoils of war," Addy said triumphantly.

"What the enemy meant for evil, God turned around for good,"[9] Payton remarked. "It's been a long time since I have seen this kind of unity in our little valley, eh Seth?"

Seth seemed not to have heard and called Logan over to him. "Logan, this is the best I could find," he said, handing the copper-headed boy several slices of rib-eye. "I'm sorry I didn't believe you at first."

Logan took the meat, a grin dimpling his freckled cheeks. "That's okay, Brother Beardsley," he said. "I'm glad you decided to let God heal Zack."

Seth's forehead wrinkled in protest. "Let God heal. . ."

"Thanks!" Logan said quickly and skipped over to his father, who was working to repair the top panel of the corral fence where the bull had busted it. Payton watched as Seth seemed to consider the statement. He looked away quickly when Seth noticed him staring.

"It's a good day, Brother Seth," he said quietly.

"Yes. It could have ended very differently," Seth remarked, his eyes still following the red-headed boy.

---

[9] See Genesis 50:20

5

Macy rested her freckled muzzle primly on her paws. Her human had not yet awakened, and she was growing restless. Spring sunlight was cautiously slanting through the windows of the little cabin. The breakfast sounds of a skillet clanking on a woodstove next door, although not easily heard by the young man sleeping in the bedroom, were loud enough for Macy's sensitive canine ears to know that it was time to get up and start looking for something to eat. When the smell of eggs began wafting through the window, she stood up and walked slowly to the bedroom door, placing a paw on the polished wooden surface. This human didn't seem to know the proper time to get up. And he certainly didn't understand how empty a dog's stomach could feel in the morning. She tentatively pressed down against the wood, her claws sliding across a crisscross of former scratches that marked numerous such occasions. No sound of stirring came from behind the door. Macy put her other paw on the door and began to scratch madly. She stopped and cocked her head to listen. Nothing. It was time for extreme measures. *"Rarf! Ararf!"*

"Macy, shut up!" a surly voice said from behind the door.

Macy cocked her head the other direction and began barking more insistently. She stopped when the sound of the human's feet hitting the floor and making their way her direction told her she had made her point once again.

"You need to go to obedience school." Garrison said groggily as he swung the door open. Macy wiggled all over and licked his hand. "Good morning to you, too," he said, and stumbled to the bathroom with Macy close behind. "You're in luck, Macy. We're going to Julie's this morning. She invited us last night after church. So you can have something besides stale bread for breakfast."

At the mention of Julie's name, Macy cocked her head again and wagged her tail slightly. She knew who Julie was. To the people of Adullam, Julie was a nurturing mother who could be trusted with any trouble you needed to discuss. To Macy, she was a soft-spoken human who had a weakness for dogs and a habit of cooking more than enough food for those sitting at the table—*and* under it. She trotted happily to the front door of the cabin, looking back at Garrison with an *"Are you coming?"* expression.

"I don't know why you don't just stay over at Julie and Mark's house all the time. It's obvious they love having you around. Of course, they love having *everyone* around. That's just how they are," Garrison said as he opened the front door. Macy danced circles around him as he walked the path to the gate. "I've never seen anyone so excited about breakfast." Garrison couldn't help but grin at the mutt's enthusiasm. *Life must seem simple when you're a dog,* he thought. *No worries about getting eaten—at least not around here. Plenty of table scraps if you look pathetic enough.* Being Adullam's only dog had its advantages.

"I just know Selah would have found you hilarious. She could see the personality in anything—even a chicken—so you would have completely amazed her with all your shenanigans." Garrison started to reach for the latch on the gate and then let his hand fall to his side. "Speaking of shenanigans, how about *you* opening the gate?" Macy cocked her head to one side and barked, waiting impatiently for her human to complete his task. "I'm not doing it. You open everyone's gate all the time, anyway. You might as well do it when it's useful," Garrison smirked and folded his arms to watch.

"Rarf!" was Macy's only reply.

"Well, I guess we won't be getting breakfast, then," Garrison said with mock sorrow in his voice and turned back toward the cabin.

"Rarf! Rarf!" Macy barked in what Garrison was sure was an irritated tone.

He motioned to the gate. "Get the gate," he said and patted the latch.

Macy looked at him questioningly. Could this human really be so stupid that he had forgotten how to do something he had already done a hundred times? She shoved her nose under the latch, pushed the gate open, and hurried through as it swung open onto the road.

"Good girl, Macy!" Garrison praised her and scratched her behind her ears.

Macy paused to enjoy the scratching, then snorted and trotted down the road in the direction of Mark and Julie's house, her tail wagging slightly. This human was more stubborn than most, she had noticed. But the Kind Man had told her to stay with him for now.

She would always listen to the Kind Man because she understood Him as much as He understood her. He had shown her where to find food before she came to this settlement, when she had followed Him here from the outer docks. He had protected her all the way as they walked past the watching eyes of mountain lions. He had even stopped her from playing with the coiled, rattling rope she came across near a limestone bluff. The Kind Man had pointed to the rope, and it had suddenly slithered away. When she started after it, He put his hand on her head; and she instantly realized the rope was a dangerous, living thing to be left alone. She trembled slightly, but when she looked up at the Kind Man, He was smiling at her out of His eyes. Macy felt safe again. She would always trust Him and obey.

Garrison followed behind Macy, wondering at how much she enjoyed smelling things. When her nose wasn't to the ground, it was up in the air, sniffing to find any interesting scents in the breeze. He watched now as her nose quivered at the aroma of goat meat drifting from an open window of the house they were passing. "Come on, Macy," he said as he passed her on the road. "Julie will have something just as good as what they're having. And we weren't invited to that house anyway." Macy gave up on the goat meat and bounded after Garrison. Their destination wasn't far. Soon she wouldn't have to settle for just the *smell* of breakfast, for Macy had her own special bowl at Julie's house.

When Garrison knocked on the front door, Julie opened it and handed him a cup of coffee. "Come in, Garrison! Mark is just pulling his biscuits out of the oven," she said warmly.

Garrison seemed surprised. "I didn't know Mark could cook," he commented.

Julie laughed. "You just haven't been over here when he was doing the cooking. Mark's a great cook," she said loudly enough for her husband to hear from the kitchen.

"Don't build it up too much until I see if these biscuits turned out ok," said a voice from that direction.

Garrison took a sip of the coffee and looked around the room. "Where is everybody?" he asked. Usually, the couch would hold a few of Mark and Julie's kids and a friend or two, while whoever was on kitchen duty would be helping with the meal.

"Hi, Gawwy," said a tiny voice from the kitchen doorway. Garrison peered around the dining table to see Laramie, who was too short to be seen over it.

"Well, hi, Laramie," Garrison said. Laramie waved at him with a fork he was taking to the table. "I setting da table."

"Good. I would hate to have to eat out of Macy's bowl," Garrison winked at him.

"Messy eat heah," Laramie gestured to a cracked clay bowl in the corner. Macy trotted hopefully over to the bowl, and upon finding nothing in it yet, licked Laramie on the nose.

"Yuck, Messy. No do that," Laramie sputtered. He picked up the bowl and went back to the kitchen. In a moment, he returned with Macy's breakfast: a cold boiled egg and some goat sausage gravy. Macy set to work on it immediately with Laramie patting her the whole time.

"To answer your question about where everyone is, a bunch of the youth went camping in the meadow last night, remember?" Julie said with a questioning smile. "How come you didn't go with them?"

"Oh, yeah," Garrison said. "I don't know. I went with them a lot last summer when I first got here. I guess I just wanted to sit this one out." He sipped his coffee. The camping trips were fun, but it was still a little chilly this early in the spring. Plus, when he was camping out under the stars, he was always reminded of the original reason he had arrived in Adullum. It reminded him of the night he left the valley and the last time he saw Selah.

"You miss your friend, don't you?" Julie remarked.

Garrison stared at her wonderingly. "It's almost like you can read my mind sometimes," he laughed. "Yeah, I guess I do. Camping reminds me of when I left home; and when we go to the river, it reminds me of how Selah and I used to catch crawdads. I've made a lot of new friends here, but Selah and I were really close."

Julie looked at him thoughtfully for a moment, and then helped Laramie refocus on his task by directing him to the kitchen sink. "Have you ever thought about going back?" Julie asked over her shoulder as she helped Laramie wash his hands.

"Sure," Garrison admitted. "After I got saved, I thought about it; but I didn't think I was ready. And also, I know there are a lot of people back home who aren't happy with the decision I made. They might not welcome me back."

"Do you think they still feel that way after all this time has passed?" Mark asked as he slid the biscuits off the pan and into a cloth-lined basket. "I know if you were my son, I would be long past being angry and would just want to see you again—or at least want to know you were ok."

Garrison's face fell. "I feel horrible about that," he said quietly. "I know Mom and Dad are either still worried sick, or maybe even have given up on me. But the people I'm thinking about who will be angry are the old timers. Well, maybe not Miss Genevieve." He wondered how the spunky old lady was doing.

"I bet she would be glad to see you again," Julie ventured.

"I bet she would be glad if I did what *she* had always wanted to do," Garrison replied.

"What? Be a missionary?" Mark asked as he set a platter of goat sausage on the table alongside a steaming bowl of gravy.

"Yeah," Garrison muttered.

"Let's pray," Julie suggested. "I'm hungry."

"I pray!" Laramie said enthusiastically. The four held hands while Laramie went into a litany of things he was thankful for, most of which were unintelligible to Garrison. The "Amen" was clear enough, though, and they sat down to eat.

"Well? Have you ever thought about it?" Mark asked.

"Thought about what?" Garrison asked.

"Being a missionary," Mark replied.

"Mark, you're being awfully nosy," Julie scolded him.

"No, it's okay," Garrison mumbled through a mouthful of biscuit. "I have thought about it because I want to do something for the Lord, but it just doesn't seem right somehow. I really had no idea I would be here this long. I fully expected to be on my way to civilization last year—before winter came. It's not that I don't want to leave. I just feel…" he drifted off, unable to explain his emotions.

"Well, we certainly aren't trying to convince you to go," Julie said gently.

"Oh, I know. Dawson told me I can stay as long as I need to. It just feels like I'm at a standstill, and I can't go anywhere."

Julie looked at him speculatively and smiled. "Are you at a standstill spiritually, or in the natural, everyday sense?"

Garrison stopped chewing for a moment and swallowed. He could feel a gentle nudging on the inside, like God was trying to get him to pay attention.

"Now *you're* the one who's being nosy," Mark said, patting Julie on the hand.

"I don't know. Maybe both," Garrison finally answered her as he swiped a biscuit across a trail of gravy on his plate. "It just seems like something's missing."

"I'm sure the Lord will reveal it to you, if you ask Him," Julie said confidently.

Garrison nodded and stuffed another forkful of sausage in his mouth. The truth was that he was fairly certain God had already shown him what he was missing. He was just too stubborn to admit it. Garrison suddenly found he could hardly wait to finish chewing before he voiced his epiphany. He washed the food down with a swig of coffee and nearly choked in his haste.

"Chew yo food an' ya don't choke," Laramie reprimanded him. "I chew," he said with bright eyes, and smacked noisily.

"That's enough, Laramie," Mark said, trying not to smile.

"It's just that I don't feel comfortable about it," Garrison said, once he was over his coughing fit. "Everyone else seems to think it's like breathing, but it still seems weird to me."

"What? Leaving here to spread the gospel?" Mark asked.

"No, no. Being filled with the Holy Spirit and speaking in tongues and all that stuff. I'm pretty sure that's what the Lord has been dealing with me about. But it makes me feel uncomfortable, not being in control," Garrison explained.

"Who says you're not in control?" Julie asked.

"Well, how can you be, if you're speaking a language you don't even know?"

"It's not like possession, where you can't control your actions. God isn't going to make you do anything you don't want to do. Acts 2:4 says that the believers began to speak in other tongues as the Spirit gave them utterance. The believers were given the words to say, but they still had to be the ones to say it. In all your time here, have you ever felt that anyone who was speaking in tongues or giving an interpretation of a message in tongues was out of control?" Julie asked.

"No," Garrison said slowly. "I've never felt like they were being used like a pawn or anything like that. I just don't understand it."

"Well, it isn't a feeling of being taken over. It's completely submitting yourself to His will and yielding the use of your tongue to Him. Which is a pretty good sign of submission, if you think about it," Julie explained. "The book of James talks about how no man can tame the tongue.[10] I think that's one reason God did something that seems so odd to us in the natural sense. How could someone speaking in a language they don't understand be something useful? Well, for one thing, it shows you are willing to yield the most stubborn part of your body to the Spirit. And of course, there are other reasons it's useful. Paul said it helps us to pray God's perfect will when we don't know how to pray.[11] And if it's a message in tongues in a service, an interpretation is given, which helps to build up the body of believers."[12]

"I just don't know if I'm ready to receive it yet," Garrison said hesitantly.

"Garrison, you've already received God's Spirit.[13] Now it's just a matter of yielding to Him completely and letting Him take you to the next level," Julie said gently.

Garrison didn't know what to say. Somehow, he knew she was right.

"Well, it's certainly something to pray about," Mark said as he gathered his plate and fork. "Hey, would you mind giving me a hand with the dishes?"

"Sure," Garrison replied. As he wiped the gravy skillet clean, he resolved to search out the scriptures Julie had mentioned and to make it a matter of prayer.

---

[10] James 3:5-8
[11] Romans 8:26-27
[12] 1 Corinthians 14:2-5
[13] See Romans 8:9-11

He smiled wistfully. Miss Genevieve would have been pleased with him for looking them up and pleased with Julie for mentioning them. If Viviana had been here, she would probably have chimed in with Julie and started badgering him to memorize them. He stopped drying the skillet for a moment as he thought of Viv. It had been a long time since she had been to Adullum…longer than usual.

"What's wrong?" Mark asked, and Garrison realized he had been frozen in thought, holding the skillet and frowning.

"I was just wondering about Viv. It's been a long time since she's come by. Do you think everything's okay?"

"Uh, let's see…when was she here last? It's been over a month, hasn't it, Jules?" Mark asked as Julie came to the sink with more dishes.

"It's been much longer than that. I'd say about three months," Julie replied. "She's been on my heart. I promised myself I wouldn't worry about her when she started coming, since I know the Lord watches over her, but sometimes it's hard not to wonder what's happening to her in her other world."

"Do you think she could be in trouble?" Garrison wondered aloud.

"From what I know about where she comes from, she's probably just laying low to avoid suspicion. Maybe she suspects someone is watching her, so she can't risk them following her here," Julie suggested.

"I wish she could just stay," Garrison said. "She's such an encouragement to the youth and the younger kids—they all love her. And she could learn all she needs to learn in a safe place without the State breathing down her neck and without having to worry about anyone squashing her beliefs."

"Hmmm. Sounds a lot like what your "old timers" were trying to do—protect their children and practice their beliefs in a safe environment. And yet, here you are," Julie said with an intense expression on her face.

Garrison was taken aback. He wasn't used to Julie being confrontational. "Well, I—" he sputtered.

"It didn't seem to work so well for them. Or maybe it did, since they seem to have passed their convictions down to you—whether you were aware of it or not," she continued.

Garrison glanced bewilderedly at Mark, who raised his eyebrows in surprise.

"But I left!"

"Yes. But you are suggesting that Viv stay here indefinitely." Julie paused for a moment and seemed to study him. "Why do you think Viv doesn't find a way to slip quietly out of society so she can just stay here? Regardless of *your* motivation for leaving, you told me you thought at least one person in your community felt like the gospel needed to be taken back to the State. And why do you think that person remained? Why do you think Genevieve stayed, if God had called her to go?" She looked at Garrison pointedly.

"Well, I'm sure it's because no one would think about leaving since it would endanger the community. No one wanted to put the others at risk. To leave would be to go against what the elders had been told to do," Garrison explained.

"Are you sure about that?" Julie asked. "Didn't you say the angel told your ancestors that if they stayed in the valley, they would be safe?"

"That's what I mean," Garrison said. "He said they would have everything they needed and would be protected."

"But did he tell them they couldn't ever leave?"

Garrison turned his back to the sink and leaned against it. "No, he didn't say that. But why would they want to leave, if staying meant they were safe?"

"What if there was something more important to them than their own safety?" Julie proposed.

"Like answering God's call—what He's asked you to do?" Mark interjected.

"Exactly," Julie said, and then looked again at Garrison with the intense expression she had used earlier. "Can you imagine the Bible without the book of Isaiah?"

The question caught Garrison off guard. "Isaiah? No. With all the Messianic prophecy in those scriptures and so many accurate depictions of Jesus hundreds of years before He was born. But what does that have to do with staying hidden in a secret community?" Garrison asked, with a feeling he was about to find out.

"Everything," Julie said promptly. "Isaiah answered God's call to be a prophet. His messages were not popular at the time. According to Jewish tradition, his life ended prematurely when he was sawed in half. All because he obeyed God. How's that for safe?"

Garrison looked at her, dumbfounded. He didn't know what to say. It went against everything he had been taught growing up: protect your own by following the rules; and if you obey God, you will be kept safe. But that's not what happened to Isaiah.

"And what about Jesus?" Julie asked. "What did He get for obeying God?"

Garrison sighed. "Torture and death—crucifixion. But that was different. The people in my community are following the rules to protect their own. They can't see God's will like Jesus could. They just remember what God's messenger said, and they stick to it."

"I don't agree with you that they can't see God's will. They have His Word, which is the main way He reveals His will. And whose rules are they following? Did the angel give them these rules from God, Himself?"

"The angel didn't give them any rules. I guess he just gave them a choice."

"So, if God asked one of them to leave, that person could still make a choice, right?"

Garrison ran his fingers through his hair, trying to think of a way he could convey the fear instilled in the people of the valley from the time they were small children. "But they think if they leave, they'll get captured and imprisoned, maybe even endangering those they are trying to protect. Jesus knew the risk when He began preaching because He knew the end result of obeying God. He knew what He was saying would ruffle the feathers of the Pharisees and the scribes because it went against their rules."

"Whose rules?"

"Their rules."

"Oh. Man's rules, which don't always coincide with God's law."

"I see where you're going with this, but Jesus didn't have to worry about protecting anyone," Garrison said. He was beginning to be frustrated with Julie's questions.

"What about His mother? His disciples? His friends? The priests threw a formerly blind man out of the synagogue because of his belief in Jesus after he was healed. They wanted to have Lazarus killed after Jesus raised him from the dead because his resurrection resulted in many people believing in Jesus. And yet Jesus continued His mission to obey His Father. He did this, knowing full well that He and other people would be in danger because of it. But it wasn't because He didn't care about their being safe. He did it because He cared about them being *saved*. He *was* protecting His own. It's just that His own included more than friends and family. It potentially included every member of the human race since *whosoever* believes in Him can have everlasting life.[14]

"So perhaps you can see why God may ask Viv to do some things that are not safe. Maybe she will be in some situations you or I would not dream of putting her in. But if the truth of the gospel is spread to those who need to hear it, Viv will have given those people the opportunity to be saved. An opportunity they didn't have before. And that is what I remember when I worry about Viv. Then I remind myself not to worry, and I just pray." Julie, who had been leaning forward with the intensity of what she was saying, leaned back against the counter and surveyed Mark and Garrison, who were staring at her as they let her words sink in.

"I don't think I've ever heard you say that much at once," Garrison finally said. "You're always listening to other people's problems. I think you just preached a sermon!"

"It happens now and again," Mark said with a grin and sidled up to Julie to give her a hug. "She's right. Ultimately, we *are* safe, even when God asks us to do things that aren't."

"Because to live is Christ, and to die is gain[15]—if we live, we are working for Him, but if we die, we get to be with Him in heaven," Garrison said slowly.

"That's right," Julie replied. "All the hard things we may go through in this life will be worth it. Even if it means suffering because we have shared our faith. At least, that's what Paul said. 'For this slight momentary affliction is preparing for us an eternal weight of glory beyond all comparison, because we look not to the things that are seen but to the things that are unseen; for the things that are seen are transient, but the things that are unseen are eternal.[16]'"

At that moment, Garrison wished Miss Genevieve could be there in the kitchen with them. She would love this family. She would love this community.

---

[14] John 3:16
[15] Philippians 1:21
[16] 2 Corinthians 4:17-18, RSV

And yet he knew even visiting other believers in another place wouldn't be enough for her. She would want to leave and take their message to the world.

"Do you think maybe Viv got in trouble for sharing too much?" Garrison asked.

"I don't know," Julie said. "But we can pray for her right now."

The three held hands and began to pray for their friend. As their prayers grew in fervency, Garrison imagined angels being dispatched on Viv's behalf. After their requests were made known, they began to thank and praise God for the protection He had offered her in the past and the answers to their prayers that were on the way. As the minutes passed, the burden Garrison had felt for Viv began to lift. He didn't know her situation, but he knew God had it under control. He was right there with her, helping and protecting her when they couldn't. The God of the universe was not hindered by distance or weakness, and He knew exactly what she needed.

6

Vɪᴠɪᴀɴᴀ Delacruz scrunched her eyes fiercely, attempting to understand the results of the diagnostic she had just run on the malfunctioning piece of equipment at the SynthaMeat Processing Plant. Making meat from cloned protein cells in order to protect the rights of animals was a source of pride for the State. But the process was not without its problems. In fact, this was the third time today this particular machine had broken down, bringing the operation to a screeching halt—quite literally. According to the monitor whose job it was to watch the machinery in question, this most recent episode had begun with a whirring noise, then graduated to a rapid *thwap-thwap-thwapping*, and had culminated in a horrendous *skreek* of metal on metal, closely followed by the automated system shutting itself down.

Viv walked to the control panel on the wall and manually flipped off the breaker to that section of the line, tagging a lockout notice on the breaker box. She walked back over to the machine where the monitor was wringing her hands nervously. "I heard it making the funny noises, but I thought it would turn off before it wrecked itself," she said timidly. Viv looked up once again from the meter she had used to run the diagnostic; and as the short, round woman seemed to shrink from her gaze, she realized she was scowling. Immediately she softened her expression.

"It's okay, Janice. This bucket o' bolts just seems to be our problem child today. It's not ya fault it didn' shut itself off in time." *Although it would have helped if the woman had taken the initiative and had manually shut off the power at the wall when she heard the commotion,* Viv thought to herself. However, if the machine was in the process of self-correcting, Janice might very well have had her pay docked for shutting down the line. Of course, she could also get her pay docked if, by not shutting it down, she had allowed a piece of expensive equipment to destroy itself.

Viv smiled reassuringly at Janice's plump-cheeked face. Normally a cheerful woman, Janice's chin was quivering slightly. "Come on, now. Nothin' to worry about. If ya shut it down when it was tryin' to fix itself, it coulda messed wit' its circuitry, don't ya know." Viv popped open the side panel and immediately saw the problem. A belt had stretched out enough to slip and get caught in the teeth of one of the gears, causing another gear to bind up. "That shoudn'a happened," Viv said.

"What seems to be the problem here, Technician Delacruz?" said a sharp voice behind her.

Viv flinched in spite of herself. Tommy Telquat was her immediate supervisor; and he seemed to watch her every move, especially lately. "A belt stretched out an' chunked up the gears," she began to explain.

"Which would not have happened if proper routine maintenance had been performed. One more incident like this and I will be forced to report you."

"I just replaced the belt last week," Viv replied, trying to maintain a calm, matter-of-fact tone. "It's in the maintenance records and was recorded by the chip in the machine."

Telquat looked surprised and almost disappointed, Viv noticed. "Hmmm. That is very strange, indeed," he said.

"That's just what I was sayin' to Janice, here," Viv said, glancing at the bundle of nerves in her SynthaBlood-proof smock.

Telquat shifted his focus from Viv to the cowering woman. "Why didn't you shut it off? Surely you could hear the gears grinding?" he said accusingly.

Janice seemed to freeze and couldn't find her voice. From behind Telquat's back, Viv pointed at the machine and made hammering motions. "Hammering noise?" Janice said helplessly.

"Exactly! So why didn't you shut it down at the panel when you heard it making a racket?" Telquat barked. Viv shook her head and pointed at the machine again, then petted and patted her arm. Janice looked at her blankly, and then her eyes opened wide in understanding. "I-I thought it might be fixing itself," she stuttered. Viv nodded and smiled at her from behind Telquat's back. The white-coated man turned around and looked speculatively at Viv, who smiled blandly back at him.

"Nothin' more irritatin' than an unwarranted shut-down," she said flatly.

"Yes. Well, explain to me why this belt, which has so recently been replaced, has already failed? You must not have installed it properly."

"Well, accordin' to the machine's li'l chip of a brain, I did. It's all here in the diagnostic. An' the crux o' the matter is, I think it was a faulty belt. But the chip shoulda caught that. So, I'm thinkin' the brain may actually be goin' bad."

"Hmmm," Telquat pursed his lips and rubbed under his nose with a blue-vinyl gloved hand. "That is expensive, but easily fixed. The mechanical part of it, however…"

"I'm on it," Viv said quickly, taking the necessary tools out of her belt. "I'll fix it, snappy as beans, but it probably won't be ready 'til the beginning of next shift."

"Next shift! That just isn't good enough, Delacruz."

"Well, it's gonna hafta be, if ya want it done right!" Viv said loudly, in spite of her previous efforts to control her temper.

Telquat leaned close to Viv and clenched his teeth. "Need I remind you that we are doing you a favor because of your questionable background?"

"Need I remind *you* that ya get a yearly bonus for each person you employ wit' a background like mine?" Viv said evenly.

Telquat's eyes narrowed. "How do you know that?"

"It's in the public records. I was readin' through 'em one day when I thought I might like to see the benefits o' climbin' up the ladder."

"Well, I hope you enjoyed your perusal of those undoubtedly boring files, because there's no way a Discard's daughter could end up a supervisor."

"There's nothing in the bylines that says that," Viv said as she removed the bolts from a junction box.

Telquat spewed air between his teeth exasperatedly. "Just fix it, Delacruz—and before the shift is over—or I'll take it out of your pay," he spat the words out, turned on his heel, and strode down the line in the direction of his office.

Janice giggled once he was out of sight.

"He's a piece o' work, that one, ain't he?" Viv said sideways to her.

"Huh? Oh, no. I wasn't laughing at him. I think he's scary. I was laughing at what you said," Janice explained, back to her old cheerful self again.

"What's that?" Viv asked. "Ya mean how rude I was? I kinda wish I'd skipped all that," Viv said regretfully. It wasn't just that she knew it didn't help anything to lose her temper, but she also felt like she had disappointed the Holy Spirit.

"No, the other thing you said. 'Snappy as beans,'" Janice giggled again. "Where did you come up with that? And what does it mean, anyway?"

Viv sighed. "I reckon I got it from my granny on my dad's side. She used to say it. I just meant I'm gonna fix this piece o' junk, real quick-like."

"Oh, I knew that—at least the part about you being quick. But what's snappy about beans? Beans are mushy," Janice persisted. She didn't get a lot of company on this side of the factory. Almost everything was automated and nearly foolproof.

"I think it's talkin' 'bout green beans—not the brown, mushy kind. When ya grow beans, they come longer than we get 'em in a can, see? Ya hafta snap 'em in two to fit a lot of 'em in a can or a jar," Viv said, and wondered where her granny had heard the expression. Surely she had never seen a fresh green bean or a garden. But Viv had. Her mind was suddenly flooded with a memory of helping Julie snap beans back in Adullam…the *snap, s-snap* and the *thunk-rattle-thunk* of the individual beans hitting the pot on the floor at their feet…the sounds of summer and laughing children who were actually interacting with each other in the here-and-now instead of wearing a Vista-Visor for a virtual reality game. The memory hit her so hard with its simplicity and sweetness that her eyes began to water. She blinked hard and stared momentarily at the gray walls surrounding her to remind herself of where she really was. *She* needed desperately to stay in the here-and-now if she was to keep from being reported.

"Did you work in a green bean cannery before you came here?" Janice asked.

"Huh? Nah. I just know someone who knows how to can green beans," Viv said carefully. Anyone listening would think she was talking about someone who worked in a cannery, Viv reasoned.

"Do Discards have gardens?" Janice asked in awe.

Well, almost anyone. Viv smiled to herself. Janice wasn't exactly a quick thinker, but she was sincere and she was cheerful—two things seriously lacking in the State.

"I never saw a Discard what had a garden," Viv said. "I don't know where my granny got that sayin'. She musta heard it from somewhere."

"I like listening to you talk. You have an interesting accent," Janice grinned.

Viv sighed. Her "interesting" accent certainly got her into some interesting situations. It immediately branded her as different. Usually, people couldn't place where they'd heard it before. And when it dawned on them that it was from the ghettos of the outer docks, there was always a momentary pause, and then one of two reactions. They either held more tightly to their belongings and excused themselves politely, or they wore a wide-eyed, sympathetic look that was a combination of wonder and pity—followed by a flood of questions about her former life or congratulatory comments for escaping it. Her background had put her under a magnifying glass the minute she made her exit from the outer docks, which is why she had to be extra careful to keep her excursions to Adullam from being discovered.

"Yeah, well, it's not all that great when it's comin' outta ya own chops, ya savvy?" Viv said.

"Well, *I* think it's great. I wish I could do something interesting. I wish I could do a lot of things—like lose weight, for instance. And be smarter…and better at my job," Janice said wistfully. "My friend Sabrina used to be fat, like me—and kind of dumb, like me. But now she's losing weight, and she's better at her job, and she makes funny jokes that everyone laughs at. Except me, because I don't get them. But she's kind of different now, too. We don't seem to have much to talk about anymore. We could laugh at the simplest things before. We always used to go out to Talk-o-lot Chocolate for a Double Marshmallow Steamer, and now she won't even do that anymore. And I wondered, 'What in the world has gotten into her?'"

Viv had only been half-listening to her coworker, but immediately she felt an urgency in her spirit that Janice was somehow in peril. She turned her full attention to the middle-aged lady. A wisp of Janice's dishwater blond hair had slipped out from beneath her hairnet. Somehow it made her look vulnerable. Viv listened with a new focus as Janice continued.

"And I said to her, 'Brina, what's gotten into you? I mean, you look great and you seem like you've got a good life now, but you're so different!' And you know what she says to me?" Janice continued without waiting for Viv to answer. "She says, 'It's because I got the chip.' And then I remembered. We had that staff meeting—you remember the one—where they said they were offering it to all employees as part of the health maintenance program. It'll make you smarter and healthier and better at your job. They made it sound like it's the answer to everything. And maybe it is, because Sabrina really seems to have a better life now."

Viv put her hands on Janice's shoulders and looked into her eyes. "Listen, Janice! Some things sound too good to be true because they *are* too good to be true. Besides, I like you for who you are. And I'm not the only one." Viv's heart was pounding. What she was doing was risky, but she had to tell Janice about Jesus before it was too late.

"Someone else likes me the way I am? I mean, you're a really nice person, Viv, so it doesn't surprise me that you would say that. You're not like anyone else I've ever met." She paused a moment and studied Viv intently. "There's something really different about you." Suddenly, the woman brightened. "Do you have the chip, too?"

"No, Janice, and I'll never get it!" Viv whispered emphatically.

Janice frowned and backed up a little. "Why not?"

"Because it's dangerous to let them put something in ya that can control ya mind."

"But if it helps you to be a better person, then—"

"Ya don't need the chip to be a better person. Ya need Jesus." Viv's pulse throbbed in her ears and her skin tingled with a sense of danger. She had just waved a red flag of treason and placed it in the hands of a chatterbox monitor with a low IQ. Even if Janice liked Viv, there was no guarantee she would keep her mouth shut.

"Who?" Janice asked, confused. "I don't think I've met him. Is he on first shift?"

"Tell ya what, Janice. If ya promise not to sign up for the chip, I'll introduce ya to 'im."

"Well, I don't know. What if he doesn't like me once he gets to know me?" Janice asked warily.

"He already knows ya. An' 'e already likes ya."

Janice beamed. "You can't be serious! I have an admirer?"

"Yup. How 'bout we meet up at Talk-o-lot Chocolate after this shift? I think I can get this fixed before third shift starts. What say we be there at twenty?"

"Twenty hundred hours? Ok. I'll be there. What should I wear?" Janice asked, blushing.

"Nothing ya wear could make 'im care about ya any more—or any less, fa that matter. Just show up," Viv said, her eyes darting to the cameras that were monitoring this section of the line. "I gotta get the chip fa this bumblebot before the shift flips. Maybe ya should go check see if anyone else needs anythin', in case they wonder why ya standin' 'round doin' nothin.'"

"Oh! Good idea," Janice said, her cheeks still rosy from anticipation at meeting someone who was purported to like her.

Viv hesitated a moment. Was she misleading Janice by letting her think she was going to introduce her to someone she could see with her eyes? At that moment, the camera aimed at that section of the line began flashing red, which meant extra sensors were being used in the recording process—probably enhanced audio. "I'm gonna go get that part now," Viv said loudly. "Don't ya worry, she'll be up 'n' runnin' in no time." She turned away and headed off the floor, leaving Janice standing there, wearing a shy smile. *It was only the grace of God that kept the audio sensors off until then,* Viv thought to herself as she strode through the gray halls.

All of the factory and much of the inner city were the same, drab gray. There was no need to paint anything. Modern concrete was formulated with a microbial additive that self-corrected any cracks, and paint would have harmed the microbes. There was no need for decorative colors since no one paid any attention to their actual surroundings anymore. Wearing a Vista-Visor, you could make the walls whatever color you wanted, which meant there was no chance of anyone being offended by someone else's color choice. And if you had the chip, it could access your likes and dislikes, making you see whatever color made you most comfortable.

Viv quickened her pace. She had put in her order for the replacement part as soon as she suspected it had gone bad, but she was doubtful the people in I.T.

would have it ready when she got there. She wanted to make certain nothing kept her from her meeting with Janice. What would she say to her? What if she wasn't receptive, or was even hostile to the idea? What if she was mad because she thought Viv had misled her into thinking she was going to have a ready-made boyfriend? "Jesus, I really need ya help wit' dis," she prayed under her breath. "I'm afraid I may have got it all wrong, the way I tol' her 'bout ya. Please make 'er heart ready to hear 'bout ya. I could really use the help of the Holy Spirit in this whole deal. Please don't let her get mad that ya not some dude what has googly eyes for 'er." Viv slowed her pace as she approached the Information Technology Lab. A poster had been plastered to the door with a before and after picture of someone who had decided to get the chip implant. "Be the *YOU* you were always meant to be," declared the poster. The depressed, overweight person in the "before" picture was in the middle of a bad performance appraisal from her boss. The "after" picture showed a thinner, prettier version of the same woman, now wearing a white supervisor's coat. "As if the ads on our Vista-Visors weren't enough. They even resortin' to ol' fashion posters," Viv mumbled. She wore a visor like everyone else, but usually kept it tilted back on her head like an unused pair of sunglasses. She opened the propaganda-covered door and stepped inside.

"Hey, Stan! How's it goin', hume?" Viv had finally trained herself not to say "man," opting for the less offensive, gender-neutral abbreviation for "human." A few cases had been won in court by those who had been called what they considered the wrong gender and had sued someone who was simply trying to be friendly.

A pudgy man at a work bench got up and came to the counter, holding a tiny plastic envelope containing the chip she needed. "Here it is, Viv. I fabricated some extras of this particular series just the other day."

"Wow, thanks! We been havin' a heap a trouble wit' this particular clunk-rot. But I can't believe ya had the time to run extras, what with all the other stuff they got ya doin'—programmin' this, fabricatin' that…. *Say,*" Viv paused as she looked more closely at the man. "Did ya change ya eye color or sumthin'?"

Stan smiled brightly. "This may actually be the first time you've seen my eye color. Always had my visor on active before. Can't see eyes very well through them when they're active, you know."

It was then that Viv noticed Stan wasn't even wearing a visor, which was tantamount to reckless for an I.T. employee. He must have seen her eyes glance at the top of his head as she looked for it, because his smile deepened as he leaned against the counter. "Don't need my visor anymore. I finally got the upgrade."

"The *upgrade*—ya got the *chip?*" Viv's breath caught in her throat and she choked a little as the words came out. Stan was one of her favorite coworkers. She was surprised that, having worked with technology as long as he had, he would ignore the risk to his autonomy by being implanted.

"I can see you had the same concerns I did: will it change my personality? Will the State take over my body? You know—all the arguments anyone has who knows anything about bio-implantation engineering. But the chip has safeguards against that. It's not a generic implant, like 2nd Sight or Audio Boost. Each chip is unique, specifically designed for the individual. This is something they don't generally tell you until you sign up, but the chip is actually *techno-organic.*" Stan said, his eyebrows raising as he leaned farther over the counter in a conspiratorial fashion.

"Meaning...?"

"The chip is a combination of your DNA and a micro computer. They harvest some of your stem cells and grow them in the lab in conjunction with circuitry that has bio-components. That's why it's so effective and why there have been no instances of anyone developing infection or rejection syndrome."

"I've heard plenty o' stories o' people goin' clean off their noggin afta gettin' a chip," Viv protested.

"That's only the people who get them on the black market," Stan explained. "You know, there's always someone willing to do the unthinkable to make some extra credits. And there's always someone who can't afford the genetic labwork who's miserable enough to risk going to a dealer. But those days are drawing to a close."

"Whaddaya mean? How so?"

"The State is going to offer it gratis. No, your Audio Boost implant isn't malfunctioning," Stan said with a chuckle at Viv's wide eyes. "You heard me correctly. Of course, factory workers have already been offered this service. But starting next fiscal year, the implant is going to be free of charge to the children of consenting parents, right along with Health 1 and 2 and Palmscan."

"Without givin' the child a choice?" Viv exclaimed.

"What child *wouldn't* choose to be the enhanced person they were always meant to be? Getting the chip so young will mean the individual will have less likelihood to mess up their physiology, like me," at this, Stan gestured to his ample gut. "They won't have the set-backs people have during adolescence when emotions are in such turmoil and hormones are out of control. They'll have a built-in guide and companion for life who knows what they need more than they do. They'll be incapable of making the kind of mistakes we made growing up because the chip won't allow it. Who wouldn't want that?"

Viv's shoulders sagged slightly. It sounded to her as if the State was trying to become a surrogate "holy spirit." Except the chip wouldn't even allow someone to exercise free will and make mistakes—or what the State perceived as such. She felt like she had been punched in the stomach. But Stan was just warming to his subject.

"And since it's techno-organic, it keeps developing throughout the person's lifetime," he continued. "With each download, the person becomes smarter— or more skilled—and the chip eventually bonds with the rest of the body on a cellular level, becoming the new genetic code for that individual. In the future, children of the chipped may not even need to get chipped themselves. Developers theorize that it will be just another part of our natural physiology. Can you imagine being always connected, never alone again? Linked to the rest of the human race simply by our DNA evolving to include neural pathways for Wi-Fi technology?" Stan gazed into space—then suddenly, his pupils grew smaller; and he straightened and handed the envelope with the repair part to Viv. "I need to get back to work. I've used all the extra time I saved by being efficient earlier," he said quickly and turned abruptly back to his workbench.

"Thanks, Stan," Viv said softly. Stan didn't answer. He was absorbed in his work, soldering a minute relay on a command chip for another piece of factory equipment.

7

Viv was convinced the broken equipment had developed artificial intelligence and had decided not to like her. Even with the new chip and belt replacement, it took an hour longer than it should have taken to get the machine operational. She barely had time to go back to her apartment and change clothes before her meeting with Janice. She hugged her arm close to her side on the subway ride. Underneath her shirt in a special belt she had made was her greatest treasure—a New Testament which Dawson had given her the last time she had been to Adullam. Although it was risky, the community's senior pastor gave her one of his Bibles because Viv was so hungry for more of the Word. "I wish I could remember it better. I wish I could memorize the whole New Testament, but I can barely remember a few verses," she lamented. When Dawson handed her the little pocket Bible, she felt as if her heart had jumped into her throat.

"You take this back with you. Maybe you could start by memorizing The Romans Road," he suggested, referring to a group of scriptures that laid out the plan of salvation.

"Oh, Dawson, are ya sure ya can part with it?" she said, trying to swallow the lump in her throat. If it was ever found, it would be immediately confiscated since it wasn't in compliance with the State's Total Tolerance Imperative, and Viv would be taken in for counseling. "Ya know if they catch me with it and chip me, they might find Adullam."

"That won't happen," the kindly man had gently smiled. Viv felt like she was carrying the fate of the lives of all the community with her by venturing out with it in the open. Even at home, she left it folded up in a pair of pants in her dresser. She almost left it at the apartment, but she wanted to be able to prove to Janice that what she was saying wasn't something she was making up. How she would actually be able to show it to her in public without getting caught presented its own set of problems. Printed books always drew attention because of their novelty. But books such as the Bible and the Koran were not only rare, they were contraband. They had all been rounded up and archived in the library of the Museum of Religious Convergence, with some historically notable copies displayed for visitors. Books making exclusive claims to the truth were not available for the general public, but were still kept for study by scholars who oversaw updates to the State's Bible Collaborative Project. However, only a few of these scholars spent time studying ancient religious documents. Most read the thousands of emails received by citizens who felt they had something relevant to add to the State Bible. Since truth was considered to be completely relative, a majority of the input was accepted and included in the next download, provided it didn't conflict with any of the State's ideals. The complete publication itself was so unwieldy that it would have been impossible to produce in a single volume in printed form, even if printed books were still made. A conglomeration of heavily edited writings of all the world's religions, continually updated with citizen comments, had created a behemoth capable of being contained only in digital form. Scholars helpfully condensed it down to the *My Truth* devotional blog read by citizens searching for spiritual guidance. Viv shook her head as she thought of the State's elaborate attempt to twist Truth to its own devices. Citizens didn't question *My Truth* because they expected the State to take care of them and to know what was in their best interests. The thought made the weight of the little New Testament feel like a pocket of lead against her side.

The next stop on the subway was hers. Viv hopped out of the car and made her way to the exit. A wiry-haired man sitting on the floor of the station platform looked pitifully up at her as he played guitar for passers by. Viv had heard stories about how people used to play for tips. This man wasn't looking for credits, though, since poverty in the State no longer existed. Viv was careful not to make eye contact with him. The case of his guitar was open, a signal that the man was in search of romantic companionship. "Don't be cold, Love," he crooned as she passed by. Viv shook her head grimly and kept walking. Her boots clopped up the steps of the exit and onto the sidewalk outside of Talk-o-Lot Chocolate.

They beat a rhythm almost as loud as her heartbeat, she thought. She tried to project a casual attitude as she swung open the door.

Talk-o-lot Chocolate was a cozy meeting place for close friends and people who *wanted* to be close friends. It was so-named because of the unusual amount of chatter that went on inside. The two-part name rhymed with itself, but everyone could see the intended intimate atmosphere by the spelling of the first part of the name. While most public eateries were silent due to the nearly incessant use of Vista-Visors, Talk-o-lot Chocolate offered lockers to its customers for the storage of visors during their visit. It added a quaint charm to the establishment that was obviously good for business, as nearly every seat in the house was taken.

Viv scanned the room and noticed Janice waving at her from a small table in a corner. She was wearing a blue, floral print dress and a worried expression, which reminded Viv she was expecting to be introduced to a man who was interested in her for who she was. "He decided not to come, didn't he?" Janice asked as Viv pulled out a chair to sit down.

Viv sighed, not really knowing what to do. "He's already here," she heard herself say. "He just doesn't want to reveal himself to ya 'til ya ready." Well, that was true, she thought to herself as Janice scanned the room. "How 'bout we get one o' those steamer things ya tol' me 'bout while we wait?" Viv suggested. Most of the servers were busy, but she managed to catch the eye of an older woman who seemed to be watching the room from the serving station.

"I just can't imagine who he would be," Janice said, still searching the crowd.

"Hello, Janice. It's so nice to see you!" The woman said as she came to take their order. There was something about her that Viv liked immediately. Her brown eyes sparked with warmth as she put her hand on Janice's shoulder. "Who's your friend?" she glanced at Viv and smiled.

"Well, hi, Luciana!" Janice jumped up to hug her. "What are you doing waiting tables?"

Despite her aging features, Luciana was an attractive woman. Her glossy white hair, pulled back in a low-profile pony tail, was in stark contrast to her dark brown eyes and tan skin. Even though she was wearing jeans and a simple company shirt featuring a steaming cup of cocoa, she managed to project an air of elegance that somehow lifted her above the other employees. "We're a little short-handed tonight. I'm just filling in where needed." Her eyes darkened with a look of concern. "I haven't seen Sabrina in a long time," she said. "Is she alright?"

Janice's face fell. "She doesn't really do stuff with me anymore. She has new friends now. Smarter friends. She got the chip."

At the mention of the chip, Viv saw an emotion flit across Luciana's eyes, one that was quickly concealed with careful practice. But she was certain it was one of anger or even outrage. She liked the woman even more.

"A lot of people are getting that thing. But I hope you don't," Luciana said, looking carefully into Janice's eyes. "I like you the way you are."

Janice perked up and sat a little straighter in her chair. "You know that Viv here—that's her name, by the way—I forgot all about introducing you! Viv, this is Luciana. She owns this place. But anyway, Viv promised tonight to introduce me to a friend of hers who she says likes me for who I am, too!"

"Should I wait to take your order until your friend gets here?" Luciana asked.

"Viv says he's already here, but he doesn't want to show himself until he's ready," Janice said with a flirtatious smile and a mysterious tone.

"Let's go ahead and order," Viv suggested.

"Ok," Janice complied. "We'll take two Double Marshmallow Steamers."

"I had a feeling you might," Luciana said with a smile.

"If Jesus wants one when he gets here, I'll take that as a good sign," Janice giggled.

"Is that his name?" Luciana asked curiously.

"Yes. Isn't it unusual? Maybe he's Hispanic or something."

Luciana glanced again at Viv with a look she couldn't interpret. Did she suspect anything? Viv had felt an immediate magnetism for the woman, but shop owners were required by law to report any conversations or activities in violation of the Tolerance Imperative, and Viv had learned that no one could be trusted. Maybe this was the wrong place to bring up the subject after all. Suddenly, Viv realized the woman had been making a quick study of her. "Ya know, if y'all are short handed an' really busy, we could just get our steamers to go," she said. "I hate to take up a table waitin' on someone who may take a while."

"But what about Jesus? What if he thinks we left because I didn't want to meet him?" Janice asked, horrified.

"Yes, indeed, what about Jesus?" Luciana said as she watched Viv. Then she smiled gently and added, "I'm certain your friend will show himself shortly, but in the meantime, we *do* have people waiting for tables. What if I let you wait in our room we save for special meetings? If he's already here, I'm sure he'll see me taking you to it. All he'll need to do is to ask me to take him there when he's ready." Luciana's eyes never left Viv.

Viv stared back at the woman, trying to decide if she could trust her. The room could be a trap. Maybe she was moving them into a place where she thought Viv would feel comfortable enough to say something that would incriminate her. But in her spirit, Viv sensed the opposite. She had been learning to listen to that still, small voice since she had been baptized in the Holy Spirit last summer, and He was telling her that she need not fear. "Ok. We'll wait for Jesus in ya meetin' room," she agreed.

Luciana gave her a slight nod that conveyed volumes. "Wait here while I place your order. I'll be back in a minute."

"Wow, this is kind of neat," Janice said. "I didn't know they had a special meeting room."

Viv looked surreptitiously around the café at the cameras the State had installed. They were in every public place. It was illegal to have a room without one. Every home had them. The only rooms allowed an exception were the bedroom and the bathroom; but even there, citizens were willing participants in their own surveillance through the use of their visors and home control units like Geeves.

Luciana returned, smiling reassuringly at Viv. "Come with me," she said, and the two followed her to an alcove that had a sign for the restroom sticking out from the wall above it on a placard. "But this is the way to the bathroom," Janice said, looking around as if she were in a brand-new world. The alcove sported two bathrooms. They both had the universal bathroom sign as required by law, but everybody knew that if an establishment had two, the unwritten rule was that the one on the left was for those who identified as women, and the one on the right was for those who identified as men. Viv could see a door at the end of the hall that appeared to be a supply closet. Luciana looked as if she were heading for that door, but at the last minute, she turned into the women's bathroom, which was apparently out of order. Janice stopped short and Viv almost stepped on her heels. "Maybe Luciana had to fix the toilet on the way," Janice giggled. After a second or two, the door opened; and Luciana beckoned them inside. Janice smiled and gave another confused giggle but obeyed, with Viv close behind. Once they were inside, Luciana turned to face them and said, "I have to admit, I think I may know this Jesus you're talking about. But I couldn't say anything where we might be heard because of His reputation."

Janice's eyes widened. "What kind of guy are you hooking me up with, Viv?" she asked. "What kind of reputation does he have?"

"Oh, it's not like you're thinking," Luciana explained. "He's the most wonderful Person you'll ever meet. But some people don't like Him because of who He says He is. He was rejected by His own people, and many people in the State don't have much use for Him, either. He doesn't ever try to force His way into people's lives and always waits to be invited. That's probably why Viv hasn't introduced you yet. She's not sure how you'll react." Luciana looked back at Viv. "Am I right?"

"Yeah. I have to be careful when I talk about Him," Viv said.

"Is Jesus a Discard?" Janice asked incredulously. She turned to Viv. "Is that how you met him?"

"No, not exactly. Jesus *was* discarded by the religious teachers as being a heretic," Viv tried to explain. "But He was no Discard."

"A hairy tick?" Janice asked, perplexed.

Luciana suppressed a laugh and squeezed Janice's shoulder. "They thought He was claiming to be someone He had no right to claim to be."

"Who did he claim to be?" Janice asked.

"Jesus said He was God's Son," Luciana said simply.

"Oh! Well, that's not bad. We're all children of God. I just read that today in *My Truth*."

Luciana glanced up at Viv. Inwardly, Viv was praying for direction. She wondered if Luciana was doing the same. Finally, Viv spoke again. "Janice, if ya read *My Truth*, ya know how it says there are many roads to God and that He has many names?" Janice nodded vigorously. "Well, He does have many names. He is called Wonderful Counselor, the Mighty God, the Everlasting Father, the Prince of Peace, the Great I Am, El Shaddai, and Jehovah Jireh, just for starters. And these names really do describe Who 'e is. But there is only one way that leads to 'im. And Jesus is that way."

"The Jesus that you're going to introduce me to—the Jesus who knows me and likes me the way I am—he knows the way to God? What do you mean, that he's one of those State scholar people?" Janice asked.

"No, Janice," Viv said patiently. "I'm tryin' to tell ya that Jesus *is* the way to God. He was God's Son and came to earth in the form of a baby. He lived a sinless life, and He healed people an' taught people how to live. An' the religious people of the day didn' like it so they had 'im killed. But He died because He was willin' to be the sacrifice for our sins. There was no way to get to God before that without killin' some poor animal to cover our sins. An' it was never good enough, because they had to do it over and over. But Jesus was the perfect sacrifice. After Him, no one ever needed to make another sacrifice. But best of all, He didn' stay dead. He came back to life, and He's still alive."

Janice's eyes clouded over and she seemed to study the tile floor. "You said you were going to introduce me to a real person who liked me, not some man who died and became part of the collective energy force."

"He *is* a real person. He's alive. An' He not only likes ya, He loves ya enough to die for ya."

"That happened thousands of years ago, Viv. I wasn't born yet, and he couldn't have known anything about me."

"Yes He did know, because He and God are the same person. And whenever anyone comes to 'im, He won't turn 'em away. He didn' turn me away, an' that's why I'm different. Remember, ya said I was different than anyone else ya knew?" Viv said desperately.

"That may be your truth, but it's not mine," Janice said coldly. She turned away and started to leave. When she reached the door, she turned back to look at Viv. "You know, I think it was mean, what you did. You got my hopes up. I didn't know you were so religious. It's almost like you really think Jesus is the *only* way to God."

Viv started to say something, but Luciana placed a strong hand on her arm. "Janice, I'm so sorry you feel hurt. If you ever need to just talk to someone, you know you can always come here and talk to me," she said.

"Oh, I don't blame you, Luciana. It's just that Viv really hurt my feelings." Tears began to collect in Janice's eyes and slip down her cheeks. "I probably won't stay mad at you for long, Viv. I like you too much. It's the same with 'Brina. No matter what she does, I still love her. But I have to go now."

Viv watched helplessly as the door closed behind her. She backed against the bathroom wall, hiding her face in her hands, and slid to the floor.

"As much as I'd like to let you stay in here and cry it out, we have to open the bathroom up again," Luciana said. "An establishment whose specialty is hot beverages can't keep a bathroom closed for long."

She looked up at the woman, who was holding out her hand to help her to her feet. "You're the only other true Christian I've met around here," Viv stated.

"Come on. We've got to go," Luciana said. Viv took her hand and scuffed her way back to the hall. She had imagined her first meeting with a Christian in the State as being very different—a joyous occasion. But Luciana seemed strangely aloof now. Once they were outside, she removed the "Out of Order" sign and tucked it away in the closet at the end of the hall. "I'm sorry it didn't work out," she told Viv as they walked back toward the serving station.

"Yeah. I wonder if she'll report me," Viv said and started for the exit.

"Wait a minute," Luciana said. "I have something for you." She ducked around the corner and came back with a travel cup and a folded-up shirt. "Here's your Double Marshmallow Steamer. And here's a shirt, compliments of the house." Viv started to protest. She really wasn't a T-shirt type person, preferring the tight-fitting body suits that were popular with people her age. "I insist," Luciana added firmly. "You've had a rough night. Take it. I hope to see you again."

"Thanks," Viv said softly, and took the drink and the shirt.

The sidewalk was well lit and full of people, but Viv had never felt more alone. She should have been ecstatic that she had met another Christian, but Luciana's behavior after Janice had left seemed strangely distant. Lost in thought, Viv barely noticed the man and his guitar until she almost tripped over him. He had moved out of the subway and was at the top of the stairway entrance now. "Careful, Love," he said in a smooth voice. "Looks like you could use some company."

"No, thanks!" Viv said fiercely.

"Easy, Darlin'. You know, I can do something for that bad mood," he said hopefully.

"Shut up, ya blinkin' chip-wipe!" she practically yelled, her frustration finally erupting to the surface. She quickened her pace and clomped down the steps to the station. The ride home gave her plenty of time to think of all the mistakes she had made trying to show Janice the way to Truth. She even began to feel bad about the way she had spoken to the man with the guitar.

"You are the only Bible those people will ever read," Dawson had said when he was trying to convince her to go back to the State.

"*Some Bible I turned out to be,*" she muttered under her breath.

Back at her apartment, she tossed the shirt on her bed and took a sip of the steamer. Under any other circumstances, she would have enjoyed the rich, creamy, chocolate drink, but her heart was too heavy. She poured it down her kitchen sink and stumbled to her bedside, where she dropped to her knees. "Oh, Jesus! Ya gotta help me. I totally messed it all up. Please help me, Jesus!" she pleaded.

Suddenly, she noticed a strange glow coming from something on her bed. It was the shirt Luciana had given her. In the steamy swirls of the cup of hot chocolate were the words, "Monday, 1900 hrs." The words glowed for a few minutes, and then faded into the background of the shirt's design. Viv stared at the shirt, holding it up to the bedroom light. All she could see were the swirls of cream and steam in the cup. The words were completely gone. "Jesus, am I seeing things?" Viv asked. "Did that really happen? Jesus, help me figure this out," Viv prayed. At the sound of "*Jesus, help me,*" the words on the shirt glowed again, becoming clearly visible. After a few moments, they faded again. Viv stood in her bedroom, holding the shirt as it dawned on her why Luciana had acted so aloof. She must have thought Viv might be a State spy. Thinking back on the night, Luciana had never said anything that would incriminate herself. She had let Viv do all the talking when it came to saying that Jesus was the only way to God. The shirt was a failsafe, a message visible only to people who prayed directly to Jesus, its electronics activated by several combinations of a few key spoken words. Her heart leapt within her. "Oh, thank you, Jesus!" she whispered, and laughed as the shirt glowed again.

8

THE rest of the week dragged by for Viv like a one-wheeled wagon. Factory equipment was running more smoothly than it had in several days, so there was less work to fill her shift. Viv made use of the extra time by spending it near Janice, checking the machine she monitored more often than was actually needed. After a few days of pretending to give her the cold shoulder, Janice had warmed up to her again and seemed to be her old self. Viv made certain to boost her self confidence any chance she got, knowing her witnessing method had dealt a serious blow to her coworker's already faltering self-esteem. Finally, Janice pulled her to the side one day at the end of the shift and looked her squarely in the face. "I know what you're doing, you know," she said. "And you don't have to keep doing it."

"Whaddaya mean?" Viv asked. She wondered if Janice thought she was looking for another opportunity to talk to her about Jesus. Just one mention of what was considered harassment to her supervisor could not only get her fired, it could result in her referral to a mental health center.

"Well, in your own way, you're trying to tell me you're sorry for hurting my feelings the other night," Janice said with a sweet smile. "I learned a long time ago not to hold grudges. And I'll never make fun of you for believing the way you do."

Viv swallowed hard. Janice was such a forgiving person. It was hard to believe she didn't already know the Lord.

"I feel a lot better now," Janice continued. "And if you want to go back to Talk-o-lot Chocolate sometime, I wouldn't mind."

"Oh, Janice, that'd be rip!" Viv exclaimed.

Janice giggled. "That funny way you talk sure makes me laugh."

"How 'bout we go tomorrow night?"

"Oh, I can't tomorrow. I'm taking a few personal days. I'll be gone for a whole two weeks!" Janice hugged herself with excitement.

"Doing anything fun?" Viv ventured. She tried to imagine what Janice would do with vacation time. She never mentioned any family or hobbies.

"Oh, just a little shopping," she said, her eyes gleaming with anticipation. "I hardly ever go on a shopping trip. Maybe I'll get a hover bike, like you."

Viv tried to imagine Janice's round little form wobbling back and forth on one of the bikes. "Well, make sure ya try before ya buy, ya hare?"

"Hair?" Janice asked, a bit confused.

"Hare. Sounds like hear. But it's hare. Like a rabbit. They has the big ears, ya savvy?" Viv tried to explain. "Big ears for hearin' what I'm tellin' ya. Do ya smell what I'm steppin' in?"

Janice nearly doubled over laughing at Viv's string of outer docks lingo. "I understand. Make sure I get on and ride the thing first before I waste any money on it. I promise, I won't do anything I'll regret later. It just always looks like such fun when I see you leaving on yours, but hover bikes may not be my thing. I know that I'm me, and you're you, and we're all special in our own way. I'll just have to wait and see."

Viv brightened. "Ya got that right. Every one of us is special to the Lord. He made each one of us with a plan in mind,"[17] she heard herself say, and flinched inwardly, wondering if Janice would take offense. But to her surprise, her face broadened in a grin.

"Oh, Viv! That is so true! It sounds just like what I read in *My Truth* the other day! We all have a part to play in the universal symphony of the Source." As she said the word symphony, Janice moved her hands like a conductor. "I'll see you in two weeks, Viv!"

"See ya, Janice. Have a great time." Viv felt like throwing up. The State's religious blog watered down the idea of God to a mindless, generic force. "Universal symphony," she spit the words out as if they left a bad taste in her mouth just for saying them. "*My Truth*. More like *Lie Truth*."

---

[17] Jeremiah 29:11

"Are you talking to yourself, Delacruz?" said a voice behind her.

Viv jumped. Usually, her enhanced hearing implant gave her fair warning about people sneaking up on her, but Tommy Telquat had a special knack for taking her by surprise.

"Nah. Just heard somethin' funny and was repeatin' it to myself."

"Well, it must not have been very funny, because you're not laughing," Telquat said, his eyes seeming to penetrate her skull. "You weren't making fun of Janice, were you?"

"Makin' fun of Janice?" Viv sputtered. "Janice is my friend! I would never do that!"

"Hmm. Good. Because someone really upset her earlier this week. I would hate to think it was anyone who worked here."

"So would I," Viv said, although she knew she was the culprit. "I'll see ya tomorrow, Tommy." Viv headed to the locker room, trying not to show her agitation. Telquat had a way of getting under your skin and crawling around like a centipede. She couldn't imagine someone confiding in him about anything, but that was Janice. She appeared to believe the best about everyone.

"Nice guys finish last, Vivvy. Ya gotta look out fa numba one," her dad had told her on more than one occasion growing up when she would catch him in a lie or see him stealing something from a neighbor he had just pretended to help. As much as she hated to think he was right, all the evidence pointed in that direction. Citizens of the State, groomed to be self-centered, were consistently told they deserved nothing but the best whenever new implants came out on the market. The "me first" culture didn't cater much to the idea of self-sacrifice. Janice, who was nice to everyone, was taken for granted and dismissed as unimportant. A feeling of anger began to swirl subtly through Viv's inner being, stirring up a bitterness she hadn't felt in a long time. What was the point of being nice if it always got you hurt?

"And whosoever will be chief among you, let him be your servant: Even as the Son of man came not to be ministered unto, but to minister, and to give His life a ransom for many,"[18] Viv said softly to herself. Jesus was the perfect example

---

[18] Matthew 20:28 KJV

of someone who gave nothing but love and was met with rejection. And yet through His willingness to die, He fulfilled the Father's plan of reconciliation of man to God.

The scripture had come to her unbidden. Dawson had said that when she hid God's Word in her heart, the Holy Spirit would bring it to her mind when she needed it; and this was one of the ones she had been memorizing. The point of showing love, even if it got you hurt, was to do the will of the Father and to be like His Son. It was a natural, outward expression of the Holy Spirit living within a believer. "Thank you, Jesus," she said. The feeling of bitterness was gone, replaced with a peace that settled deep into her being.

Although Janice didn't know Jesus, Viv understood why she consistently tried to connect with others and win their affection, even if her kindness wasn't reciprocated. Janice was lonely. Viv could certainly identify with that. Being a Christian in the State meant traveling a solitary and dangerous road. Viv didn't spend much time with old friends because she didn't want to hang out in clubs anymore, looking for shallow relationships and one-night stands. Her time at Adullam was precious to her, but her current work schedule only gave her two days off in a row every other week, making it impossible to visit for the past three months. Modern transportation was streamlined as long as you stayed in the cities and the causeways between them. Viv's excursions to Adullam took her through thick forests and along rivers and creeks where trees arched their branches over the water in a protective shield from vantage points above. It made for good cover, but was slow going. It took the better part of a day to make it from Saint Louis to Adullam. That left just a few hours to visit the next day before she had to be on her way again, and the difficult and hazardous journey outweighed the small amount of time she could stay there.

Viv mounted her bike and headed home. On her way, her thoughts turned to the secret message hidden in the design of the shirt from Luciana. Since there was no location given, she assumed the logical place for the meeting must be at Talk-o-lot Chocolate. Would they all cram into the women's bathroom and hold a service there, she wondered? How could they keep from being discovered? Even if bathrooms were devoid of camera surveillance, surely it would be suspicious for a crowd of people to show up at the same time and all head for the toilets. She laughed at the thought, but her stomach flip-flopped in anticipation of meeting new brothers and sisters in Christ, no matter where the meeting was held. It was worth the risk, and Monday couldn't come soon enough for her.

9

"Good morning, Piper. Did you sleep well?"

Piper opened her eyes. It was no use pretending she was asleep, because somehow they could tell when she wasn't. Something to do with the wires they had attached to her scalp. She sighed. They had shaved her bald to make it easier to put the little sticky things on her head. The image of the long, golden-brown locks falling to the ground was imbedded in her mind. It wasn't so much that she minded losing her hair—even though it had turned out much prettier than she had realized, now that it was clean. What bothered her was that they didn't give her a choice. She turned her head on the pillow to look at the man who had entered the room. "When can I go home?" she repeated the question she had asked every day for the last two months. "I didn't do nothin' wrong."

"By the word of your testimony, you did indeed break the law," said the slim man in the white coat, with a touch of irony in his voice. "But since you are underage, I wouldn't expect you to understand completely the implications of what you've done. That's why you're here, Piper. That's why we're trying to help you and why we have tried to give you a chance to change."

Piper couldn't understand it. Being raised in the outer docks, she had never had any proper schooling, so she wasn't aware of very many of the laws enforced by the State. In fact, she didn't remember State authorities having much dealings with Discards at all unless they left the outer docks and wandered into the Preserve. Even those who managed to sneak into the cities were simply returned home unless they had committed a heinous crime.

"I didn't hurt nobody. I was trying to save 'em, to show 'em they don't *hafta* hurt no more, that they don't hafta do drugs or nothin' to be okay. Cuz when ya got Jesus, ya don't need nothin' else. He's everything! If ya knew 'im, ya'd know what I'm talkin' 'bout!" Piper said desperately. She had tried time after time to show the love of Jesus to this man, and he just wouldn't listen.

"How many people did you make depressed by telling them they weren't 'okay' without Jesus?" the man asked quickly. "How many people did you tell there was something wrong with them on the inside, and they needed to be fixed?"

"Ya mean how many people did I tell about needin' to be born again? Just about everyone I met," Piper said, her eyes gleaming. She felt that peculiar warm feeling she experienced when she knew God was pleased with her. No matter what she was going through, knowing that He was pleased made everything alright.

"Don't you have any remorse that your words caused them pain? To be told there was something wrong with them?" the man snapped.

"Nah. They was already in pain, see? They really did need fixin'. I was offerin' the answer to their problems. I was offerin' hope," she tried to explain. "I done tol' ya this—I don' know how many times."

"And how many people believed you?"

"I tol' ya that, too. Thirty-two, best I remember."

"Names, Piper. I want names," the man said firmly.

Piper's eyes narrowed. "Ya know I won't do that, even if I could remember all their names. Ya think I want 'em to end up here, away from their families, with their heads shaved & wires glued to their noggin?"

The man leaned casually against the wall. "What wires?" he asked.

Piper sat up in bed. Some of the drugs they gave her while she was here made her head foggy. She felt a little dizzy sitting up, but she made herself do it anyway. *"What wires?* Whaddaya mean, '*What wires?'* The wires ya done glued to ma head for weeks on end," she said, reaching gingerly for her scalp. But instead of the medusa-like tangle of wires she expected to encounter, all she could feel was the slight stubble of her hair trying to grow back. Her eyes grew wide. "They gone! Ya took 'em off when I was sleepin'," she said in surprise. "How did I sleep through all that?" she asked herself.

"You had a little help sleeping. And now you'll have a little help remembering. Because even if you don't think you remember the names of all those people, we have discovered the mind usually has those names stored somewhere. It's just a matter of recalling them to the surface of consciousness," the man said smugly.

Half the time, Piper couldn't understand what he was saying. But she understood when someone did not truly have her best interests in mind. "Why don't ya want people to be happy, Dr. Joe? Why don't ya want 'em to have peace in their hearts?" she asked. "That's all I was doin'. I was introducin' them to the only One What can give 'em peace. Ya see, we're all lookin' for our real Dad. And until we find 'im, we ain't got no peace."

"I told you that I know all about your Jesus. And I don't want to hear about it. Man has evolved to the point that we don't need mythology to explain things away or use as an emotional crutch to face the unfairness of life or to combat loneliness. We have moved beyond the idea of a benevolent, all-knowing imaginary friend," Dr. Joseph Moses said angrily. "We have the technology to never be separated from anyone again, should we wish. We no longer need to be bound by the chains of religion. And now, you too, can experience this freedom. Since you remained recalcitrant concerning your practice of insisting your belief system is the *only* way, you left us no choice but to go forward with the procedure we spoke about last week."

Piper sat very still. She remembered now how she had begun to feel groggy right after the nurse had given her what she had assumed was her weekly vitamin booster they had been giving her ever since she had been taken here. She reached tentatively behind her head at the base of her skull. Something foreign met her fingertips; something small and rigid. A wave of nausea swept over her as she realized what they had done.

"Get it out! Get it out, now!" she whimpered, digging at the piece of titanium.

"I wouldn't do that, if I were you. It's surgically fastened to your spine, and the connections lead all the way to your cerebral cortex, with the help of nanotechnology—the tiny robots I told you about when I explained all this. The chip drive can only be opened and accessed by a technician with the proper tools. To try to remove the chip by other means would have unfortunate results," Dr. Moses explained.

Piper shuddered. She remembered the videos she had been shown of the patients who had unsuccessfully attempted to remove their own chips. Most of the drooling, tube-filled bodies had been euthanized, but a few had been kept alive for instructional purposes. She drew her small hands slowly down to her lap. "It doesn't matter what ya put in ma head. I'll never change my mind about Jesus."

"We'll see," Dr. Moses said with a smile, and left the room. His smiles never seemed to indicate friendliness, Piper reflected. Of course, she was used to the misuse of body language when it came to people trying to get what they wanted. When her mom wanted Piper to leave her alone so she could get high, that's when she would smile the brightest and tell her eight-year-old daughter she was free to go play in the Shaw by herself. Shaw "Park" was an open space between two rows of buildings. It used to be part of a nature preserve that had been engulfed by the growth of St. Louis suburbs years ago, and it contained the only tree in a three-mile area. The tree was a shaggy barked, scratchy branched cedar that stubbornly refused to die. Its greenery gave her a rash when she climbed it, but Piper loved it. Being small, she could climb almost to the very top, where others who sometimes came after her were too heavy for the upper branches to support. It was one of the only places she felt absolutely safe. Often, no one even noticed she was there until her mother came to get her. It was from this vantage point that she was able to observe the interactions of others from a comfortable distance. Watching the way people treated each other—how what they said didn't match what they did—had opened her eyes to what her mother was actually doing when she let her go off and play by herself. The realization had taken a while to set in, because she hadn't wanted to accept it. But when her mother got angry the first time Piper said she wanted to stay with her when she was supposed to go to the Shaw, that's when she had to face reality.

From that point on, she knew the only person she could really trust was herself. She had never known her father, only a string of men and women who stayed for a short time, bartering with Piper's mother for the only tender she had. For as long as she could remember, it had just been the two of them and a revolving door of faces who came and went. Of course, she still loved her mother. The only thing that had changed was that she didn't trust her anymore, and she began to hone her own survival skills instead of depending on someone else.

Dumpster diving was the way her mother had taught her to gather scraps to eat or items to sell for food. The State relocated most of its trash to the outer docks, with workers refilling dumpsters from the safety of armored trash trucks. Discards lined the sidewalks of the alleys designated for dumpster refilling, which ran on a schedule known only to the State workers. Waiting on a dumpster was a game of chance intended to spread out not only the State's generosity, but the amount of people waiting at each alley. Fighting over rubbish was reduced with lower numbers at each dumping point, but small folk like Piper were still in danger of being trampled. The safest bet was to wait until the end when everyone else was finished.

However, as Piper branched out on her own, she had begun to test new sources of food. Her biggest find came quite by accident, on a day when the dumpsters were picked clean of anything desirable, and her stomach was growling like a trash panda guarding a crust of bread. She was walking down an alley, her eyes scanning from side to side, looking for even a crumb that may have been dropped by a rat. Suddenly she saw a French fry, but before she could reach it, one of the ever-present starlings had snatched it up and flown away. She went to the spot where it had been, anger and despair welling up in her heart, and began to cry. Huddled with her back to the wall, she cried for a good, long time, looking at the brick wall across from her through her tears. After her sobbing subsided, she remained there, staring at the blank space, until a shot of color in the middle of the monotonous brickwork caught her eye. A dandelion seed had managed to find purchase in years of dirt collected in a crack in the wall, and its blossom was like a miniature sun shining in the alley. Another blossom had already headed out and sent its seeds on a mission of propagation. Piper slowly rose to her feet and crossed the alley. She had never really thought about dandelions much before, except to blow on their seed heads or to use their yellow blossoms as makeshift sidewalk chalk. As she stood there, she decided it was indeed a beautiful sight, with its blazing bright color in the middle of all the drab walls. She leaned over to smell it, and her stomach growled again. And suddenly, without any thought, she had bitten the blossom right off the plant and chewed and swallowed it. It was bitter, but it was something in her gut. She began to slowly try each part of the plant. The flower stem was awful. The bigger leaves on the outside were almost unbearably bitter. But the smallest leaves weren't too bad, she decided. And the tiny green blossom heads that had not yet developed were almost sweet. She looked around the alley and found another flower, and another. Before she knew it, she had eaten three or four of them, leaves, roots, and all. Everything except the little buds tasted bitter to her, but as her mother had always said, *beggars can't be choosers.*

A few starlings had gathered nearby to watch, assuming she had found some tasty crumbs from a lucky Discard's fast-food throw away. Piper chewed thoughtfully as she watched them, wiping away a bit of green juice from her chin. Killing animals was illegal in the State, this much she knew. But this wasn't technically the State. This was the outer docks. She had once dined on roasted trash panda when one of her mother's friends had dropped by. She had heard about people catching and eating pigeons. Starlings were much smaller, but there were so many of them; and when they got greedy, they lost all sense of caution. No one she knew of ate starlings, so there would be no competition or worry of treading on anyone's turf.

She began to collect old shoelaces and bits of yarn. Her mother yelled at her when she unraveled part of her grandmother's afghan to complete her project, but Piper didn't let that deter her from her plan. The net was eventually complete. Her first attempts were unfruitful, but from her vantage point in the Shaw, she had watched how other trappers had successfully lured in pigeons under a netted canopy. One pull of a string, and the weighted ends of the net collapsed, usually resulting in a few trapped birds. Piper weighted her net with misshapen bits of concrete. She set it up in an alley that was seldom visited because it had no dumpster, and baited her trap with crumbs and other bits of food that were so moldy, even the poorest Discards left them alone. After her intial few unsuccessful attempts, she decided she would have to earn the birds' trust. For two weeks, she faithfully scattered her bait and allowed the birds to devour it. As time went on, they began to lose their fear of the girl who watched nearby and began to fight amongst themselves as greed outgrew their caution. Finally the day came when a large flock of squabbling starlings gathered under her low lying canopy, paying not the least bit of attention to Piper. With one sharp tug, she yanked the trip string, and down came the net. Piper lunged forward with a blanket, immediately covering the net to prevent exit through any larger holes and to confuse the birds further from their path of escape. She had only expected to catch one or two, but she had succeeded in catching almost the entire flock! Carefully, she extracted them one by one, stuffing ten of them into a cage which had housed a guinea pig her mother had given her for her birthday on one of their more bountiful years. The next year was a meager one, and her pet had disappeared from his cage one morning. Piper had kept it, hoping Marshmallow would come home someday. Now the cage proved useful, its occupants, she realized with a lump in her throat, soon to meet the probable fate of her guinea pig.

There were still five birds left in the net. They wouldn't fit in the cage, and Piper was immediately faced with the dilemma of what to do with them. She didn't want to let them go, because she wasn't certain when her next meal would be. She didn't want to kill them either, she suddenly realized as the terminality of her plan finally set in. But hunger finally outweighed her squeamishness. One by one, she killed them the way she had seen the pigeon trappers do it, wringing their necks clean off of their bodies in some instances. The squawking was unbearable at first, but she steeled herself to her task. These were the creatures who competed with her for food. They had brought their fates upon themselves by being so greedy and careless, she reasoned. As she pulled the last head off, she felt like something inside her had died as well.

Piper then realized she had no idea what to do next. How did you cook them? Did you skin them, or pluck them? She put the dead birds in her pocket and wrapped the cage up in the net and the blanket and made her way to the Shaw. Today was Tuesday. It was Zelda's day to trap. She was the oldest trapper of the bunch, and she had allowed Piper to watch her trap from close by when she realized the girl could keep still.

When Zelda saw her approaching with a blanket wadded around what appeared to be a box, she squinted her eyes suspiciously and leaned back on her haunches. "Whatcha got dere girl, hum? Stay back ovah dere wit dat package, ya hare?" Zelda's accent was thick and hard to understand, even for someone who had been born here. She was one of the oldest people Piper had ever met, a mind-bending fifty years. She came from the outermost edge of the docks, right on the border of the Preserve. Most people didn't initiate conversation with her, and all had learned to keep their distance. Zelda could spit with frightening accuracy.

Slowly, Piper unwrapped a bit of the blanket so Zelda could see its contents. The trapper leaned forward; and for a moment, her eyes opened wider. Then they went back to their perpetually skeptical squint. "Where'ja git dat, girl? Where'ja git dem rat birds?"

Piper pulled out a bit of the net from under the bundle so that Zelda could see. "I made a net. I caught 'em, see? I's powerful hungry," Piper explained. Then she reached in her pocket and slowly pulled out one of the dead starlings. "But I don' know hows to fix 'em." She looked steadily at Zelda, the unasked plea for help evident as she bit her lip and waited.

Zelda rocked back on her haunches again, her eyes moving from the net made from bits and pieces of string and yarn to the gaunt face of the small girl. A look Piper had never seen before flashed across her face. "Well, I'll be. I'll be," Zelda said slowly, and suddenly Piper realized with a rush of pride that the unidentified look was that of respect. "Ja come 'ere girl. Gimme dat rat bird, an' I shows ya whatcha do," Zelda said with a snaggle-toothed smile. She showed Piper how to remove the bird's breast and told her different ways she could cook it. "Rat birds, dey's small, but dey's sump'n, hum, girl?" Zelda said as they parted ways. Piper offered her a few of the birds as payment, but Zelda refused. "Ya take some where ya dock, hum? Gotcha fambly somewheres, hum?" Piper nodded, although she didn't know what her mother would think about eating the rat birds, as Zelda called them.

They offered little meat, but it was more meat than she and her mother had seen in a month; and it was fresh. From then on, Piper visited the dumpsters mostly to search for bait. Her health improved with the better diet, but for some reason, her mother started growing weaker. At first, she blamed the starlings. "Them birds you is bringin' home's done ailin' me," she said, and refused to eat any more of them. A visit to the traveling hospital sent out by emissaries of the State told a different story: cancer. It had already metastasized. In a month, she was gone. Piper had always worried she would die from an overdose or from taking drugs that had been stretched with something dirty. Cancer had never entered her mind as a possible killer.

Although Piper had already made strides toward self sufficiency, the weight of her mother's sudden death left her dazed. She didn't even have the strength to hold vigil over the body, feeling that in a strange way, allowing the scroungers to take her was a way for her to live on. Loneliness shrouded her days; and later, she was overshadowed by the guilt of letting the body be cannibalized. Finally, she could stand it no longer and in desperation began to look to the thing she had vowed she would never do to kill the pain. She began to dig through the dumpsters again, searching for anything she could use to trade for dope. On one of these dumpster dives she found it, smeared with barbeque sauce and puffed out like a miniature accordion from sopping up whatever slop the citizens of the State deemed unfit to consume. It was a little book with a picture of a tiny lamp on the front. Piper could read it—the one legacy her mother had given her was to teach her daughter how to read. "New Testament. Psalms, Proverbs," she read. She had never heard those words before—except *new*, of course. Well, it was in bad condition. But it was a book, and books were rare. Maybe someone would pay something for it at the Pawn Shop near the Shaw. She opened the book on her way and began to read. It had been a long time since she had read anything except old grocery ads from dumpsters when she used to dream about being able to eat the food in the pictures. Some of it was hard to understand, but there was a fascinating character called Jesus who seemed to be the hero of the book. Piper kept reading until she got to the shop. She sat down on the steps to read some more because she wanted to find out what happened. Something had flickered inside of her when she began to read about Jesus, and she was curious to know more about Him. And then the words seemed to jump up off the page. "For God so loved the world, that He gave his only begotten Son, that whosoever believeth in Him should not perish, but have everlasting life. For God sent not His Son into the world to condemn the world, but that the world through Him might be saved."[19] Piper's heart pounded. If anyone needed saving in the world, surely she did. "Oh, God," she prayed quietly, "I don't know

---

[19] John 3:16-17, KJV

Ya, but Mama said Grandma did. If Ya really out there, can Ya save me? If Ya Son really came, can 'e help me? I really need someone to help me. No one else is here for me now. How 'bout it, You an' me? I don' know why, but I believe that bit 'bout Ya Son, an' all. I know I ain't perfect, but I don' know hows else to be. If Ya kin look past my messin' ups and somehow see it in Ya heart to be wit' me, I sure would be glad of it." And all of the sudden, the heaviness in her chest began to lift. Something deep within her began to build. It felt like light shining inside of her…like a fresh, strong wind from the top of the cedar tree …like when you have enough water to take a bath and finally get clean. Except this was an inward clean. She felt clean from the inside out, in places and ways she had never known she was dirty. Piper smooshed the fanned-out, swelled-up pages back into a book shape as best she could and started for home. She needed to gather her things, because her mother's friends who gave them rent money would be coming around for payment soon. She didn't know where she was going, but she knew she no longer needed to be afraid. She would never be alone again.

10

IRA stared out the window of his high-rise apartment at the sluggish Mississippi as it oozed past the Gateway Arch like a giant, muddy brown salamander. The morning sun was shining brightly on the monument, but the oily sheen of the river could barely reflect the relic of the old republic. The governing body of the State had considered changing its name to the Causeway Arch as a nod to one of the features of the landscape that typified the new era; but in the end, Congress had decided the term *gateway* also lent itself to an appreciation for the way things were done now. It was a symbol of a gap that had been bridged, which is what the causeways had done for modern transportation.

While causeways are generally thought of as raised passageways over expanses of water, the State's causeways were so named because they were not only raised above the landscape, but they had revolutionized the car industry. Land vehicle abilities were lifted to the same level as that of a jet plane, all due to technology that was a symbiosis of the computers in modern vehicles, a network of Wi-Fi linking the roadways much like a combined system of air traffic controllers, and the types of material used to make both the causeways and the vehicles. Motorists using the system were not actually in control of their vehicles at all as the result would be disastrous. One bobble of the steering wheel could result in a 2,000-car pile-up. So once the driver entered his destination into the causeway itinerary and was given access to the transit system, he became a passenger. The programming in the causeway Wi-Fi linked the car's computer with that of every other vehicle en route, creating a sort of vehicular internet. The new cars didn't have wheels; they hovered. And on the causeways, they no longer used fans to project themselves above the road, but were buoyed along by a material in their frames which worked together with the causeway similarly to how superconductive magnets in Maglev trains reacted with their tracks. However, the new material was more efficient even than the magnetic fields used to float trains in the past. Programming had to be installed to limit the amount of g-forces created during acceleration and deceleration. People could now go from one end of the country to the other by land as quickly as by air.

However, the methods used to create the materials in the electronically-lined transit routes had a devastating effect on the health of the environment as companies competing in this particular tech race secretly disregarded environmental laws in their haste. The result was fishless rivers, choked with industrial sludge as the byproducts of mining and manufacturing caused a strange bonding of water, oil, and chemicals similar to the cohesiveness of mercury. Anyone living near the Mississippi or the other affected rivers developed a severe form of asthma, and cancer rates skyrocketed. Citizen outcry demanded retribution for damages to the health of humanity and the environment. The end result in the courts was that power was taken out of the hands of big corporations once and for all and given over to the management of the government.

This took a considerable amount of control out of the hands of not only greedy, unscrupulous corporations, but eventually out of the hands of individual citizens. Private land had already been abolished by the global directive of the Free Land Initiative, which declared that the earth belonged to everyone as a whole and to no one as an individual. All land was public land and was therefore under the jurisdiction of the governing body of each respective country. Now that the big, private corporations were abolished, it was a small step from there to require individuals to run all proposals for small private businesses through the State, which placed restrictive limits on their expansion. Businesses which grew beyond their "ability to conduct themselves responsibly" were absorbed by the State and either expanded or shut down. The political evolution that followed was slow but steady as the media (which was also State-owned) continuously fed the public believable propaganda that made the restrictions easier to swallow. One by one, citizens found themselves willingly giving up more freedoms to protect themselves and their children from their own mistakes. The lack of governmental divisiveness formerly in play due to the tugging of individual viewpoints in a healthy democratic republic disappeared, replaced by a suave new form of socialism. After all, what good was freedom if you weren't healthy or safe enough to enjoy it?

Former fears that the abolishment of private health providers would be a fiasco where the medical community was spread too thinly and no one got adequate care were quickly put to rest by the newly lubricated political machine that was becoming the modern State. With the advent of implants that detected and corrected many health problems before they became an issue, the average citizen was likely to never encounter high blood pressure, diabetes, or cancer. Women pregnant with infants who had cerebral palsy, muscular dystrophy, genetic deformities, mental retardation—or any other deviation from what was considered healthy—never need know why their implant had instigated a "miscarriage". It was enough to know they and their child had been saved a lifetime of hardship and suffering. Antidepressants were quickly administered to the would-be mother to prevent any psychological setbacks. The result was a lower, healthier population and a better standard of living for all who embraced the new system. If you didn't embrace it…well, you could leave for the outskirts of the city and cope with disease, harsh living conditions, and whatever genetic mutations life handed you.

"Ira. Your breakfast is ready," said a soothing voice seeming to emanate from the gray walls.

"Thank you, Geeves," Ira said absently. Even though Geeves was just the home control unit with no need of common courtesy or affirmation, Ira found it hard to do away with social niceties. There was no one else in the apartment. Sometimes he felt the need to talk to someone, and Geeves was the literal wall off which he bounced his ideas. To take the artificial intelligence for granted or treat it as a mere tool seemed somehow rude. He turned from his vantage point of the river and sat down at his small dining room table where his heated, prepackaged breakfast had been deposited by a slide-out tray from the microwave embedded in the wall.

He glanced around the apartment as he chewed his rubbery French toast. It was a nice set-up—better than most, he realized. The apartment had been given to him rent-free for working as a monitor for the State. The grand view out the window was probably a perk for having worked with Dr. Moses, who had taken an interest in Ira even before they met. Ira's lack of optional implants was a source of curiosity for most people, and the foremost authority on bio-implantation technology was no exception. He seemed to respect it somehow; and Ira was never asked to take the chip or get any of the implants people normally opted for when they turned sixteen, even if it would have made his job easier. Ira always suspected he might have been viewed as a sort of failsafe if the interconnectivity of technology backfired and produced a cascading, cataclysmic systems failure. At least there would have been one State employee with a solid grasp of computer systems and tech interface programming whose brain wasn't affected by their absence.

Which was why he was sometimes confused as to the reason he was still watching a monitor screen eight hours a day. He was capable of so much more than was required of his job. The drone readout rooms were thought of as a way to "get your foot in the door" of the State tech positions, and having been there for two years, now at the age of thirty-five, Ira had somehow gotten his foot stuck. But he faithfully came to work and rarely complained. In his free time, he kept up on the latest trends in tech interface programming (his area of expertise) and learned the new languages associated with its advances. He did it not only to keep abreast of what was happening in the programming world, but immersed himself in it for sheer enjoyment. Not many people understood his love of programming, so he mostly kept it to himself. Anyone who did find out about it marveled at the fact that one so proficient in tech interface took pains to avoid integrating it into his own body's systems. But it was precisely his knowledge of the subject that kept him at arm's length of acquiring it personally. Ira could see the way technology was evolving, and he could see the way many programmers were attempting to force a similar type of evolution in humanity. The more absorbed in technology people became, from games to social media to augmented physical systems, the less able they seemed to connect with each other as human beings. Despite the promise of connectivity touted by emissaries of the chip, Ira was skeptical. They never talked about the pros and cons—only the pros. And there had to be cons along with the pros. "More than one kind of con, too," Ira said out loud.

"I'm sorry, Ira, I didn't understand that request."

"Nothing, Geeves. Just thinking out loud," Ira said, and went into the bathroom to finish getting ready for work.

As he brushed his teeth, his mind wandered to the Pod-Op he had been monitoring. He wondered about hygiene out in the Preserve, where clean water wasn't readily available. Could she brush her teeth, take a bath, or even wash her hands? Not all rivers and streams were polluted like the Mississippi and the Missouri, but few of them were safe enough for drinking or even hand-washing. It was quite a sacrifice to be wandering around out there, far from the comforts of home, he reflected. Of course, if the Pod-Ops were originally Unspokens, they might feel they owed their lives to the program for saving them from exit. Ira nearly choked on his toothpaste as he pondered the possibility. *Was Jo-Mo using Unspokens to further his research on chip advances and community connectivity?* Ira had never voiced this question, not even to Geeves. Dr. Moses was one of the most powerful men in the State. If he had any inkling that someone was questioning the ethical stability of his research, that person might be obligated to undergo counseling. Then suddenly Ira remembered. All the Unspokens were scheduled for exit. What difference did it make to the State if they were used for feeding zoo animals or running experiments or creating Pod Operatives? A wave of anxiety swept over him. It made a difference to Ira. He had never been able to shake the feeling that it was morally wrong to treat human life with so little respect. He would never be able to adopt the cavalier attitude so popular with his coworker, Vicey, and others. That much he had expressed in the think tank at the Conference of the Mid-south Chapter of Tech Interface. His shoulders sagged. Why hadn't he kept his mouth shut? This could be the very reason he was still stuck in a monitoring position. If he had been more subtle, maybe he would still be involved in current tech interface programming. Maybe he would be able to exert an ethical influence, or at least present what he felt was the ethical side of things.

"Your shuttle is nearing the stop, Ira," Geeves said. "Estimated arrival in three minutes."

"On my way," Ira said as he grabbed his jacket and waved his palm over the scanner at the door to be let out. He repeated the process at the scanner outside his doorway to lock it. Behind him in the empty apartment, lights went out and the water he had absent mindedly left running in the bathroom was shut off. Ira hurried down the hall, scanned his way into the elevator and eventually out the front door. He could see the shuttle was just pulling up at the stop down the street. He ran the short distance and caught it just in time. If he was going to be so deep in thought in the mornings, he was going to have to ask Geeves to give him a shuttle notice at the five-to-ten minute mark, he decided.

When he arrived at the Mid-south Sector Drone Readout Room, Darst, the night shift monitor, was wearing a grin. "I almost hate to leave," he said. "It's starting to get interesting."

"What? What happened?" Ira asked quickly.

"Pod girl looks like she's running out of things to eat. She took a shot at a rabbit earlier. Must be pretty hungry."

Ira squinted at the screen. "It's more likely she thinks she's being watched and is trying to get someone to trust her. In any case, I'm not sure the rules about killing animals apply to Pod-Ops who are trying to blend in with the people in their surroundings."

Darst shrugged, stood up and stretched. "I don't know, hume. I'm pretty sure that a couple nights ago, I saw her eat the last bite of whatever that brown, chewy stuff was that she's been gnawing on. Since then, she's been picking leaves off of plants along the side of the road and eating them. That doesn't seem like it would be very filling, if you ask me."

Ira nodded. He had seen her eating certain plants as well—even the small, young growth off of those green, prickly vines that grew at the forest's edge. But if she was out of supplies, surely her supervisor would understand if she needed to ask for help. Was it that crucial that she maintain her ruse of being a defector of the State? Couldn't her superiors make a secretive drop of a food cache she could retrieve later without breaking her cover? And why was she steadily heading toward the city?

"Morning, Ira," Vicey said in her nasal voice.

Ira looked up, unaware of having ever sat down. He had been so engrossed in the girl that he hadn't even realized Darst had left. "Hello, Vice," he said.

"So what's our Pod girl up to today?" Vicey asked as she settled into her station.

"Well, looks like she's almost made it to Rolla."

"I heard she ran out of provisions. Nothing for her to eat in that old ghost town, that's for sure," Vicey said. "She sure puts on a front, acting like she's never seen civilization before."

Ira smirked and rubbed his chin. Indeed, she did. When she came to the first abandoned town on her route, she had been so convincing in her bewilderment that he almost believed she was the child of a defector and it was the first time she had laid eyes on a city block. Then he saw her talking to her supervisor again and realized it was all an act. He couldn't make out what she was saying, but she was definitely talking to someone on a secure link.

A thought suddenly occurred to him. Maybe she wasn't asking for help because she didn't want to admit she needed it—she didn't want to look weak. Maybe he should let his supervisor know that she was in need of supplies. Rolla had plenty of distinguishable landmarks in which a drone could make a food drop before she got there. She could be notified of its location and retrieve it without any hidden defectors who might be following her knowing anything about it. Maybe her superiors hadn't been informed of her situation, although he was certain Darst must have reported her shot at the rabbit. He decided to call it in.

"I'll inform them of her situation. Thank you, Ira," his supervisor said.

The rest of the day, Ira kept an eye on the Rolla surveillance readout screen, expecting his drone in that area to detect a supply drop at any moment, but none ever came. As the girl entered the outskirts of the old city, he realized they expected her to take care of herself. Once again, she looked up at the buildings as if they were a marvel to her. Smiling in wonder, she kept making comments to her supervisor as she gazed at the glass and concrete structures. She didn't seem upset about not having any food. As she wandered down what had been the main thoroughfare, she kept looking from side to side, occasionally peering into the buildings. Eventually, she called out something loud enough that he could hear her over the monitor.

"Hello? Is there anyone here?"

She repeated the phrase at several different buildings; and then, seeming to give up, she resumed her regular pace. She was approaching what appeared to have been a fountain at the entrance of a park. The pool was filled with muck and leaves from years of neglect and was brimming with water from recent spring rains. Her face brightening, the Pod-Op took a pouch out of her back pack and began filling it with the water. Ira had seen her do this before, during a rainstorm when the ditches at the roadside were flooded. It was a sort of filtration system she was using. He watched as she gulped down the last of the water in her canteen before filling it up again with the newly acquired water. She drank each portion she filtered until finally, her thirst slaked, she filled the canteen and capped it. She splashed some of the water from the fountain on her face and sat down on an old stone bench that was part of the fountain wall. The couple days walking with nothing but leaves from various plants to eat had seemed to take its toll on her energy level, and she was just resting her head on her arm on the fountain wall when her eyes opened wide; and she looked in the direction of the park entrance. In its day, it must have been a pleasant place to jog or take children to play. Now the park was just a mass of overgrown shrubbery and thickets, with a few open places here and there. From the drone's vantage point, Ira could see what was making the noise she had heard. A rabbit was chewing on some tender young leaves of low-lying branches on a bush just beyond the park entrance. With each bite, it tugged at the shrub, which must be creating a rustling sound. Ira watched as the girl slowly reached for her bow, her eyes never leaving the direction of the noise. She nocked an arrow and slowly crept along the wall, moving only as the rabbit was busy tugging at the shrub. Finally, she stopped and waited. At the next tug of the shrub, she drew her bow. Ira's heart pounded. Was she really going to try to shoot it?

Suddenly the arrow was released, and the rabbit squealed and jumped. The girl was upon it before its second feeble jump, clobbering it in the head with a rock. Ira was stunned. He had never seen an animal killed before. He was even more spellbound when she gutted and skinned it and set to work making a fire in one of the abandoned buildings near a broken window, using an old wooden chair for fuel. As he watched, she roasted pieces of the rabbit over the fire and proceeded to eat it. Ira swallowed to keep the stomach bile from coming up in his throat. He wasn't certain which was more barbaric: killing and eating an animal, or the fact that she had been forced into that position by supervisors who refused to come to her aid. Whatever the case, she was smiling, talking once again to whoever was on her feed. Apparently, she didn't consider it an unforgiveable oversight on the part of her superiors. She devoured the entire rabbit and another canteen of water, then curled up on the floor by the fire to spend the night.

11

"PHOEBE! Phoebe!" A squeaky voice and a fluttering of wings awakened Selah as gray daylight found its way through the broken storefront windows. Selah opened one eye from her bed of broken tile. "Phoebe, Phoebe!" insisted the bird of the same name. As Selah rolled to a sitting position, the slate and white colored bird dived out of her nest above the doorframe and swooped onto a tree branch across the street. "I'm not going to hurt you, silly," she mumbled and slowly stretched her arms and legs. Her neck and shoulders ached from the weight of the packs pulling on them. She knew her feet would feel like she was standing on pins and needles as soon as she stood up, so she delayed getting up for as long as possible. As the Eastern Phoebe squeaked out its territorial proclamations, she drew her feet in and massaged them thoroughly.

This was the biggest town she had come across; but it, too, was devoid of people. Had something happened to them all? Perhaps something so catastrophic that no one was left? She shook her head. No, it couldn't be that. Otherwise, who was controlling the drone that had been following her since she started walking the road? Unless it was simply automated. What if all that remained were machines? And if that was the case, had the machines destroyed humanity? Selah laughed at herself. Her thoughts sounded like an old fairytale her father had made up to tell her when she wanted to hear a ghost story. She always suspected he had taken his idea from a classic movie in the Old Country. Now that she was actually *in* the Old Country, the fairytale seemed eerily believable.

A swish of wing beats roused her from her reverie. The Phoebe was peering inside the window, its beak full of moths. "Ok, Phoebe. I realize I'm not the only one who wants breakfast," Selah said and put on her boots. She wearily pulled the pack and her bow to her shoulders and staggered out the door. Behind her, the nestlings cried shrilly as breakfast was served. Her stomach rumbling, Selah briefly thought that if she were desperate enough, she could actually eat them. The thought was abhorrent to her, and she decided she clearly wasn't that desperate. As she stepped off the curb, she hopped over a thick black cable she hadn't noticed the night before. Suddenly, the cable moved, and Selah jumped three feet into the street and whirled around as she realized it was a snake. "Just a black snake," she panted. Snakes by surprise were never welcome to her, no matter if they were harmless. She watched as the six-foot long rat snake slithered over the curb and through the open door of the building, stopping every once and a while to test the air with its tongue. Selah had raised chickens long enough to know exactly what it was seeking. And then the thought occurred to her that there was a fair amount of meat on a snake that size. Besides, she had always been partial to Phoebes. They ate a tremendous amount of insects. She wasn't going to stand by and watch while the snake ate a nest full of their babies, so she picked up a piece of rebar she found lying next to the door; and in a few minutes, she had procured her next meal. Breaking apart a little display shelf from a store, she made a fire from the wooden pieces in a sheltered corner between a building and a retaining wall. She wanted to make certain the meat was cooked well, because she knew reptiles carried a disease the old timers called salmonella. Her community had been protected from many diseases, but the old timers didn't believe in throwing caution to the wind, and neither did she.

As she bowed her head to thank the Lord for her food and bless it, she couldn't help but think the whole situation wasn't a coincidence. The Lord had been providing for her during her journey, reminding her of edible plants when she ran out of jerky, and showing her the rabbit and the snake. The rabbit was admittedly better eating than the black snake, but Selah wasn't going to complain.

Her breakfast over, Selah decided to sit by the fountain and read from one of the Bibles she carried in her pack before she started on her way. Spiritual food was as important to her as a physical meal, and although her daily rituals had been altered drastically since she left the valley, this was one part of her routine she was unwilling to give up. She took off her boots and socks again and let her feet soak in the cool, leafy water of the old fountain as she read. For the last two days, they had felt like they were baking in miniature ovens as they clomped on the asphalt in her old leather boots. She decided to look up scriptures that had the word "feet" in them for her study that morning, since hers were at the forefront of her mind. The concordance in the back of her Bible listed several, but a few jumped out at her. 2 Samuel 22:32-34 said "For who is God, save the Lord? And who is a rock, save our God? God is my strength and power; and He maketh my way perfect. He maketh my feet like hinds' feet and setteth me upon my high places."[20] As a child, Selah had always laughed when she heard this passage read. She didn't understand it until her mother explained to her that a hind was another word for a deer. David, who had written this particular song, was painting a picture of a surefooted deer set on precipitous mountain heights, far above those who would pursue it. The psalmist was safe because his God had brought him to a place of rest in the presence of the Lord, the rock of his salvation.

Psalm 40:2 also spoke of a person's feet being set upon a rock. "He brought me up also out of a horrible pit, out of the miry clay, and set my feet upon a rock, and established my goings,"[21] Selah read. "Lord, please establish my goings. If I'm going in the wrong direction, let me know. I'm just following this road because it seemed the obvious choice. If I'm wrong, please show me," she prayed.

The last scripture listed in her concordance was Isaiah 52:7. "How beautiful upon the mountains are the feet of him that bringeth good tidings, that publisheth peace; that bringeth good tidings of good, that publisheth salvation; that saith unto Zion, Thy God reigneth!"[22] Selah looked down at her feet, which were starting to get wrinkled as they soaked in the water. A couple of her toes sported blisters, and they were red from the constant walking and the coldness of the water. They were anything but beautiful. *"They are beautiful to me,"* she felt a voice say deep in her spirit. *"You are carrying My most precious message of peace to a people who have forgotten where to find it. Tell them that I still reign. Tell them that I am still their God, the One who came down and brought salvation to them."* Selah swallowed and blinked back tears. Every time she felt like

---

[20] 2 Samuel 22:32-34, KJV
[21] Psalm 40:2, KJV
[22] Isaiah 52:7, KJV

this was a fruitless quest, the Lord took time to show her otherwise. She closed her Bible and put it back in her pack, thankful that she had not neglected her morning devotions. Since she had taken time with Him, He was taking time with her.

Selah dried off her feet as best she could, put on her socks and shoes, and gathered her gear. Maybe today she would meet someone, she thought hopefully. The thought put butterflies in her stomach, but that was the purpose of her mission, after all. "If this is the day I meet someone, Lord, please help me to know what to do and what to say," she prayed. She started down the road once again, singing to the Lord as she went. One block later, a sign on a building stopped her dead in her tracks. "Hog Jaw Café –voted the best BBQ in Rolla three years straight." So this was Rolla. This was the city her ancestors had come from—Miss Genevieve's home town! Where was everyone? It was then, in the quiet, that she noticed the humming.

At first, she looked up to see if she could get a glimpse of the drone. But this was a different, deeper sort of humming. Selah walked cautiously forward, keeping closer to the buildings as she traveled. The farther she went, the louder the humming became. Intermittently she could hear sharp little bursts of sound in the midst of the hum, like the time she had gotten too close to a hornet's nest and wasn't aware of it until they started zipping past her ear. Finally, as she came to the end of the block and looked down the street, she could see the source of the sound. Just above the buildings, gleaming in the bright morning sunlight, was what looked to Selah like a giant, silver serpent suspended in the air.

She stayed motionless, trying to make sense of it. Was it a bridge of some sort? Why was it making that noise? Surely it couldn't be a plane, hovering so perfectly still in the distance. Selah shifted her pack to a more comfortable position. There was only one way to find out.

Miles away in St. Louis, in a room full of monitors, Ira watched the girl steadily approaching the Texas Transit Causeway. The TTC began in the consolidated city of Austin-San Antonio and ended in St. Louis, from where it branched to other consolidated cities in the eastern half of the continent. If she went to the southwest, the girl would take a long, long time to reach Tulsa, the first consolidated city in that direction. She would pass out of Ira's sector before she reached what used to be Oklahoma. But if she turned northeast and followed the causeway, she would reach the outer docks of St. Louis in approximately 25 miles. He found himself hoping she would turn northeast. Then he paused to wonder—why would she follow a causeway? If her mission was to seek out isolationist outposts, why would she take a route that precluded finding one? Shouldn't she be heading deep into the Preserve, where people would be likely to hide? Ira frowned and drummed his fingers on his chin. Maybe she was just passing under the causeway to another sector. Or maybe she was going to stay close to it, betting that whoever may have been following her would want to keep their distance. This would ensure she could be picked up and returned home to report on her findings without blowing her cover. Ira watched closely as the girl neared the causeway. She seemed overly cautious, as if she sensed a trap. He zoomed in on her face in time to see her talking to her supervisor again. It was a fair day with low humidity, and the drone was able to get a crystal clear, close-up view. He couldn't hear what she was saying, but she seemed a little bewildered and was speaking slowly. He was able to lip-read the words, "Which way do I go?"

Ira leaned back in his chair. Was she really that turned around, that she didn't know? All the Pod-Ops he knew about had been implanted with a GPS device. She couldn't be lost. Maybe she was no longer sure of her next assignment. Or maybe….

Ira's heart fluttered. He quickly returned to that morning's footage of her sitting on the fountain wall. Zooming in on what he had assumed was a book she had taken from a secret commune in the wilderness, he could see the words on its spine: *Holy Bible.* So she had stolen an ancient religious text from some cultish community. She seemed to be reading it. At one point, she paused, and he could see tears running down her cheeks before she smiled and placed the book back in her pack. He backed up the footage to her morning meal. Right before she ate, she bowed her head and said something. He zoomed in on the footage until her lips were nearly the size of the screen. Ira was no professional lip reader, but he could clearly see the words "thank you," and then something more. He enhanced the audio linked to his earpiece, and was able to isolate the sound of the girl from the calls of the annoying, squeaky-voiced bird which had kept him from hearing her earlier. And then he heard it very clearly in his earpiece: "Thank you, Jesus. Thank you for providing this food. Please bless it to the nourishment of my body, and help me as I serve You today. Amen." Ira's blood ran cold. This was no Pod-Op, and that was no superior officer she had been talking to this whole time. He didn't know how her home had remained hidden, but she was walking to her own demise and that of her family if she continued. His superiors were allowing it. They probably hadn't intercepted her in the hopes she would lead them to her home or another outpost besides the one of her origin.

His heart pounding, Ira knew what would happen next. They would eventually pick her up. If she didn't tell them everything, they would chip her, and her community would be discovered. She would probably live the rest of her life in prison for having killed and eaten not one, but *two* animals. The State turned a blind eye to Discards eating the occasional pigeon or rat when the garbage truck offerings were meager, but the outer docks were a gray area. The animals this girl had killed were in the Preserve, which by its very name implied the seriousness of her offense. Why was she traveling the roads and the causeways? Didn't she have any idea of the danger she was in? Was she *trying* to find civilization, unaware that her actions had already doomed her to a life of imprisonment, experimentation, or chip-induced personality adjustment? *Well, of course, if she was born in the Preserve, she would have no knowledge of any of those things,* Ira chided himself.

And then, his nerves prickling with adrenaline, he knew what he had to do. But he had to do it at the right time, near the end of his shift, when it would arouse the least suspicion. The rest of the day was interminable as he watched the girl head northeast and follow the causeway, as he had suspected she would. He spent some time subtly and meticulously erasing his review of the footage and the close-ups that led to his discovery, leaving only the original, unenhanced footage intact. His proficiency as a programmer served him well. Only the most skilled analyst would be able to detect his deception. And then, half an hour before his twelve-hour shift was over, he overwrote the drone's programming. Covering it up with a scheduled maintenance download, he coincided the drone's new protocol with the causeway's sonic vibrations. If the girl stayed within distance of the audible noise of the transit route, she would be unde-tected. He hovered over the point he knew to be her exact location. It worked. She was invisible. Of course, so were any other heat-producing life forms. But since he could detect birds and the occasional squirrel when he took the drone out of the causeway's sonic range, it would not appear suspicious.

The girl had slowed her pace considerably, frequently stopping to rest and to look for things to eat within the roadside vegetation. She was between the towns of St. James and Cuba. Due to urban sprawl and city consolidations, Cuba was just a few miles away from the outer docks. He scanned the surrounding countryside as though he were looking for any sign of her. The makeshift glitch would probably be discovered soon, but hopefully he had covered his tracks well enough that his subterfuge would remain unnoticed for a few hours. He had bought her some time. In order to be believable, he would have to report that he had lost sight of her, which would be difficult to explain. Ira made himself breathe slowly and meditatively until he felt he could speak without his voice shaking. Then he called his supervisor.

"You lost sight of her after a maintenance download?" the voice in his ear-piece asked.

"Yes. Sometimes when we download next to the causeways, we temporarily lose visual. I was aware of that possibility, but she hasn't been exactly unpre-dictable or hard to track. I didn't think there was any risk of losing her. But she's nowhere near the causeway now. I think she may have put some distance between it and herself to get away from the noise for a while. You know how loud they can be from the outside," Ira said in what he hoped was a calm voice.

"Well, keep looking. She can't have gone far. Use the heat sensors."

"I will. I'm certain I'll find her," Ira said confidently.

"Make certain you do," said his supervisor in a firm voice.

Ira spent the last half hour of his shift making a pretense of looking for the girl in drainage ditches, under overpasses, even up in trees and under bushes. He knew his supervisor would check back with him soon, and when he did, Ira wanted to sound rattled. He didn't think he would have any trouble with the performance, and he was right.

"I've used heat sensors, I've enhanced the audio, I've done everything I can think of, and I haven't been able to locate her," Ira said, his voice quavering slightly.

"Get Vicey to help you. With two of you, it shouldn't take long. I would advise one of you to stay close to the causeway, though, since that was her last known location."

"Of course. I'm planning on it. It's just…we'll be changing shifts soon. Do you want me to explain the situation to Darst? Or do you want me to stay on into the next shift?" Ira paused, hoping he sounded worried enough to want to stay and fix his mistake, but emotionally unsuitable to complete the task. Drone pilots had been known to overcompensate when they were under pressure, alerting targets of surveillance to their presence and in some cases, annihilating the subject.

"Darst can handle it. It's the end of your shift, and I think you're ready for a break."

"But I can fix this!" Ira exclaimed, pounding his fist on his desk in mock frustration.

"Absolutely not. Go home. But before you do, tell Darst to hug the causeway and have Angelo pull in the nearest drone from his region."

"Certainly," Ira said, inwardly relieved. Darst would keep the reprogrammed drone close to the causeway, where the girl was sure to be, while Vicey's night-shift counterpart would be kept busy looking where she was not. In the meantime, he had some more reprogramming to do when he got home…and some ground to cover.

When Darst arrived, Ira explained the situation and their supervisor's instructions. As they walked out of the readout room together, Vicey put her hand comfortingly on his arm. "Don't worry, Ira. They'll find her," she said sympathetically.

"I hope so," he lied. *And I hope I get to keep my job,* he thought to himself. He forced himself not to think of the consequences of his actions if they were ever discovered. Losing his job was the least of his worries.

Upon arriving at his apartment, Ira waved his hand over the palm scanner outside the door, stepped inside, and immediately pried open the scanner on the inside of the apartment with a pocket multi-tool passed down to him by his great grandfather. He had to work quickly, so that the other connected subunits in the building would not be alerted. After entering a program he had written at work to convince Geeves he was in the apartment, going about his regular routine, he bypassed the connection between his unit and the cameras in the hall, running a playback loop of the empty hallway into their memory. Donning a hooded sweatshirt, he scanned his way out of the apartment, smiling with satisfaction when the soft blue life-sign light on the wall next to the door stayed illuminated —indicating that Geeves, indeed, thought he was still inside.

When Ira stepped out of the elevator into the basement docking garage, he kept his head down. His Vista-Visor, although not turned on, obscured most of his face, and the hood covered his hair. To the surveillance cameras, he would be unrecognizable. He regretted that he hadn't had time to reprogram the cameras in this section of the building, but hopefully his act would be convincing. Being careful not to let his implanted Palmscan come into contact with the scanner on his car, he broke into his own vehicle using a program hack he had seen used by car thieves when he was in a required criminal justice class. Once inside, he deactivated the car's GPS unit, his fingers shaking slightly as he typed in the commands. This particular crime was a federal offense, but he just added it to the mental list of felonies he had committed that day and kept working. All of them paled in comparison to what he was about to do.

Ira backed out of the docking port, drove out of the garage and headed toward the causeway. Hopefully, Darst would still be searching close to St. James. His car had no way of detecting drones, and if it was spotted by the one Darst was piloting, it wouldn't matter that the drone couldn't detect a life form; it could still detect a vehicle. He would have to park it under some sort of cover near where he suspected her to be, and then search for her on foot. But first, he had to make it through the outer docks.

The State didn't mind its citizens occasionally visiting the poverty-stricken area. It was a powerful reminder of the way things could be if you decided not to comply with all the implants, chips, and the restrictions on personal free-doms. However, except for the compassionate few in the medical profession and the Discard Outreach Emissaries, most people opted to live their lives as if that segment of the population didn't exist. It was an unpleasantness better left forgotten. Besides, it was rumored that Discards could come in mobs and overtake your vehicle if you slowed down in the wrong area at the right time.

Ira's knuckles whitened in their grip around the steering wheel as he neared the border and passed through the gate to the Dead Zone, a buffer area so named because no one was allowed to live there. He gave a perfunctory glance to the cameras on the wall as he passed through. The hood and the visor still concealed his identity. On either side of old Interstate 44 under the causeway, the zone stretched in its emptiness like a lifeless, cement desert. Its barrenness made the efforts of any Discards trying to sneak through nearly impossible as they were easy to spot. If one of them did manage to make it through the Dead Zone undetected, they would have to scale the wall to enter the city. And yet somehow, every year, a few managed to make it through. The State had not yet figured out how. Underground tunnels led into the city, but they were flooded with toxic Mississippi runoff. A few minutes of exposure to its fumes in such a confined area, to someone without implants, would render permanent lung damage. After an hour's exposure, the body would later be found floating in one of the outlets created to disperse some of the river's toxins over a wider area and through a filtration system in the outer docks.

Ira was approaching the gate. He held his breath and accelerated, halfway expecting Discards to leap out at his car as he throttled through the entrance. But it was uneventful. No one was there to meet him except a startled crow that flew up out of his path in a frenzy of black wing flaps.

As he motored by dilapidated old buildings, he began to notice a few faces peering out the windows. There weren't many people loitering in the streets. Peering down the side roads as he passed, he thought he could see one or two pedestrians, but he was going so fast it was difficult to see many details. From the tales told to him by the monitors in charge of the street cameras, he had thought the place would be crowded with people slowing his progress, begging and clamoring for help or holding signs protesting what they felt was un-fair treatment. But this stretch of the road seemed almost deserted. The lack of activity should hardly have been surprising, as prolonged exposure to the sonic and infrasonic vibrations of the causeway in the city were known to cause headaches, even with soundproof housing and the soundproofing of the cause-way, itself. Such safety measures, however, were not provided in the outer docks. Probably only the poorest of the poor lived near it.

He turned his attention back to the road. It would take him less than twenty minutes to reach the place he had decided to hide his vehicle—an area just be-yond the wall that marked the edge of civilization. There was an overpass he had noticed from his hours of monitoring that had always seemed like a good place for Discards to hide when they wandered into the Preserve, which was seldom.

For generations now, the government had made certain its citizens were con-fined to consolidated cities, the causeways, and a few minor designated routes between them to comply with the Global Directive that Mother Earth be re-turned to a more natural state. Cancer and disease rates had increased steadily with the population, but with the condensing of society, the world had also become ripe for any pandemics—manmade or otherwise—which might come along. After the third global pandemic within a five-year span, the world's pop-ulation took an alarming nose dive. Countries came together to combat viral threats, forming the strongest union of nations yet seen worldwide and ushering in the age of implants. The result was that individual governments held loosely to their nationalities, deferring to a singular governing body representing them as a whole. Citizens increasingly looked to both their national governments and the newly forming world government for more of their needs and for protection from threats to their health.

The use of weapons—even for self-protection—had been abolished long ago. To wander out into the Preserve and turn your back on society, even as a Discard without implants, was not only to refuse all medical help, but to make yourself vulnerable to whatever dangers might be out there. Fear of predatory animals, a total disconnect from self-reliance, and a general aversion for the natural world kept most people within the walls, which did not sport a conventional gate. The gateways were open gaps at various places in the wall, but they kept predators at bay through a sonic frequency that repelled wild animals. The open space gave the illusion of free choice, but of course, by making the decision to leave a designated route and enter the Preserve by any other means than one of the

State-sponsored sightseeing tours was to forfeit one's rights to live free. Offenders were forced into the manual labor of toxic river waste clean-up, and they didn't live long after that.

Ira breathed a sigh of relief as he passed through the outer gateway. With his GPS disabled, the car couldn't be tracked, but it would be caught on camera at the wall. Later, he could report it stolen. He pulled off the road three miles past the view of the wall cams and just before the overpass, where invasive autumn olives and Bradford pear trees choked a narrow draw. A creek, nearly obscured by the brushy trees, meandered under the bridge, providing water that might look good to someone desperate and on the run. He had never found any fugitives there, although he always did a fly-by when he was in the area. "Humph! Maybe that's why they never hide there," he said out loud to himself.

Satisfied with his hiding place, he grabbed a satchel of provisions he had prepared, left the car and climbed back up to the interstate under the causeway. He would travel on foot to remain undetected by the altered drone. If the girl had kept her usual pace, he estimated he would meet her just before she reached Cuba. What would it be like to meet someone from a community totally independent from the State? Someone who knew how to start a fire without a lighter or matches, who knew what plants could be eaten from the wild and how to kill and prepare animals for food? Would she trust him? Would she even listen to him? He could try to warn her, maybe even transport her safely for a short distance, but eventually he would have to say goodbye to his car and somehow make it safely back to the city. That's where his plan got fuzzy. Since the wall cams had detected a vehicle that couldn't be tracked, border security would be actively looking for it. He couldn't just drive it back inside. He was planning on somehow sneaking into the outer docks and bartering with the Discards for safe passage back into the city with a few choice items he had brought, but what would stop them from killing him and keeping the items? Or even worse, they could turn him in for a reward, and he would be made an example for all others who thought of defying the State. Ira smiled grimly. After all the brilliantly deceptive programming and planning, his act of compassion could end with a simple double-cross that could be performed by any third grader. "I should have thought of that," he said to himself with a joyless laugh.

"Thought of what?" said a voice to his left.

Ira jumped in spite of himself, but regained his composure and turned with what he hoped was a friendly, welcoming expression. There, standing beside one of the causeway support columns, was Pod-Op Jayka.

12

Time stood still for a moment as Ira's breath caught in his throat. So this was it. He had been apprehended before he even had a chance to warn the girl. All his efforts were for nothing, and now he would probably spend the rest of his life inhaling toxic gases in a river clean-up penal colony. It wouldn't seem quite so horrible if he had actually accomplished what he had set out to do, but he hadn't. Ira finally exhaled as a crushing feeling in his lungs reminded him that he had forgotten to breathe. His heart was pounding in a fight-or-flight physical response, but there was no sense in fighting or fleeing against an expertly trained, highly skilled Pod-Op. He had seen Jayka take down male volunteers almost twice her size at one of the demonstrations given at work. And although he had never seen them carry one, he suspected Pod-Ops were exempt from the law prohibiting the use of weapons. "Hello, Jayka. What are you doing here?" he heard himself ask in a voice that sounded absurdly casual.

"As you do not have Level 5 clearance, I am not required to provide you with information regarding my purpose at this location," Jayka clipped. This must be what a Pod-Op sounded like when they were on duty, Ira decided, remembering the Meet-and-Greet reception during which he had conversed with Jayka and the others as if they were at any coffee house or cocktail party. He waited for her to say something else, but instead she stared silently past him into the surrounding woods, all the while shifting her position in response to the sounds of squirrels and birds or noise made by wind in the autumn olives. She reminded him of films he had seen of mountain lions or wolves in the Preserve, responding to every sound and movement without any trace of fear, ready to spring into action after their prey.

"Where is the rest of your team?" he asked, at a loss for what to say next.

"Again, I am not required to give you their location," she said automatically, her green eyes darting suddenly back to him. "It seems strange you should continue to ask questions I am not required to answer, all the while ignoring the obvious fact that you are required to tell *me* why *you* are here. Why have you ignored the law against trespassing in the Preserve? Why are *you* here, Ira Owens?"

The Pod-Ops were looking for the girl. She didn't stand a chance unless he could distract them or convince them to look in the wrong direction. Ira cleared his throat. "As I'm sure you know, a girl I was monitoring disappeared on my watch. I am unaccustomed to making mistakes—at least not of this magnitude. Finding her is of utmost importance to me, and I think I know where she is. But my supervisor ordered me to leave at the end of my shift. I can't leave it unfinished like this. I can't let her get away."

"Because of the danger to the security of the State, or the danger to your reputation as a Level 3 readout room monitor?" Jayka asked, her eyes narrowing.

Ira ignored the jab at his position. As long as he could keep her talking, he was distracting her from her mission. "What difference does it make? I admit, I'd rather not have this mark on my record, but I wanted to fix my mistake—for the good of my reputation *and* the security of the State."

"Enough to risk being sent to a penal colony or a reconditioning center?"

"It's that important to me," Ira stated emphatically. "But the longer we stand here talking about it, the more likely she is to get away."

Jayka studied him for a moment. "You are a narrow-minded people, making decisions solely based on your individual welfare. I find it highly unlikely that you are doing this for any other reason than to keep your job and save your skin. However, if you think you have some explanation as to where she may be hiding and why we have been unable to locate her, I must insist you divulge any information you may have on her whereabouts."

Ira relaxed slightly. Maybe his efforts wouldn't be a total failure after all. "There's a creek north of here. Follow me," he said confidently and turned sharply to the right, scuffling down the brushy bank on the shoulder of the interstate. From his surveillance of this area, he knew that the creek where he had left his car was a tributary of another creek which would intercept the road in a short distance; but he was trying to move Jayka as far away from the causeway as possible. The girl was likely to take refuge in Cuba for the night, and this was farther from the main part of town.

"Where are we going?" Jayka demanded, catching up to him and putting a firm hand on his shoulder. "I was instructed to stay near the causeway as she has been following it since she encountered it in Rolla."

"And by this time, she must have a splitting headache and is looking for relief from the constant humming as well as water and something to eat," he explained, wincing as her fingers dug into his muscle.

This seemed to satisfy her. "Stop talking. And stop crashing through the brush like a buffalo. I will alert my team." She paused momentarily with a faraway look, then refocused on his face. "They are on their way. I have downloaded a detailed map of the creek and no longer require your assistance. Return to the causeway. You will only slow us down and possibly alert her to our presence with your inept efforts of traversing the Preserve." She started to leave and then turned abruptly back around. "I don't need to tell you to await my return. You will be handed over to the authorities, and attempting escape is pointless. *I* don't lose my subjects." With that snide remark, Jayka disappeared into the trees.

Ira watched for a few moments, pondering her comment that he and other citizens of the State were a narrow-minded people—as if they and the Pod-Ops occupied totally different planes of existence. Well, perhaps they did, he mused. He had never seen Pod-Ops mingling with citizens outside the confines of the Meet and Greets. He wondered—did they ever leave their base and venture out into the real world when they weren't on assignment, or did they just sleep in coffins when they were off duty? Ira managed a smile at his own joke. Even with whatever programs and advanced chip technology they had, the Pod-Ops were human beings, just like everyone else. They could think of themselves as an elite and separate race if they wanted to, but deep down—Ira was sure—they must have retained some spark of humanity.

He turned back to the causeway and scrambled up the bank. Jayka had told him to go back and await her return. She hadn't told him exactly *where* to wait. He was already in over his head; he might as well make it worthwhile. There might still be a way to warn the girl—to let her know the State was not the haven she must be expecting. But if he left her a note, there was no guarantee she would find it; and if someone else did, the true nature of his actions would be revealed. Unless….

Because of his state job associated with surveillance and retrieval of wayward citizens, Ira had access to certain records unavailable to the general population. Even literature that was considered inflammatory or subversive was made available to readout room monitors (with the understanding that it was only to be used for work purposes) if it helped them understand a fugitive's behavior or to anticipate their next move. He slipped his Vista-Visor down over his eyes and began accessing any unaltered passages of the Christian Bible that he could use to give the girl insight to the danger she was approaching. Surprisingly, he found one almost immediately. After a few minutes searching, he found two others that might encourage her to change her route. Ira copied the scripture references down with pencil and paper he had brought in case he needed to draw a simple map for the girl, who would obviously not have access to the internet. "Follow your dreams," he added for good measure. If she found the note, would she understand what he was trying to convey? If it was recovered by State authorities, would they guess its meaning? It was pointless to speculate. He needed to get the contents of the pack to a point in the causeway somewhere before she would reach Cuba, where she would find it but where it wouldn't be noticeable from the air. Leaving the backpack, itself, wasn't an option, because Jayka would notice if he no longer carried it.

Ira caught movement out of the corner of his eye, and could see a Pod-Op —was it Tyrell? —crossing the causeway ahead of him, en route to rendezvous with the others. As Ira watched, the young man glanced his direction and nodded to acknowledge his presence. Apparently Jayka had conveyed the whole situation with that uncanny link they shared. He supposed it wasn't actually that uncanny since it was a simple Wi-Fi connection with each other, just as people who had the chip were connected to the internet. It was mostly just unsettling since it didn't seem foreign to them at all, as if they were born with it. He waited until Tyrell was out of sight and began to walk quickly down the road. When he was fairly certain he was out of earshot, he began to run.

Because Ira's occupation usually required him to sit in a chair for literally half of a day, he tried to make up for the lack of physical activity by taking up long distance running. Before he came to work for the State and moved close to the river, he had been a frequent participant in 5K and 10K races. Now he had a regular route he took from his neighborhood to a less polluted part of the city where the river gas fumes dissipated enough to allow large gulps of air when necessary. The Health 1 and 2 implants he had been given at birth and early childhood helped his lungs become more efficient at normal, everyday filtering of the fumes, but that didn't mean breathing them was a pleasant affair. In contrast, the Preserve's air was rich in oxygen with all the surrounding trees and vegetation, and it lacked the heaviness attributed to chemical particles in the city. He smiled as he caught his stride. This felt amazing.

Cuba was only about a mile away. If he increased his stride, he could drop the items just west of the town and be back before Jayka and the others knew what he had done. His pace lagged for a second as he thought of the girl's slim chances. The "glitch" in the drone's heat-seeking capabilities would be discovered and corrected in the next maintenance download just before 0600 hours. With 24-hour drone surveillance and a team of Pod-Ops looking for her, there was nowhere for her to hide. What had he been thinking? He gritted his teeth and pumped his legs harder against the pavement. The girl had made it this far. Her origin was still a mystery, though drones constantly combed the Preserve for deserters of the State. Maybe her people had some special power no one knew about—a power to keep them hidden until they wanted to be revealed. Maybe their collective consciousness had created a protective barrier surrounding their location. The State published a great deal about the power of collective consciousness, but Ira had always dismissed it as political propaganda to promote the use of the chip. He had seen the girl praying. Maybe their secret wasn't some fabled result of combined willpower. Maybe there *was* a Higher Power somehow watching over them? He forced his legs to move faster. If there was a Higher Power, Ira was sure he had never seen it in action. If a Higher Power was benevolent enough to protect a community from the prying eyes of the State, surely it would care enough to save the Unspokens from being used as meals for zoo animals and as lethal demonstrations in Pod-Op training exercises.

Ira slowed his pace. He had been deep in thought as he passed Cuba and was a half-mile past it now. As he jogged, he began scanning the area for a good hiding place. Where could he put the cache of goods so that they wouldn't be seen from the air but would still be obvious to someone walking by? If he found a big enough rock, he could carry it up to the causeway and hide them under that. Suddenly he noticed a bit of turquoise in last year's tall, dead grass on the shoulder of the road. An old car door, crunched from a wreck of yesteryear, lay at its final resting place. Well, almost final. Ira dragged the door up close to the pavement and dumped the contents of the pack underneath it, keeping a couple of the bottles of water. Jayka would wonder why he carried a pack if nothing was in it, and he knew the girl had a water filter of some sort that she could use for water from the creek. He looked back at the car door. If Darst was any kind of a monitor, he might wonder why he had never noticed it before. Hopefully the girl would see the items and recover them before then. Ira looked around to see if there was any sort of natural-looking material he could use to cover the door and make it less conspicuous from the air. The weeds which had partially obscured it in the first place would do nicely. He began ripping off armfuls of the stuff and piling them around it. He backed up and surveyed his work. From a drone's vantage point, it would look like a pile of dead grass as long as the wind didn't blow his camouflage away. But to someone walking along the causeway, it would look like exactly what it was—something someone was trying to hide. And what was more enticing than that?

Ira turned and began to run back up the causeway. He had only gone a few paces when he spotted a Pod-Op running his way. He increased his speed, wanting to put as much distance as he could between himself and the car-door cache. The Pod-Op, however, was in much better shape and closed the distance in no time. He could tell it was Jayka by the way she moved. There was something animal-like in her unforgiving pace, like a cheetah on the savanna running down a gazelle. "I told you to await my return!" she nearly shouted when she reached him, grabbing him by the arm and handily clicking his wrists into club cuffs. "I'm assuming you know how club cuffs work," she said, her eyes fierce. Ira nodded quickly, but Jayka explained anyway. "Now that you're wearing them, you and I are members of an exclusive club. And if you try to leave the club by stepping more than five feet away from me, you'll instantly feel as if you've been *hit* by a club. So I suggest you take advantage of your membership and stay close. Were my instructions unclear earlier? Did you think you could escape?"

Ira pretended to still be catching his breath as he considered what to say. "You said to return to the causeway and await your return. But I got scared. I—I heard something in the brush, and I thought it might be a mountain lion or a bear. And then I thought it might be the girl, and even though I came out here to find her, I thought she might shoot me. She carries a weapon, you know, and she killed something with it just yesterday. I guess I panicked and just started running. When I came to my senses, I realized I should have been running back toward the city, so I turned around. It was such a relief to see you coming —really it was."

Jayka glared at him. "You have caused me a lot of trouble. The girl hasn't been anywhere near the stream, so that was a dead end. Then when we got back, you were gone. We've wasted a lot of time because of you."

"I'm sorry. I've really made a mess of things," Ira said, feeling the truth of it deeply. He had tried to help, but it hadn't worked out. But at least she hadn't been discovered yet.

"Excuse me…um, hey, could you wait up, please?" said a voice behind him, sounding rather out of breath.

Ira turned around and his heart sank. There she was, despite all his efforts. She must have seen him right before he started running back up the road.

"You're a really fast runner," she continued pleasantly. "I have blisters from walking so far, and it was hard to catch up. My name is Selah, by the way." She waited for them to respond.

"Try to keep up," Jayka said suddenly.

Ira whirled around and looked at Jayka. Was she just going to trust the girl to walk back with them, unrestrained?

"I know you can run fast. But it is difficult to run wearing club cuffs, so for your sake I will slow the pace," Jayka continued.

Ira spun around to look again at Selah. Suddenly, he felt an excruciating pain in his wrists and arms and stumbled to his knees.

"I told you what would happen if you let too much distance get between us. Now, keep up," Jayka snapped.

Ira scrambled awkwardly to his feet, looking confusedly at Jayka and then back at Selah.

"What do you keep looking at? Are you dehydrated?" Jayka asked. "Do you have any water in that pack of yours?"

"I do, actually," Selah offered, her voice trailing off and sounding suddenly very small and scared as Jayka completely ignored her.

Jayka spun Ira around and unzipped his backpack, while Ira stared at Selah in disbelief. Jayka couldn't see her. She couldn't see *or* hear her. "I do, actually," Ira repeated Selah's words, and winked at Selah. "I'm really glad I brought it, too. I had originally planned to bring a lot of other things, but I changed my mind. If I had brought them, I would have just had to leave them somewhere down the road, because they would have just weighed me down." Ira winked again, and tried to use his head to gesture in the direction of the car door.

"Stop your incessant babbling and drink this water before your nonsensical thought processes get any worse," Jayka demanded.

"Yes. You're right. I'm starting to see things that you can't see, so I must be dehydrated," Ira said, looking at Selah meaningfully just before Jayka shoved the water bottle in his mouth. He drank noisily and sputtered and choked as Jayka forced him to drink more.

"All of it. That's good. I don't want you coming back sick on my account. One of the reasons I wanted you to wait for me at the causeway was for your own safety. Aside from the risk of being attacked by a predator, as as you mentioned, there is always the possibility of falling and being injured in the rugged terrain or getting lost and dehydrated. Staying near the road could prevent all of that since you wouldn't get lost, and there's even footing, and wild animals tend to stay away from the irritating resonance produced by the causeway. But there is always the chance one of them will be brave enough or hungry enough to come around anyway, which is why I question your logic in moving farther away from me and my team. We could have protected you."

"That's really thoughtful of you to think of my welfare. I didn't know Pod-Ops cared about their captives," Ira said.

"We don't. I just don't want you dead before we get a chance to question you," Jayka quipped.

"Oh, I see. That kind of makes me understand why most Discards don't want anything to do with the State," Ira said loudly in Selah's direction.

"Come on, Citizen Owens. Let's go."

Ira glanced behind him and saw Selah start to follow. He shook his head vigorously and turned his full attention to keeping up with Jayka. When he looked back later, he could still see the girl watching them, looking bewildered and confused. He didn't blame her. He had no idea why Jayka couldn't see her. And then he wondered…if the Pod-Ops had linked with the drone to retrieve its footage, did the glitch he had installed carry over to the Pod-Ops' programming, interfering with *their* ability to see her? Ira snorted at his preposterous theory. If that were the case, Jayka wouldn't have been able to see *him*, either.

As they made their way back to the others, he studied Jayka with furtive glances. He remembered the first day he had seen her, at the demonstration with the Unspoken and the poison gas. Although he had tried to erase it from his memory, he had been unsuccessful. The sight of the infant, gasping for breath…and then Jayka picking it up and dropping it as if it were a sack of trash when she was told to leave it alone—those images were still vivid in his mind. "Do you remember when you did the demonstration with the poison gas?" he asked suddenly.

"Of course, I remember. I remember all my missions and assignments. The chip makes me incapable of forgetting, unless my superiors deem it necessary to have a memory erased," Jayka said brusquely.

"They can do that? They can erase your memory?"

"Of course. Once someone has the chip, the majority of their memories are stored there. But you already know that, being top of your class in tech interface programming."

"Yes, I know you can designate the chip as the main storage for memory, but I can't imagine erasing someone's memory without their consent. Doesn't that seem unethical to you?" Ira asked, flabbergasted.

"Rather, it seems unethical to leave a citizen with painful memories they would rather forget, or a Pod-Op with memories that might cloud their judgment during future assignments," Jayka said. "Some Pod-Ops even request to erase their kills. But I do not."

Ira swallowed. He was beginning to think his imagined scenario of Pod-Ops sleeping in coffins was close to the truth. "Why not? I, for one, would rather forget the sight of that baby taking its dying breaths. But I can't."

The hardened veneer of Jayka's expression seemed to fade for an instant, and Ira thought he detected some emotion—something softer than the indifference she had displayed so far. "Why did you go pick it up?" he ventured.

"I don't know what you're talking about."

"Yes, you do. You just said you don't erase the memory of your kills. So you remember going and picking it up and then dropping it when they told you to leave it."

"That was not my kill. I did not kill that baby—that Unspoken," Jayka quickly corrected herself, midsentence. "The poison gas killed it. But I retain that memory and memories of other kills because the first time I killed another human, it was very…*difficult*. I do not want to lose the coping skills I have gained in dealing with this process. I do not want to relive the *first* time every time I make a kill. Each one gets a little bit easier. Any Pod-Op who wants to succeed keeps their memories for that reason, or merely for the reason that it would be hard to retain what you have learned on a mission or from pursuing a subject if you wiped your memory every time."

"Do you know any Pod-Ops who do erase their memories?" Ira ventured.

"I knew one who did."

Ira waited for an explanation, but Jayka wasn't forthcoming. "Well?" he finally prodded her. "Purely for scientific curiosity," he added quickly, when she shot him a look that would whither crabgrass.

"That information is classified. All I can tell you is that it didn't work out very well for him since we are all linked—as you know," she said carefully.

"So, he must have come across the incident he had erased in one of your memories?" Ira guessed. When Jayka didn't answer, he took that as a yes. "That must have been extremely difficult for him to see if he had taken the pains to erase it," Ira said. After a few minutes of reflection, he added, "I can see why you choose to retain your memories. It forces you to take responsibility for your actions. That is commendable, I suppose. Even admirable."

"I do not need your admiration," Jayka said sharply.

"No, of course not," Ira said. He decided to venture a little further. "But what do you do if your actions cause you emotional duress?"

"We have counselors, reconditioning therapy, and drugs for that."

"But would reconditioning therapy involve erasing or at least altering the memory?"

"Reconditioning therapy doesn't necessarily change a memory. It changes the affected operative, giving them a personality more suited to adapt to the memory. It instills programs which provide appropriate coping mechanisms. Have you been behind a monitor screen so long that you have forgotten the basic principles of tech interface?"

Ira ignored her question. "But what if it doesn't help? What if you can't get rid of the guilt?" he persisted.

"What guilt? Guilt is a tool to use on the weak-minded. I have no guilt for the orders I have followed for my State," Jayka said proudly.

"If you say so," Ira mumbled under his breath.

"You must be aware that I have Audio Boost," Jayka said. "I heard what you said. Perhaps you don't believe me that I harbor no guilt."

"If that is true, then you must also harbor no conscience," Ira said before he could stop himself.

"Quiet!" Jayka snapped. "Your pointless questions make this trek back intolerable. If you don't stop, I will increase the pace."

Ira clamped his mouth shut and hurried to keep up, as Jayka had sped up slightly anyway. After a few seconds, she glanced in his direction. "I had heard you were different," she said, and sped up even more so Ira wouldn't be tempted to talk. But he wondered about her comment the rest of the way back.

Behind them in the distance, Selah watched in disbelief. It was clear that the man called Ira had been able to see her, but the young woman was either unable to do so or was doing a very good job of ignoring her. She walked back to the grass-covered piece of metal she had run past in her attempt to catch up with the man. It was a strange affair of crumpled color heaped up with bunches of dried grass. He had nodded in its direction and winked at her as if to say, "Go ahead. Take it." She looked underneath and her heart jumped when she found three rectangular pouches labeled *Meal: Ready to Eat.* Beside the pouches was a small, red and silver-colored object that looked vaguely familiar, a bottle of water, and a smooth-surfaced black container the size of a person's hand. This last item appeared to have designs on it arranged in a row. As Selah picked up the box to study it more closely, she discovered a folded-up piece of paper beneath it. She unfolded it eagerly, hoping for some explanation of the items and the strange behavior of the people she had just encountered.

What she saw written there took her completely by surprise. "*1 Peter 5:8. Matthew 7:13-14. Matthew 2:1. Follow your dreams.*" Selah stood staring at the note for a few seconds before she reacted. She knew 1 Peter 5:8 by heart: "Be sober, be vigilant; because your adversary the devil, as a roaring lion, walketh about, seeking whom he may devour."[23] Even as she recalled it to mind, she had a sense of urgency that she needed to take cover. Gathering up the items and stowing them in her pack, she scrambled down the bank to the ditch and crept into the cover of some autumn olives. As she did so, she could hear the approaching sound of a drone over the low humming emitted by the bridge overhead. As of yet, they had seemed unable to see her, even though she had waved her arms frantically and jumped up and down a few times to attract their attention. But Selah couldn't shake the feeling that she needed to hide, so she stayed put. After the drone had gone, she dug a Bible out of her pack and looked up the other scriptures. "Enter ye in at the strait gate: for wide is the gate, and broad is the way, that leadeth to destruction, and many there be which go in thereat: Because strait is the gate; and narrow is the way, which leadeth unto life, and few there be that find it."[24] Selah sat back on her haunches. Surely this man wasn't trying to witness to her and warn her about the wiles of the devil. There had to be another explanation. What was it supposed to mean, in reference to her current situation? Spiritually, the broad way was the easy way to go—the one that didn't challenge your selfish nature or your tendency to sin. But it led

---

[23] 1 Peter 5:8, KJV
[24] Matthew 7:13-14, KJV

to death. The narrow way, or living for Jesus, led to life; but it was harder to follow, and fewer people chose it. She looked up the last scripture. "And being warned of God in a dream that they should not return to Herod, they departed into their own country another way."[25] After this particular reference, the words "Follow your dreams," had been written and underlined. That clinched it. He was warning her to go back home, to avoid the roads where she would be easily seen, and to be aware that she was being hunted. Selah had known before she left home that she would be hunted. She was counting on it. More than that, she was counting on being found. But her strange encounter with the man named Ira and the bossy woman who seemed to be holding him captive had unsettled her. The messages he had left her seemed to confirm the fears of the elders in her community. Yet she knew she had been called as a missionary to the Old Country.

She thought back to the instance where Paul had been determined to go to Jerusalem, even though he was warned by the prophet Agabus that his journey would end in imprisonment.[26] Everything she had experienced so far resonated with her spirit that she should continue in her quest. But obviously some people would be ready to hear her message, while others weren't.

What was it the man had said? *"Most Discards don't want anything to do with the State."* Was a Discard exactly what it sounded like—a person who had been discarded by society? The longer she thought about it, the more of a burden she felt for these people who were so reviled that they had been given a name which meant "cast out" or "rejected." She knew she had to continue on her journey, but maybe for now, like the Discards, she should keep a low profile. The man's last clue, "Follow your dreams," was meant to make her think of the wise men, who (because of a dream) avoided reporting back to Herod and returned home by another way. Undoubtedly, he was telling her to go home and avoid the authorities. Instead, Selah was reminded of all her dreams that led her to leave the valley in the first place. God loved these people and wanted to save them. She would avoid the State for now and start with the Discards until she felt God's assurance that she should move on. But where would she find them? She looked

---

[25] Matthew 2:12, KJV
[26] Acts 21:10-14

in the direction Ira and his captor had gone, and couldn't help thinking she should follow, albeit while remaining hidden.

But first, she would investigate the food. Her stomach was rumbling, the shadows were growing longer, and she needed to rest. The town which she had seen from the elevated position of the road was out of the question for spending the night as it would be an obvious place to seek shelter. She turned into the forest, walking just far enough away to barely hear the annoying hum of the suspended bridge. A particularly bushy cedar tree offered cover and a bare place to sit underneath it. Eagerly, she took out the meal pouches. *"Chicken Chunks, White, Cooked. 1st Strike Bar. Cheese Spread, Cheddar, Plain. Tortillas, Plain. Trail Mix, Recovery. Candy II. Beverage Powder, Carbohydrate Electrolyte,"* one pouch promised. Selah cut it open with her pocket knife, wondering how all that food could be contained in the rectangular package. The individual pouches inside were labeled with directions for mixing certain items with water, and there was even a flameless heater to cook the entrée. She had no idea what a 1st Strike Bar was and laid it aside, but she quickly opened the tortillas, globbed the cheese spread over them and crammed them into her mouth. It took a lot of water to wash them down—but she was so hungry, she didn't care. Selah looked dubiously at the pouch that claimed to be a heater, decided she was too hungry to wait for the food to warm up anyway, ripped open the package of chicken and shoveled it down with a spoon made of something similar to the linoleum in Miss Genevieve's kitchen floor. She moved on to the trail mix and stirred up the beverage powder. Afterward, she felt slightly sick. It was the most food she had eaten in several days, and whoever had the audacity to call what was in the pouch "chicken" should have been beaten with a switch. But on the other hand, she was full for the first time since she had left home. She laid back against the packs and stared at the fading patches of daylight between the cedar branches. Before she knew it, she was asleep.

13

ZELDA nervously ran her tongue in and out between the gap in her smile where one of her front teeth used to be. In an attempt to steady her nerves, she had been humming the same tuneless song for the last hour as she hobbled toward her destination. Since she was always alone, she was annoying no one. Not that she cared if she was. Zelda had stopped caring about what other people thought a long time ago.

The wall loomed ahead of her in the dim morning sun—a dingy, gray barrier between herself and freedom. She sighed and darted her tongue in and out like a snake trying to catch a scent. No one had come to make repairs so far, but every time she made her visits, she breathed a little easier once she saw her project was undisturbed. The site was out of view of the wall cams, partially due to a depression in the landscape. Because of this depression, the wall was actually a little taller at this location, making it an unlikely place for Discards to try to escape or predators to try to invade. Surveillance simply wasn't necessary. Zelda smiled smugly as her prized possession came into view. There it was, undisturbed and thriving. She scuttled down the slope and toddled to the wall. The State didn't want water collecting around the base of the barrier and had built grates and underground drainage systems, carefully maintained to be free of debris and clogging vegetation. Most of these outer docks drainage ports were several hundred yards behind her, leading to tunnels that emptied out into the Preserve. Additional, smaller drainage ports were located at intervals along the wall's foundation.

It was at the base of one of these smaller ports that Zelda had planted her secret weapon: *Wisteria floribunda*. Known for its aggressive nature, the plant was rarely planted beside structurally supportive walls or near sewer lines, as its thickening girth and prolific nature had been known to disrupt drainage systems and separate roofs from houses. For eight years, Zelda had tended her plant, pruning it vigorously to keep its climbing on the inside of the wall to a minimum. She had chosen this spot not only because of its lack of surveillance, but because she had discovered a larger than normal space at the junction of the drainage port and the wall—a space which the wisteria's roots and meandering vines had also discovered. Each year, the gap in the wall widened. As Zelda kept the plant pruned on the inside, it worked furiously to find a less restrictive environment as it grew through the port and under the wall. Three years ago, Zelda noticed significant cracks around the port. Finally, earlier this year, the stones surrounding the drain had buckled as the girth of the vine swelled in diameter. Zelda sat down by a pile of rocks and took a drink from her canteen, smiling in satisfaction at her well-crafted plan. For the last two years, she had hidden a small crowbar under the rocks, using it to help the wisteria in its destructive journey. She had always been careful not to bang or chip at the concrete, as the wall was monitored for sudden, jarring vibrations. But now, there was no need to disassemble the rock pile, retrieve the crowbar, and pry at the stubborn brick. Zelda had been going in and out of the wall for the last few months, catching such delicacy as raccoon and rabbit.

She had shared her harvest with those she knew needed it most, but she had to be careful not to arouse suspicion. Often, she would leave the gift in a bundle at the recipient's door, knock, and quickly leave. Some Discards were snitches and would rat out their dockmates for medical care or even a week's plan of the garbage truck route, so her offerings were always anonymous. No one would suspect anything. Most people were afraid to approach her and wouldn't suspect her acts of kindness. After all, she was one of the few who caught things and killed them. It was a living that set her apart from others.

The more she thought of the bounty beyond the wall, the more time she spent formulating a plan to leave permanently. Zelda was a survivor, and unlike most Discards, she knew how to go out and catch a meal rather than waiting for it to be delivered by a garbage truck. She didn't need much: her traps, a knife, a lighter or some matches, a pot to boil water, and a tarp for temporary shelter until she could find a suitable cave or could build something more permanent. Everything ran smoothly in her mind until she remembered the lion.

One day last week, she had set her traps and was returning to check them the next morning. The trap on the game trail by the creek was the farthest away from the wall, but it had yielded the best results: four coons, six possum and a hapless rabbit. Cantaloupe rinds were apparently tasty treats in the Preserve and caused normally wary animals to abandon caution. She was almost to the spot when she thought she heard a commotion in the brush. She had crept closer, listening carefully, as the noise from the creek had masked any sounds until now. An explosive snarling was erupting from the location of the trap. Zelda recognized the snarl as a raccoon, and the scene played out in her head before she reached the drama that was unfolding. "Dern coyote tryn' ta git ma panda!" she hissed under her breath and rushed down the trail. What she saw stopped her dead in her tracks. A full-grown mountain lion, its back to her, was clawing at the trap, trying to get at the raccoon inside. It was so fully absorbed in its task and the raccoon was so noisy in its growling that it didn't realize she was there, only a few yards away. Zelda turned silently back up the trail and hurried to the safety of the wall. When she returned a day later, she found what was left of the trap in a dense thicket twenty yards from its original location. A few wads of fur and chunks of hide left no mystery as to the demise of the coon.

Zelda had heard stories about the lions from her grandfather. He said you didn't need to worry about being able to get away from them because they were quiet and attacked from behind, and you wouldn't know it until it was too late. It should have been a story that kept a small girl from wanting to escape the outer docks; but in her mind, Grandfather was just trying to scare her enough to keep her out of trouble. She had dismissed the warnings about the lions, bears, and wolf-dogs as State scare tactics that her grandfather had adopted as his own —except maybe for the wolf-dog and coywolf hybrids. She could hear them at night, yipping and howling. Zelda had decided she needed some sort of defense against them and had made preparations. She wondered if her puny defenses would be enough against a pack of wolves, much less an animal as stealthy and powerful as a lion. She had a fixed blade knife from the black market and had whittled a channel in the end of a stout stick, binding an old, sharpened screw driver into the depression to make a spear. Her pocket knife she had given to the girl a few years back and had never regretted it.

A tightness gripped her heart as she thought about the girl. "Pipah," she said sadly. "Pipah girl." That little slip of a lass had watched her catching pigeons and had made a net of her own for starlings. And she was good at it, too. Zelda had taken her under her wing, teaching her all she could. It was young folks like that who gave her hope for the future in an otherwise bleak and hopeless world.

When Piper's mother had died so suddenly, Zelda didn't see her for a while. She knew the girl must be taking it hard, so she didn't worry. People needed time to grieve, and she didn't think Piper was the type to run away from her sorrows or bury them deep under something else like her ma had done. When she saw Piper again, she thought maybe she had been wrong. The girl seemed so happy—not like someone who had lost her mother. She seemed to glow from within like she knew a secret.

"Zelda! I gots sumthin' to tell ya. Sumthin' amazin'!" she had said.

"Ja founds a food stash?" she asked in a whisper.

"Nah, nahhh. It's way better than that."

"Da hydrant at de Shaw git fixed?"

"It's even better than that."

Zelda looked at her crossways. The source for drinking water in the Shaw neighborhood had been broken for over a year, forcing locals to walk several blocks to the next hydrant. What could be better than fresh water? Suddenly Zelda moaned. "Aww, no girl. Ya ain't packin' a chile, are ya?" Being pregnant was not Zelda's idea of something wonderful and amazing, but to a young teen who had just lost her mother, it might seem an escape from sadness and loneliness.

Piper's eyes widened. "Oh, Lawdy, no!" she exclaimed. "I gots to tell ya 'bout someone I just met! He saved me! He took my sad feelin's and made 'em glad feelin's. I still miss my ma, but now I got someone to be with me all the time."

Zelda looked at her speculatively. Right after a loss was not the time to start up a relationship. Anyone who could see the state she had been in would be able to take advantage of her loneliness. But she was so happy now, it probably wouldn't do any good to talk her out of it. "He good to ya?" She finally asked.

"He's better than good. He changed ma life! I'm a differ'nt person now!" Piper exclaimed.

Zelda eyed her from head to toe.

"Oh, I know I looks the same. But I'm differ'nt on the inside. I'm clean, where I used to be dirty." She paused, searching for the words to describe her experience. "I know I sounds like I'm jittered out, but it's the truth. His name is Jesus. He's the Son of God. I read 'bout 'im in a book, an' it said He came to save us an' give us life that lasts forever! So when we die, we don't hafta go to Hell. We can live up in Heaven with *Him!*"

Zelda let out a sigh that puffed out her lips. "Girl, dis *is* Hell. Hows ya think it could get any worse? Who tol' ya all this trash?"

Piper looked as if she had been punched in the gut. "I done tol' ya. I read it in a book."

"Well, ya can't believe ever'ting ya read," she said dismally, and then inwardly cussed herself for saying it. The girl was so happy. Why should she go and spoil it? But to her surprise, Piper smiled like a kid who had just found a half-used bar of soap in a dumpster.

"I can believe it, because it happened to *me*," she said with finality. "I met 'im myself, an' I'll never be the same. An' I wants *you* to meet 'im, too."

"Nope," Zelda said, and clamped her mouth shut.

"How come? How come ya don' wanna meet 'im?" Piper asked, confused.

"Cuz I don' fall in wit' no religions. De only one I can depend on is *me*," she said with finality.

"Won't ya even let me tell ya 'bout 'im? I mean, you should hear the stories in this book!" Piper said, taking out the tattered little Gideon New Testament.

Zelda held out her hand and Piper passed it over to her. It was in rough shape, but it was still a real book, made of paper. "Dis book seen better days, but it still bring ya sump'n at da pawn shop."

"That's what I thought, 'til I started readin' it," Piper said. "Then I knew I had to keep it. When I found out how much God loves us, I asked 'im ta forgive me for all I done what's bad, and to be with me forever. An' then sumthin' happened to me on the inside. A big shadow left me, an' sumthin' inside o' me woked up, an' I been seein' sunshine ever since."

Zelda opened the book and looked at the pages filled with symbols she had never been taught to interpret. She stroked a page, closed the book and rubbed its textured cover, turning it over and over in her hands. As bad a shape as it was, it was still valuable, but it was the girl's. She handed it back to Piper. "Ya keep dat outta sight, lest ya want someone take it from ya."

"Can I read ya some o' the stories in it?"

Zelda started to protest, but looking at the girl, her heart softened. "If'n ya wants ta read me sump'n whilst I'm a waitin' for da pigeons ta come in, go ahead. I do likes a good story."

And thus began Zelda's introduction to a world she never knew existed, full of marvelous stories she didn't necessarily believe, but found entertaining. And if it made the girl happy to read them to her, so be it. She would listen, or at least pretend to listen. For the next three years, while setting up traps and waiting, she listened to Piper read about Jesus. To her surprise, she liked some of the stories so well, she asked for them again. When that Jesus fellow fed five thousand people with just a few loaves of bread and two fish and there were even leftovers—well, obviously that couldn't really happen. But wouldn't it be something if it were true?

On one particular day when the pigeons seemed overly cautious, Zelda asked Piper to read the story of Jesus feeding the crowd. When she was done, Zelda tilted her head sideways and squinted at the girl. "Now, datted be a dude ya wanna have 'round," she said. "All da food ya wants. No dumpster divin'. No pigeons too skeert ta come in to da bait. Just fish an' bread. Fish!" Zelda exclaimed suddenly, with a faraway look in her eyes. "I wonder what dey taste like?" She turned again to Piper. "If ya really knows dis Jesus dude, why'nt ya ast 'im for us, ta git us some grub? Maybe ya could ast 'im for some fish, even, if you's astin'."

Piper turned away, resting her head on her knees. After a few minutes, Zelda was sorry she had said anything. "Hey, girl. I's sorry. I didn' mean ta make fun. It's jus'…well, wouldn' it be sump'n ta be able ta just ast for whatcha need when ya can't git it fo' yaself, an' dere it is?"

Piper turned around, and Zelda could see that she wasn't upset at all. In fact, she was grinning. "Ya betcha it would. That's why I asked 'im just now."

"Ast who?"

"Jesus. I asked 'im if 'e could git us some grub somewhere's, cuz we's havin' trouble gittin' it today."

"How can ya ast 'im ta do anything? Where is 'e, so's you can ast 'im?"

"He's in here," Piper said, patting her chest, "and He's all aroun' us. He can hear us, no matter where we are."

"How's ya know he keers ta answer? How's ya know all that astin' gonna do ya any good-wise?"

"Cuz it say right in here, 'Ask, an' ya shall receive. Seek, an' ya gonna find. Knock, an' the door be open to ya,'[27] Piper said with confidence, tapping the little New Testament with her index finger.

"Hmmph." Zelda eyed Piper skeptically and resisted the urge to say anything. Even if the book was actually true, all the stories in it were ancient history. How could a person who died thousands of years ago help them today? Zelda didn't believe in God, much less His Son. And even the book about Him said He died, so how could He be around to hear what they were asking for? How could He be everywhere at once? Piper claimed it said He rose from the dead, too, but that *had* to be made up.

Zelda looked resolutely at her net and the untouched bait. There were no pigeons in sight. The shadows were starting to stretch, and the birds would be going to roost soon anyway. "Well, girl, I's done today. Dem birds ain't comin'." Zelda said, stretching her back and slowly unfolding her legs.

"Let's wait jus' a lil bit longer," Piper begged.

Zelda sighed. "It time to go home, Pipah."

"Jus' five more minutes," Piper pleaded. "I'll count 'em, an' I won't cheat," she said, because neither one of them had a time piece to tell when the five minutes were up.

"Well, okay. But we're cuttin' it close," Zelda said. It was better to be off the streets before nightfall.

---

[27] See Luke 11:9-10

The minutes wore by, with Piper counting silently, looking skyward for the pigeons she knew Jesus was sure to send. But none came. When the five minutes were up, the net was still empty. Zelda sighed and looked over at Piper. "It's ok, girl. Sometimes people let ya down. Ya shore know dat, eh? Mebbe Jesus, he busy right now. Da world's a big place, ya savvy? He got's lots ta take keer of," she said reassuringly.

But Piper wasn't listening. She was sitting up tall, straining to hear something.

"What is it, girl?"

"I hears a food wagon," she said simply.

"Nahh. Dem's already left for da city. An' anyhows, dere ain't no dumpsters out dis way," Zelda commented, but now she could hear it, too. She scrambled to gather her nets, as technically, trapping anything was illegal. But it was too late. The garbage truck rumbled out of the alley and into the Shaw, coming to a halt just a storefront away from them.

Zelda couldn't grab her nets, but she wasted no time scooting around the corner. She was halfway down the alley when she realized the girl wasn't with her. She leaned against the wall, panting. Had she been apprehended? She had never known of a garbage truck to take a prisoner—but then again, she had never seen a truck in the Shaw, either. She waited, and after a while, she could hear the girl's voice. Zelda crept back to the corner of the building and peeked into the square. The girl was right there next to the garbage truck, talking to the men inside! "Oh, Lawd. I hopes she not gabbin' 'bout dat Jesus stuff. She git herself reported!" She watched as Piper and the driver conversed, and then the man reached into the truck and handed her something in a sack. Then he waved, started up his truck, and rumbled out of the Shaw and into another alley. Zelda cautiously stepped back out into the square. It could still be a trap.

"Zelda!" Piper called as she turned back to her friend, waving the sack around.

"Hush, girl," Zelda scolded her. The square was empty, but that didn't mean someone wasn't watching from a window. She hobbled over as fast as her hips could take her, but Piper was skipping in happiness, so she didn't have to go far.

"Zelda. I jus' tol' them guys about Jesus!"

"Shoot, girl, ya gonna git yaself reported an' taken away, if'n ya keeps dat up! It's one ting ta tell folks in da outer docks 'bout Jesus. But when ya starts tellin' State folk, dat's a differ'nt story."

"Oh, the driver didn' mind. An' look what 'e give us," She held out the sack. "They picked up someone else's lunch order by mistake, so they's headed back into the city ta grab some dinner. They said they ain't no way they eatin' this garbage."

"Garbage?" Zelda huffed. "Dey don' know what it *is* ta eat garbage. Ya tellin' me dis is fresh food, what's not been molderin' in da sun all week?" Zelda crept closer, pulling the girl into the shelter of the alley to hide their treasure.

"It only been molderin' in the food wagon all day. But it cold in there! I could feels cold air comin' outta it! How they do that, Zelda?" Piper asked in amazement.

"I don' keer. Let's eat!" Zelda exclaimed. "An' if God is real, Lawd, bless dem souls what give us dis grub!"

"Thank ya for the food, Jesus!" Piper exclaimed and pulled two sandwiches out of the sack, handing one to Zelda.

What happened next, Zelda would never forget. For as she unwrapped the plastic from around the sandwich, she realized the synthesized meat was one she had never eaten before. It was battered, like chicken. But when she bit into it, it was a flaky texture. She looked over at Piper, her eyes wide.

"I think they got this chicken wrong at the factory, an' that's why them guys didn' want it," Piper was saying. "But it still taste good to me. It ain't spoiled. I don' hafta worry 'bout no belly ache."

"Pipah, dis ain't chicken," Zelda said wonderingly.

"What is it, then?"

"It's fish. I knows, cuz I saw a guy find a piece of it once. It was flaky, like dis, an' it smelt kinda funny, like dis."

"But it taste good," Piper insisted.

"Ya betcha it taste good."

"I told ya He listens ta me," Piper said, her mouth full of fish.

"Who? Da driver?"

"No! Jesus. Jesus listens. Cuz I asked 'im, right when ya tol' me ta ask 'im. I says, 'Jesus, we's hungry. An' Zelda wants some fish. But pigeons 'd be jus' fine.' Guess He jus' want ya ta know He listenin', when ya ask 'im an' believe 'im fo' sumthin.'"

Zelda stared at the sandwich and back at the girl. "Hmmph." She crammed more of the fresh food into her mouth, but something was stirring in her heart. Could the girl be right? Zelda had never seen a trash truck in the Shaw before. And this one had delivered exactly what she had jokingly asked for.

From that day on, she began to look at things differently. If there was really a God out there, listening to everything she said, she certainly didn't want to offend Him. She didn't feel like she could talk to Him personally, because she didn't know Him like Piper did. But the possibility of there being a God who was willing to help a young girl who believed in Him—that added a whole new perspective to life.

It wasn't long after the incident that Piper was taken. She stopped showing up at the Shaw, and when Zelda asked around, she found out the girl had been picked up by the Department of Mental Health. One of the men in the truck must have reported it and given a description. Zelda wondered that if Jesus was everywhere, as Piper claimed, where was He when *that* happened? The stirring in her heart died down, and she spent more time outside the wall trapping and planning to leave.

Now she had to be more careful than normal. There had been a lot of activity at the gateway yesterday afternoon. Her sources said that a special forces car had headed out into the Preserve, and then later that day, a man from the city had driven out the gate like he was being chased by the devil, himself. If he was trying to escape the city, it was certainly bad timing. There was much more chance of him being noticed if one of the new chipmate teams was out and about. She debated with herself about whether she should go, but she had left several traps in the Preserve. If they were found, the authorities would probably suspect it belonged to someone in the outer docks who had somehow managed to evade detection. A thorough search of the wall would result. Repairs would be made and security, tightened. She couldn't let that happen. She could only hope they hadn't already been found.

Zelda sat down beside the drainage port and placed her feet on the wall, pushing with her legs. The damaged brick around the wisteria vine gave way, and Zelda quickly scrunched her way through the opening. She replaced the chunks from the outside and looked warily around her. She could not afford to be seen. The hum of the causeway was faint in the distance, but not loud enough to keep her from hearing if someone or something approached. Sunlight was beginning to make its way through the trees, dappling the forest floor with gold. Zelda swallowed her fear like a bitter spring tonic and made her way silently into the woods.

The first trap was still there. An animal had managed to take the bait and spring it without getting caught. She tucked it away into her bag. The second one yielded a squirrel. She put it into the bag, wincing slightly as the traps rattled together. The last one was in the game trail just across the creek, about a mile away. Zelda walked slowly, carefully placing each step so as not to snap a twig or crackle leaves. It was a painstaking process, and it took her three times as long as it normally did to reach the site. The trap was empty. It was just as well, since it was a live trap, and scaring or killing something would have meant making noise. She tucked it under her arm and looked in the direction of the causeway, wondering if the chipmates were still crawling around in the underbrush. Suddenly she froze. Something was moving around just upstream of her, about fifty yards away. Not something, some*one*. It was a girl, and for a moment, her heart jumped. Could Piper have escaped instead of being caught? But no, it wasn't Piper. Piper had brownish blond hair, and this girl had dark brown hair. She was bigger than Piper, and was dressed strangely—not like a chipmate, but she definitely wasn't wearing the State's hand-me-downs, either. Zelda watched quietly as the girl gathered water into a pouch and then squeezed it from the pouch into a canteen. She did this several times until the canteen was filled. Zelda dared not move to give away her position; but as the girl finished her task, she looked up and down the creek, and their eyes met. Zelda could see her flinch and shrink away slightly, and then she stopped as if she didn't know what she should do. The two stared at each other, and Zelda suddenly wondered…could this be who they were searching for? Zelda clutched her sack and turned back silently into the woods. She couldn't afford to have the chipmates who were chasing this girl finding her, too.

"Wait!" she heard a voice behind her. "Wait! Can you help me? I have things to trade."

Zelda turned quickly back to the stream and held her finger to her lips. If this idiot girl kept talking, they would both be found. She beckoned for her to follow and moved back into the trees. To her surprise, the girl knew how to be quiet. In fact, she was better at it than Zelda. When she came near, the old woman once again raised her finger to her lips. The girl nodded silently. Good. Apparently, she wasn't stupid. Zelda led her into a thick grove of cedars and said in barely a whisper, "Don' ya know dey's lookin' for ya? Dem chipmates? Dey's after ya. An' if ya tags along wit' me, dey might find me, too."

"Shipmates?"

"Special forces. Pod-Ops, I tink dey calls 'em. Dey's all chipped togedder, connected somehows."

The girl's forehead wrinkled in confusion. "I'm sorry. I don't understand," she whispered back. "I just need to get to the city. I need to meet the—the Discards, I think he called them."

Zelda cocked an eyebrow and tilted her head. "Why?"

"I have a message for them. I want to tell them about Someone," the girl whispered, after some thought.

"Who?"

She seemed to hesitate, and then a look came over her face that for a moment reminded her of Piper. "His name is Jesus. He wants to save them."

Zelda couldn't believe what she was hearing. "Ya know dis Jesus dude, too?"

The girl brightened. "Do you know Him?"

"Nahh. But I had a friend what did." Zelda paused, looking around them into the woods. "Listen. Ya don' wanna go tellin' folks about Jesus. Dey don' like it. Dey take ya and mess wit' ya head. Dat's what happen ta ma friend. Leastwise, dat's what I tink happen."

"But I *have* to go. I've come so far, and that's why I've come."

"To tell Discards 'bout Jesus?"

"To tell anyone who will listen. But I think I'm supposed to tell the Discards first."

Zelda sighed. The girl was a fool, after all. But as soon as she had started making a ruckus, Zelda had known she had no choice but to take her with her. It was that or be discovered. "Ya gots to be quiet. No gabbin.'"

The girl suddenly held out her hand. "Thank you. I'm Selah," she said.

Zelda looked down at her hand and sniffed. "Discards don' got no Palmscan," she said, with an air of propriety. "Zelda," she nodded, giving the girl's hand a dismissive glance before turning around. "Follow me."

The trek back to the wall went at a snail's pace. Selah carefully planned each footfall, and she could tell Zelda was trying to be quiet, but her hobbling gate and the occasional jingling of the contents of her sack seemed to announce each step. Of course, Selah's bulging packs weren't much help either. Being stealthy was nearly impossible. "Lord, make us invisible to those who would harm us," she prayed silently. "Let any noise we make be as silence to them."

At one point, Zelda stopped so suddenly Selah almost crashed into her. Up ahead through an archway of branches bowed low by a tangle of grapevines, Selah could see what had brought Zelda to a halt. A young man was crouched in the underbrush. His camouflage was uncanny, blending in with his surroundings nearly perfectly. Although there was much growth on the forest floor, there was nothing between their line of sight. If it had been a deer, Selah had reflected later, she would have taken the shot. The two remained motionless as the seconds ticked by, waiting for the inevitable, but it never came. Instead of spotting them, the man was distracted by something in a stand of sassafras saplings to his left, and never even looked their direction. Once he was out of sight and earshot, they continued.

Finally, Selah could see a change in the trees ahead—a grayness like a mist that swallowed light. She put a hand on Zelda's shoulder, pointed in that direction and raised her eyebrows in a questioning glance. Zelda nodded. A shiver ran down Selah's body, immediately followed by a foreboding she couldn't shake. The closer she got, the stronger her fear became. It pervaded her senses. Every crackle of a twig was a trigger for the release of adrenaline. The wall which loomed before her was identical to the gray walls in her dreams. *"Once inside, you will never leave these walls,"* hissed a voice in her ear. Selah twisted sideways to face her attacker, but no one was there. The sudden move caused her bow to slip down her arm and bang against a branch, which caused Zelda to turn around with a wild-eyed glare. Selah touched her ear where she had heard the whisper. Zelda watched her with eyes narrowed and once again placed her finger to her lips. Selah nodded apologetically, realizing the source of the whisper wasn't her imagination, but was someone known by her and all her brothers and sisters in the body of Christ. Of course, his minions had been lurking about on this journey, trying to discourage every step, bombarding her with thoughts of doubt when she was tired and hungry. She steeled her mind against them with a scripture: "Ye are of God, little children, and have overcome them: because greater is He that is in you, than He that is in the world."[28]

In a few moments, they were at the base of the wall. Selah looked up. It was at least forty feet high, made with smooth bricks that had very little evidence of mortar between them. Scaling it seemed out of the question, so they must be going under, she rationalized. Zelda turned right and walked a few paces toward a healthy vine that had attached itself to the wall. But even it seemed to be struggling up the surface, as if it had difficulty conquering the grim brickwork. On closer inspection, Selah could see places where it had been trimmed here and there. Zelda knelt down and carefully began removing pieces of the wall that seemed to have crumbled away around the vine's monstrous base. Soon there was an opening big enough for a person to crawl through. Zelda stooped down and peered through the hole. Satisfied, she poked her sack through and motioned for Selah to do the same. Then she put her head and arms through and inched her way to the other side as fast as her old joints would allow. Selah followed quickly, keenly aware that all of her supplies were now on the inside of the wall. As Zelda carefully replaced the damaged bricks, Selah marveled at the vigorous vine that had opened a doorway for them. Zelda brushed the frizz of her ginger-gray hair away from her sweaty forehead and smiled when she noticed Selah admiring the plant. "Wisteria," she said, grabbing one of the gracefully drooping leaves. "Gits purty flowers on it, too, in da summer. Flowers

---

[28] 1 John 4:4, KJV

don't matter none, for breakin' down walls, though. I sho didn' brung it all da way out here ta be purty."

"You planted it?" Selah asked. "How long did it take to grow that big?"

"Not soon enough ta save Pipah," Zelda scowled. "I shoulda tol' her 'bout it. But I was waitin' 'til I was good an' ready. Den I was gonna show 'er. Was gonna ast 'er if'n she wanted to come wit' me. But da trash boys, dey turned 'er in. Dey tol' someone she was gabbin' 'bout dat Jesus fella you so fond of." Zelda paused. "Tell me, now. If Jesus is real, why didn' 'e save Pipah from da loon dockers? Why'd 'e let da girl down?"

"Loon dockers?" Selah repeated. She could barely understand the woman's words through the thick accent, much less decipher any unknown terms.

"Crazy people doctors. For da loonies. Dey done took Pipah ta where da loony people dock. If only I had worked harder, mebbe I coulda saved 'er. Mebbe at least I coulda convinced 'er ta shut up 'bout religions," Zelda said miserably.

"If she really loved Jesus, I doubt you could have stopped her from talking about Him," Selah said. "Jesus saved me from myself, from my own sinful, self-ish ways. He gave me purpose in life, and protected me on my journey here. He's been with me every step of the way, and even pointed me in the right direction to find food."

Zelda stared at her silently for a moment, and then motioned for her to follow. After they had gone a few paces, she said over her shoulder, "One time 'e give me fish." Then she added quickly, "Leastwise, dat's what Pipah said. She ast 'im for me, an' den da trash boys pulled up wit' a coupla fish sammiches!"

"Isn't He amazing? No request is too small for Him," Selah bubbled enthusi-astically.

Zelda scrunched her wiry eyebrows together as if trying to figure out a riddle. "Didja hear what I said? Dem was *fish* sammiches. Sammiches ain't nuttin' ta sneeze at, expecially when da pigeons ain't comin' in an' ya belly's gnawin' at ya back bone. An' dey was *fish*, an' dey was *fresh*—not from da dumpster."

"I like fish too, but where I'm from, we either can them or smoke them, if we're not eating them fresh out of the creek," Selah said. "I'm not familiar with a *duhdumpster.* Is that a type of smokehouse?"

Zelda stopped for an instant and looked at her as if she had just landed from another planet. "Girl, you sho do talk funny. An' where ya live, dat da fish in da creek ain't full o' pyson?"

"Pyson?' asked Selah helplessly.

"Stuff dat make ya sick. Cuz da water be bad."

"Oh…*poison*. Are all your rivers and streams polluted here?" Selah asked apprehensively. She had been drinking filtered water from wherever she could find it, but wasn't sure how effective the old filter could be against chemicals.

"Only good drinkin' water 'round here come from a hydrant. If it's workin', dat is," Zelda said, eyeing Selah up and down and plodding to a halt. "Listen, girl. I can't jus' drag ya into da docks like *dat*."

"Like what?"

"De way ya all garbed up. Looks like ya been playin' at cowboys an' Native 'mericans. An' dat weapon ya got 'round ya arm, an all da stuff in ya sacks. Dey liable to jump ya an' make off wit' ya loot, an' I can't do nuttin' 'bout it. We gots to stop where I dock, whenever I'm outta da *main* docks. Mebbe den we can sorts ya out an' find ya sump'n presentable ta wear, an' stash some o' ya stuff. An' den," Zelda added almost guiltily, "ya did mention sump'n 'bout tradin'. I wouldn't ast, but I'm plannin' a journey o' ma own. I need supplies."

"Of course," Selah said.

Zelda grinned. "Good. Hardly no one lives in dese docks where I'm takin' ya, cuz dey's no dumpsters out dis way, an' no hydrant for miles. We be safe dere." With that, she led the way up to the lip of the slope that had shielded them from the wall cams, pausing to look around for signs of activity. Satisfied, she again motioned for Selah to follow.

As the depression in the land flattened out, Selah began to see the towered ghettos of the outer docks, looming in a sickly haze.

"Is that mist, or pollution?" Selah asked, gesturing to the buildings.

"Dat's da choky fog what come up from da river every mornin'. Dey still tryin' ta clean up dat mess. Sometime's when ya mess wit' stuff ya ought not ta mess wit', ya gits mo' trouble den ya can handle," Zelda said sagely.

Eventually, Selah was able to see details of buildings, most of them more of the depressing gray color like the wall behind them. What immediately struck her about the area between the wall and the buildings was the lack of trees. "No trees means no sneakin' out to da wall. Dey know if ya go, an' dey know if'n ya come back," Zelda explained. "Dey's watchin'. Dey might see us right now. Which is why we gots to make ya blend in. An' we gots to convince anyone what knows 'bout ya not ta turn ya in. State probly come lookin' for ya, cuz dey see me go to da wall by mahself, an' see two come back. What I can't figure is, if'n dey saw ya was out in da Preserve, why didn' dey grab ya when dey had a chance? How come dey let ya git so close? Didja stay hid 'til mebbe yesterday?"

"No. I think they've known about me for several days. I was following an old road at first, and then I started following that huge, humming bridge," Selah said.

"Dat's da causeway," Zelda informed her.

"What is it?"

Zelda shrugged. "Sump'n ta do wit' State folk gettin' from one place to anudder real zippy. Stay by it long enough, ya gits a headache. But if'n you was followin' da causeway, I don' see no how, no ways, why dey didn' pick ya up. Dey had to seen ya."

"Well, that's the crazy part of it," Selah said, remembering her encounter with Ira and the young woman. "Someone did see me. There was this man and a woman who had taken him prisoner. She had some sort of power over him, but I don't understand how. I just know when he didn't follow her like he was supposed to, she did something that caused him to be in pain."

"Datted be da club cuffs," Zelda nodded. "I seen 'em used once."

"Anyway, I tried to talk to them—"

"You *what?*" Zelda interrupted. "Girl, you's an idjut. No one from da State is ya friend, an' ya need to learn dat right now. How were ya able ta gits away after ya talked to 'em?"

"That's the thing I'm trying to tell you. The man could hear me and see me, but the woman couldn't. The man gave me a lot of the stuff I have to trade, and he just pretended he was delirious from being dehydrated so the woman wouldn't get suspicious. The only way I can explain it is that Jesus hid me from the woman, but let the man see me," Selah tried to explain.

"Dat's ri*dick*las," Zelda humphed. "Dat sound like sump'n outta Pipah's book. Like when Jesus got 'imself away from dem peoples dat was gonna trow 'im offa da cliff. Somehows, 'e jus' pass right by 'em an' dey don't see 'em."[29]

"It was exactly like that, except the man could see me," Selah said enthusiastically. "Kind of like when Elisha could see God's army protecting them, but his servant couldn't until his eyes were opened."[30]

Zelda's brow furrowed. "I don' know dat story, an' I heard most all of 'em. Anyway, I wonder if da dude ya saw was him what bursted out da wall yesterday afternoon," she said. "What was he tinkin' I wonder—dat 'e could jus' waltz on outta here through one o' da gates? Took me years ta make ma hole in da wall. Dat fool jus' blows past it like 'e tinks 'e can git away wit' it. Dey always gonna come for ya, if dey know ya git out." She paused and studied Selah. "Girl, ya gotta lay low. If'n dey find ya, ya won't be tellin' no Discards 'bout Jesus. But I tell ya what ya will be tellin'. Ya be tellin' 'em bout ma plant an' ma hole in da wall, an' dey be comin' after me next."

"I wouldn't tell them about any of it," Selah began.

"You say dat now, but all dey hafta do is put da chip in ya head. Den ya gonna tell 'em everyting dey wanna hear, whether ya wanna or not," Zelda said fiercely.

"What do you mean? What's a chip?"

Zelda sighed. "Girl, ya gots a lot ta learn. Just promise me ya won't start preachin' 'til at least a week after I makes it back to da udder side o' da wall. Den ya on ya own. Go ahead an' gab 'bout Jesus all ya want. Git yahself caught. Git yahself chipped, like dey prob'ly done ta Pipah. Just promise me dat ya wait a week. An' promise..." at this, her eyes welled up suddenly with tears, and she swallowed before she could continue. "Promise dat if'n ya sees Pipah, tell 'er I love 'er. Tell 'er I hopes it's true, what she say about Jesus an' heaven. Cuz if'n it is, mebbe she can meet 'im someday, face ta face."

The Holy Spirit rose up inside of Selah as she said with confidence, "It *is* true. Someday she *will* see Him face to face. And if you believe in Him and decide to trust Him, you will too. Even if you never get to see Piper again on this earth, when you both get to heaven, you can tell her that you love her, yourself."

---

[29] See Luke 4:24-30
[30] 2 Kings 6:8-17

Zelda regarded Selah silently. There was something about this girl. She looked nothing like Piper, but it seemed like they could be related by blood somehow. There was something on the inside that was similar, something that tied them together. It made her miss Piper even more. "Come on, girl. We's almost dere. Den ya can tell me all 'bout it. Mebbe tell me more 'bout dat Elisha dude, too," she said, and trudged up to the edge of a road that appeared as they neared the outcroppings of the dismal gray buildings.

Selah followed, praying for Zelda's eyes and heart to be opened to the gospel. As she did, she could feel the Lord's presence settle around them like a cloak. Selah felt humbled and honored at the same time. It was finally beginning— the reason she had come! She looked over her shoulder at the wall that had filled her with so much dread earlier, but now she could only feel the warmth of God's approval. Maybe someday she would be caught, as Zelda predicted, but not until the Lord had allowed her to complete her mission. Even then, she knew He would be with her, as a scripture came to her mind: *"Fear thou not, for I am with thee: be not dismayed, for I am thy God: I will strengthen thee; yea, I will help thee; I will uphold you with the right hand of My righteousness."*[31]

---

[31] Isaiah 41:10, KJV

14

Passengers bobbed to rhythmic bumps of the subway car bound for the Soulard District. All but one were wearing their Vista-Visors—a swaying sea of half-hidden faces in designer colors. Catching her reflection in one of the windows, the occupant with her visor flipped up over her head pulled back her silver and crimson hair into a pony tail. A small lock of royal blue escaped and stubbornly hung down in front of her line of vision as she pulled her visor down over her eyes. The reflection had betrayed her dazzling smile. Being that happy was suspicious behavior for someone who was unhooked. Now that her eyes were hidden and she appeared to be accessing the internet, she looked down at the cup of steaming hot chocolate portrayed on her shirt and attempted to quell her excitement. This next stop was hers.

Smoothing the rumples out of her T-shirt, she stepped out of the subway car and made her way to the exit. To her relief, the man who played guitar near the stairs was absent tonight. The last time she had seen him, she had lost her temper and regretted it. Perhaps he had found companionship elsewhere.

A dreary fog had begun to creep up from the Mississippi and thicken the air with its toxic particles. The girl slid the built-in air filter down out of her visor and secured it below her chin, because sometimes health implants were not enough to combat this particular St. Louis weather phenomenon. She had never experienced acid fog in Adullam. Perhaps the river that flowed by the little community had remained unaffected, or perhaps they had asked God to heal their river. She would have to ask Dawson when she saw him again.

"Viv?" called a tentative voice from the shadow of an awning.

Viv stopped and recognized Luciana from the Talk-o-lot Chocolate Café as she stepped out of the darkness to meet her. "Luciana, it's great to see ya again!"

she began, offering her hand.

"Let's avoid that," the older woman whispered, putting her arm around Viv's shoulders instead. "It's great to see you, too. But Palmscans are recorded in a database every time they are activated, meaning there would be a record of our meeting if we scan each other. When we get inside, I'll give you a glove to wear to remind you not to slip up and flash someone your palm."

"I had no idea they could track us with that," Viv said uneasily.

"Only when you flash someone. Otherwise, the only way they can track you is if your visor is turned on or you have the chip. I assumed from our previous meeting that you haven't been implanted?"

"No way, hume. And my visor is off."

"I didn't see anyone following you. Let's get out of this fog. I wanted to make sure you would recognize me," Luciana said, and it was then Viv realized the woman wasn't wearing a breathing mask of any kind.

The two hurried past the entrance of Talk-o-lot Chocolate, which had a "closed" sign in the window of the antique wooden door. Once past the storefront, they ducked into an alley and came to a side entrance. After a series of knocks, the door opened, and they slipped into the darkness inside.

"We can turn on the lights now. Viv is the last one," Luciana said.

When the lights flickered on, Viv could see they were in a small, windowless room with seven other people. "Welcome to our church!" Luciana said warmly. "We call ourselves *The Closet.*"

"The Closet? You mean like a prayer closet?" Viv asked, remembering one of Dawson's sermons about spending time alone with God.

"Well, yes, but also because that's where we're meeting," Luciana laughed, gesturing to a mop in the corner and other cleaning supplies on the shelves of the tidy little space.

"Is this the janitorial closet I saw by the restrooms?" Viv asked.

"Yes. We just enter by the alley because there's no camera there. This is an extremely low crime area, and surveillance is minimal. That is actually why I chose this location for the café. That and a lot of seeking the Lord for direction," Luciana explained.

"Ya mean ya planned ya whole business around whether or not it would make a good location for an underground church?" Viv asked, amazed.

"Yes. And we stagger peoples' arrival time so as not to arouse suspicion," said a man about Luciana's age. He was wearing the uniform of a garbage truck operator.

"You'll have to excuse my husband's attire. He just got off work," Luciana said as she noticed Viv looking at the uniform.

"I didn't mean to be starin'. I guess I thought we all might show up wearin' these T-shirts," Viv explained, noticing that she was the only person sporting one.

"That would draw too much attention," said a familiar-looking teen with caramel skin and hazel eyes. Viv realized she had seen her waiting tables at Talk-o-lot Chocolate the other night.

The group then introduced themselves. Stasi was the girl who had just spoken, and there were three other workers from the café: a dark-haired boy named Celidor, a tall, slender girl named Contessa, and Melford—a chubby, sandy-haired man in his twenties who was sporting an acoustic guitar. Chester was Luciana's husband, but everyone called him Chess. Ranger was a man from Denver, Colorado who wanted to start a cell church in his neighborhood. His slight build and humble nature didn't seem to match his name. Viv was impressed he took the Colorado Connection Causeway from Denver to St. Louis every Monday to attend. But the most surprising member was a man named Rhys, who was a curator at the Museum of Religious Convergence.

"Luciana caught me reading a bit of original text I had copied from Paul's letter to the Philippians," Rhys explained. "When she asked me about it, I tried to witness to her. That's when I got one of the shirts," he grinned.

"What happens if another customer sees ya handin' out shirts and wants one?" Viv asked suddenly. "Aren't they suspicious when ya turn 'em down?"

"We don't turn them down," Luciana said. "Anyone who wants one can have one. It's a little expensive because of the encoding, but there's no risk, for the same reason. Only someone who uses the name of Jesus in conjunction with the phrases 'Help me,' 'I love you,' 'Thank you,' and 'I praise you,' ever knows about the message encrypted in the fabric. Actually, Ranger has been able to supply us with the shirts through his business in Denver, and he bears most of the expense."

"It's worth it," Ranger interjected. "I'm glad Rhys got a shirt and decided to take the risk to join us. He's given us a wealth of original scripture—all copied by hand so it doesn't leave a digital trail."

Rhys smiled and cleared his throat. "I'm happy to be able to help."

Viv's heart pounded as she realized she had something these people only obtained in bits and pieces. "I may be able to help, too," she said, and carefully withdrew the New Testament from the pouch underneath her shirt. A collective gasp was heard in the tiny room.

"Where did you get that?" Stasi asked wonderingly.

"That's incredible! A paper version, still in circulation!" Celidor exclaimed, crowding closer to examine the little Bible.

"I-I'm kind of sworn to secrecy," Viv stammered, not willing to reveal the sequestered community of Adullam.

"As well you should be," Luciana said firmly. "The less we all know, the less likely your source can be exposed if we get caught. But since you have brought it, would you mind if we copied some of the scriptures from it while we're here? We've all been trying to memorize as much of it as we can."

"Same," said Viv. "I'm not very good at remembering, so my friend just went ahead and gave me one of his copies."

"*One* of his copies?" Celidor asked incredulously.

"There are more out there than you might think," Chess said. "I've heard of a few people who have hidden and passed down copies in their family for generations and have somehow avoided the purgings. Just a few months ago, I met a girl in the outer docks who had one."

Viv brightened. "I wonder if it was the same girl who first told me about Jesus two years ago. She was from the outer docks, and she had a little Bible."

"But *two* New Testaments, owned by the same person?" Rhys questioned. "That is rather remarkable."

"He actually has more than two. He wanted to give me a complete Bible with the Old Testament but was afraid it would be hard to hide," Viv said.

"How is he hiding them all?" Celidor asked excitedly.

"Celly, come on. The more we know, the more dangerous it is," Melford cautioned.

"Yeah, I know. It's just…I've never met anyone who owned an unaltered version. It's incredible he's gotten away with it," Celidor remarked.

"You don't know just how incredible," Chess said sadly. "The girl I mentioned earlier was reported by my coworker and picked up by mental health providers. She's probably chipped by now, and maybe she's believing everything they're feeding her."

"No!" Viv said emphatically. Something rose up in her as she remembered the young girl who had witnessed to her, and she suddenly recalled what Dawson had said when she told him she was afraid she might be caught and implanted with the chip. "Even if they chip her, nothin' is too powerful to overcome what we have in our relationship with Jesus. 'For I am persuaded that neither death, nor life, nor angels, nor principalities, nor powers, nor things present, nor things to come, nor height, nor depth, nor any other creature, shall be able to separate us from the love of God, which is in Christ Jesus our Lord.'[32] It says so in Romans 8:38 and 39." Viv quoted.

"That's powerful," Contessa said, her brown eyes shining. "Can I copy that one tonight?"

"It's alright by me," Viv said. "But I'm not in charge. I don't wanna take time away from the service."

"Anyone can copy any scripture they want as long as it doesn't take so much time that others don't get a chance," Luciana said.

"Are you the pastor, then?" Viv asked Luciana.

"I provide a place to meet," Luciana began.

"Don't let her fool you. Luciana does more than provide a meeting place," Stasi said quickly. "She looks out for us. When she sees we're struggling, she offers hope through the portions of the Bible that she's memorized. And she can *preach!*"

"Don't I know it," Chess said sheepishly. "I get it at home."

The group laughed.

---

[32] Romans 8:38-39, KJV

"Luciana doesn't like to brag on herself. But she knows how to extrapolate the scriptures I bring her," Rhys confirmed.

"I just pray and let the Word of God shed light on my understanding, and then I share what I've learned," Luciana said.

"Luciana's prayers are how this church began," Chess said. "She told me about Jesus when we were still dating. I thought she was taking a big risk by doing that, but then I found out she had prayed for me for months before we even met. Then after we got married, she started spending hours in prayer in the evening when she would get home from work. She wanted desperately to reach others, but wasn't sure how. That's how this business was born—and from there, we were able to start this church."

"Well, since the church is all here now, let's give God some praise," Luciana said, redirecting the conversation away from herself and toward the Lord. Melford began strumming some chords, and the group was soon singing. Viv didn't know all the words, but she didn't care. The same kinship she felt with the people of Adullam could be felt in the small room that was hidden in plain sight at the café. Tears began streaming down her cheeks as she lifted her hands in praise and thanked God that she had found brothers and sisters in Christ right here in her own city.

At the end of the service, the group prayed for Piper, although they didn't know her name. "The Lord knows," Luciana said confidently.

"Indeed, he does," Rhys agreed. "I just read it at work the other day in Nahum 1:7. 'The Lord is good, a stronghold in the day of trouble; and He knoweth them that trust in him.'"[33]

"Now, there's one for *me* to memorize!" Viv said eagerly. "Can ya help me write it down?"

"Sure!" Rhys said affably and proceeded to record the verse on a scrap of paper.

The group stayed as long as they safely could, recording as much scripture as possible onto the pieces of paper Rhys had provided. Then they decided on arrival times for next week according to their schedules and departed one by one. "I can't thank ya enough, Luciana," Viv said as she left.

---

[33] Nahum 1:7, KJV

"You coming to be a part of us is thanks enough," Luciana replied. "And if you see Janice, please tell her hello for me. She's really been on my heart lately."

"She's been off for a coupla weeks, but I'll tell 'er when I see 'er," Viv promised.

When she stepped outside, Viv discovered the fog had cleared. The sense of guilt that had plagued her since her attempts to witness to Janice seemed to have lifted with the fog. It may not have gone the way she wanted it to, but there was no more important thing she could share with her friend than the love of Christ. "Lord, I know all things work together for good to them who love Ya and are called according to Ya purpose.[34] I'm holdin' onto Ya promise for Janice's sake. I'm trustin' that You can somehow even use my mistakes to reach 'er." She hugged the Bible close to her side in its secret pouch, remembering the wonder in the eyes of her brothers and sisters when they saw what she possessed. If only Dawson and the people of Adullam could realize the role they were playing in strengthening Christians they had never met, simply by providing a Bible to a girl who had never had one.

Across town in a small, windowless cell with no furnishings, Piper leaned against a padded wall. "You will find that if you trust the chip and stop resisting, this will be much less painful. Although your headaches will still persist for a while, they will gradually lessen. The confusion you are feeling will disappear, and you will be able to experience more than these dreary, drab walls—much more than you could ever imagine. Everything you have ever wanted to know will be available to you. Even useful things you think you have forgotten will be as fresh in your mind as the day you first learned them because the portions of your brain where these memories are stored will be available for you to access again. You will be able to live out fantasies in your mind that go beyond the shallow premise of a daydream. You will be able to visit any place in the world right from the confines of this cell. But then again, once you embrace the chip, you will find you won't want to spend your time in daydreams. Life will be so much richer you will want to experience it to the fullest." The words of Dr. Moses repeated over and over in her mind. And how could she forget his added

---

[34] See Romans 8:28

warning? "If you persist in being stubborn, we will simply extract the needed information ourselves. The only reason I have held out this long is because of your tender age and my sense of decency. It turns out your mother did, indeed, sign a Declaration of Intent to Nurture, despite your deplorable upbringing. So although your crimes have negated many of your rights, you have *this*, at least, in your favor. My advice to you is not to wait much longer—for there is a limit to my patience."

Piper squeezed her eyes tightly shut and cradled her throbbing head in her hands. "Jesus, I love Ya. I know Ya saved me. But I don' know how much more o' this I can take," Piper whispered.

"Then why don't you let Me take it for you?" said a voice above the confusion in her head. Piper opened her eyes. This was not like the other voices she had been hearing in her head. This sounded like it was coming from someone right beside her. She turned around and was surprised to see a man standing in the room with her. His eyes were full of compassion, and His arms were stretched toward her as if He were waiting to receive something from her.

"Who are you? How didja get in here? Are you another one of their tricks?" Piper asked—but in her spirit, she knew she could trust this man. She felt like she was talking to an old friend.

"I came because you called upon Me, and others have called upon Me on your behalf. I know you are at the breaking point. I have come to ask you to hold out a little longer. But I have also come to take some of your pain and confusion away. Remember, Piper? You've read it before. Cast all your care upon Me, for I care for you."[35]

And then Piper knew who was speaking to her. "Oh, Jesus! Is it really You?" She leaned into His embrace and immediately her head cleared and the pain ebbed away. "Can Ya get me outta here?" she pleaded.

"I have a mission for you here, Piper. But I will protect your mind from them. And I will use their own devices against them. You remember how Dr. Moses told you that you will be able to remember things you thought you had forgotten?"

---

[35] See 1 Peter 5:7, KJV

Piper nodded.

"Very soon, the people who work here will attempt to make you reveal the names of my servants. I want you to surprise them by using the chip in your mind before they use it forcefully against you."

"But I don't wanna be possessed by no chip in ma brain!" Piper exclaimed.

"You won't be. Instead of them taking control of you, you will take control of the tool they have given you. Your brain is a much better thinking machine than the one they have constructed. It is capable of building walls they cannot break through. If you make the pathways in your mind the way I show you, you will be protected from their efforts, and any attempts to invade your conscience will result in their own confusion. Are you willing to do this?"

Piper laid her head against His chest. "I know I can trust Ya, Jesus. An' I wanna do what Ya want. But I's so tired. I wanna see that city John wrote about in Ya book. Can't I jus' go home wit' Ya today?"

"It's not time for you to come home yet, daughter. And what I'm asking you to do isn't easy, but it will be worth it. There are others who need to hear the message you have. Since you've lived in the outer docks your whole life and have never had any implants, your body and mind aren't as willing to let technology take control. That gives you a natural advantage over them. But you also have Me and My Holy Spirit, and you will find that I am more than enough to guide you in this process. And you will also find that all My Word you have hidden in your heart will be a light unto your path as you go forth in this mission."

Piper leaned back and looked into Jesus' eyes. "I *have* memorized a bunch of Ya book. I read it so much to Zelda that she can nearly tell some o' Ya stories from memory. But there's so much left I don't remember. I read the whole thing through once, but I can't say it all by heart."

"Don't worry. Do you remember the scripture you memorized about how not to worry?" Jesus asked.

Piper stood up straight and said confidently, "Be careful for nothing; but in every thing by prayer and supplication with thanksgiving, let your requests be made known unto God. And the peace of God, which passeth all understanding, shall keep your hearts and minds through Christ Jesus. Philippians 4:6 and 7."[36]

---

[36] Philippians 4:6-7, KJV

"Very good. Now, do you believe what you just said? Do you believe My peace will keep your heart and mind safe?"

Piper was quiet for a moment and looked in the stillness of her heart. "I believe it because Ya Word says it, and because Ya done showed me before that it's true." She looked up at Jesus once again. "I trust Ya. Ya said Ya would go wit' me, to show me what I need to do. If Ya go wit' me, I can do anything, cuz Ya also said in Ya Word that I can do all things through Christ, Who strengthens me."[37]

Jesus threw back his head and laughed in sheer delight. "Oh, daughter! You give me such joy. I am looking forward to this journey with you. Now, take My hand."

Piper reached out to clasp His hand and noticed that He had a deep, horrible scar. She hesitated for an instant. "Is that…is that where they put the nail?" she stammered.

"Yes," Jesus said gently, and looked deep into her eyes. "But you were worth it."

Piper swallowed the lump in her throat and grasped the nail-scarred hand. Suddenly the walls of the room faded away. They were in a meadow with more lush, green grass than she had ever seen before. For some reason, the place seemed familiar to her, although she knew she had never been anywhere like it. A beautiful tree with patches of white, cream and gray bark stood nearby, and a stream flowed softly through the tall grasses. "Is that a sycamore tree?" She asked. Her grandma had seen one when she was a little girl—before the people were evacuated from the Preserve to consolidated cities. She had told Piper about its beautiful white bark.

"It is," Jesus said. "It likes to live by sources of water. Let's go over and sit down by it."

"Okay," Piper said, still clinging to Jesus' hand. When they arrived at the base of its trunk, Piper saw something that made her heart jump. Her old Bible was there, but the stains on it were gone and the pages were in perfect condition. It looked as if it had just been printed. "It's ma Bible!" Piper exclaimed. "What's it doing here in this meadow?"

---

[37] See Philippians 4:13

"This meadow is what you imagined in your mind when you would read Psalm 23. And just like the green pastures where a sheep can eat or lie down to rest and the still waters where she can feel safe to drink, this is a place where you can come and be refreshed. All the words you have read in your Bible are available to you here. When you need to remember something for any situation, all you have to do is to think of this spot in your mind, and you can read about it in My Word," Jesus said.

"But what about when I need to make paths like Ya tol' me 'bout? How will I know what kinda path to make—and where to go?" Piper asked.

"Hmmm. Why don't you look in My Word and see what it says about paths?" Jesus suggested.

"Okay," Piper said. She picked up the Bible and tried to remember where to look. "I can't remember where I read it," she said at last.

"You could always try the reference section in the beginning. Look under the word, 'trust.'"

Piper found it. Proverbs 3:5-6. "Trust in the Lord with all thine heart; and lean not unto thine own understanding. In all thy ways acknowledge Him, and He shall direct thy paths."[38] Piper smiled and looked up at Jesus. "When can we start makin' paths? This is gonna be fun!"

Jesus filled the meadow with deep, hearty laughter. "I agree. It *is* fun! But we've already started."

"We have?"

"Yup. You already have the tool necessary for making these pathways and building these walls you need to build. It's right there in your hands. Whenever you need advice, just think of this place, and you can access whatever part of My Word that you need."

Piper scanned the meadow, which was surrounded by a protective wall of tall trees. "Can we go in there?" she asked, pointing to the forest.

"We can," Jesus said.

The two waded through the billowing ocean of grass and came to the forest edge. Light was swallowed up in the dark shadows of the arboreal canopy. It was unsettling.

---

[38] Proverbs 3:5-6, KJV

"There's no path in there," Piper said in a small voice. "And it's dark."

Jesus waited, knowing Piper already knew what to do. She raced back to the sycamore tree and returned with the Bible in her hand.

"Thy word is a lamp unto my feet and a light unto my path!"[39] Piper exclaimed. "I didn' even hafta look that one up!"

Jesus' laughter pealed across the meadow once again. "You're a fast learner," He congratulated her. "That was one of the abilities I really enjoyed giving you when I formed you in your mother's womb. You've already figured out that you can take this spot in your mind with you wherever you go."

Piper held out the Bible, and its light splashed brightly against the tree trunks. There didn't appear to be a path, but as she stepped out in faith, one appeared. Each step was a creation in the making. Jesus smiled and placed His hand on her shoulder, walking beside her all the way and encouraging her when she wasn't certain where to go. Around them, as the trees grew taller, God's Word blazed like a torch in the darkness.

---

[39] Psalm 119:105, KJV

15

GARRISON'S stomach grumbled noisily. "Sorry stomach. You'll have to wait," he said, and continued picking his way through fallen limbs in the grove of cottonwood trees. It was last summer when he had followed Macy through this stand of giant cottonwoods to the edge of the meadow. He stood there now, scanning its gentle dips and rises until his eyes came to rest on a grouping of boulders on a swell of ground. Goats grazed in the thick, green grass, and the bell of the lead goat tinkled softly in the distance. The night Macy had led him here, he had a dream about this place that had trailed the boundaries of his subconscious for weeks like a relentless hound tracking a scent.

Garrison sighed and ambled slowly to the gray slabs of rock. He had come here many times since the dream, trying to make sense of it. But this time was different. This time, he had been fasting and praying as he looked for answers. He carried a Bible, a notebook, and a pencil in his satchel. Craig Goforth, the youth pastor of Adullam, had recommended he keep them handy during his fast. "You may see different things in a scripture that you may not have seen before, even if you've read it a hundred times, just because you are ready to receive it *this* time. Be ready to write down what God reveals to you as you seek Him," he had told Garrison. "The most trustworthy source of revelation is God's Word. You may have a dream that was just the result of eating jalapeños the night before. But unlike our emotions or physical state, God's Word doesn't change. It changes *us*. You can count on its promises and its truth, even when our lives are confusing or situations around us are changing. Hold onto it, and let all other revelations you may have fall under the light of its scrutiny. If what you think God is telling you doesn't line up with the Word, then you haven't heard from God."

Garrison knew it was solid advice. He had heard something similar from Miss Genevieve right before he had left the valley. "The Almighty is always speaking to us," she had said, "but we are rarely in a position receptive enough to listen. He most often speaks to us through His written Word, but through the ages, there have been times when He used other methods." Just as Pastor Craig had explained, Miss Genevieve told him if he thought he had heard from God, to always make sure it was something already promised in the Bible. Garrison grimaced. Even back then, before he had given his life to Christ, he had been getting sound, Biblical teaching that he had handily ignored. He was ready to listen now.

The rock formation rose up before him, cool to his touch in the morning shadows. He put his foot on the familiar indention that always acted as his first step in climbing to the top. Suddenly he paused. Why should he always climb up the same way, his behaviors ingrained in the same predictable pattern? Maybe if he approached from the other side, he would see something new. Maybe his spiritual state would mimic the physical realm, and he would see things differently and understand what God was trying to tell him through the dream.

He followed the edges of the boulders along an outcropping of smaller rocks that looked like little gray loaves of bread. "Lord, is that what the stones looked like when the devil told you to turn them into bread?" he asked with a chuckle. "A lot of things are looking good to eat, after only three days. I can't imagine what it must have been like after forty days in the wilderness with no food."

The anatomy of the boulders changed as he reached the eastern side. An hour of daylight had already warmed the rock face. He put his hands on the smooth surface and remembered why he always ascended from the western side, which had myriad pock marks and cracks that acted as natural stair steps. The eastern side had no existing footholds that he could see. He sighed and looked up at the wall of rock. It wasn't very tall—only about ten or twelve feet, but he wasn't an expert climber like some of the other people in the youth group. This was a popular destination for their outings, and he had seen a few of the kids find places to put their toes and grip with their fingers where there appeared to be nothing to hold onto. His recreational time in the valley where he grew up had been spent fishing, catching crawdads, and playing basketball, not climbing bluffs. And the weakness he felt from fasting wasn't encouraging him to look for challenging ways to do something physical. He backed away from the rock and stood there for a while, the sun warming his back. With a sigh, he followed the edge to a point where it was almost facing the cottonwoods.

Perhaps because of the thickness of the understory trees and bushes, he had never studied this part of the landmark before. This side of the rock was girthed by a thick stand of aromatic sumac. But through the brushy barrier, he could see that the rock face appeared to have been cleaved in two by the blow of a giant's ax. He pushed his way through the tangle of undergrowth. Two smooth sides of the rock rose fifteen feet above him, and he realized this was the place the others had warned him to avoid while walking around on top because of the danger of falling into the crevice. He stepped closer. The space was just large enough to accommodate him. He squeezed inside and felt the instant coldness of the stone against his skin. Above him, the golden light of dawn was slowly deepening to azure. The outside of the boulders and the meadow around them were warming up in the late spring sun, but here in the cleft of the rock, it was still pleasantly cool. A song starting playing in his head, complete with Ethel Rosales, the song leader back home, belting out her scratchy soprano: *"He hideth my soul in the cleft of the rock that shadows a dry, thirsty land."*[40] The people of Adullam had never sung that hymn. It was an old one, even to the people back home, who had left the Old Country much earlier.

He leaned with his back against the stone, put his hands on the wall in front of him, and suddenly had an idea. Using his feet on one wall and his back on the other, he slowly began inching his way up. The space gradually widened as he climbed. In a few minutes, he was sitting at the top, his legs dangling down into the crevice. He looked across the meadow and back down into the cleft of the rock. "He hideth my life in the depths of His love, and covers me there with His hand,"[41] Garrison sang softly. He couldn't get the song out of his head. *"Where did the person who wrote that get the idea?"* he asked himself. He seemed to remember something in scripture about someone hiding inside a crevice of a

---

[40] From the hymn "He Hideth My Soul," words by Fanny Crosby
[41] Ibid.

rock. Grabbing the Bible out of his satchel, he turned to the concordance in back and looked up the word, "rock." There were several references about the Lord being a Rock, but nothing about someone hiding in one. He tried the word, "hide," but there wasn't anything about someone hiding in a rock and being covered by God's hand. Finally, he decided to look up the word, "cover," and there it was: Exodus 33:22. Garrison flipped over to that portion of scripture and read it and the surrounding verses, thankful that when he was being taught in Sunday School by Miss Genevieve, he had learned how to use a concordance. "If something about the Bible is stuck in your mind like a cocklebur, then the Lord wants you to understand it better," she had said. "Don't give up if you can't find it the first place you look."

The scriptures in Exodus referred to a time when Moses was asking the Lord to go with him as he led the children of Israel. The Lord had assured him, "I will do this thing also that thou hast spoken: for thou hast found grace in My sight, and I know thee by name."[42] The implications of that statement staggered Garrison. To know, from the very lips of the Almighty, that you had found grace in His sight, and that He knew you by name—it was astounding! To realize that the Creator of galaxies would recognize such a fragile element of creation was humbling.

But Moses wasn't content with that. He wanted more. "And he said, I beseech thee, shew me Thy glory."[43] Garrison's stomach flip-flopped, and it wasn't from hunger. He suddenly felt an excitement akin to the feeling he had one day when he had jumped from a feed bunk onto one of the steers in Payton Hamby's pasture. He was thrilled that God had saved him. He had been searching for answers to what he should be doing next, wondering about the strange dream he had, and had even been seeking the baptism of the Holy Spirit—although he had never spoken in tongues. But he suddenly realized the simple fact that Moses' desire and his were the same. Just knowing that God had promised to be their guide wasn't enough for Moses. He wanted to see the glory of God— to be as close as any human could possibly be to his Creator.

---

[42] Exodus 33:17, KJV
[43] Exodus 33:18, KJV

Garrison resumed reading. The Lord continued the conversation with Moses, explaining that Moses couldn't see His face and live. "And the Lord said, Behold, there is a place by Me, and thou shall stand upon a rock: And it shall come to pass, while My glory passeth by, that I will put thee in a clift of the rock, and will cover thee with My hand while I pass by."[44] That was the scriptural basis for the hymn that had been playing in his mind since he had seen the cleft in the rock face.

Suddenly the air around him seemed to close in, and Garrison felt cocooned in a wave of excitement. "*What is this?*" he wondered to himself. "*Where have I felt this before?*" And then he remembered: it was during the worship services here in Adullam. Sometimes, when everyone was praising God, the air around them seemed electrified. Some of the youth reacted by jumping up and down. Some people spoke in tongues. Some knelt down and bowed their faces to the ground. It was a feeling of awe, of power, of *presence*. And he was feeling it now, all by himself, on the rock in the meadow. He realized suddenly that not only did he want to be near God and feel His presence, but God wanted to be near *him. God* wanted *Garrison's* presence. The startling realization made him dizzy, and he scooted away from the edge of the drop-off. A heaviness descended on him that felt like the weight of a thick comforter. He laid down on the rock and began to weep as the world around him seemed to fade away. All that mattered was God's presence and God's love. It swept over him like waves rushing across the meadow and crashing over the rock. It no longer mattered to him if he spoke in tongues or ever left Adullam to return home or explore modern civilization. At that point, it didn't even matter to him if he ever left the meadow. It was enough to be with the Lord… in His presence. "*You are more than enough,*" he prayed silently. A warm feeling of approval settled over him.

Garrison wasn't certain how long he had lain there when he was roused by a wet, slobbery tongue swiping across his face. "Ugh, Macy!" he exclaimed, but laughed and pulled the dog to him in a hug. He looked around and grabbed his notebook, scribbling down the scriptures he had read and the revelation he had. The weightiness of God's presence he had felt earlier had lifted, but the

---

[44] Exodus 33:21-22, KJV

deep joy in his heart remained. He clambered to his feet and stretched before climbing down the boulders by his normal route, feeling somewhat like Moses descending Mt. Sinai. When he reached the floor of the meadow, he promptly stepped in some goat manure. "Nothing like poop to bring you down to earth again, eh, Macy?" he commented while the dog sniffed eagerly at his boot. "Quit it, dog. Let's go."

That night there would be a youth meeting, and the minutes dragged by until service time. He had been getting a garden plot ready for Dawson and Sophia and was glad for the distraction. Although he still felt weak from the lack of food, his spirit felt energized. He was hoeing away at the dirt, throwing rocks into a pile, when Sophia came outside and handed him a cup of water. "Thanks," he said, and thirstily gulped it down.

"You don't have to go at it like you're killing snakes," Sophia laughed. "You can take a rest now and then."

"Keeping busy like this is good for me, though. It passes the time until service starts," Garrison explained.

"Sophia, tell that young man to come inside and take a break," Dawson called from the porch.

"It's two against one," Sophia chided him. "Just come in for a minute, and then you can get back to work."

Garrison relented and left the hoe leaning against the fence.

"We just had soup and sandwiches for lunch. Would you like one?" Sophia asked as they walked through the front door.

"No, thank you."

"It's no trouble," Sophia added. "In fact, I insist!"

"No, really, I'm fine," Garrison said. He had made a commitment in his mind to fast until the next morning, and he intended to keep it.

Sophia started to protest, but Dawson patted her on the shoulder. "Honey, maybe he has a reason for refusing," Dawson said knowingly.

"I was trying to be private about it, but I'm fasting," Garrison explained.

"Oh! I'm sorry I kept insisting," Sophia apologized.

"I thought it was something like that. I hadn't seen you in the cafeteria lately," Dawson said, and gestured for Garrison to take a seat in the front room.

"Yeah, I've been seeking the baptism in the Holy Spirit and the answers to some questions," Garrison explained as he settled himself down next to the fireplace. "I think I may actually have found some answers today. Even if I never get filled with the Holy Spirit and speak in tongues, I don't feel left behind anymore. Today, I had this experience where I felt the presence of God like I've never felt it before. And I realized that God is enough. Whatever He has for me is enough." Garrison's voice quavered with emotion as he remembered his time on the rock.

Dawson smiled gently. "Sometimes when we feel left behind, it isn't because God doesn't want to use us. It's because He's taking time to perfect something in us." He paused for a moment and looked in the direction of the kitchen. "Do you smell that soup in there? Doesn't it smell good?"

"Yes, and I'm trying not to think about it too much!" Garrison laughed.

"Sorry about that! I'm not trying to make your fasting more difficult. But that soup really lends itself to a point I'm trying to make. Sophia put that soup together yesterday. The vegetables and chicken were ready to eat then, but we waited. Have you ever heard that old expression 'putting something on the back burner?'"

"Yes. I always thought it was for when you had something you wanted to do, but it wasn't really important and you didn't have time for it, so you set it aside for later," Garrison answered.

"Well, that's one way to look at it; but if you take it quite literally, why do you think Sophia would keep cooking her soup after it was done the day before? Why not just make it the day you're going to eat it and serve it as soon as it was ready?"

"Soup doesn't really taste good until it simmers a long time. My mom used to cook a pot of vegetable beef stew almost all day before we'd eat it. She said it helped the flavors to meld. And it was even better the next day," Garrison responded.

"Ahh. I see. So you don't think it was a waste of time and fuel to cook it longer?"

"Not if you want good stew," Garrison said.

"So when something or someone is 'put on the back burner,' so to speak, it's not necessarily because they aren't important enough to take time for. It's actually the opposite. They are worth the extra time it takes to get it right." Dawson paused. "Now, let's stop talking about soup. I can hear your stomach growling from here!"

Garrison laughed. "I'd appreciate that."

Dawson leaned forward as he warmed to his subject. "Just look at David, for instance. I'll bet that every time his brothers went into battle and he had to stay home and take care of the sheep, he must have felt like he was being 'put on the back burner.' After all, he had been anointed by Samuel to be the next king of Israel. Why should he always be left behind? But you know what he was doing out in those pastures with that flock of sheep?"

"Keeping them safe? Making sure they got the food they needed?" Garrison ventured.

"Yes. He was learning to look after things that needed leadership and protection. And he was probably singing and playing his harp. He was known for his skill in playing instruments.[45] All that time out there, he was learning about leading, and he was cultivating his relationship with the Lord through worship. God hadn't forgotten that he was anointed to be king. David wasn't left behind at all. He was a man after God's own heart, and it was worth the extra time to prepare him for what God wanted him to do." Dawson stood up and walked to the mantle, his eyes resting on a picture of his son. "I tried to explain all of this to Yosi when he became a teenager and grew so restless. He had such a gift— I might even go so far as to say he had a calling on his life, where technology was concerned. He felt so limited here, unable to reach his full potential. I told him that someday, in God's timing, it might be possible for him to return to the State. His walk with the Lord was always a tenuous one, though. As far as I was concerned, he wasn't ready. But then he took matters into his own hands and left anyway." He turned back to Garrison and smiled wistfully. "I admit, I have wondered if you had been his age and had come to Adullam during that time of his life, would it have made any difference? Would your story and the

---

[45] See 1 Samuel 16:17-19

life change you experienced upon arrival have had any bearings on his develop-ment and decision?"

Garrison wasn't certain what to say. "I'd like to think I could have made an impact. Our stories sound pretty similar. I can relate to feeling limited. I used to talk to Selah about it all the time. But now that I've given my life to Christ, my motivations for leaving my community seem so shallow. To be honest, though, I don't think anyone could have talked me out of leaving the valley. Selah couldn't, and she tried."

Dawson shook his head. "I think it was your time to leave home. If you hadn't, you would have grown resentful—and who knows? Maybe you never would have come to know the Lord as your Savior. But now, you really know what it means to be born again.[46] I've watched you grow in the Lord, and I'm convinced that now you are in a time of preparation."

"So you're saying the reason I haven't been filled with the Holy Spirit is be-cause God wants me to learn something else first? I thought maybe God was disappointed in me because I didn't want to speak in tongues earlier."

Dawson chuckled. "Let me assure you that God isn't disappointed in you, and He doesn't withhold His Spirit from His children. Jesus said that if we, as humans, know how to give good gifts to our children, how much more will our Heavenly Father give the Holy Spirit to those who ask Him?"[47]

Dawson studied Garrison for a moment before continuing. "I remember you had this dream you told me about in which you were a sheep, and Jesus was your Shepherd. He wanted you to eat a certain plant, but you were afraid to eat it. When you told me about that dream, I was certain it was referring to you receiving the baptism of the Holy Spirit. There's no reason why He wouldn't want you to have this experience. The power of the Holy Spirit is a promise He made to everyone who believes.[48] Even though you initially wrestled with the idea of speaking in tongues because it seemed so strange to you, that won't keep God from fulfilling His promise. It's a gift you simply need to reach out and receive, even though it may seem you are trying and getting nowhere."

---

[46] See John 3:1-8
[47] See Luke 11:5-13
[48] See Acts 2:39

Garrison nodded. He had spent what seemed like hours on multiple occasions seeking the baptism of the Holy Ghost while people prayed with him. He had felt bad that he was taking so long, and he even considered faking it a few times so he wouldn't be inconveniencing people. But in the end, he had just left feeling defeated, like he was missing the point somehow. "I don't know what I'm doing wrong," Garrison said at last.

"I don't think you're doing anything wrong, Garrison, except maybe being too hard on yourself. Some people try so hard they make it difficult. Many times, it is just a matter of yielding and stepping out in faith by uttering the words that come to you. After the experience you have had today, I think you are truly learning to yield your will to the Lord's. Just allow Him to lead, and trust Him as He works in you."

Garrison leaned back against the hearth and sighed. "The people where I'm from don't talk much about the Holy Spirit. They would probably think I was just going through another kind of rebellion by seeking the baptism in the Holy Ghost."

"Some believers think the gift of tongues is not for today. They may not believe in any of the gifts except teaching, helping, administrating, and apostleship. Maybe most of the people where you're from believe this way. And that's ok. We don't need to argue with them. They are our brothers and sisters in Christ, and God did not call us to argue with each other. 1 John 4:7 begins 'Beloved, let us *love* one another"—not 'Beloved, let us always prove our point.'" Dawson said with a wry smile.

Garrison nodded thoughtfully, finished his cup of water, and went back outside to work on the garden. The hoe seemed to have picked up weight since he had rested. After a while, Dawson came outside to carry rocks and noticed his slower pace. "Son, why don't you go back to the cabin and get some rest before service?" he said. "Pastor Craig won't be very happy with me if you fall asleep during his message. Not to mention, a bath would do you some good," he winked.

Garrison grinned and handed him the hoe. "Ok, Pastor. That's not a bad idea."

"But before you go, why don't you allow me to pray with you?" Dawson suggested, laying the hoe aside.

"That would be great, Pastor," Garrison said thankfully.

Dawson put his hands on Garrison's shoulders and looked skyward. "Father, I thank You for my brother. Thank You for the hunger he has for more of You. I know that You see the desire of his heart is to be closer to You, and it pleases You so much. Thank You for Your presence that He felt today out in the meadow. And I know that no matter how hard he is seeking You, You are seeking Him more."

Garrison opened his eyes in surprise as he realized that Dawson was relaying the revelation he had earlier, even though he hadn't mentioned it. It was confirmation that God really did want to be with him as much or more than he wanted to be with God. The reality of it stunned him, and he began to praise the Lord and tell Him how much he loved Him.

Dawson was praying again, but Garrison hardly heard what he was saying because he was lost in worship. "Lord, give him the words he needs to worship You as he desires in his heart," Dawson said.

Suddenly, Garrison felt as if he would burst if he didn't express how he felt about the Lord. "There's no one like You, Lord. You are wonderful! You are mighty! You are omnipotent! You are holy!" He continued to offer up praise, but he simply couldn't find enough words to proclaim the goodness of God. "I wish I knew the words to say to tell You how wonderful You are," Garrison said.

"Then just let Him help you. Yield your tongue to Him, and He will give you the words," Dawson said.

"Lord, help me to praise You like you deserve," Garrison cried. And then he felt something on this tip of his tongue. It wasn't a word yet. It wasn't even a sound. It was like he was about to say something, but he didn't know what he was about to say. His tongue began to quiver. He opened his mouth, and a word that sounded like nonsense came out.

"Go ahead. Keep praising Him," Dawson encouraged him.

Garrison opened his mouth again and more sounds came out. They didn't make sense to him, but Dawson didn't act like he was doing anything wrong. In fact, he was encouraging him. "That's it, Garrison! Tell the Lord how much you love Him in whatever language He gives you!" Dawson was almost giggling with happiness for his friend.

"So, this is it! I've just received the baptism of the Holy Ghost!" Garrison thought incredulously as he continued to speak the words he didn't understand. The more he spoke, the more of God's power and love he felt welling up within him, and the less hesitant he became to speak. He kept praising God right out there in Dawson's yard, and the longer he praised, the louder he got. When he finally stopped, the joy was indescribable. He opened his eyes and looked around to see Dawson beaming at him. Sophia, who had come outside when she heard the commotion, was clasping her hands together in happiness.

"That was beautiful, Garrison!" Sophia exclaimed. "When were you two going to tell me?"

"Well, it just now happened," Garrison said. "We didn't have time yet."

Sophia looked at them quizzically. "No, I mean when were you going to tell me you were learning Tagalog? Dawson didn't tell me anything about teaching you how to speak it."

Garrison stared confusedly at Sophia and then turned to Dawson, who was laughing joyfully. "Honey, he has no idea he was speaking my native language. He just got baptized in the Holy Ghost."

Sophia's mouth dropped open and she clapped her hands together. "Praise God! I've been praying for you about that for so long!"

"Wait, what?" Garrison asked in wonder. "I was speaking a language you *know?* Was I making sense?"

"Indeed, you were," Dawson said, still grinning from ear to ear. "You were praising God and telling Him how wonderful He is, in perfect Tagalog!"

"But I thought that when we spoke in tongues, it was a holy language just between us and God," Garrison said.

"Most of the time, it is," Dawson explained. "However, if someone in a service gives a message in tongues that is meant for the congregation, usually an interpretation will follow by someone who operates in that gift. But sometimes He uses a language that is already known to someone around us, as He did on the day of Pentecost.[49] He may do this to speak to that person who understands, or to confirm something through them."[50]

"Oh! I didn't realize that could happen," Garrison said. His head was reeling.

"And sometimes, I think He just does things like that because it's fun. Perhaps He just wanted you to know that what you experienced was the real deal," Dawson continued.

"Oh, I have no doubt about that!" Garrison exclaimed. "I've never felt like this before! I haven't had food in three days, and I feel like I could run to the meadow and jump to the top of that rock!"

Dawson and Sophia laughed. "Just the same, why don't you go home and take a rest," Dawson suggested.

"I'll try, but I'm not making any promises," Garrison said with a broad smile. He turned and walked back to the cabin with a spring in his step. Macy trotted ahead of him, her tongue lolling out the side of her mouth as she panted in the heat. The quiet coolness of the guest quarters was a welcome respite from the sunshine that had been beating down on them, but Garrison still wondered how he was ever going to settle down enough to get any rest. He bathed quickly and lay down on the bed, joyfully thanking the Lord for filling him with His Spirit. Tears ran down his cheeks onto the pillow as he began praising God again in tongues. He wasn't certain how long he had been praying when the elation he had felt earlier dimmed a little and the weariness of his body began to creep back in. His eyelids became heavy, and he drifted off to sleep.

He could hear a voice calling him. It was a familiar voice, but it was hard to distinguish the words. He arose from the bed and went outside. It was broad daylight, and he had trouble remembering why he would be sleeping in the daytime. The whole town seemed to be asleep until he looked more closely. As he walked down the streets of Adullam, he could see into the windows of each home. Some people were lying down upon their beds, asleep, while others were already awake, kneeling in prayer. He could hear the voice calling to each one. Some of

---

[49] See Acts 2:6-11

[50] On a certain occasion, Ora Morrison, an Assembly of God pastor and missionary to the Apaches, spoke in tongues during a church service. Immediately afterward, a Chinese man ran to the altar and gave his heart to the Lord. Ora had no way of knowing she was speaking Mandarin Chinese until the man came to her after the service and told her.

the people who were asleep rolled over and ignored the sound of the voice. Others awakened and sat up, listening intently before getting out of bed and kneeling in prayer. Sometimes the voice would call to an individual who was already praying. That person would get up, come outside of their home, and join him as he walked from house to house. After a while, Garrison had a small group of people walking with him. They all walked to the center of the village, and Dawson was there. He walked up to each one of them and placed his hand on their heads and smiled. Then he turned around to a table behind him where a large Bible sat. It was opened to a scripture which was underlined. Garrison could see the scripture from where he stood: "Go ye into all the world, and preach the gospel to every creature."[51] Suddenly, Dawson tore a page out of the Bible and wadded it up into a little ball. He took the wadded-up page and poked it into Garrison's mouth. "Chew!" he commanded. Garrison began chewing, and suddenly the paper burst into flame, but he wasn't burned. He began speaking, and what came out was the truth of the gospel. As he spoke, the space around him became brighter. Dawson repeated this process with each of the people who had come into the center of the village until they were all preaching the good news of Christ and illuminating everything around them. "Now, go," Dawson said, pointing away from the town center. The group left and walked until they reached the edge of their community. Although it was bright in Adullam, it was dark outside of its boundaries. "Go," Dawson's voice called out from behind them. Garrison wanted to comply, but he wasn't sure where to go next. Suddenly he heard the voice that had called to him earlier. He obediently stepped forward to follow it, and the darkness around him fled from the light he created as he spoke the good news. He looked around at the others. Each one was surrounded by a halo of light as they stepped forward into the darkness.

Garrison slowly opened his eyes. What a strange dream! It had been so vivid, and he felt it must be significant. He was wondering if he should share it with Pastor Craig when he realized the shadows around his room had deepened. Suddenly he was wide awake. He was almost late to the youth meeting! He freshened up as quickly as he could and rushed out the door. Macy barked excitedly as he ran to the church building, bounding along beside him and nearly

---

[51] Mark 16:15, KJV

tripping him as she ran around him in circles. When he arrived, he was nearly light-headed. "Are you okay?" Pastor Craig asked as he stumbled in the door.

"Pastor Craig, you're not going to believe this!" Garrison panted. "I just received the Holy Ghost this afternoon in Dawson's back yard!"

"Wow, that's incredible! Thank You, Jesus!" Craig exclaimed. "I want you to testify about it sometime in the service."

"No problem," Garrison said, looking around the room. "Am I late?"

"Well, we don't always exactly start on time around here," Craig grinned and clapped him on the shoulder. Garrison could see that most everyone else had already found a seat.

"Garrison! Over here!" Thom, a boy about Garrison's age, was motioning to an empty chair beside him. Garrison hurried over and sat down, just in time for the worship service to begin.

Some of the other teens were distracted as the singing began, whispering and teasing each other. It bothered Garrison, but his flesh felt too weak to be angry. Instead of being irritated, he prayed for the rowdy ones and that the whole group would become united in worship. Eventually, he was so focused on the Lord that he didn't notice the others gradually begin to seek the Lord in earnest as well. After one particularly quiet moment between songs, Garrison felt a stirring inside of him. It was an urgency, as if he was supposed to do something. *"Lord, help me to yield to You,"* he prayed silently. He opened his mouth and began speaking in tongues, his voice gaining strength as the Spirit moved upon him. As he spoke, the images of the dream he had during his nap came vividly to mind. There was a silence throughout the room. Garrison realized the group was waiting for someone to operate in the gift of interpretation of tongues. But no one said anything. All the while they waited, Garrison kept seeing the images in his head, coupled with the sense of urgency that made him feel like if he didn't do something, he would burst. "If someone has the interpretation, be obedient and speak it out," Craig said from the platform. "Just listen to what the Spirit of God is showing you and begin to speak."

With a dawn of revelation, Garrison realized *he* was the one who was supposed to give the interpretation. He focused on the images and prayed for the Lord's help in conveying the correct meaning. Immediately, a scripture came to mind; and he began to say it from memory. "And that, knowing the time, that now it is high time to awake out of sleep: for now is our salvation nearer than when we believed. The night is far spent, the day is at hand: let us therefore cast off the works of darkness, and let us put on the armour of light."[52] Garrison paused, and then with the images clearly in his mind, he began again. "The Lord would have you know that some of you are asleep, even though it is time to get up and work. Others of you are already awake, working fervently in prayer. I hear your prayers, and I am preparing you to go forth with My message. With the blessing of My leadership, I am sending you out. Take My message of light to those who are lost in darkness. Speak out the words that I give you, so My light will shine brightly. You are My representatives, My image bearers. Show My Son to the world." Garrison stopped speaking, and, shaking with emotion, wilted to his knees.

"Thank you for speaking to us, Father!" Pastor Craig whispered into the microphone. He directed his next words to the crowd. "If you feel that message was for you, I want you to come down to the front. I want to pray with you right now."

A few teens came forward immediately. Garrison felt a hand on his shoulder. "I'm going down there, buddy," Thom said.

"Help me up. I'm coming with you," Garrison replied. Thom helped him to his feet, and the two made their way to the front.

Garrison stood for a while, waiting for his turn to be prayed for; but eventually, he sank to his knees again. It wasn't weakness from fasting, but rather an overwhelming sense of God's presence and power similar to what he had experienced on the rock earlier that day. Soon, Pastor Craig was kneeling beside him, praying.

"Thank you for being obedient to the Spirit," Craig told him.

"I wasn't sure what to do," Garrison admitted. "I just felt like I was supposed to do something, and this dream I had earlier kept playing over and over in my mind. So I just tried to say what I thought God was trying to tell me through the dream."

---

[52] Romans 13:11-12, KJV

"People sometimes see interpretations of tongues in the form of images in their mind," Craig explained. "You did the right thing in speaking out."

"But how do I know if I got it right?" Garrison asked.

"What do you feel in your spirit?" Craig asked.

"I feel like everything's okay."

"So do I. Of course, we can't rely on feelings. But your interpretation used scripture, and it lined up with the Word of God. And besides that, it's confirmation that I'm preaching the right message tonight. The interpretation goes right along with what I'm preaching," Craig said.

After the prayer time was over, everyone returned to their seats, and Craig went back to the platform. "The Spirit of God wants us to hear what He is saying to us. That message in tongues confirms what the Lord gave me to share with you tonight. Not everyone is called to preach or to be missionaries. But everyone is called to share the gospel somehow. I don't want those of you who don't feel called to preach to feel left out. Many of you are called to pray for those who will go forth. Your job is just as important as those who share the gospel directly, because without someone preparing the soil of people's hearts through prayer, the seed of the gospel will fall on stony ground that cannot accept it. The time for us to wake up is now. The time for us to pray is now. Turn with me in your Bibles to Ephesians chapter 5, starting with verse 6."

The sound of pages rustling could be heard from some areas, while some faces were illuminated by the lights of their phones or tablets as they accessed the scripture electronically.

> "Let no one deceive you with empty words, for it is because of these things that the wrath of God comes upon the sons of disobedience. Therefore do not associate with them. For once you were darkness, but now you are light in the Lord; walk as children of light (for the fruit of light is found in all that is good and right and true), and try to learn what is pleasing to the Lord. Take no part in the unfruitful works of darkness, but instead expose them. For it is a shame even to speak of the things that they do in secret; but when anything is exposed by the light it becomes visible, for anything that becomes

visible is light. Therefore it is said, 'Awake, O sleeper, and arise from the dead, and Christ shall give you light.' Look carefully then how you walk, not as unwise men but as wise, making the most of the time, because the days are evil. Therefore do not be foolish, but understand what the will of the Lord is. And do not get drunk with wine, for that is debauchery; but be filled with the Spirit, addressing one another in psalms and hymns and spiritual songs, singing and making melody to the Lord with all your heart, always and for everything giving thanks in the name of our Lord Jesus Christ to God the Father."[53]

Craig looked up at the crowd and waited a while for the words to sink in. "I cannot express to you how important it is that we understand and receive this message. This is a critical time. There are wars being waged in the spiritual realm, and if we are not praying and obedient to what God has called us to do, souls may be lost forever." Craig's voice was strained with emotion. "I know that walking into the unknown is scary. You don't know how the world will receive your message. Maybe they'll think you're crazy. Maybe people will laugh at you. Maybe they will put you in prison, or worse. But remember—it may be the unknown to you, but it is not unknown to God. He is already there waiting for you, because He is the God Who is, and was, and is to come."[54]

Garrison glanced around the room at the others he had seen come forward to declare their calling. The time he had been waiting for was almost here, and how different it was from what he had imagined! Gone were the shallow dreams of an easier life and the excitement of seeing a different world. In their place was a heart to do the will of his Father, to share the good news that Christ was still bridging the gap between humankind and its Creator, and to seek out and save those who were lost in darkness.

---

[53] Ephesians 5:6-20, RSV
[54] See Revelation 4:8

16

SELAH peered upward out of the small window of Zelda's little apartment in the outskirts of the outer docks. She had awakened early with her host to see her off on her journey. Back in her home hidden away in the Ozark hills, Selah would have been able to see the stars. She used to gaze at them on cloudless nights from her bedroom window. Jackson Meritt had taught his daughter how to find Orion and the Big Dipper and had shown her which stars were really planets. But here, on the edge of the mega-metropolis of the consolidated cities of the eastern half of Missouri, tall buildings and light pollution made star viewing a literally dim possibility. She sighed and wondered how her parents were doing. What did the rest of the community think? Were her parents outcasts now? Had Seth Beardsley locked them up because they had helped her escape?

She looked at the bedroll on the floor where she had been sleeping. On it were piled all her belongings in the world: the leather knapsack made by her father, the pocket knife she always carried, her fire-starting kit, and Miss Genevieve's satchel with her Bible and study materials. Selah's heart jumped suddenly when she recognized for the first time that her bow was missing from the pile. She had given that to Zelda, along with the water filter. God had called her to be a missionary here. Surely he would provide for her needs, and Zelda would need the items more than she did.

The spunky old woman had looked dubiously at the bow when Selah had offered to teach her how to use it a few days after she had arrived. "I's a trapper," she said adamantly. But after Selah shot an unusually large rat they saw scampering around the edge of the apartment building, her interest was kindled. "Well, mebbe I could give it a go—just for funzies," she relented. In a week's time, she was hitting a cardboard box stuffed full of trash at thirty yards. Selah insisted she take it when she left.

"You're going to need it more than I do," Selah said. Zelda wasn't accustomed to receiving handouts unless it was from the State. She was much more comfortable trading. Upon their arrival at the apartment, Selah had spread out her belongings and negotiated for her room and board. Zelda had quickly latched on to the MREs. "Don't eat too much at once," Selah cautioned her. "The one I ate gave me a sour stomach."

"Reckon dat's cuz of all da chemicals dey pump it full of ta keep it good so long," Zelda explained. "Ya probbly don' git much o'dat where ya dock. But I's raised on dat crud. An' now I eats pigeons what've been eatin' dat crud. So it don' bodder me none." She eyed the pile of belongings eagerly. "What else ya got dere, girl?"

Selah showed her the bar of magnesium and flint and the char cloth. "It's for starting fires," she explained, when Zelda looked at it quizzically. Then she quickly demonstrated by flaking off some of the magnesium and sparking the flint to light it on fire.

Zelda nodded appreciatively, but instead pointed to the red and silver object Ira had given her which Selah had been unable to identify. "I'll take dat instead," she said, looking up at Selah for permission to retrieve it.

"Okay," Selah agreed, and the old woman snatched it up. "But what is it?"

Zelda looked at her as if she were seeing her for the first time. "Ya trades me sump'n ya don' even know what is? How ya know I didn' jus' take da bes' ting ya got?"

Selah shrugged. "That's one of the things the man I told you about left for me. I've gotten along without it so far. I can probably manage without it now."

Zelda held up the item and rolled her thumb against the top. A small flame appeared opposite her thumb. "Dis is a lighter. Very handy. An' much quicker'n dat ting ya got. Be a long time 'fore I runs outta fluid. Besides, I gonna settle down, find me a place, keep some coals burnin'."

Selah suddenly remembered why it had looked familiar to her earlier. "Miss Genevieve had one of those in a drawer in her kitchen. She said it didn't work anymore—out of fluid, I guess."

"Who?" Zelda started to ask, and then interrupted when Selah began to answer. "Nevermind. Show me what else ya got."

"Well, I've got this little black box," she said as she handed Zelda the item Ira had left. Zelda took the box and pressed a button on its shiny surface. A beeping sound was heard, and a display panel on the front lit up.

Zelda looked up at her under hooded eyes. "You can keep dis. I don' need it where I's goin'. But if'n ya hold onto it, ya may be able to pay someone ta tote ya into da city, if'n ya really serious about wantin' ta go dere." She paused and turned it over in her hand before handing it back. "It's against da law ta have one o' dem tings."

"What is it? Some sort of weapon?" Selah asked apprehensively.

"Nope. It's a locater. It scans da area and tells where da nearest State-owned vehicle be. So's ya can steer clear of de police is why dey sell 'em on da black market in da State. But here, people use 'em to locate da trash trucks. Gives an unfair advantage to da dumpster divers. I never much keered for 'em. But dere's some people what'd trade most anyting ta get one."

Zelda nodded toward the Bible that was visible peeking out of the knapsack. "What about dat? Whatcha got dere?"

"Oh—I'm keeping that," Selah said quickly. "That's my Bible. I need it for when I start telling people about Jesus."

"Dat's illegal too, ya know," Zelda said, her eyes narrowed. "An' I guarantee —no one'll be wantin' ta read it. But since it's a real book made o' paper an' all, it'd bring a high price at da pawn shop in da Shaw, 'cause it's a genuine antique. You could probbly trade it fah most anyting ya need."

Selah shook her head.

"Suit yaself," Zelda said.

"The last thing I have to trade is this pocket knife," Selah began.

"Girl! Shame on ya. Ya don' jus' go tradin' a knife to a complete stranger," Zelda scolded her, but her gaze never left the knife.

"You can have it," Selah assured her, but Zelda refused.

"Much as I want it, I can't take it. Knives is meant to be given to kinfolk an' such. Besides, I already gots a knife. You needs ta keep it, 'cause a person can always use one." Then she leaned toward Selah and winked at her. "Dey's illegal too, by da way."

Selah raised her eyebrows. "What *do* they allow you to have here?" she asked.

"Garbage. Clothes nobody wants no more. Medicine—but nuttin' fancy. An' if ya willin' ta git implants and play da State's games, dey gives ya citizenship an' a job, an' most whatevah else ya want." Zelda leaned back and surveyed the items she had acquired.

Selah's brow furrowed. "Sounds like a good trade. Sounds like a better way of life than being here in the outer parts."

"Outer docks," Zelda corrected her. "An', no, it ain't no good trade. Once ya git Palmscan, dey can track ya whenever ya use it. Once ya git implants, ya gits powerful healthy. But how ya know what else dey puttin' in along wit' it? Trackin' devices? Pyson dey can release whenever dey want? Pretty soon, dey probly gonna be puttin' in da chip without people knowin' it. Too much techno. Even people in da outer docks got Vista-Visors or at least a phone, an' dey's all addicted to 'em. Dey lives deir whole lives wit' deir eyes glued to a screen, just watchin' stuff dat ain't real, while da real world passes 'em by. An' who can blame 'em, since life is so *bad?* But at least it's not plugged direckly in deir brains, like da chip." Zelda waved her arms in a broad gesture. "People feel sorry for us in da outer docks. '*O, all dem poor Discards. Dey's trapped in da outer docks an' wishes dey had a better life. Look how much better we 'ave it 'ere in da State!*' But at least we 'ave *some* freedom. We don' 'ave no one tellin' us ta git da chip. We don' 'ave no one puttin' trackin' devices in us when we's born. Don' git me wrong, we's got it rough, an' we depend on da State for da garbage we eat. But pretty soon, I's gonna be free o' dat, too." She leaned back against the wall and sighed. After a few moments, she fixed her gaze on Selah. "Ya sure ya don' wanna come wit' me?"

Selah smiled grimly and shook her head. "God called me to come here—to tell others that there's still hope in such a hopeless place, if they will believe in His Son."

Zelda's eyes narrowed. "Why is dat so important to ya, eh, girl?" she asked.

Selah leaned forward. "Did Piper ever tell you the story about the man who found a treasure in a field?"

Zelda shook her head slowly. "I don' recall dat one," she lied. Piper had read her all the parables of Jesus several times, but Zelda liked a good story. Besides, she had never understood that particular parable.

Selah got out her Bible and turned to Matthew 13:44. "Again, the kingdom of heaven is like unto treasure hid in a field; that which when a man hath found, he hideth, and for joy thereof goeth and selleth all that he hath, and buyeth that field." [55] She closed her Bible and looked at Zelda steadily. "Before someone knows Jesus, their life feels empty—hollow. That's because their spirit is dead on the inside. But when they meet Jesus and decide to follow Him, Jesus puts His Spirit inside of them. He brings their spirit to life with His Spirit. He gives them eternal life, so that when they die, their spirit will go on living forever with Him in heaven. There is no greater treasure. That's why I'm willing to give up everything to tell others about this priceless treasure He has given us."

"What's in it for *Him?*" Zelda asked. "Why's 'e so bent on us livin' forevah?"

"It's because He loves us," Selah explained. "He doesn't want to be separated from us. Humans were created to be in relationship with God. But when the first man and woman disobeyed God, sin came into the world, and that perfect relationship with humankind was broken. God didn't want that separation. He wanted to be able to talk freely with us. But since God is holy and perfect, He can't live alongside sin. There had to be a way to get rid of our sin in order for Him to be able to be friends with us again. So God came to earth as a little baby—"

"I 'member dat story!" Zelda interrupted. "Dat's da Santy Claus story. Jesus came an' da wise men played Santy Claus."

"Well, sort of," Selah said slowly. "But the important thing is that Jesus lived a perfect life. He never sinned. But when He went to the cross, He made a trade."

"Jesus was a trader?" Zelda asked skeptically. "I thought He was a carpenter, like His daddy."

"He was a carpenter like Joseph, who raised Him as his son. But Jesus was into trading. And so was His Heavenly Father." Selah opened her Bible to Isaiah. "This is from part of the Bible that Piper didn't have. It happened *before* the

---

[55] Matthew 13:44, KJV

part she read to you. It looks ahead to what God is going to do through His Son, Jesus. Listen to this verse: 'The Spirit of the Lord God is upon Me; because the Lord hath anointed Me to preach good tidings unto the meek; He hath sent Me to bind up the brokenhearted, to proclaim liberty to the captives, and the opening of the prison to them that are bound; To proclaim the acceptable year of the Lord, and the day of vengeance of our God; to comfort all that mourn; To appoint unto them that mourn in Zion—'" at this point, Selah stopped reading and explained, "And here is where the trading part comes in. 'to give unto them beauty for ashes, the oil of joy for mourning, the garment of praise for the spirit of heaviness; that they might be called trees of righteousness, the planting of the Lord, that He might be glorified.'[56] You see, even hundreds of years before Jesus was born, God was using people like Isaiah to explain what His Son was going to do for us all." She flipped forward in her Bible to the New Testament. "Now, here's a verse that you might have heard before. It shows how God traded His Son. 'For He hath made Him to be sin for us, Who knew no sin; that we might be made the righteousness of God in Him.'[57] The curse of sin was destroyed when Jesus died on the cross. Jesus traded His righteousness for our sin."

"Dat's a stupid trade." Zelda said in disgust, and spat over her shoulder.

"Not for us!" Selah said. "He takes our sin and offers us His righteousness."

"What exackly is righteousness?" Zelda asked.

"It means being restored in your relationship with God—to be in right standing with Him," Selah explained.

"You mean ta tell me dat Jesus died so He could take our bad doin's away, an' all da guilt what goes along wit' 'em, jus' so Him an' His Dad could be friends wit' us?"

"Yup. That's basically it," Selah said, watching how Zelda would react.

"If'n dat really is true, He musta loved us sump'n powerful."

"He did. He does. Would you like to know Him like Piper did?" Selah asked.

Zelda looked at her knobby hands and rubbed her knuckles thoughtfully. "I tink I's prob'ly too old."

"Nope. John 3:16 says that God loved us so much that He gave His only Son, so that *whosoever* believes in Him will not perish, but have everlasting life.[58] It

---

[56] Isaiah 61:1-3, KJV
[57] 2 Corinthians 5:21, KJV
[58] See John 3:16

doesn't say just young people. It says whosoever," Selah insisted.

"Pipah used to say dat one to me all da time," Zelda said, misty-eyed.

"God doesn't stop saying it, either. Listen to this: 'And the Spirit and the bride say, Come. And let him that heareth say, Come. And let him that is athirst come. And whosoever will, let him take the water of life freely.'[59] It says that right at the very end of Bible. So you see, God never changed His mind about it. He wanted everyone to know about it, and He wanted everyone to come to Him. That's why I'm here." Selah looked at Zelda intently.

Zelda stared back at her. It was a shame this girl was going to throw her life away on a bunch of Discards who cared nothing about what she had to say. But there was something about her words that made Zelda hungry to hear more. "Mebbe. Mebbe God is jus' waitin' for us to turn aroun' an' see 'im standin' dere," she finally said.

"Well?" Selah asked, her heart beating faster. "Are you going to turn around? Are you going to make the trade?"

Zelda sighed and inspected her treasures as she placed them inside of her bag. "I'll tink about it."

Late in the afternoon of the day before Zelda left, Selah heard a commotion outside. Zelda had gone deeper into the outer docks to retrieve a few items she had stashed in her hiding place at the Shaw. Maybe the old woman had returned and tripped over the trash can just outside the door. From the window, Selah had a good vantage point of the street. Zelda was nowhere to be seen, but a big raccoon was peeking out of the garbage can, holding the empty packet that had contained the chicken chunks from her MRE. Selah had always considered coons to be a little greasy, but beggars couldn't be choosers. She shot it and raced outside to make certain it didn't run off where she couldn't find it. It was a good shot. The coon had merely fallen back into the can and was almost dead when she got there. Selah carried the can to the back of the building, put the coon out of its misery and gutted and skinned it. Since she had arrived there, she hadn't seen another soul besides Zelda—but she wanted to play it safe, since killing things was frowned upon. The coon would make a nice farewell dinner for her new friend.

---

[59] Revelation 22:17, KJV

When Zelda returned later that evening, she cackled happily when Selah showed her the meat simmering in a skillet. She excitedly pulled two round, brownish lumps out of her bag. "Taters!" she exclaimed. "I got 'em from da guy what traded me da wisteria. He's always tryin' ta grow stuff." She got a bigger pot from underneath the counter and dumped the contents of the skillet into it. Then she carefully poured in enough water to cover the meat, quickly diced the potatoes, and added them to the pot. "Trash panda stew! Now we's eatin' high on da hog." After adding the salt and pepper packets from Selah's half-eaten MRE and simmering the concoction for another hour, Zelda declared it done. It wasn't anything like Asha's venison stew, but it was the first home-cooked meal Selah had eaten since she left the valley.

After they were finished, Zelda patted her stomach and settled herself down on a couch cushion she had found by the side of the road. "How 'bout ya read me one o' dem stories outta dat book? How 'bout da one where Jesus feeds five tousand people wit' just a few loaves o' bread an' a coupla fish?"

"I could read that. Or I could read one you haven't heard before," Selah suggested.

"I likes da ones about food. Is dere one 'bout food comin' outta nowheres?" Zelda asked eagerly.

"There are several like that, actually," Selah said. "There's one about God sending food from heaven. There's one about a widow pouring oil out of a little bottle to fill a bunch of other containers. And there's one about a woman who had a barrel of meal that never ran out as long as she needed it."

"Read me dat un. Da one about da barrel o' meal."

"Okay," Selah said and turned to 1 Kings 17. Zelda sat transfixed as she heard the story of Elijah the prophet, who showed up on the doorstep of a starving woman and her son during a time of drought and asked her to give him their last bit of food.

"I can't believe he'd ast her ta make 'im a cake an' give it to 'im before she even fed her own chile," Zelda growled.

"The story's not over," Selah assured her. "Just listen to what happens next. Elijah said to the woman, 'The barrel of meal won't run out, and the bottle of oil won't run dry, until the day God sends rain," she paraphrased.

Zelda puffed air out of her lips through the gap in her teeth. "Ri*dick*las. Take a lot o' nerve ta say sump'n like dat to a starvin' lady an' her chile."

"Maybe so, but she did what he asked," Selah said.

"Idjut woman. She deserve ta starve, den," Zelda said emphatically.

"But she didn't starve. The barrel of meal and the bottle of oil didn't run out,"[60] Selah explained.

"It really say dat in dere?" Zelda asked skeptically.

"Yup."

Zelda cocked her head and thrust out her chin. "Tell me *dis*, den. How come God don' do stuff like dat today? How come he don' help people like dat no more?"

Selah thought for a moment. "Didn't you tell me He gave you and Piper some fish sandwiches after Piper asked Him?"

"Well, dat *did* happen," Zelda relented. "But just da one time. Not time after time."

"I think God helped out the woman like He did because she was obedient. She put someone else's needs before her own and did what the man of God asked her to do, even though it seemed unreasonable. She stepped out in faith that what God said He would do, He would do," Selah suggested.

"Well, wouldn' it be sump'n if dat would happen here, in da outer docks? If'n ya really is God's messenger, den mebbe you could ast 'im ta do sump'n like dat. Cuz people 'round here is powerful hungry. An' it sho would draw a big crowd ta hear what ya has ta say," Zelda said, using her knife to work at a splinter in her thumb.

"I would imagine people around here are hungry for a lot more than just food. They need hope," Selah replied.

"Mebbe so," Zelda said as she laid back on her couch cushion. "But hope is a lot easier ta swallow on a full stomach. An' who wants ta hear stories 'bout Jesus when deir gut is growlin' so loud dey can't hear nuttin' else?"

Selah was quiet for a while. Zelda was right, of course. It would be terribly hard to concentrate on anything but surviving when you were always on the

---

[60] See 1 Kings 17:8-16

brink of starvation. She hadn't even considered the physical needs of those to whom she would speak. Shouldn't she make some sort of effort to help meet their physical needs as well as their spiritual ones? After all, Jesus had compassion on the multitudes that came to listen to Him teach. He made certain they were fed before He sent them away. And God had spoken of helping those in need through Isaiah: "Is not this the fast that I have chosen? To loose the bands of wickedness, to undo the heavy burdens, and to let the oppressed go free, and that ye break every yoke? Is it not to deal thy bread to the hungry, and that thou bring the poor that are cast out to thy house? When thou seest the naked, that thou cover him; and that thou hide not thyself from thine own flesh?"[61] Selah was disappointed that she hadn't thought of this aspect of being a missionary. But then again, she had thought the people she would be ministering to would have no lack of material provision. She had no knowledge of the disenfranchised segment of society known as the Discards before she set out on her quest. "That's a really good point, Zelda. I can't believe I didn't think of that before," Selah said.

Zelda's only answer was a ragged snore from her corner of the room.

The old woman departed well before daylight. Selah had pressed the water filter into her gnarled hand as she went out the door. "I can always find a hydrant," she told Zelda, as she started to protest.

"Suit yaself," Zelda said as she slung her cumbersome sack over her shoulder and picked up Selah's bow and her homemade spear with her other hand.

"I hope you'll think about the trade Jesus offers," Selah said awkwardly.

Zelda turned to fix Selah with her gaze before she went out the door. "I hopes ya gits whatcha came 'ere for, girl. I hopes dey hear ya. I know dere's some what heard Pipah and made da trade. Mebbe dere's some dat'll hear you, too." With that, she nodded her farewell and disappeared into the early morning darkness.

After that, Selah couldn't go back to sleep. She stayed up and paced the floor, praying for Zelda's safety and that her heart would turn completely to God. She prayed for her next contact with the people of the outer docks. And she prayed for Garrison and her parents and her community back in the little valley she had left behind.

---

[61] Isaiah 58:6-7, KJV

When first light came, her stomach growled and she was reminded of the left-over stew in the dingy little cold box Zelda had explained to her was a refrigerator. She opened the door to get out the pot to heat it on the stove and hesitated. Maybe there was someone nearby she could share it with. And maybe over the meal, she would be able to tell them about Jesus. She slid the pot back inside the fridge. She had never seen another person in this neighborhood, but she often had the feeling she was being watched. Zelda said there were a few neighbors, but most were too scared of her to associate with her. "Dey know I kills stuff," Zelda explained. "Dat ain't natural 'ere. Ain't too many pigeon trappers aroun'. People used ta gettin' food in a package or in a dumpster. People is used ta meat what's been growed in a factory, not runnin' aroun' somewheres."

Then she remembered she had promised not to preach until Zelda was gone for a week. Well, maybe if she shared a meal with them, she could gain their trust, she reasoned. On the other hand, if they were afraid to approach her, how should she even begin?

Outside, the sky was beginning to turn a dismal gray which passed for dawn in this part of the world. Soon, the toxic fog that came from the river every morning would be creeping through the window. She left the refrigerator to shut the window and stopped short when she saw a figure standing at her door-way. Small of stature, the person didn't appear to be much of a threat, although Zelda had warned her not to trust anyone. Their hair was matted into dread-locks that were the same color as the dirt that had collected on the sidewalk, and a tattered ball cap was pulled down over their eyes. Their clothing was much too large for the small frame and everything they wore looked as if it had been dropped in the mud and trampled. Sending a needy child to her door might be a way for someone larger to gain entrance. She breathed a silent prayer, but felt no warning from the Holy Spirit that a threat was imminent. "Hello," Selah called out the window tentatively, hoping not to scare the little person away.

The figure jumped slightly but then quickly regained their composure. "I was just about to knock on ya door, but I can come back if it's a bad time," said a voice that squeaked alternately with the low and high tones of a boy going through puberty.

"Just a minute. I'll be right there," Selah said, and went to the door.

"I got sump'n ya might be interested in tradin' for," said the boy as the door opened.

"Well, okay," Selah said, taken off guard. "What is it?"

A small hand extended out of a dirt-encrusted sleeve and opened to reveal five buttons of varying sizes, styles and colors.

"Well…that *is* something," Selah said encouragingly. "You never know when you're going to need a button."

The boy nodded vigorously. "I know. Dat's why I collect 'em. Ya just nevah know when ya gonna need one. And of course, dese is high quality buttons."

"Oh, I could tell that much right away," Selah said. Looking at the gaunt face, she wondered if the boy's growth had been stunted from malnutrition. She thought of the stew in the refrigerator. "Would you be willing to trade them for some stew? I was just thinking of having some, myself."

"Dat'd probably cover it," said her visitor, trying to be nonchalant, but the hunger in his eyes betrayed his excitement.

"Okay. Come on in and sit down," Selah said.

"Um, I'll just eat outside, ma'am."

"Ma'am?" Selah had never been called that before. "My name's Selah. What's yours?"

"Andrew. But most people call me Mouse."

"Well, what do you prefer to be called? Andrew, or Mouse?"

The boy wrinkled his forehead in confusion. No one had ever cared what he preferred. "Whatever ya wants ta call me, I guess," he said.

"Andrew it is," Selah declared. "Are you sure you don't want to come inside? The fog is starting to come up from the river."

Andrew's dark eyes darted down the street, where the fog was starting to lick the corners of the buildings.

"You could sit right by the door. I'm just going to be over here by the stove, heating up the stew," Selah suggested.

"Ok," Andrew squeaked, and came in the door as Selah moved toward the stove.

"It sure is nice to have such good electricity," Selah said as she turned on a switch and marveled at the responsiveness of the burner on the stove. There was no comment from Andrew. "Where I lived before, we didn't have reliable power. I usually cooked over a fire."

"Risky," Andrew muttered.

Selah was quiet for a moment. Maybe open fires were illegal here as well. She was going to explain that dry wood didn't smoke much, but then Andrew would wonder where she got her wood, and the question of her origin might come up, so she changed the subject. "I've just been here for a few days, and you're the first person I've seen besides Zelda."

Andrew shifted uncomfortably on his haunches.

"I take it Zelda doesn't have very many friends?"

"Zelda's a scary ol' woman. She kill stuff. She disappear for weeks at a time, cuz she go where da birds go. When she traps a place out, she go where she can find mo'. Don' come back til da pigeons come back. She don' come 'round here much. Spend most her time at da Shaw, 'cause o' da hydrant an' da birds. An' da tradin'. Zelda scary, but she do like a good trade. An' da people further in toward da city ain't as skeered ta trade wit' 'er."

"But people out here don't trust her as much?"

"Just ain't as many people out here. If she cheat ya out here—or worse—who gonna see it? She gotta stay honest when dere's mo' people around."

"Well, I'm glad you feel you can trust *me*," Selah said cautiously.

Andrew scratched his nose with the back of his sleeve. "Who say I *do*? I sittin' by da door, ain't I?"

Selah said nothing as she stirred the pot. Finally, Andrew added, "I know dis one ting. Zelda tinks you's a good trader. An' I smelt dat stew cookin' yestaday, when I's walkin' down da street. I's just hopin' ya had some left an' ya might trade."

Selah nodded. She wondered how he knew Zelda thought she was a good trader since he obviously didn't have any dealings with the old trapper, but it didn't matter. What was important now was that she gained his trust. She scooped a generous portion of the stew for Andrew into the chipped bowl Zelda had used the night before and ladled a modest amount into a tin cup for herself. She sipped some of the stew from the cup while Andrew watched and then handed him the bowl and a spoon. Selah tried not to stare as the young man ravenously shoveled the savory food into his mouth and licked the bowl clean. He scrambled to his feet and deposited the buttons onto a large square of stained cardboard atop a stack of pallets Zelda used for a table. "There might be some more left," Selah offered quickly.

Andrew looked in the direction of the stove. "I's outta buttons just now."

"Buttons last longer than stew. I didn't figure it was an even trade yet. I don't want to be known as a cheat," Selah said quickly.

Andrew's eyes never left the pot of stew. "Dey *is* good quality buttons," he said and handed her the bowl.

Selah went back to the stove, hoping she could scrape up enough to fill the boy's belly. There was more left than she had realized, and she filled the bowl to the brim. "This ought to even us up a little," she said as she carefully walked the bowl back to him.

"Tanks," said the boy, after he had gobbled up every morsel and licked the bowl clean again.

"Thank you for the buttons," Selah said as Andrew covered his face against the fog and began to slip out the door. On an impulse, she added, "How did you know Zelda thinks I'm a good trader?"

Andrew paused on the door step and tapped on the right side of the doorframe before turning quickly and disappearing into the fog. Selah stepped outside to close the door against the fog and squinted through watering eyes to see some markings scratched into the brickwork. It looked like an arrow going both ways. On one side of the arrow was a box with four lines sticking out of the top of it and one line coming out of the lower right corner at an angle. On the other side was an upside-down mirror image of the same symbol. The one on the left reminded Selah of a child's drawing of a turkey. Of course! The symbols on either side of the arrow were hands. The arrow between them must symbolize trading. The markings weren't there the day before. Zelda must have made them just before she left. Selah sputtered and choked in a coughing fit and slipped back into the apartment before the fog could make her throat sore. She thanked the Lord for Zelda, who had paved the way for her to gain the trust of the people of the outer docks.

The rest of the day, she tried to find things she could use for trade, but all she could bear to part with was the satchel which had contained Miss Genevieve's books and drawings. She could store all of her belongings in the larger bag her father had made. Genevieve's satchel was in good shape, but it was just one item. She wanted to keep the little black scanning device for passage into the city when she was ready. If only she had kept one of the MREs, she could trade parts of it a little at a time—but those had all been given to Zelda. When evening came, she decided she should probably try to locate the place known as the Shaw. Perhaps she could trade the bag for some food items and form some more trading relationships there.

The evening meal was a meager one as there didn't seem to be much of the stew left. Reluctant to eat it all when she knew it was all she had, she left a small amount in the pot and put it back in the fridge. A movement out of the corner of her eye made her jump. She relaxed as she realized it was a cockroach crawling up the wall. "If worse came to worse, I suppose I could eat *you*," she said to the insect, curling her lip in disgust. "Lord, please don't let it come to that," she prayed earnestly and squished it with the piece of rebar Zelda always kept by the front door.

Suddenly, she heard a knock at the door. She furtively glanced out the window and could see Andrew with a couple other people. Praying under her breath, Selah wondered if she should trust them. What would keep the three from ganging up on her and taking whatever they wanted? For a moment, fear overwhelmed her as all the worst scenarios played out in her mind. But when Andrew knocked again, her fear suddenly subsided. *"Knock, and the door shall be opened unto you,"* she thought. Except that by bringing people here, Andrew was actually opening a door of opportunity for *her*. Selah opened the door.

"Haydee Selah, Ma'am. Ya gots any more o' dat stew ta trade?" Andrew said, his lips curving into a shy smile. The people he was with turned out to be an older woman and a girl a little older than Andrew. "Dis here ma mama an' sis. I done tol' dem 'bout ya stew. Dey brought sump'n everyone need," he said, and held out a dirty plastic bottle filled with water. "Nearest hydrant two miles away. Dat oughta be worth sump'n, eh?"

Selah hesitated. "It certainly is. But I don't have much stew left. I do have this bag," Selah offered, reaching for the satchel on the table.

Andrew's face fell, and the women looked down at their feet and began to back away from the door. "I understand if'n ya don' gots much left, but even a little would be worth sump'n." Andrew said hopefully, motioning with his hand for the women to stay.

"Well, okay, but don't get your hopes up," Selah said doubtfully, praying silently as she went to the fridge, *"Lord, you brought these people to me. Please give me an opportunity to show them Your love."* Maybe there would be something somewhere in the apartment that would pique their interest, she thought as she reached in the fridge to pull out the nearly empty pot. But when she picked up the pan, it seemed heavier than earlier. She opened the lid. There was more in it than she had remembered. She turned on the burner and pulled up some buckets and a crate to the table of pallets. "Come on in," she offered.

Andrew nodded encouragingly to his family and motioned for them to come inside. "Where'd ya'll meet Zelda?" the older woman asked as she settled herself down on a bucket.

"It's a ways from here," Selah said. "Just one of the places she goes looking for birds and such."

"Hmmm," was the woman's reply. Selah could tell she didn't believe her. "Ya'll don' sound like you is from 'round here."

"Mama," Andrew protested weakly.

"Hush, chile. I jus' wanna know where dis girl is from," said the woman in her hoarse, gravelly voice. "Cuz she sho do talk funny."

"That's what Zelda said," Selah laughed. "I'm from quite a ways away. But we trade there just the same as you do here."

"How we know ya ain't from da State?" said the younger woman.

"Bally! Shut *up!*" Andrew said loudly.

"I's got a right ta know. Afore I go eatin' food dat may or may not be pyson," Bally said sharply.

"I done et it dis mornin', and I's still here," Andrew squeaked.

"Bally. That's an interesting name," Selah said, trying to change the subject.

"Dat's not my real name," the girl said in the same sharp voice.

"It's short for ballerina, cuz she like to dance so much when she was a kid," Andrew explained.

"Shut *you* up, Mouse," Bally commanded and crossed her arms, still standing in the doorway.

"Well, I like it," Selah said. "It's a friendly-sounding name."

"Humph. What *you* know," Andrew chuckled in Selah's direction. "Selah may be a good trader, but she don' know nuttin' 'bout big sistahs."

"That's probably true. I'm an only child," Selah said as she located three mis-matched spoons in a drawer by the stove. She ladled the stew into the chipped bowl, a tin cup, and an old, cleaned-out pickle jar to serve her guests. To her surprise, there was enough left to fill each container to the top.

Andrew eagerly dipped his spoon into the bowl. His mother's hand swiftly closed around his fingers, stopping the mouthful before it reached his lips.

"It's okay, Mama," he said reassuringly.

Selah quickly grabbed a fork—since there weren't any spoons left—and scooped it into the tin cup, sampling the stew herself to prove it wasn't poisoned. "Yup. It's hot enough," she said, ignoring the obvious lack of trust. Andrew's mother released her grip and tasted her jar of stew. Her eyes widened as she nodded at her daughter. "Come sit down," she ordered. Bally hesitated just long enough to let everyone know she was only coming because she had decided on her own, and then the family began to eat. The room grew quiet except for the clinking and scrapings of spoon against bowl, jar and cup.

When they were finished, Bally looked toward the pot on the stove. "If ya can wait 'til tomorrow for me ta bring it, I can bring ya some mo' water, if'n I can have a lil mo' o' dat stew."

"Bally! Mind ya manners. Da girl *say* she don' got much, den she don' got much," said Mama.

"She said she didn' have much before, an' it was enough ta feed us all. Don' hurt to ask," Bally said indignantly.

Andrew looked at the floor in embarrassment. "Bally, I can't take you nowheres," he said exasperatedly.

"I'm afraid your mama may be right," Selah said, but Bally had already leapt to her feet and whisked past Selah to the stove.

"Hah, girl! I knew you's holdin' out on us," Bally said with a wicked grin. "I trade ya two mo' bottles a water if ya give us all anudder helpin'."

Selah's brow wrinkled in confusion. If the spoonful of stew that was left in the pot looked like three more helpings to the girl, it must have been more food than they had seen in a long time. She collected the empty serving dishes and made her way to the stove. What she saw made her nearly drop the pickle jar. The pot of stew was simmering merrily. It was at least half full. "But that's impossible! I know how much was left," she began, and suddenly stopped as she remembered the story she had told Zelda about the barrel of meal. Her breath caught in her throat as she remembered Zelda's words. *"Wouldn' it be sump'n if dat would happen here, in da outer docks? If you really is God's messenger, den mebbe you could ast 'im ta do sump'n like dat. Cuz people 'round here is powerful hungry."*

"Thank you, Jesus," Selah said out loud.

"Who you call me?" Bally asked.

"I was just thanking the Lord because He just provided some more food," Selah explained. "When you first showed up and asked for it, I didn't think I had enough, so I prayed. And it turned out to be *more* than enough," Selah said, her eyes tearing up as she realized a miracle had just taken place in a pot on the stove.

"Uh-huh. I understan' ya gotta watch out fa yaself," Bally said knowingly. "I don' blame ya none. Now, is ya willin' ta trade, or ain't ya?"

Selah swallowed hard. "Of course. But I'd like to thank the Lord first."

Bally raised her eyebrows and stared at her mother and brother as Selah said grace. "Strange doin's where ya come from, Selah," Bally remarked, but sat down at the table and waited to be served.

Selah watched in wonder as the family ate two more servings of stew apiece. "We'll be back tomorrow wit' da water," Andrew promised when they left. Selah watched as the family walked down the street together. She had assured Zelda she wouldn't preach until a week after her departure, but just praying over the food and treating her visitors with kindness could be a witness.

"Don't get your hopes up," her own words echoed in her mind. She shook her head. "God, use whatever it takes to bring people in to hear Your Word. And forgive me for my lack of faith. I didn't even think about You multiplying the

food!" she exclaimed—and since she was hungry, she sat down to another bowl herself.

17

IRA sat on the cool, concrete floor, staring at the gray bricks of his isolation cell. There wasn't much else to look at in confinement at the sentencing center in downtown St. Louis. The administrators had stripped him of his Vista-Visor, even though its link to the internet had been suspended, so he couldn't choose the color of the walls to make his surroundings appear cozy and welcoming. Ira knew this was supposed to have a demoralizing influence on those in confinement, but the effect was lost on him since he avoided using the visor as much as possible. After looking at screens all day at his job, the idea of being practically plugged into one during his free time was unappealing. Unless he was programming. That was a different matter—a synthesis of logic and creativity he found intellectually stimulating. Years ago, when he had begun his studies in tech interface programming, he had been captivated by the advances made in combating disease, viruses and debilitating health conditions through the use of implants. The field of bio-implantation engineering promised a future where humanity learned more quickly, adapted more easily, and found solutions to environmental, political, and economic problems that plagued the globe. He had entered advanced studies in the subject and excelled in his abilities, eagerly adding his skill set to the pool of tech-interface knowledge.

At first, the advancement of the chip seemed a miraculous boon to humankind. Early models had worked in conjunction with natural neural pathways, aiding the individual to use formerly unused parts of the brain as they learned. Newer pathways were formed organically, and the subject who worked at it could gain knowledge more quickly and even access artistic and problem-solving areas of the brain that had been previously untapped.

But as time went on, the field had taken a disturbing turn. Instead of using the technology to enhance brain function, top programmers had found ways to bypass the brain's natural connections and replace those functions with the chip. A human being with low IQ could be implanted and suddenly become a completely different person, capable of superhuman calculations and thought processing. However, if the individual's chip malfunctioned, they were in the same state as before implantation. Ira suspected that relying so heavily on the hardware was making the brain's natural function become sedentary. How many natural connections would stagnate and become lost from inactivity? Or perhaps they would not be lost forever, but would simply become increasingly difficult to access.

And then, as if other programmers had been wondering the same thing, the issue was addressed in the chip's latest incarnation. A nearly seamless blend of technology and organic function, the chip was not so much *manufactured* as it was *grown*—bioengineered using stem cells from the host and circuitry designed with bio-components to aid in the symbiotic process. People with the latest version did not simply have a computer chip in their brain. They had a piece of technology that gradually grew throughout their brain. The technology was so new that Ira was certain it hadn't been thoroughly tested for possible side effects, and yet it was being touted as the end to all suffering and the evolution of modern humanity. The fact that it was being thrust upon the public with such vigor meant the State was very keen on making it the standard for all citizens, which was cause in itself for Ira's unease. The process was time consuming and expensive. For the State to offer it free to the next generation meant there was an even greater payoff for the government. If the whole world could be chipped and neurologically linked together, would freedom of thought still exist? Surely the combined thoughts of billions of lives could not go unregulated, or chaos would ensue. Citizens would consent to being regulated gradually… incrementally, so that it was barely noticeable—all for the sake of organized thought in an unwieldy sea of collective consciousness. But who would make the decisions? Who would do all the organizing?

Ira's thoughts were interrupted by the sound of footsteps approaching his cell. In a moment, the locking mechanism was deactivated, and the door swung open. "Good morning, Ira," said a dark-haired man in the doorway. Ira scrambled to his feet, and the guard behind the man rushed forward to place himself between Ira and the visitor. "That isn't necessary," said the man with a dismissive gesture to the guard, who gave an obedient nod and departed. The man's dark blue, almond-shaped eyes narrowed in an amused expression as he watched the guard walk stiffly down the hall. "Good ol' Atticus. He was a Pod-Op once, but didn't last very long. The rigors of maintaining a balance between duty and conscience leave some individuals mentally and emotionally …*compromised.*"

Ira swallowed and met the gaze of his visitor, who was leaning casually in the doorframe now, his hands tucked into the pockets of his charcoal gray, double-breasted suit. "So it's morning, is it?" Ira asked in what he hoped was an indifferent tone. He surveyed the man's attire, noting the suit was expertly tailored to his build. "The last time I saw you, you were wearing jeans and a tee-shirt. In fact, that's all I've ever known you to wear. What's the occasion?"

"Your release," said the man as he straightened to his full height, which was one inch shorter than Ira. "Although I *have* been enjoying experimenting with different clothing styles lately. A silly hobby, perhaps, but it is a refreshing departure from the exacting project in which I am currently involved." The man brushed a bit of dust off his sleeve and again turned his full attention to Ira. "This whole business of your confinement has been a gross misunderstanding. We can stand here discussing my wardrobe, if you prefer, but I assumed you might want to get out of here?"

"Indeed," Ira said, immediately wondering what the condition of his release would be. "I would be most interested in going home, provided my conscience can live with the price."

The man laughed as if he were genuinely entertained by the exchange. "Ira Owens. Always moralizing the issues." He backed away from the doorway, implying he was waiting for Ira to follow. "There's no price. It's more of an offer, really. And as to going home, I'm not sure that will be possible. Your Geeves unit seems to think you're still there, and I don't think it would let you in. Not without another reprogramming session."

Ira blanched slightly as he realized all his misdeeds had certainly been discovered by now. "Oh, don't worry. You've been completely exonerated. In fact, it was the testimony of the Pod-Op who apprehended you that rendered your need to stand trial unnecessary."

"Jayka testified on my behalf?" Ira asked incredulously. "I thought she would just as soon have seen me dead."

"Jayka has a distinct appreciation for duty and justice. She understood what you were trying to do—correct your mistake and apprehend a renegade member of society. She was not as impressed by your attempt to save face, but that is beside the point. And I must say, that bit of drone programming—absolutely brilliant," the man said with an air of respect. "It's just the sort of move I was waiting for you to make before I brought you onto my team. That is, if you're willing?"

Ira's heart skipped a beat. This conversation was definitely not what he had been expecting. When the door had opened, he had expected to be taken to a hearing, where he would be sentenced to work in a river clean-up penal colony. But now he was being offered his dream job—or at least, what had been his dream job at one time. He was certain that if he accepted, he would be walking on ethically unstable ground. But wouldn't it be better for everyone concerned if there was some sort of moral check in that field—the input of someone who hadn't totally bought into the State's idea of a biotechnological evolution of humanity?

"I would be honored to be on your team, Dr. Moses," Ira finally said.

"Glad to hear it. And please, call me Joe." He gestured to the hallway. "Shall we?"

18

Piper looked over her shoulder down the pathway she had just created. Beyond the halo of light radiating from her Bible, she could faintly distinguish the outlines of leaves and branches arching and intertwining over the trail to create a shelter against howling winds, scorching sun, or torrential rain—symbols her mind had created for the attempts of those who would seek to penetrate her peace and influence her thought processes. In the distance, the sound of someone banging against a heavy, wooden door reverberated through the trees, causing the leaves to shake slightly with each impact. "The thuddin' noise is gettin' louder," she remarked.

"Don't let your heart be troubled," said a soothing voice beside her.

Piper looked gratefully up into Jesus' face and placed her small hand into His, wondering at the sensation of the jagged scar against her smooth palm. "I'm so glad Ya here. I don' know what I'd do if Ya wasn't," she said.

"Remember I said that I am with you always, even unto the end of the world,"[62] Jesus reminded her reassuringly.

"I remember Ya said that. Right here in this Bible."

Jesus smiled. "That's right. And whatever I said in My Word is true. It is a promise, and I will keep it—even if it is something I said to my followers thousands of years ago. It is also meant for *you*, for today. I don't go back on My Word."[63]

Piper smiled back at Jesus and once again concentrated on the task at hand: creating pathways. It wasn't easy, because sometimes she was reminded of specific things that had been troubling her since she was little girl—things about

---

[62] See Matthew 28:20
[63] See Numbers 23:19 and 1 Samuel 15:29

her mother and why life was so difficult and people could be so cruel. Sometimes Piper didn't want to think about the things Jesus was trying to teach her, but she tried. One day she asked if they could stop making paths for a while and just go back to the meadow and play in the creek. Jesus had patiently placed his hand on her head. "I know you are tired. We can go back and rest for a while." The two made their way back to the meadow, and Piper washed her face and hands in the creek and took a good, long drink of water. She decided to take a nap in the tall grass while Jesus rested with his back against the sycamore tree. It was all so peaceful and refreshing. When she awoke, Piper felt so much better that she had a wonderful idea. "Why don't we just stay here? We can make paths in the meadow if we want, and take naps, and enjoy the sunshine."

"We could. But if we don't make paths and build walls, there won't be any protection against the storm that is coming," Jesus said.

"What storm?"

Jesus tilted his head to one side of the meadow. Piper looked in that direction and could see a bank of clouds rising above the tree line. They were inching slowly toward the meadow, swirling brown and sickly green like a mud puddle in an alley.

"If this is what Dr. Joe is sendin', why don' we just use Ya Word like a sword, like it says in Ephesians chapter 6? We can fight 'em off with the sword of Truth!" Piper exclaimed.

"Ok. Here. Take your Bible," Jesus said, handing her the little New Testament. Piper obediently took it and turned to face the wind.

"What verse should I read?" she asked as the wind began to pick up speed.

"How about Matthew 6:14 and 15?" Jesus suggested.

"Ok!" Piper said excitedly, flipping eagerly to the scripture. "For if ye forgive men their trespasses, your heavenly Father will also forgive you: But if ye forgive not men their trespasses, neither will your Father forgive your trespasses."[64] Piper frowned. "I don' really like that one. How 'bout one from Psalms, where it talks 'bout how Ya destroy all my enemies for me?"

"Those clouds are made by someone I am not willing to destroy," Jesus explained. "In fact, I'm working on her behalf."

---

[64] Matthew 6:14-15, KJV

"Whaddaya mean? How couldja *do* that?" Piper said, genuinely hurt. "And whaddaya mean by *her*? Is it one o' them nurses workin' with Dr. Joe?"

"No. Those clouds are of your making. Dr. Moses has nothing to do with them. But he will be able to use them to his advantage if you don't take care of them soon," Jesus said gently. "The verse I asked you to read is about something you're having trouble doing. By holding onto resentment against people who have hurt you, you have built a different type of wall than the ones we are going to build together. You can't see it, but it is something you carry with you all the time. It makes it harder for me to help you sometimes because you are keeping me away with it."

"Why would I do *that*?" Piper asked. "I don't ever want to be separated from Ya. Jesus, I think maybe Ya wrong about that, cuz here we are, talkin' together. We ain't separated none."

"It's true that you are My child. Nothing can separate you from My love.[65] But you have been hurt so badly and have been protecting yourself for so long that you won't let anyone into this area of your life to help you—not even Me."

Piper was silent for a moment. There were hurtful things that had been done to her—things she had almost convinced herself had never actually happened. She knew Jesus was right. "But it's not my fault. *I'm* the one that got hurt! Why should I have to do the hard part?" she said angrily.

"By not forgiving those who hurt you, you think you can keep them from hurting you again. You have made a little prison cell for them in your heart. But what you don't realize is that you have locked yourself in there with them. All that hurt is trapped deep inside, binding you together with them, because you won't let them out of that cell,"[66] Jesus explained.

"I just don't think I can do it. There's lots o' things I don' wanna remember, an' lots o' people I don' wanna remember. I can't do it. I'm not strong enough," Piper said in an attempt to justify her unwillingness to obey.

"You're right. You aren't strong enough. But I am. And I am going to lend you My strength—the strength to forgive those who hurt you," Jesus said and quietly awaited her response.

---

[65] See Romans 8:38-39
[66] With thanks to Bro. Lee Allen for this analogy

Piper turned away, her eyes resting on the stream that meandered through the meadow. She tried to regain the feeling of refreshment she had experienced earlier, but the dark clouds on the horizon kept drawing her attention. Suddenly she turned around to face Jesus. "When I first met Ya, things were so wonderful. I knew Ya'd saved me and I just knew everything was gonna be alright. But now, Ya askin' me to do stuff that is just *hard*. Why's it hafta be like this? Why can't we just have fun together?"

Jesus smiled gently. "I'm so sorry this is hurting you. Do you remember when I asked you to help Me that I said it wouldn't be easy?"

Piper nodded. She had agreed readily because she was willing to do anything to escape the pain inflicted upon her by the mental stress of fighting the chip implant. But she hadn't been aware she would have to face the pain inflicted upon her by the bitterness she had cultivated in her heart. She hadn't even been aware of its existence, until Jesus had shown her in His Word that she needed to forgive. Then the bitterness rooted deep within her had sprouted and pushed itself to the surface of her consciousness, scratching her with its barbs as it emerged.

"Unforgiveness can grow into a wall of thorns that restricts your growth as a new creation in Me. You may reach out in your attempts to help others, but there will be a thorn blocking your path. Then you may try to reach out in other areas, and you will find another thorn. Your growth will be diminished and altered by the thorns—and even if you push through the pain, the source of it will still be there, festering underneath. What I am asking you to do is to forgive those who planted the seeds of those thorns in the first place. I am not asking you to relive the painful experiences you have had. In fact, I want you to give those to Me, right now. I paid for them at the cross, so they are rightfully Mine. The chastisement of your peace was upon Me. It says so in My Word, in the book of Isaiah, chapter 53,"[67] Jesus explained.

"The chastisement of my peace?" Piper said, hopelessly confused. "What does that mean?"

"It means that I took upon Me everyone's punishment, so that all who receive Me could experience peace. I fought for your chance to be free from the turmoil

---

[67] See Isaiah 53:5

you feel deep inside. You don't have to go back and watch the person plant the seeds of hurt. You just need to stop watering and cultivating that bitterness and pull it up by the root."

Piper didn't like the idea. But she loved Jesus. He had brought her spirit alive with His Spirit and had saved her when she had been ready to give up. Even when her mother had done things that hurt her or had allowed others to do things that hurt her, Piper hadn't abandoned her or stopped loving her. She hadn't been able to trust her mother after so many disappointments, but Jesus had never disappointed her. Everything He had told her in His Word had always been true. She decided to keep trusting Him. With a tremor in her voice, she said, "Ok, Jesus. I'll try. But where do I start?"

Jesus placed His hands on her shoulders and gently directed her to a still part of the stream where the water filled a deep, tranquil pool. "Look at your reflection," Jesus said.

Piper obediently looked into the water. There she was, with Jesus standing behind her, their images rippling gently back and forth in the slow current. But something was partially obscuring Jesus' reflection.

"What do you see?" Jesus asked.

Piper squinted. "I see us in the water, but it's harder to see You. Something is in the way."

Jesus squeezed her on the shoulder. "That's what we're going to get rid of," He explained.

Piper looked at the strange tangle of briars that was sprawling up behind her and blocking her perfect view of Christ. "Ok. Time ta git rid o' this mess," she said, and turned around to face it, but it wasn't there. She could still feel its branches hooking into her as she moved. She spun around faster, hoping to catch a glimpse of it, but it remained out of sight. Piper looked back into the mirror of the stream. She could still see the thorny vine rising above her head. "Jesus, how am I supposed to do this?" she sobbed. "I can't even see it or tell where it's comin' from."

"You don't have to do it on your own, daughter. Let Me help you," Jesus said, and took hold of Piper's hands, guiding them behind her back. To Piper's surprise, the thorns were actually growing out of her back, sprawling out in all directions.

"If I was an angel, I'd have wings. But since I'm just Piper, I have thorns growin' outta ma back," she remarked dismally.

"Since you are Piper and not an angel, you can sing the song of the redeemed when I take you to the city I have prepared for us. Did you know the angels are fascinated by this arrangement? They have been curious about it for ages,"[68] Jesus said. "Now we will begin. Just think of each person who hurt you and tell them you forgive them. Then I will help you pull out the bitterness that is weighing you down."

"Ok. But what if it hurts?" Piper asked fearfully.

"Then I will be here to heal your pain," Jesus reassured her.

Piper thought for a moment. There was one man especially, a boyfriend of her mother, who had hurt her very much. She decided to start with all the easier names she could think of. But after naming one person and forgiving them, she realized she didn't feel any different than before. "If I don't feel any different, does that mean I didn't really forgive them? Does it mean I'm lying?" Piper asked.

"When you said you forgave them, you made the choice of your own free will. The heart doesn't always want to agree with the choices we make, even when they are the right ones. Leave that part to me," Jesus reassured her and helped her reach behind her back to locate the source of the hurt. She grasped the vine and pulled. At first, nothing happened. But then she felt Jesus' strong hands enveloping hers—and with one long tug, the vine was pulled out and lying in a scraggly heap on the stream bank. Piper felt a little lighter. She named another person and another, until one by one, the vines were lying there before them, yanked out by the root.

Only one vine remained, and Piper realized that all the other vines had been light as feathers compared to this one. She knew that its roots ran deep. If she turned her head slowly, she could see that this particular vine had wicked thorns

---

[68] See 1 Peter 1:12

and spiny offshoots that trailed behind her like a train on an old-fashioned wedding dress. "I don't think I can do this one, Jesus," Piper finally said as a cold, miserable feeling began to seep into her heart.

"This is the worst one," Jesus said, "but it needs to come out."

"This man hurt me real bad. I get sick just thinkin' 'bout it, so I usually just try not to remember."

"What Slater did to you was a horrible thing. I don't like thinking about it, either. But did you know I also came to save Slater from his sins?"

Piper froze and stared hard at Jesus. "Ya know his name, and Ya know what 'e did, and Ya *still* wanna forgive 'im? Why?"

"Because My Father so loved the world, that He gave Me, His only Son, so that *whoever* believes in Me will be saved."

"Even *Slater?*"

"Even Slater."

Piper sighed. "That's some crazy kind o' love! How couldja love someone like *that?*"

"He didn't start out that way. I didn't create him for darkness. Piper, you yourself have been called out of darkness into marvelous light. You have received mercy, while you knew nothing of mercy before you met Me.[69] Slater has never been exposed to My Light. But My Holy Spirit is actively seeking him and others like him. I am not willing that *any* should perish, not even Slater. I desire for all to come to repentance.[70] And as long as you keep and nurture this vine, it will continue to grow and rob you from your own growth in Me."[71]

Piper scrunched her eyes shut and willed herself to say the words. "I forgive you, Slater." Then, before she could change her mind, she reached behind her back and gripped the vine at its spiny base. Piper gasped in pain as the thorns pierced her hands, but Jesus was there to lend her His strength. The extraction was not easy, because the hurt was rooted deep within her. It had affected every part of her life without her even knowing about it. But suddenly it was over, and Jesus was placing his hand on the open wound where the hurt had been. And

---

[69] See 1 Peter 2:9-10
[70] See 2 Peter 3:9
[71] See Hebrews 12:12-15

then something strange happened. A warm, soothing sensation spread over her, like sunshine that breaks through clouds on a cold day. "What *is* that?" Piper asked in wonder. "It feels like firelight or sunshine, or suddenly being dry and warm after bein' out in the cold, wet snow all day."

"That is the absence of pain and the feeling of My presence in a closer way than you have experienced before," Jesus explained.

Piper stood in wonderment at the new sensation. She whirled around to face Jesus and reached to take His hands. It was then that she noticed blood was dripping from her palms where the thorns had cut her deeply. She drew her hands away quickly, but Jesus swiftly cupped them in His own. "Forgiveness can be costly, but if you want to experience true peace, it is necessary," He said. Piper watched as Jesus' nail-scarred hands healed the cuts in her own. "Now, there is only one person left to forgive," Jesus said.

"But I thought we were done! All the thorns are gone," Piper said, rubbing her hands on her back experimentally.

"We are *almost* done," Jesus said. "Come with me and I will show you the last person you need to forgive."

Piper started to protest but quickly shut her mouth and followed Jesus to the edge of the stream. "Look into the water," Jesus said.

Piper did as she was told. Once again, she could see their reflection. This time, the thorns were gone and could no longer obstruct her view of Christ. But a shadow covered His face. Suddenly she realized that *she* was the source of the shadow.

"You may find this hard to believe, but *you* may be the person who is hardest for you to forgive," Jesus said.

"Whaddaya mean? Why would I need to forgive myself?" Piper asked. And then she remembered. Before she had learned to trap the birds, when she and her mother had been very hungry, an older boy had told her he would give her food if she would do certain things for him. She hadn't wanted to, but she didn't want to starve, either. She had finally agreed, but the memory made her so angry that she hated herself for it. "But You forgave me for that a long time ago," Piper protested.

"Yes, I did. But *you* didn't," Jesus explained. "Look at yourself in the reflection and tell yourself that you are forgiven, just like you did for all those other people."

Piper looked at herself. "Isn't it just enough to *know* that I forgive myself?" Piper protested. It seemed silly to talk to her reflection. She waited for Jesus to say something, but He was silent, letting her make up her mind for herself. *"Well, if it's silly, it shouldn't be that hard,"* Piper said under her breath and stared at her reflection wavering back and forth in the water. She opened her mouth to say the words but suddenly choked as a ragged gasp escaped her lips. Jesus was right. This hurt ran deeper than all the others. She was suddenly aware of Jesus' hands resting comfortingly on her shoulders. It gave her the strength she needed to complete the task. "Piper, I forgive you!" she cried. Violent sobs wracked her body as she released her pain, and the tears dripped down her cheeks to be carried away by the stream. Then Jesus' arms were encircling her. After her jerking sobs had subsided to a few quiet sniffs, Jesus smiled down at her and said, "Well done, daughter. Look at your reflection now."

Piper looked again. Her face was red and blotchy from crying, but behind her was Jesus, His image perfectly visible. "Thank You, Jesus," Piper said gratefully. "I didn't even know about all the stuff I was draggin' aroun' with me."

"We've struck a blow to the enemy with the work we accomplished here," He said, pointing to the tree line where the dark, ugly clouds had been approaching. In their place was a clear, blue sky.

Piper breathed deeply and squeezed Jesus' hand. "I'm ready to build some walls and make some paths now, as long as Ya promise to be right here with me the whole time."

"I will never leave you nor forsake you,"[72] Jesus promised.

"Then let's get ta work!" Piper said, thrusting out her chin with determination.

Jesus grinned, and His joyful laugh filled the meadow. The two headed back into the forest, hand in hand.

---

[72] See Hebrews 13:5

19

THE middle-aged woman sat hunched in front of the mirror in her room at the St. Louis Life Renewal Center. A dumpy caricature of a figure with dirty-blond hair and dull eyes stared back at her: a stranger to her, now that she had the chip. The weight problems and the feelings of everyone else being smarter than she was—all would soon be a thing of the past. How had she managed to live with herself like this for so long?

A knock at the door distracted her from the self-assessment.

"Citizen Druthers?" called a voice from behind the door. "It's Sharlotta. I'm here to take you to Image Revamp now. Are you ready?"

"Am I ever!" the woman said gratefully as the door to her room was opened by the slender-built chip tech. "I can't stand the way I look anymore. Are we going to be able to change any of that today with the revamp process?"

"We can do a few things immediately with a simple adjustment of wardrobe, hair color, and even contact lenses to correct or amend eye color, if you want. But the majority of what we will do to rebuild your image depends on how you want to look and the lifestyle changes you will need to make to achieve that look."

"Lifestyle changes…" Druthers said worriedly. "I've tried dieting and exercising, and I can never stick to it."

"Yes, but that was *before* you had the chip," Sharlotta said brightly. "Now you have everything you need at your disposal to lose weight and get in shape. After revamp programming, you will have the will power you previously lacked. Plus, the chip can integrate the thyroid correction implant you were unable to afford earlier. With so many companies offering the chip to their employees as a bonus, older implants like those will soon be obsolete, anyway. All we have to do is program these directives into the chip, along with some exercise programs and a sensible diet plan, using the guidelines you provided to us when you filled out the initial questionnaire. Just follow me."

Druthers followed the young technician down the hall to the elevator for the trip to the third floor, where procedures were performed. The last time she had been there was a week and a half ago, when the chip had been implanted. She had been put under anesthesia for the process, so she didn't remember anything. But she had awakened with a throbbing headache and a small, titanium port at the base of her skull. Nurses had quickly administered drugs to counteract the pain, so she shouldn't have had any apprehension regarding her time spent on the third floor. However, as they stepped out of the elevator, an uneasiness gripped her gut.

"Citizen Druthers? Are you alright?"

The diminutive woman looked up at the chip tech, unaware she had momentarily frozen in her tracks, wringing her hands fretfully. "I'm just a little nervous," she replied.

Sharlotta smiled reassuringly and placed a hand on her shoulder. "That's perfectly normal the first time. After all, we *will* be altering your thought processes. But we are altering them to *correct* them—to make you the *you* whom you were always meant to be."

"About what you were saying earlier…are you telling me that you can help me to actually *want* to exercise?"

The technician smiled patiently. "Absolutely! In fact, you will be incapable of refusing to exercise. No more procrastination and no more excuses! Here, take a look at this," the trim, perky girl said proudly as she flipped her name badge around. On the back was the picture of an obese woman wearing scrubs. "Do you recognize her?"

"Am I supposed to?" Druthers said, staring hard at the photo.

"Look very closely," Sharlotta instructed, and increased the magnification of the digital photo badge so that Druthers could see it more clearly.

There was something familiar about the eyes, she realized. Suddenly, she noticed the name badge on the woman's scrubs: SHARLOTTA. She gasped as she looked back into the beaming face of the chip tech. "That's you?"

"Yes, it is! Isn't that incredible? And it's all because I got the chip two years ago. They offered it to us here at no cost if we wanted to participate in a clinical trial. It changed my life. Now, it's your turn to have your life turned around," Sharlotta said warmly.

Druthers nodded and gulped. It was a very convincing testimonial. So why did she still feel the urge to turn around and get back in the elevator? "Can I have a drink of water?" she asked suddenly. Her throat was terribly dry.

"Not before this procedure. But you can have one two hours afterward," said the technician in an upbeat voice.

"Two hours! There's no way I can wait two hours before I have something to drink!"

"Remember, we told you not to eat or drink anything last night after 1900 hours to make certain there wouldn't be any nausea during or after the procedure."

Druthers remembered. The nurses had removed any food or drink last night, and the only plumbing that still worked in her room was the toilet. They had even locked her door from the outside to make certain she wouldn't wander out and find a water fountain or a snack from the vending machine in the middle of the night. "That's the problem. I haven't had anything to drink since then, and now you tell me I'll have to wait for two more hours *after* the procedure?"

Sharlotta smiled again and patted her arm. "I know it seems like a long time now, but after we install this programming, you won't have any problems resisting the temptation. In fact, you'll be unable to do anything detrimental to your health or anything outside the parameters of your desired programming."

Again, the fear hit Druthers in the pit of the stomach. "I don't think I want to do this after all. I think maybe this was a mistake," she began.

"I know it all seems unsettling now, but once the chip is programmed, you won't be afraid at all. You'll look back and find the fear you're experiencing now to be laughable," the technician said, gently but firmly ushering her forward.

"I've changed my mind," Druthers said, stepping back toward the elevator.

"Well, I'm sorry, but you signed the consent form. You already have the chip, provided to you at no cost," the technician said, an edge of irritation creeping into in her voice.

"Well, I've decided I don't want it after all," Druthers said, giggling slightly as hysteria threatened to take over. She fought to keep control of her emotions. The unassuming woman had never been one to stand up for herself, but this all seemed horribly wrong. She couldn't afford to let others run over her this time. "Just take it out and I'll be on my way," she said, in the firmest voice she could manage.

"Citizen Druthers, I know you remember the videos we showed you of those who had their chips removed. The process of reversal is not easy, or successful, for that matter."

"Well, then leave it in—I don't care. Just don't program it to do anything. I can live with being fat. I can even live with being stupid. Just take me back to my room to get my things, and I'll leave," Druthers said, her voice rising in pitch.

"As we explained earlier, the chip is the property of the State. You are merely the beneficiary of the opportunities it creates. You can't leave without the chip being programmed. And you can't realistically have it removed, unless you want to be left in a drooling, catatonic state. Just think of how much better you'll feel when your thinking is corrected."

"I don't want my thinking corrected!" Druthers screeched.

"We can even correct your tendency toward anxiety and hysteria."

"I've never been hysterical before now," Druthers said and began giggling uncontrollably as she bounded back to the elevator, with Technician Sharlotta close behind.

"I could use some help here!" Sharlotta called loudly, and several techs immediately stepped out of the preparation room to come to her aid.

"Now, Citizen Druthers, just try to calm down," Sharlotta said breathlessly as the woman shoved her against the elevator wall with a strength that belied her unimposing stature.

"Surely there's a way I can get out of this. I didn't understand what I was signing up for," Druthers pleaded.

"Look at me, Citizen Druthers," Sharlotta began.

"Call her by her first name. It has a calming effect," said one of the other technicians who had just arrived at the elevator door.

"Ok, Janice. Just relax, and we'll get this all straightened out," Sharlotta promised.

"Really? You'll help me?" Now the pretty, young tech had her full attention.

"Of course," Sharlotta answered in a soothing voice. "Just look at me and concentrate. Remember why you came here in the first place."

Suddenly, Janice felt a stinging sensation in her neck as one of the young men administered a sedative. "Noooo! I should have listened to Viv…." she cried, her voice trailing off as she lost consciousness.

"Whew! That was rough. I hate it when they react that way," said one of the male technicians.

"You're telling me. But as soon as they're programmed, they find the memory amusing—even absurd," Sharlotta said. "It'll be so much better for people when they start offering it free to parents for infants and toddlers. Things like this are much less traumatic when you're young—like when parents choose to have their baby's ears pierced." Sharlotta paused and glanced over at Janice, slumped against the wall of the elevator. "We really should do something about this one's anxiety, though. Maybe a leveling off of her emotions across the board. I think I'll mention it to Dr. Mahanes before we begin."

"Good idea," said a tech with bulging muscles that couldn't be hidden underneath his scrubs. "We don't want to take the chance that she might not have the same results as everyone else."

"Harley, that Bodybuild program you had downloaded last year has done some incredible things for your physique," Sharlotta said admiringly as the ripped tech helped her to her feet.

"Thanks, Shar. I could say the same thing for you and the Trimfit program," he said, his eyes traveling up and down her body.

Sharlotta blushed as the group deposited Janice onto a gurney and headed down the hall toward the preparation room. "In a year or so, you'll probably be saying the same thing to Citizen Druthers, here," she scolded him playfully.

"Maybe so," Harley said with a wink and a sideways grin. "Although she's a little short to be my type."

"Well, that's *one* thing the chip can't fix," Sharlotta muttered as they wheeled the gurney into the prep room. "Dr. Mahanes, we may need to incorporate some additional programming for this patient to make a successful transition," she said to a man who was doing a last-minute check of the individualized revamp plan.

The chip interface programmer listened with interest as Sharlotta relayed the scene in the corridor. "Well, I'm apt to agree with you. She signed consent allowing us to do anything possible to help her transition successfully." He rubbed the titanium port on the back of his neck thoughtfully. "Incorporating those programs shouldn't be a problem at all."

20

"A_{LL} employees must report to their stations in five minutes," a smooth, feminine voice said pleasantly over the intercom of the SynthaMeat Processing Plant. "Failure to report will result in demotion or immediate dismissal."

Viv's palms were sweating as she flashed her hand across the scanner at the factory entrance. She knew she had been cutting it close by staying in bed an extra fifteen minutes after a late-night service at The Closet. To make matters worse, a combination of heavy traffic and exceptionally thick fog had made for a difficult commute. After all the trouble she had been taking to avoid scrutiny by her superiors, she may have blown it by sleepily telling her Geeves unit to "snooze."

She rushed to the locker room to grab her coveralls and sped to the monitoring room, flashing the palm scanner just before the first-shift buzzer blared throughout the factory. Accessing her assignments on the electronic whiteboard, she downloaded them into her Vista-Visor and glanced at the monitors to see how the day was beginning. *So far, so good,* she thought, as she donned her coveralls and suddenly noticed she hadn't changed into the required factory boots. Well, of course she hadn't. She had barely managed to grab her coveralls on the way. With a tingling residual of adrenaline, she whirled out the door and plowed directly into someone coming down the corridor from the opposite direction.

The short, dark-haired woman staggered sideways, caught herself against the wall, and smiled.

"Oh, I am so sorry!" Viv sputtered.

"In a hurry this morning?" she offered in a friendly manner.

"Yeah! *I forgot ma boots!*" Viv whispered. She began to circle around the woman, who was still holding her with an intense gaze. "You're new, ain't ya?" she asked, wondering if the new hire would be fired on her first day for not reporting to her station on time.

"I'm new to this shift. I used to work second."

"Me too," Viv said. There was something familiar about her. She could tell she wanted to chat, but Viv couldn't afford to be caught in her street shoes. "I really hafta go," she said apologetically.

She was about to rush back to the locker room when the woman placed a hand on her arm and said wonderingly, "Do you really not recognize me, Viv?"

Viv turned and for the first time, looked carefully at her. "By Jovies!" she exclaimed. "Is it Janice? You're back! And ya changed ya hair an' eye color!" Viv stared at the lustrous auburn hair, dark eyebrows and deep brown eyes. "When ya said ya were goin' shoppin', I didn't know ya were goin' for a whole new identity!"

Janice smiled. "You think it looks ok, then?"

"It's really different seein' ya with dark hair an' brown eyes, but it actually works," Viv said carefully. "Some blonds can't pull off a color change like that, but I guess ya have the right complexion for it."

"Thanks," Janice said. "Sorry to keep you. I just wanted to say hello. But I really have to get to my new station now. They kept me a little late in training."

"Ya startin' a new station?" Viv asked. She wondered if Janice's poor work performance had finally earned her a demotion.

"Yes. I'm in Protein Analysis now," Janice replied.

Viv's mouth dropped open, and she tried to think of something to say to hide her surprise. Protein Analysis was a pay grade above Viv's position as a machine technician. It required a degree in biochemistry and a secondary degree in nutrition, and Janice had barely made it through high school. "Con—congratulations!" she stuttered, and then paled as the reality of what had taken place sank in. There was only one way Janice could have risen to this position. Everything —the time she had taken off and the change in her physical appearance—now made sense.

"Well, maybe I'll see you at lunch," Janice said. Viv thought she detected a note of sadness in her voice. Did she feel bad she had revealed her higher position? Was it awkwardness that her promotion was not due to hard work, but the fact she had gone against Viv's advice and taken the chip?

"See ya then!" Viv suddenly remembered to call out as Janice hurried purposefully toward her new station. With a gut-wrenching feeling, Viv reasoned the turning point for Janice was probably that night at Talk-o-lot Chocolate when she had felt so humiliated. "Oh, Jesus. I don't think I can take this. This is all my fault!" Viv said under her breath, her eyes welling up with tears.

"Technician Delacruz, is everything alright?"

It was Tommy Telquat. He had poked his head out of the office one door down, and now stepped into the hall to study her more closely. "You seem upset."

"I'm just a little rattled," she tried to explain, hoping Telquat would focus on her tears instead of her shoes. "I just ran into Janice, and I didn't even recognize 'er."

Telquat smiled triumphantly. "She looks great, doesn't she? She told me that in a few months, she would look even more different, since she's on a new lifestyle plan."

"I thought she looked fine the way she was," Viv began, but stopped short when she saw her superior's expression change.

"Janice is becoming the person she was always meant to be. She needs our encouragement and support, not criticism for her decision." He eyed Viv speculatively; and a smile again crept onto his lips, as if it had to sneak aboard and hijack his face. "If I didn't know any better, I'd think you were jealous."

"Jealous?" Viv spat out the word.

"Yes, of course. Janice goes away for a couple of weeks, and she comes back a new person, in a higher pay tier than yours. She didn't need the years of schooling or training to do it, either. All she had to do was accept the free gift offered to her by SynthaMeat, and it just fell into her lap. Why *wouldn't* you be jealous?" Telquat said pointedly.

"Maybe because I value freedom of thought," Viv said before she could stop herself.

Telquat's neck began to turn red. "Is that what you think happens to people who get the chip implant? You think they lose their ability to think for themselves? Didn't you listen to the tutorial at the last assembly? Citizens are intimately involved in their own specialized image revamp plan. Their journey to a better life is one that is set into motion by their wishes. Each desire for improvement is taken into account by programmers, who put together a plan that ensures each individual achieves their goals." The well-rehearsed litany was punctuated by gestures and Telquat's propensity to turn red when he got angry.

"If ya so keen on it, why haven't ya gotten it yaself?" Viv asked, wincing as she heard the words spill out of her mouth.

Telquat straightened to his full height, which was still two inches shorter than Viv's. "I'm on the list for the Level 2 version," he said loftily.

"What makes it different from the regular chip? Are ya saying you're gettin' a better version than everyone else?" Viv asked.

Telquat scowled at her. "Of course not. The chip is the Great Equalizer. Every one of them is designed to make its host the person they were always meant to be. But as a supervisor, I require a different version, that's all."

"Why?" Viv persisted.

Telquat squinted at the question, and his gaze dropped to Viv's shoes. "On a note of more immediate importance, why are you still wearing your street shoes?"

"I forgot to change out of 'em."

"Well, then, you had better do so. We can discuss the consequences later." Telquat grimaced out another smile and turned stiffly into his office.

Viv walked resolutely down the hall to retrieve her boots. The consequences, which were most likely docked pay or being moved to the graveyard shift, seemed trivial compared to her knowledge of what Janice had done. *"Oh please, Jesus,"* she pleaded silently, *"don't let Janice be lost forever. Somehow use someone to reach 'er, even though she got the chip."*

When the lunch buzzer sounded, Viv wondered if Telquat would summon her to his office to discuss consequences, effectively curtailing her chance to eat. But there was no sign of him. That in itself was rather unusual. Telquat didn't fraternize with his underlings, as Viv jokingly called herself and the other workers. However, he did often use the time to flirt with Doris, the cafeteria supervisor. Doris was gazing out her office window into the lunch room, looking lonely, so he wasn't in there, either.

"Hey Viv," called a familiar voice. "You can sit here if you want."

Viv looked around to see the new Janice, sitting at a table with a few other lab techs from Protein Analysis. "Well, ok," she said hesitantly. The techs in P.A. had never been very friendly to her. It was a cliquish department, being staffed by people who seemed distinctly aware that their position was a result of higher intelligence and advanced schooling. She had seen them roll their eyes at Janice's naivety and her overly friendly personality in the past. She wondered if they were still treating Janice as a second-class citizen.

"So, how's ya new job goin'?" Viv asked as she slid into the seat beside her. The man sitting opposite her flinched slightly at her outer docks accent, and Viv flashed him a sickeningly sweet smile.

"It's ok," Janice said dully, taking a bite of her sandwich. Viv stared at the mushy, green paste oozing from between the thin slices of bread.

"What kinda sandwich is *that?*" she asked, wrinkling her nose.

"Kale-a-cado. It's kale, avocado and lemon juice blended with protein powder and a vitamin supplement. Oh, and the bread is carb-free," Janice replied.

"Sounds nasty," Viv said.

"It's okay."

"I thought maybe ya'd be celebratin' ya new position with macaroni and fried chicken, like when ya first got offa the graveyard shift."

Janice's gaze lingered momentarily over Viv's roast beef sandwich and potato chips, and then she turned back to her own sandwich. "This meets my nutritional requirements and keeps me on track with my weight loss goal," she said in a dull voice.

Viv couldn't help but stare. She had another friend who had taken the chip; and if anything, her personality seemed more vivacious and engaging. This version of Janice seemed the opposite, as if someone had turned off her emotions. "Janice, are you alright?" she asked.

Janice daintily blotted her mouth with her napkin and stared blankly at Viv. "I'm fine. Why do you ask?"

"Well, ya just seem so different. I figured out ya got the chip, but ya don't seem happy about it."

Janice looked at her intently, seemingly trying to focus her thoughts. For an instant, Viv thought she could see a look of desperation in her eyes. "I'm on track to be the person I was always meant to be," Janice finally answered.

"But ya were so bubbly before. Ya seemed happier then. I liked ya just how ya were."

"Well, *I* didn't," Janice said matter-of-factly.

"Are ya sure ya don't wanna talk? We could meet afta work."

"I don't have time. I have to go to exercise class."

"Maybe another day this week?"

"Between exercise class and meditation, I don't have much free time."

"Meditation?" Viv asked cautiously.

"It helps with the integration of my new components and the pathways they're forming in conjunction with my existing neural network," Janice said automatically.

"Janice, are ya still in there?" Viv whispered.

"Of course. They warned me my old friends might have trouble making adjustments to the new me. It takes time for everyone to relearn how to act around each other; but eventually, it becomes commonplace. I know you're worried about me because you don't like the chip. But look at me. I'm different now—in a good way. I have a better job. I'm smarter. I can converse at a higher level. My coworkers respect me. Soon, my life will be just what I've always dreamed of."

"Ya just don't seem very happy about it, is all," Viv persisted.

"You're the one who doesn't seem happy about it," said the man who had flinched earlier. "I would think that, coming from the outer docks, you would understand why someone who has the chance to make a clean start of their life would take it, no matter how difficult the transition. It seems to me you're only making her transition *more* difficult, with all your questions and innuendos."

Viv bit her lip and looked down at her plate. She knew she was in danger of being reported for technology discrimination. "I didn't mean to make things difficult. I'm just concerned, is all."

"Really, I'm fine," Janice said in a flat tone.

"She's fine," repeated the man, looking hard at Viv.

Viv picked up her tray and got up from the table. "I guess I'd better leave," she said carefully.

"Okay," Janice said as she stared straight ahead, dutifully taking another bite of Kale-a-cado.

"Well, I'll see ya 'round," Viv said softly. She turned around and nearly dropped her tray when she saw Tommy Telquat had been standing behind her.

"Delacruz. My office. *Now.*"

Viv didn't bother to take her sandwich with her. She had completely lost her appetite. She followed Telquat, slowing her strides to keep from stepping on his heels.

Once they reached his office, Viv was surprised to see another person already there, in a seat that had been pulled up beside Telquat's chair. "Hello, Viviana," said the person, whom Viv assumed identified as female. But no matter how strikingly feminine or masculine the individual, it was never safe to assume anything about preferences.

"Ainsley Abbot is an Employee Interrelations Specialist assigned to us by the State," Telquat explained. Viv smiled and said hello. She couldn't remember if Ainsley was strictly a female name. Not that it mattered. Anyone could have any name they wanted, provided they registered it with the State under their Social Security Number and had it synched with their Palmscan. As long as Viv didn't refer to the specialist in the third person, she was unlikely to cause offense. "We're very lucky to have her. She is spearheading a new program, destined for success, I am certain," Telquat said with an obsequious smile.

Viv exhaled slowly. So Abbot identified as a woman. At least she was on firmer ground in that respect. "Nice to meet ya, Specialist Abbot."

"Oh, please! Ainsley will do just fine," said the woman, her dark eyes sparkling out of a spotlessly smooth ebony face. She appeared to be in her late 20s. Her short, Jet-black hair was carefully sculpted around high, refined cheekbones. The fact she was employed by the State rather than SynthaMeat was made obvious by her attire—a black and white stylish pant suit that accentuated her svelte figure. Viv glanced self-consciously at her own unisex coveralls.

"Grab a seat, Viviana," Ainsley said, and motioned for Viv to sit down in one of the uncomfortable chairs Telquat kept in his office for the uncomfortable conversations usually held there.

Telquat raised his eyebrows at the lack of formality, but settled himself behind his desk and solemnly steepled his fingers in front of pursed lips. "I've been keeping an eye on you, Delacruz. And although your skill as a worker has been satisfactory, your interactions with some of your coworkers have been less than exemplary. As you know, discrimination of any sort will result in consequences. I have long suspected you of technology discrimination, among other violations, but I have never had the proof I needed to recommend you for reconditioning until today."

Viv blanched. Ainsley glanced quickly back and forth from Viv to Telquat. "I think we're getting ahead of ourselves, Tommy." She smiled reassuringly at Viv. "We haven't come to discuss any violations but rather to give you a unique opportunity."

"That was before these most recent events came to light," Telquat began, but Ainsley silenced him with a hard stare before once again turning her attention to Viv.

"Viv—may I call you Viv?" Ainsley asked politely.

Viv nodded.

"What we are offering is a position as a liaison in Outer Docks Transition—our pilot program to help citizens such as yourself to transition smoothly into their new role in the State."

Viv caught a glimpse of Telquat's mouth dropping open before he quickly shut it and assumed an expression of calm. "Although we are aware that your service record may not be perfect," Ainsley continued, with a look of deference to Telquat, "we are prepared to give you any training you need to succeed. You see, we have been watching you as well. Out of all the other people who have chosen to leave the outer docks, you have shown the most promise in mental health and adaptability to change. And who better to show the people of the outer docks that they can succeed in their transition than someone who has done it successfully, herself?"

Viv was stunned. She had been certain she was going to receive a demotion, or—if Telquat had his way—forced reconditioning. But this woman was offering her a government job helping Discards to become citizens. "What's the catch?" she heard herself ask.

Telquat clinched his fist and pointed a bony finger at Viv. "You see? That is exactly the kind of response I'm talking about. Delacruz has a disregard for authority. She is always speaking her mind, whether or not it lines up with company policy or differs from everyone else's opinion."

"A candor which my supervisors and I find refreshing. It is often one of the marks of a true leader," Ainsley said, with a glint in her eye.

Telquat's mouth hung slack for a moment. "But I have hard evidence against her for technology discrimination. I am going to recommend she be sent for reconditioning."

"Your recommendation is noted…and ignored," Ainsley said, with a slight curve of a smile. She rose from her chair and turned to Viv. "If you'd like the position, it's yours. But the offer ends when I leave this room."

Viv was dumbfounded. There was no time to deliberate over the decision, but the choice seemed clear, since staying at SynthaMeat would mean being sent to a reconditioning center where she would likely be forced to take the chip. She jumped up from her chair. "I accept ya offer," she exclaimed and reached out to flash Ainsley's extended hand in the State's gesture of shared good will. To her surprise, Ainsley clasped her hand in the antiquated manner of a handshake.

"Marvelous. So glad to have you on board," Ainsley said warmly. "Gather your things and meet me at the location I just sent your Visor. I'd take you myself, but I assume you rode your bike today?"

Viv nodded and wondered how closely they had actually been watching her. She looked back at Telquat and started to say goodbye but was met with an icy stare. "I have what I need to bring you down, Delacruz," he said softly after Ainsley had exited the office and he thought she was out of earshot.

"Oh, what rubbish!" Ainsley called from the hallway with a musical laugh. "Come on, Viv."

Telquat's face reddened, but he held her gaze. "I have friends, Delacruz. Friends who listen to me."

"I'm glad for ya, Tommy. Everyone needs a good dockmate," Viv said as she left, then immediately regretted the catty remark. She wondered if Telquat actually had any friends besides Doris and the workplace acquaintances to whom he reported. Even though he had made her life miserable, she knew she should have prayed for him more and done a better job of showing him the light of God's love.

"Idle threats," Ainsley said, with a sidelong glance at Viv as they strode down the hall together. "You needn't worry about Tommy. He's a Level 2 drone, at most."

Viv sighed. Once again, she was relieved her thoughts weren't on display, even if her emotions apparently were. "A drone? He said he was on the list for a Level 2 version of the chip, but he made it sound superior."

Ainsley smiled broadly and tilted her head to one side. "Of course he did." She paused as Viv turned to go to the locker room. "I'll see you there, Viv. I have to make a stop on the way, but I'll be there shortly."

Viv watched as Ainsley continued down the hall. She needed to keep on her toes if she was going to be working directly for the State. They would watch her even more closely than Telquat had—indeed, they had already been watching her. She left her coveralls in her locker and grabbed the few personal items she had stored there. With one last look around the room, she suddenly remembered her first day at work. She had come with high expectations about leaving her background behind and blending in with a society where everything was taken care of for her and she didn't have to resort to stealing or scrabbling for scraps in a dumpster to survive. She had tried to fit in since she was fourteen, but her accent and expressions of speech were daily reminders to fellow citizens that she was a product of the Discards. Fear and prejudice were hard to overcome, and acceptance wasn't won easily. She had tried everything she could think of, including getting the voluntary implant, Audio Boost, to blend in. She had then decided to get a good-paying factory job at SynthaMeat so she could afford more implants. That was all before she had met Jesus and had realized her self-worth didn't have to be bound up in the acceptance of others.

Being able to help those who had been in her position seemed like a worthwhile cause and was a cushy government job as well. Maybe she would even have more opportunities to witness to her old dockmates about the real reason for her successful transition. But something strange was churning inside of her. *"Am I doin' the right thing, Jesus?"* she prayed silently. Now that she had time to think about it, she wondered if she should actually refuse the offer, even if it meant the risk of receiving the chip. *"Is there any reason why I shouldn't be doin' this?"* she prayed again. She didn't sense the leading of the Holy Spirit to refuse the job, but she did feel an overwhelming sense of caution. And she couldn't shake the feeling that she needed to stay vigilant in praying for the people who worked at SynthaMeat.

As she walked down the hall, she wondered if she might still be able to say goodbye to Janice and Stan. They had always been friendly to her and made her feel like she fit in. When she looked in the cafeteria doorway, she was surprised to see Ainsley sitting at the table across from Janice. Was this the stop Ainsley had to make before she left? Was Viv being investigated for technology discrimination after all? She started to walk into the cafeteria, but stopped short when she felt the Holy Spirit warning her against it. As she turned to go, she could see Stan sitting at another table, but she got the distinct impression she simply needed to leave. *"Please watch over the people who work here, Jesus,"* she prayed as she left abruptly. *"Please send someone here who can reach 'em and open their eyes."* She had always thought she would be that person, but as she walked toward the exit, she felt a sense of release from her assignment there, and a scripture came to her mind: "I have planted, Apollos watered, but God gave the increase."[73] She had done what she could to plant the seeds of the gospel. Maybe it was someone else's job to water what she had planted. She had to trust that eventually, God would give her and her fellow laborers in Christ the harvest they desired: souls for the Kingdom.

---

[73] 1 Corinthians 3:6, KJV

21

MACY watched as Garrison shifted his backpack to a more comfortable position. The late spring morning was crisp, cold and slightly damp with mist from the nearby river. Dewdrops beaded the edges of the leaves. They caught the sunlight that pooled through the trees, making them sparkle like diamonds. Macy glanced at the other members of the group. Behind Garrison were Thom, Lydia, Chandra, Lelah, and Dania, with Pastor Craig bringing up the end of the line. Macy had not been dissuaded by Craig's repeated commands of *"Go home!"* Finally, he had thrown his hands up in the air and said, "If God wants her to stay in Adullam, she'll stay. If He wants her to come with us, she'll come. Personally, I give up. She's always had a mind of her own."

Macy had waited with her lopsided smile until Craig stopped yelling at her, and then her gaze shifted once again to the Kind Man, Who had beckoned her to follow. He was right in front of Garrison, at the head of the line. She had just assumed they were all following *Him*. Several times, though, the humans had veered off the direction He was leading, and He had to wait until they found the way. It was so much easier just to follow Him, but maybe they couldn't see Him like she could. Those times when they strayed from the path, Macy would wait patiently with Him and bark gently until they noticed her. When they paid attention and came to see what she was barking about, they usually discovered a way that was easier to traverse through the thick woods. The Kind Man was pleased with her when she helped them find the way, so she tried to do it as often as she could. She was glad to help and glad He had asked her to come along so she could stay with Garrison. Garrison was her friend, and she had grown attached to him. But the Kind Man was her *Master,* and she loved Him and wanted to obey. There was nothing better than pleasing Him.

She had waited outside the sanctuary that morning, watching through a window as Pastor Dawson laid hands on the team of young people to bless them and send them out on their journey. The alpha male and female of each team member's pack stood beside them. Macy could sense that they found the departure of their offspring difficult. But she had also seen the Kind Man spend much time with each couple in their home, while they dreamed, and during their quiet time with Him. He had prepared the leaders of each pack for this day, and their offspring were leaving with their blessing.

It was slow going with humans, especially when they were so stupid about following the Kind Man when He was obviously leading them the best way. It helped that He was patient with them. He scratched Macy's ears so that she would also be patient as she waited for the humans to stop stumbling around through the brush and rocks to notice her soft little barks. Eventually, they began to follow her as a matter of course. When this finally happened, Macy put her head down and followed in the Kind Man's exact footsteps, her tail wagging slightly. She made certain to go slowly enough that the humans could keep up. Once she looked up with her lopsided grin to see the Kind Man grinning back at her.

When the shadows began to lengthen, He led Macy to a stand of pine trees near a creek. Pine needles thickly blanketed the forest floor, making a soft bed for the weary travelers. Pastor Craig chuckled as he helped set up a tent. "The children of Israel had a cloud by day and a pillar of fire by night. We have a mutt named Macy," he said with a bemused expression. Macy cocked her head to one side and wagged her tail at the sound of her name. These humans were loud and completely oblivious to their surroundings. They had never seen the mountain lion that had circled around them, planning to intercept the last in line until the Kind Man had scared it away. Macy had cowered in the brush as she watched. The Kind Man was, indeed, kind, but He could also be terrifying. Amazingly enough, the humans never saw any of it. They were impatient with her as she waited for the scene to unfold and even started to go around her when she didn't immediately move. She had to growl to get their attention. And then He was back, leading the way again. Humans were so clueless. It was incredible they had survived for this long, what with their propensity for taking the worst route and ignoring their Leader. She would never understand why they stubbornly went their own way. There was no greater joy than following Him.

22

A thick, choking haze was crawling up from the Mississippi, reddening eyes and tightening lungs with its acrid fumes. Selah almost regretted her morning walk, since the fog had come earlier than normal today. She trotted the last block to her apartment with her shirt pulled up over her nose and tears streaming from her eyes. People from the outer docks had learned to cope with the fog, but Selah still struggled, having grown up in the fresh air of the Ozark Mountains. Her vision was so blurred by the time she reached her destination that she didn't see the group of people clustered by her front door until she was nearly upon them. "Oh!" she exclaimed as she nearly ran into Andrew.

"Sorry to scare ya, Miss Selah. I brought some friends by. Dey hasn't et anyting fo' a coupla three days, an' I jist thought ya might have some mo' o' dat stew," he said with a winsome smile. She noticed with irritation that Bally was with the group. Since Andrew had introduced Selah to his family, Bally had made an appearance at her door nearly every day, whether she was with Andrew or not. She had a way of making her presence known and dominating the conversation, leaving little room for discussions to be directed toward Christ. Even in Zelda's apartment, which everyone now considered Selah's, Bally took command in a not-so-subtle way that left no question as to who would set the tone. The neighborhood youth looked up to her as older and wiser even though she was only nineteen. And Selah wasn't in the habit of exerting authority over people her own age or older.

She swallowed her annoyance and tried to look welcoming. "Of course! Come on in." Selah managed to choke out the words before she had a coughing spasm. She opened the door to allow her guests inside

"Ya gonna live?" drawled a giant of a teenager as he stepped past her.

"I think I'll survive," Selah joked, and then started coughing again. Aside from the tall boy, there was a boy called Bester whom Andrew had brought by earlier, and a pale girl with orange dreadlocks and freckles. Selah gritted her teeth as Bally pushed past her. Bally was used to being first and rushed in to take charge of the situation. Selah was almost glad she had another coughing fit so she couldn't tell Bally what was really on her mind.

"Maybe ya'll needa go to da clinic," suggested the freckle-faced girl, who looked just a little younger than Andrew.

"Why? So's dey can bodysnatch 'er? Drey, you shorely got some dumb *idees*," said the tall boy.

"Lay off, Tunes. She got better *idees* in her little toe den what *you* got in ya cagey brain," snapped Bally.

"Hey! We's Miss Selah's guest. Let's act peaceable," Andrew pleaded.

"Ok, Mouse. I can be powerful peaceable when it comes to seein' stew from a magic pot," said the boy called Tunes.

"A magic pot?" interjected Selah. "Andrew, what have you been telling people?"

"Ohhhh, *Andrew*, is it?" jeered Bester.

"Well, that *is* his name, right?" Selah asked as she got the stew pot out of the fridge.

"Only to his mama," Bester chortled.

"You can just call me Mouse," Andrew squeaked in Selah's direction. A chorus of laughter erupted from the group.

"I think I'll stick with Andrew," Selah insisted. "Do you know what your name means?"

"Whaddaya mean, do he know what it means? It's a name. Like Mary or Charlie. It don' mean nuttin'—it just a purty word to call someone by." Bally said condescendingly.

Selah willed herself not to give a snippy reply. Once again, she wished Bally had stayed home. "Actually, all names mean something," She said as she stirred the pot, and glanced up at the tall boy. "Why do they call you Tunes?"

"Cuz I likes ta sing, baby," Tunes said, and began a spontaneous, melodious review of the group and how they earned their nicknames. "*Bester always*

stumpin' ya, cuz he's always one uppin' ya. Drey, she climb high—like a squirrel to
'er nest in da sky. Bally, she prances like a ballerina dances. Mouse, he as potent
as a itty bitty rodent!"

The group laughed again, all except for Andrew. "Ya tink ya funny, Tunes, but someday I get ma full growin' height an' I won't be Mouse to ya no more. An' dat ting 'bout Drey an' da squirrel nest don' make no sense. I mean, I know she climbin' along window ledges an' fire escapes all da time like a squirrel, but Drey don' mean nuttin'. It's jist a name, like Selah."

"Drey does *to* mean sump'n," Drey retorted. "Ma grampa done give me dat name. He said it's what dey call a squirrel nest, back when we had lotsa squirrels an' da parks had trees. Da squirrels'd make nests outta leaves way up high in da tree tops."

"So, judging by your nicknames, you all know exactly what I mean," Selah grinned from her station by the stove. "Names *mean* something. And the name Andrew means manly, strong, and courageous."

"Manly!" Bally guffawed from her seat at the pallet table. "Strong and courageous! Dat's a good one." The others fell into fits of laughter while Andrew turned red in the face and looked away.

"It's the truth," Selah insisted. "It took a lot of courage for him to be the first one to come here since this was Zelda's place. It took courage for him to bring his family and courage for him to tell you a story which you might not believe. He may not have gotten all the details right, but he got the main idea across— that if you came here, you would be fed as much as you want, from one little pot of stew."

"Yeah, an' we's still waitin' to see if 'e's right 'bout dat," Drey said.

"He right," Bally and Bester said in unison.

"I done seen it," Bester added. "I brought my folks here two nights ago. Dey ate 'til dey was full to bustin'. I don' know how she done it, but she did."

"Actually, I didn't," Selah said. "It was Jesus."

"Who dat?" Drey asked. "Where he at?"

Selah prayed silently and took a breath. "He's the One Who brought me here, to this part of the outer docks. He's the One Who keeps me safe and provides for my needs. And He's the One Who keeps putting more stew in this pot."

"So ya sayin' he ya old man," Bally said matter-of-factly. "But we ain't never seen 'im come 'round. I never seen 'im show up an' put mo' stew in da pot, an' I been here plenty o' times when it shoulda been empty. It's nevah empty. It may get kinda low sometimes, but I ain't nevah seen it run out. But I nevah seen dis Jesus dude."

"That's because I'm not talking about an ordinary man—" Selah began.

"Oh, I'm sure he's da *ultimate*, but we jist never seen 'im, dat's all," Bally interrupted. "Anyway, dese folks is hungry. How 'bout some grub? We'll see if Jesus shows up to put mo' stew in da pot, cuz it look like ya runnin' low like last time. Tunes, Drey, Ya'll come up here an' look. I want ya to see how much she has."

Selah sighed as she gathered empty bowls and cups from the cabinet. She wondered if she would ever get to explain to these people who Jesus really was. *"Lord, please give me another opportunity. And please keep Bally from ruining it by running her mouth!"* She prayed silently.

"Ya never told us what *your* name meant," Bally said to Selah as the others ate.

"It means, basically, 'Pause and consider,' or 'Think on these things,'" Selah explained. "It was used in the book of Psalms to show people when to pause during the music so that people could think about what had just been sung."

"Oh. Ok," Bally said in a dismissive tone. "Dat's a kinda weird ting ta name someone."

"Bally, do ya ever tink afore ya open ya mouth?" Andrew said exasperatedly.

Bally shrugged and then glared at Andrew. He was the only one who could get away with talking to her that way because he was her little brother.

"Well, I tink it's an interestin' name," Tunes said. "'Specially since it's about music." He looked hesitantly at Selah. He had wolfed down his portion before all the others were half finished. "Dat shore is some powerful good stew."

"Would you like some more?" Selah offered.

"Yes, ma'am," he asked politely.

"She don' like it when ya call 'er ma'am," Bally said. "She da same age we are, if'n ya hadn't noticed."

"Well, she differ'nt somehow. And I want 'er to know I got respect. And I gotta come clean, Miss Selah. I don' have nuttin' to trade just now," he said apologetically.

"That's ok, Tunes. You can pay me by listening to a story," Selah said as she refilled his bowl.

"But everyone else has sump'n to trade," Tunes said, looking longingly at the stew. "Go 'head an' give 'em seconds 'fore ya fill mine again."

"Don' you worry none, Tunes," Bally reassured him. "Everyone here gonna be full up to da gills." She took the steaming bowl out of Selah's hands and gave it to him. "Besides, what's it gonna hurt ya ta listen to a story? Shoot, if I'd known all she want is a dockmate ta listen to 'er, I'd a quit bringin' 'er water weeks ago." She grinned at Selah as if she were sharing a joke. It was the first friendly gesture Bally had made.

"I'd be glad ta listen to ya story, Miss Selah," Tunes said between mouthfuls.

"Good! I'll be right back," Selah said, and retrieved her Bible from the other room. The group suddenly fell silent.

"Oh my *gawd*!" Bally exclaimed. "Is dat a *book*? Where'd you *git* dat, girl?"

"Dat ain't just any book, either!" Bester said, upon closer inspection. He looked warily at the windows to see if anyone might be peeking inside. "Dat's a *Bible*, y'all."

"Dang, Miss Selah," Tunes said, his eyes wide. "Ya got *some* nerve, totin' *dat* aroun'. Ya know how much trouble ya can git into fo' havin' *dat* book?"

"Last person I saw wit' a Bible got bodysnatched," Bester said, keeping his voice low.

"Are you talking about Piper?" Selah asked.

"Yeah, dat who he talkin' 'bout," Bally said, backing toward the door. "Zelda's little friend. Long-haired little trapper girl. Nice kid. Went kinda nutty after 'er mama died. Den after she found dat Bible, she went really loony."

"I liked Piper," Andrew said. "She wadn't loony. She just got happy. We couldn' figger out what dere was ta be happy about. She said it was cuz o' Jesus dat she was so happy."

"Is *dat* da Jesus ya been talkin' 'bout?" Bally asked incredulously. "Dat ain't ya ol' man! Dat's a guy in a contraband story book!"

"Miss Selah," Andrew said fearfully, "It's real dangerous for ya ta have dat book. Ya can't be takin' it out where people can see it. O' course, none o' us'll say nuttin," he said, looking hopefully at the others, whose eyes were still glued to the Bible, "but if anyone sees us here wit' ya readin' dat ting, we's all in a heap o' trouble."

"Y'all can stay here if'n ya wants to, but I tink I'm gonna leave," Bally said, her hand on the door knob.

"Please stay, Bally," Selah was surprised to hear herself say. It would be nice to be able to read without being interrupted, but she knew if Bally left, the others would certainly follow. "This story I'm going to read explains why the stew pot never runs out."

Bally took her hand off the door knob, but peeked through the window down the street to make certain no one was coming. "Ok. I'll be da lookout. If anyone comes, you git dat book hid, ya hear?"

Selah nodded, and turned in her Bible to Matthew 14. "This story is about when Jesus got done teaching a huge crowd of people," she began.

> *"When it was evening, the disciples came to him and said, 'This is a lonely place, and the day is now over; send the crowds away to go into the villages and buy food for themselves.' Jesus said, 'They need not go away; you give them something to eat.' They said to him, 'We have only five loaves here and two fish.' And he said, 'Bring them here to me.' Then he ordered the crowds to sit down on the grass; and taking the five loaves and the two fish he looked up to heaven, and blessed, and broke and gave the loaves to the disciples, and the disciples gave them to the crowds. And they all ate and were satisfied. And they took up twelve baskets full of the broken pieces left over. And those who ate were about five thousand men, besides women and children."*[74]

When she was finished reading, she looked up at the group. "So you see, this isn't the first time Jesus made a lot of food from a small amount. He did it thousands of years ago, back when He first came here."

---

[74] Matthew 14:15-21, RSV

"Wait a minute," Bally said. "Ya talkin' 'bout dis Jesus dude like 'e's still alive. But 'e can't be alive if 'e was here thousands o' years ago."

"Like I said earlier, He's not an ordinary man. He is the Son of God. He came down here to teach us how to live and to save us from our sins," Selah explained.

"Sins? What dat?" Drey asked.

"Bad doin's," Tunes said suddenly. "Dat's what da old folk call it when ya do somethin' dat ain't right."

"Like killin' fo' no reason," Bester suggested.

"Or sellin' a dirty batch o' dope," Drey added.

"Or like whoever snitched on Piper. Cuz she may've drove us crazy wit' talkin' 'bout Jesus, but she don' deserve ta have da loon dockers drag 'er away," added Bally. She put her hand on her hip and cocked her head back, her eyes squinted speculatively. "Hey, now—you tell me dis. How did Jesus tink he could save us from bad doin's?" she asked. "No one can keep from doin' bad now an' den. I don' keer how good y'are, everyone done sump'n wrong sometime."

"You're exactly right," Selah agreed. "It says so right here in this book in Romans 3:23. '*For all have sinned and come short of the glory of God.*' And it doesn't matter if the sin is something huge, like killing, or something that may not seem as bad, like telling a little lie. Sin has a price. Later on in the same part of the Bible, it says that the price is death."[75]

"Well, everyone dies someday," Bally said, rolling her eyes.

"Yes, but it's where we go *after* we die that's important," Selah said. "If you ask Jesus to forgive you of your sins and believe that He is the Son of God Who died for us, then you can live with Him forever in Heaven. If you choose to follow your own way and ignore His free gift of life, you are choosing to go to hell."

"Hell? Dat's where da boogy man parties, eh?" Bally cackled, and Drey joined her.

"Hush, ya'll," Tunes said, his brow furrowed in concentration. Bally glared at him, but Tunes ignored her. "Miss Selah, is dis Jesus da same one dey call Jesus *Christ*?"

"Yes," Selah said, her heart quickening. "Have you heard of Him?"

---

[75] See Romans 6:23

"Sure we have. Dat's da same name everyone yells out when dey mad," Bally laughed.

"Not aroun' my granny, ya couldn't," Tunes said. "When my granny was alive, she'd blister ya backside if 'n ya said dat."

"I don't see why. Your granny was funny dat way. It's just a name, like anybody else's," Bally said.

"Not really. The name of Jesus is a name above every other name. There's power in that name. There's healing in that name. There's forgiveness and re-demption and deliverance in that name. Mighty things can be accomplished through His name when you believe in Him and trust Him," Selah said boldly.

"Like what?" Drey asked.

"Maybe like havin' a stewpot dat never runs out?" Bally asked, her voice tak-ing on a serious tone. For a moment, her sarcastic smile disappeared.

"Exactly that," Selah said. "Do you think *I* could make the stew keep coming? No one can do something like that except Jesus. He wanted me to show His love to you so much that He made that happen." The group was quiet for a moment as they studied Selah.

"My granny used to sing dis song about him," Tunes began. "We used to hafta tell her to *shut it* when da State police come 'round, cuz she'd start singin' it to 'em when dey standin' there guardin' da clinic. It don't actually say *Jesus*, but it calls him by his last name in da end." Tunes then began to sing, his mellow voice filling the room:

"Before the throne of God above
I have a strong and perfect plea,
A great high priest whose name is Love,
Who ever lives and pleads for me.
My name is graven on his hands,
My name is written on his heart;
I know that while in heav'n he stands
No tongue can bid me thence depart,
No tongue can bid me thence depart.

When Satan tempts me to despair
And tells me of the guilt within,
Upward I look and see him there
Who made an end of all my sin.
Because the sinless Savior died,
My sinful soul is counted free;
For God, the Just, is satisfied
To look on him and pardon me,
To look on him and pardon me.

Behold him there! The risen Lamb,
My perfect, spotless righteousness;
The great unchangeable "I AM,"
The King of glory and of grace!
One with himself I cannot die,
My soul is purchased by his blood;
My life is hid with Christ on high,
With Christ, my Savior and my God,
With Christ, my Savior and my God."[76]

When Tunes had finished, a hush filled the room, and the Holy Spirit settled on them like a blanket. Suddenly, Bally broke the silence. "What does dat all mean? What's it mean—'bout 'im dyin' an' bein' a lamb and buyin' our souls wit' his blood?"

"When sin first came into the world, it separated man from God," Selah began. "The only way people could make up for doing wrong was by sacrificing animals to Him. But the blood of the animals would never really get rid of people's sin. They would have to keep offering sacrifices to make themselves right with God and were never really free. God wanted to have a relationship with us —so finally, He sent His Son, Jesus. Jesus never sinned. He lived a life in perfect relationship with His Father and healed people and taught them and even fed them by multiplying food, like I read to you earlier."

---

[76] "Before the Throne of God Above," by Charitie Lees Bancroft

"I bet everybody loved him," Drey said.

"Many people did, but not everybody. Some people were jealous. And the religious leaders thought He was out of line because He said that He and God were the same person," Selah explained.

"Was he serious? Did 'e really tink he was God?" Bally asked.

"He was serious, and He was *right*," Selah said. "He was more than just a man. He was God, in the form of a man. He came so that we would know He understands what it's like down here, because He's been through it. And He came because no one else would have been able to live a perfect life and be the perfect sacrifice."

"Are you tellin' me dat *God* came down an' died for *us*?" Bally asked in disbelief. "Well, I've always heard dat God is dead, an' I guess dat explains it, y'all." She laughed and looked around at the others; but they were quiet, waiting for Selah's response. However, before she could formulate an answer, Bally whirled around to face her. "Wait a minute. Dat jist don' make no sense. If'n he really is God, how can 'e die? And if 'e's dead, how's 'e makin' da stewpot work?"

"Well, He didn't stay dead," Selah explained. "He laid down His life for us by going willingly to the cross. Then they put Him in a tomb, and three days later, He rose from the dead. And He's still alive! And if you believe in Him, He'll forgive you from your sins and put His Spirit inside of you. He'll bring your spirit to life with His Spirit," Selah said, her eyes shining.

"Well, I don't understand all dat, an' dat's powerful hard ta believe," Bally said. "But I know what happen wit' da stewpot ain't normal. An' I know sump'n else. Piper was different after she found Jesus. And Tunes' granny, I met her once, and dere was sump'n different about her, too. Now here *you* are, tellin' us 'bout Jesus an' all. An' ya got da same look on ya face dat Piper had when she'd talk about 'im. It's like ya so happy, ya glowin' or sump'n."

"Happiness comes and goes with whatever you're going through at the time," Selah explained. "But Jesus gives us joy that stays with us. That's what you're seeing in me, and what you saw in Piper and Tunes' granny. Jesus said He would give us joy that no one could take away."[77]

---

[77] See John 16:22

"Well, I sure could use some o' *dat*," Bally said. "Dat sound like a drug too good to be true."

Selah's heart skipped a beat. "Well, then, let me introduce you to Him," Selah offered. "Why don't we just kneel down right here and you can ask Him to be the Lord of your life? If you really believe in Him and ask Him, He'll forgive you from anything you've done wrong and welcome you into His family." And right there by the pallet table and the pot of stew, Selah led Bally to Jesus.

When they were finished praying, Bally looked at Selah, an expression of surprise on her face. "Sump'n happened, y'all," she said in a hushed tone. "I feel differ'nt. Sump'n happened inside!" She clapped her hand on her chest.

"That's Jesus," Selah explained through tears. "He put His Spirit inside of you and made your spirit come alive."

Bally's eyes were wide as she surveyed the group of teens. "Y'all gotta do dis," she said, clambering to her feet. "Dere ain't no feelin' like dis."

"Well, it has to be their choice," Selah began.

"But why wouldn't dey want it?" Bally insisted. She looked around at the others. "Ok, ok. Miss Selah said it's y'all's choice. But if'n ya turn down dis deal, y'all is missin' out. I'm tellin' ya, I feel differ'nt inside. An' not weird, like when ya buy dat stuff down da street from da Shaw. I feel good. I feel…*new*," she said after some thought. And then she giggled and grabbed Selah in a bear hug.

Tunes cleared his throat and stood up. "Miss Selah, whatevah my granny had was real. We used ta make fun of 'er for it, dat she would believe sump'n like dat. An' it used ta make us nervous dat she would get caught an' hauled off by da loon dockers. But she really believed it. An' she always wanted me ta believe it, too. An' I don' know why I'm feelin' dis way now, but I tink *I* need it. Can ya make introductions for me to dis Jesus Christ?"

"I'd love to introduce you to Jesus, Tunes," Selah said through tears.

As she and Tunes and Bally were praying together, she felt someone standing next to her. It was Bester. As soon as they were finished, he said, "I never met no one like ya, Miss Selah. Ya give us grub, an' I can tell ya don' really care if'n we trade ya nuttin' fo' it or not. And you's willin' ta risk ya life to tell us 'bout Jesus. Dis meetin' Jesus ting, it really makes a mark on a person. I mean, Bally, *she's* an old *hide*. I ain't nevah seen 'er happy unless she's bein' sarcastic 'bout sump'n." At this, Bally laughed and grabbed Bester around the shoulders. He flinched, but she was only giving him a hug. "Ya see whut I mean? Bally just ain't like dis, normally!" he exclaimed.

"Well, like I said, God's Spirit lives inside of her now. He gave her His joy and His peace. The Bible says she's a new creation.[78] And as long as she keeps following Him, she'll become more and more the person He created her to be," Selah said.

"Dis is really real, ain't it?" Bester said, looking from Tunes to Bally. "Y'all let me in on dis. I wanna give it a go." One by one, each teen gave their heart to Jesus. Selah couldn't believe it. She was having a revival, right there in Zelda's living room.

"Thank You, Jesus," Selah said through tears as she surveyed the smiling faces.

"Yeah, tank You, Jesus!" Bally echoed. "Now, what's next? Is dere sump'n else 'bout Jesus in dat Bible o' yourn? I mean, If'n we all gonna break da law, we mise well do it up big."

"Yeah, read us some mo' o' dat," Tunes said eagerly. "Is dere any songs in dat book?"

"As a matter of fact, there is," Selah said. "I mean, *are*," she corrected herself. "Oh, well, it doesn't really matter," she laughed, and opened the Bible to Psalm 22. "This is a song about Jesus. It was written hundreds of years before He was born."

As Selah read to them, the Spirit of the Lord moved softly among them like a gentle breeze. When she was finished, Bally, who had been on the edge of her seat, leaned forward even more. "Can y'all explain dat to us more, Miss Selah?" she asked.

"I'll do my best," Selah said.

"Do you still wish Bally would shut up and go home?" she felt the Holy Spirit ask. She could almost hear the laughter in His voice as His presence rested sweetly in the room.

---

[78] 2 Corinthians 5:17

23

Ira Owens ran his fingers nervously across a day's growth of stubble on his jaw. Dr. Moses was counting on him to figure out the glitch in this system, and he hadn't yet made any progress. It was unlike any system he had encountered before—much more complex. But then, JoMo *had* warned him about the difficulty of the task. "Even with the benefit of the chip, I haven't been able to crack the encryption code. I'm hoping a new set of eyes will be the key to understanding this particular problem," he had said. "The fact that you don't have the chip shouldn't hinder your progress, since we have recreated the interface for this artificial virtual link with a Vista-Visor. You will be able to experience everything someone with the chip experiences when they are attempting to form a neural link with another implanted individual. The only difference will be your reaction time, since you will be inputting commands and coding with a keyboard, rather than with your thoughts."

When it became clear he wasn't expected to take the chip, Ira had breathed a sigh of relief. "Ira, you're too valuable a commodity to corrupt at this point!" Moses had laughed. "Do you know how rare it is to find a tech-interface programmer of your ability who hasn't been chipped? I'm laying odds that in this case, biotech may be our Achilles' heel. And you, my friend, being unsullied by any except the most basic implants, are our Trojan horse!" With this pronouncement of faith in him, Dr. Moses had left him alone in the small, dimly-lit room.

Ira was relieved, even flattered, that Moses believed in his abilities to perform the task. He had been given everything to ensure his success: a private room with no interruptions, dim lighting to enhance his focus with the visor, a suit designed to assist his sensory perception of the virtual world, an ergonomically designed chair you could almost forget you were sitting in, and a mini-fridge fully stocked with snacks and drinks. The only thing he was lacking was a clue as to what he was working against.

Moses had told him it was a rogue program—something which had popped up in their research on chip interface that could be detrimental to an implanted subject since it could interfere with their ability to connect to the internet or to other users with a Virtual Private Link. The inability to use a VPL seemed to be JoMo's chief concern, for whatever reason. Ira couldn't imagine wanting to step right over the bounds of privacy to be immersed in someone else's mind, but that was one of the State-promoted benefits of the new chip: enhanced intimacy and the ability to engage emotionally with loved ones over long distances. It meant never again having to be alone. Perhaps someone else also found it hard to imagine, and that is how the rogue program came into being, Ira reasoned. Or perhaps it was spawned by the commingling of biology and technology resulting when someone was implanted, and it was the user's subconscious way of protecting themselves against a total annihilation of privacy. Self preservation was only natural, but Dr. Moses was concerned this program had the possibility of morphing into malware, with the potential of attacking the hosts' own systems and spreading to others. This was yet another reason Moses had abandoned the pursuit of this particular project, himself. Being chipped and a member of several Virtual Private Networks, he ran the risk of losing his ability to link and infecting multiple networks in the process.

The problem was not only the complexity of the code, but its foreign structure. It was completely different than any Ira had worked with before. It didn't match any type of computer language he had ever encountered. He was reminded of a movie his grandfather had told him about in which the United States Marines had utilized members of the Navajo Nation to convey secret messages using their native language. Japanese intelligence couldn't decipher the intel. Ira had always wanted to see the film, but it had been banned because of its treatment of something called Nazi Germany during World War II. Grandfather always quietly insisted that this war had been worth fighting and that the State was now in danger of exterminating Christians in the same way he claimed Nazi Germany had exterminated thousands of Jewish people. Of course, he never said these things in public, since he would have been arrested for maligning the State. Nowadays, all nations worked together for global peace and cooperation. Adolph Hitler was viewed as a visionary who was before his time. His methods may have been somewhat militant, but State schools mentioned none of the atrocities Grandfather Owens claimed were committed.[79]

Ira had loved his grandfather despite his quirks and had accepted his stories as truth until a Global History class in junior high. The teacher had warned students that any history other than the one taught in that class—especially if it was something claimed by a member of the older generation—was leftover misinformation taught by the Foundling Fathers. "That's *Founding* Fathers, Ira, not *Foundling*," Grandfather had corrected him when he had confronted him about it. But the teacher had said "Foundling." Ira was sure of it. Besides, it had been discussed in their text book. The United States of America was begun by renegade foundlings—troublemakers of civilized society whom nobody wanted. It was only when the neo socialist movement rose up and finally overthrew the Foundling Constitution that the Declaration of Dependence had been created and signed. He still remembered the parts he had memorized for class:

> "When in the course of human events, it becomes necessary for one people to form political bonds which connect them to another, and to assume among the powers of the earth, the blended and equal station to which the Laws of Nature and of Nature's Source entitle them, a decent respect to the opinions of humankind requires that they should declare the causes which impel them to the bonding.
>
> "We hold these truths to be self-evident, that all humans are created equal, that they are endowed by their Source with certain unalienable Rights, that among these are Healthcare as deemed necessary

---

[79] Revisionist history is not futuristic. It has taken place in many countries, including China, North Korea, Germany, the Netherlands, and most recently, the United States. America's providential history is well-documented, although it is being ignored in public schools today. The dangers of socialism and communism are also historically verifiable, although these systems are being touted as the wave of the future in America's public schools. The Jewish Holocaust is a historical, documented fact. One need only look at an old, unaltered history book or speak to a veteran of World War II to realize the truth. Unfortunately, veterans of this war are nearly all deceased, and the digital books offered to students today are easily altered to suit the agenda of whatever socio-political force is currently in power.

for the good of the majority, Liberty within the boundaries of the law, and the pursuit of Happiness as deemed appropriate—that to secure these rights, Governments are instituted among humans, deriving their just powers from the consent of the State—that whenever any group of people becomes destructive of these ends, it is the Right of the State to alter or abolish them, laying its foundation on such principles and organizing its powers in such form, as to the State shall seem most likely to effect their Safety and Happiness."[80]

He still recalled how he had puffed out his puny, seventh-grade chest with pride as he recited it to his grandfather. The white-bearded man had listened gravely. "There's another version of that…" he had begun when Ira finished.

"Oh, we know," Ira said. "We know all about the misinformation left behind by the Foundling Fathers."

"Oh, *we* do, do *we?*" Grandfather said and looked Ira up and down. "Who's *we?*"

"Well, you know. Everyone at school. Our teachers. Society. Today's State." Ira fumbled around verbally before finally settling on the last choice.

"Today's State. How do you know today's State isn't just telling you what they want you to believe and holding back all the rest?" Grandfather paused as Ira looked nervously around the room. "Stop looking around for that newfangled Geeves Unit you've been squawking about. You know I had mine uninstalled the minute I moved into this apartment. And you can't tell me anymore that it's not a surveillance device for the State—not the way you looked just now, like a Discard caught in the Capitol building." Grandfather had settled back in his recliner and scowled gently at him. He was the only person Ira had ever known who could somehow convey his love through a scowl. "You've got a brain, Ira. Don't let them use it *for* you. Use it *yourself.*"

Ira had reservations about his grandfather's view of the world, but the words had stuck with him. He later made it a personal principle never to have an elective implant or the chip. And as time went by and he observed the trends

---

[80] With sincere apologies to the Declaration of Independence and all who hold it dear

of the world around him, he was more inclined to reconsider the elderly man's worldview.

Now he was working for the very entity the old curmudgeon had warned him about, against a program he had been told had the potential to undermine links of neural networks that worked for the cohesion of society and mental stability of its individuals.

He had been told.

Ira sighed. As he reasoned with himself before, it would be good to have someone such as himself, who upheld an old-fashioned moral and ethical standard, working for the State. And it was immeasurably better than being sent to a penal colony. Besides, even if he managed to crack the code, that didn't mean he had to expose his findings immediately. If it turned out to be something that was somehow beneficial for humanity, something someone had created to protect the rights of the individual—surely he could keep its secrets and claim inability to complete his objective. Maybe people really should have a right to privacy. He seemed to remember his grandfather saying something about that once.

Suddenly, the viewscreen of his visor flashed, bringing him back to the present. The lines of code he had been studying had vanished. Towering before him in the virtual world of the visor was a vast, formidable wall. Dr. Moses had told him this was the first thing he had encountered when he had discovered the rogue program. He had been trying to establish a link with another user in a controlled virtual environment when the wall had suddenly appeared. This in itself was not unusual. The wall icon was a part of each user's identity in a VPL. It set the boundary for each person's neural network. Anyone in a VPN could simply approach the wall of the one with whom they were attempting to establish a link and "knock" on the door in their wall. Even though he had never formed a link, Ira had seen examples of virtual walls before. He had even helped construct them, in the fledgling era of biotech interface. Some people liked to personalize them with sculpture, or even graffiti. Others preferred a more reserved look with simple red bricks, while others showed a scholarly flair, using cut stone and ivy. But this was unlike any wall icon he had ever seen. It didn't appear to be a manmade structure at all, but rather the sheer, red stone face of a cliff, its top obscured by a misty swirl of clouds. There was no sign of the door Dr. Moses had described—an immense wooden one made of thick, dark planks secured by metal battens. Moses had knocked on it, but it never opened. He had mentally input lines of code that were a failsafe for entrance when a user's interface experienced a glitch, but nothing worked. Finally, in frustration, he had thrown himself against the door repeatedly. Surprisingly, it had suddenly given in; but instead of interfacing with the user, he was immediately surrounded by darkness and rows upon rows of the foreign coding.

The surrounding blackness and indecipherable code were what Ira had seen the moment he took his seat in the room and put on the visor. The wall had never reappeared since Dr. Moses had broken through the wooden door icon —until now. Ira wondered if he should notify someone that the wall was back but decided against it. It would be better to wait until he made actual progress, rather than report he merely had *opportunity* to make progress.

He was about to use the arrow keys on his keyboard to approach the wall when something remarkable happened. He was suddenly closer to the wall without having touched any keys. Of course! This visor was probably equipped with the enhanced ability to read cues from eye movement and pupil dilation. Ira relaxed and watched through the visor as his virtual hand reached for the wall. Funny, it even looked like his hand: knobby finger joints and all, with the freckle on the knuckle of his middle finger. He watched as his virtual hand touched the rock face, and to his surprise, he could feel it in his real hand. He rubbed his palm experimentally along the rough, reddish-brown surface. It was cool to the touch. The clouds above kept the wall shaded from sunlight—if the sun even existed in this world.

Ira backed away and looked to the left and right. Where was the door Dr. Moses had described? No sooner did the thought cross his mind than the door appeared before him, large and imposing in the eerie stillness of the desert scene. It was much broader and taller than he had imagined it would be, even though its size was dwarfed by the massive, cliff-like wall. Ira jumped slightly, for something was happening to the door. He leaned in as close as he dared and watched letters begin to take shape on the metal bands as if being engraved by the unseen beam of a laser. He peered even more closely at the inscription. "Enter ye in at the strait gate: for wide is the gate, and broad is the way, that leadeth to destruction, and many there be which go in thereat: Because strait is the gate, and narrow is the way, which leadeth unto life, and few there be that find it."[81]

Ira frowned. What a strange little saying. What an odd thing to carve into a door. A very large door. A very *wide* door….

Ira backed up. Could the key to breaking the code lie in this statement? If this was the wide gate mentioned in the inscription, was there a small one — a "strait" one—as well? He had never heard of a wall icon with more than one door. He looked to the left. The wall stretched on for what looked like miles. A broad path skirted the base of it. He looked to the right. There appeared to be a narrow path along that side, strewn with boulders and the occasional cactus, just to make things interesting. Ira looked back to the left and was about to take that route, when something drew his attention to the inscription on the door. "*Broad* is the way that leadeth to destruction, but *narrow* is the way which leadeth unto life," he mumbled. He turned back to his right and began slowly working his way up the narrow trail. He could almost believe he felt the pebbles rolling under his feet and the desert air sucking the moisture out of his body. He decided to avoid the cacti, just in case he was able to feel their spines. How were the visor and the suit managing all this? He could almost smell the air— as fresh as when he had been running along the causeway in the Preserve.

Ira stopped momentarily as he recalled the girl. He wondered where she was now. As far as he knew, they hadn't apprehended her. What in the world was she thinking, trying to reach the city? Was her community in trouble? Had her family died of some plague? Was she all alone and seeking human companionship? Ira leaned against a log that was blocking the path. He hoped they never found her.

At that exact moment, he noticed an unusual discoloration in the rock face up ahead. He scrambled over the log and approached what appeared to be a crack in the wall. No, not a crack. A small recess that had been hewn into

---

[81] Matthew 7:13-14, KJV

the rock. Tucked within the rich, red stone was a door that completely ignored compliance with modern construction standards. It wasn't much more than a foot wide, and was shorter than Ira. "Well, it certainly fits the bill for narrow," he said to himself. He looked for a handle, but finding none, he put his hands on the weathered wood and pushed gently. The door was solid. It felt immoveable as the wall itself. As he ducked down to study the doorframe for any clues to possible entry, he noticed an inscription in the stone above: "Matthew 7:7." That was strange. He knew it was in reference to the Christian Bible, but he had no idea what it said. He would have to access it from the visor. Ira scrolled through the suggestions the visor offered and finally found what he was looking for: an unaltered version of the Christian Bible, containing both Old and New Testaments. This version was only available for State employees on official business. It was the same version he had used when he had been looking for a way to leave a message for the girl in the Preserve. Ira glanced behind him. A slight breeze had begun to disturb the stifling silence of the desert air, gently brushing the back of his neck. He made a mental note to himself to ask Dr. Moses about the tech used in the virtual suit, for it was unparalleled in its detail. Returning to his task, he typed "Matthew 7:7" into the search bar, and the verse appeared: "Ask, and it shall be given you; seek, and ye shall find; knock, and it shall be opened unto you." Knock. Of course. That was standard protocol in forming a link. Ira looked back at the door and put his knuckles close to the weathered surface, wrapping them hesitantly against the wood. Immediately, the door opened inward. But before he could step inside, he felt the breeze behind him pick up speed. He turned around in time to see a disturbance in the sand as the wind suddenly jumped to gale force. A blinding light was rushing toward him—brighter than the sun. He scrunched his eyelids shut and covered them with his hands, crouching in terror before the door. This storm—whatever it was—was already upon him, and there was no time to step through the wall before it hit.

But instead of impact, he heard a voice, or voices, all talking at once. There were so many of them and so many things being said simultaneously that it sounded almost like the rushing of a river or the crashing of waves against a rocky shoreline. The onslaught of words and light rushed over and around him and through the door like a tornadic wind. Even though his eyes were shut and covered, he could see and feel an intense glow that appeared momentarily from within the confines of the wall; then everything returned to normal. Ira cautiously opened his eyes and inched his way slowly up the side of the rock door frame. He had never felt such power before. Was this what it was like to experience a power surge during a link? He ducked his head and looked through the opening, wondering if the bombardment of light and sound had completely fried the circuits and destroyed the artificial VPL. But inside, he saw no signs of devastation—no damage whatsoever. The first thing he noticed was lush, green grass. He stepped through the door and could feel the soft, cushiony thickness of it beneath his feet. The next thing he noticed was a peaceful stream meandering through this virtual meadow. In the distance, he could make out a large tree with white and gray bark. Beneath the tree was the slim figure of a girl. When she saw him, she jumped up and down and began running toward him, her long hair bouncing in little rivulets of golden brown. "Ira!" she cried. "Ira, we've been waitin' for ya!"

24

Iᴿᴬ stood frozen in the grass at the edge of the meadow. This was supposed to be an artificial VPL created by Dr. Moses to house the rogue program. So who —or *what*—was this girl running toward him? He took a few steps backward, then stopped. Even if she were some artificial intelligence with intent to protect the program, there was no way she could harm him. He wasn't chipped and therefore didn't have an actual link that could be used to infiltrate his mind. Being merely an observer, he could interact without fear.

"Hello," he said cautiously. "How do you know my name? Did Dr. Moses tell you I was coming?"

"Ya mean Dr. Joe? Even if 'e had, I wouldn'a believed 'im. He hasn't been exactly truthful with me. An' 'e's kept us pretty busy, even before 'e started tryin' ta break down the door. So we didn' have much time fa anything except buildin' walls an' makin' paths. But we was restin' one day, an' Jesus tol' me He was bringin' someone here who looked at things differently—someone who could help us," the words tumbled out of the girl's mouth like water over rocks in a river.

Ira's brow wrinkled in confusion. "Who did you say was helping you? I didn't catch the name."

"Jesus. Have ya met 'im?" she asked. She was positively glowing.

"Well, no…I mean, I just arrived, and I'm not actually *in* here to have been able to meet him." Ira stopped short, wondering how much information he should divulge. "Can you explain to me who or what you are, exactly?"

The girl smiled patiently at him. "Ya don't have to be in ma brain to get ta know Jesus. I met 'im on the outside when I was readin' His book."

"On the outside?"

"The outside world—the one we live in, *usual*. I'd still be there if Jesus hadn't tol' me He had a job for me to do. So I came inside and started buildin' walls and makin' paths with 'im."

"You mean you're a real person?" Ira said, his heart sinking into the pit of his stomach. "Dr. Moses told me he had been trying to decipher a rogue program that was keeping him from establishing a link with another user. I assumed you were a virtual representation of that program—like the wall I just broke through."

The girl laughed. "You didn' break through. We let ya in."

"Why did you let me in? And why didn't you let Dr. Moses in?" Ira asked.

"If 'e was tryin' to force 'imself into *your* brain, would *you* let 'im in?" the girl asked.

Ira swallowed. Moses had lied to him—tricked him into working on breaking through the boundary of an individual's neural network by telling him it was a rogue program. Who was this girl? How and why had she been so heavily protected? More importantly, why had Dr. Moses been so set on breaking through the protective coding and hacking into her mind? Suddenly he feared for her safety. If the lab was somehow monitoring the visor, surely they would realize the link had been established.

"Listen, you may be in danger. They probably realize we've established a connection," Ira began.

"Don't worry, Ira. They don' know nothin' about it," the girl reassured him.

"How do you know? And how do you know my name? And why did you let me in?" Ira asked again.

"They don' know 'cause *we* were the ones who let ya in. An' like I said earlier, I know ya name 'cause Jesus tol' me you were comin'. Dr. Joe didn' bring ya here. *Jesus* worked that all out," the girl explained.

"But I don't understand who this Jesus is. And who are you, that Dr. Moses would find it so important to violate your will by trying to break through your neural boundaries?"

"My name is Piper. But who I am isn't important. Who *Jesus* is—that's the only really important question," Piper began. "Actually, He's the reason Dr. Joe is tryin' ta hack ma brain in the first place. He's got somethin' personal against Jesus. I just don't understand why."

"Is Jesus a part of your personality? Is he the one who created the rogue program—uh, I mean, your boundary wall?" Ira asked, wondering if he was dealing with a genius with dissociative identity disorder. Jesus might be a protective alternate personality.

"Jesus and I built that wall together using the promises in His Word. An' I'm learnin' ta be more like 'im by followin' His Word and believin' what 'e says. But Jesus ain't part of my personality or my imagination. He's real. He's the Son of God Who came into the world to save us from our sins," Piper said in her plainspoken manner.

Ira was quiet for a moment, letting this information sink in. "So you're telling me the Jesus you're talking about is the deity of Christianity and that he helped you build your wall?" The girl might be a genius, but she was certainly delusional, which meant she could be dangerous. Perhaps this is why Dr. Moses felt it necessary to access her mind—to assess if she was a threat to herself or anyone else.

"Deity? I don' know that word."

"Deity means divine being…or God, if you will. Nowadays, people call it the Source," Ira tried to explain.

"Jesus isn't an *it*. He's a *He*. An' He ain't that mumbo jumbo the State calls the Source, although He *is* the source of all life. He isn't just the God of *Christianity*. He's the God of *everything*," the girl said emphatically.

"Well, don't let anyone else hear you say that, or you'll be branded for intolerance," Ira cautioned her.

"How do ya think I got chipped in the first place?" Piper asked.

Ira was stunned. "How old are you?" he finally asked.

"Fourteen."

She was older than he had guessed. Her growth must have been stunted by malnutrition. "What about your parents? Do they know you're here?" he asked gently.

"I never knew my dad. Mama died almost three years ago."

"So how did you end up here? Did your mother sign a D.I.N.? Because if she did, I don't see how they can hold you here." Ira assumed most Discards didn't even know about the Declaration of Intent to Nurture. The State passed out literature on the subject, but few Discards could read. They were warned about it at the clinics, but many avoided medical treatment of any kind, choosing to give birth at home since they didn't trust the State.

"Sure, I got a D.I.N. Mama made sure ta do that. But they said they had 'just cause' to go 'round it. They said they gave me plenty o' time to tell 'em what they wanna know. An' since I told everyone about Jesus, an' since I told these loon dockers I wouldn't *stop* tellin' people, they said they had 'just cause.' So they chipped me," the girl said matter-of-factly.

"What kind of information could they want from a fourteen-year-old girl?" Ira asked. "Did you see some horrible crime? Are you protecting someone?"

"They say I'm the one who committed the horrible crime. I was just tellin' people 'bout Jesus. They wanna know who got saved, but I ain't tellin', cuz they'll likely end up here like me, with a chip in their heads. So I guess I *am* protectin' folks. But I don't think what I did was a crime."

Ira leaned back against the red stone. His grandfather had been right, all along. The Declaration of Dependence laid the foundation for altering or abolishing people who interfered with others' inalienable rights. Christians could be seen to fit that description, if they were saying there was something wrong with you—and that their God was the only way to make it right.

Ira had never heard anyone openly insisting that *their* faith was the *only* way, as Piper was doing. Most people were reluctant to talk about their faith, even when you asked and they would have been within their rights to tell you. Still, altering a young girl by chipping her without her consent seemed wrong. Wasn't she too young to fully understand the unstable moral ground she was treading? The State had often turned a blind eye to what happened in the outer docks. Why was Dr. Moses so bent on changing this girl's mind about her faith? What was so important about getting a list of people she had converted to Christianity? Assuming, of course, she was telling him the truth.

"What's wrong with tellin' people how ta get saved?" the girl was saying. "What's wrong with showin' 'em the way to get clean inside?"

Ira cleared his throat. "Well, telling people how to get clean implies that they're dirty. There are a lot of good people out there, trying to do good things. Telling them they're dirty isn't only insulting, it also just isn't true."

Piper scratched her nose and cocked her head to one side. "So, I s'pose ya think ya might be one o' them good people?" she asked.

"Well, yes. I suppose. I mean, I don't go out of my way to *hurt* people. I keep to myself, mostly. But I *have* gone out of my way to *help* people," he said, vividly recalling how he nearly lost his career and went to prison to help the girl in the Preserve. "Surely that counts for something."

"In Romans chapter 3, God's Word says 'There is none righteous, no, not one: there is none that seeketh after God. They are all gone out of the way, they are together become unprofitable; there is none that doeth good, no, not one.'"[82] Piper said in a solemn tone. "I learned that one a long time ago. But here's one I learned just now. It's from the Old Testament ya brought with ya. 'But we are all as an unclean thing, and all our righteousnesses are as filthy rags; and we all do fade as a leaf; and our iniquities, like the wind, have taken us away.'"[83]

Ira pondered this for a moment. "Well, that's a very picturesque way of saying it. But if I understand you correctly, you're telling me that no matter what good I do, it's never enough. Don't you see how that might make people feel bad— might interfere with their pursuit of happiness?" Ira asked. "This is the legal grounds on which they implanted you with the chip. If you would just present your faith in a non-threatening way and offer it as a choice—"

"But I *am* offering a choice," Piper insisted. "If ya accept the free gift Jesus gave us by paying for our sins when He died on the cross, ya can have eternal life in heaven. Or ya can pay for ya sins yaself by spending eternity in the Lake of Fire.[84] That's a choice. And it seems like a really simple one, to me. Ya don't hafta work ya way into heaven. Ya couldn't, even if ya tried. An' if gettin' into heaven depended on whatcha did, how fair would that be? Some people got lotsa smarts. They could prob'ly do lotsa things ta help people. An' others are just simple-minded. Maybe they can do some stuff, but not as much as someone like yaself. An' what about people who just don't have any chance to do

---

[82] Romans 3:10-12, KJV
[83] Isaiah 64:6, KJV
[84] See Revelation 20:15

anything cuz they's born in the State where ya bein' watched all the time? That just wouldn't be fair. But how easy is it to accept a gift? That makes it fair for *everyone*. An' Jesus gave it freely! No one made 'im do it. He loved us that much, that 'e would die for us and give us His righteousness for free."

Ira sighed. "But don't you see how your views might be seen as intolerant?" he asked.

"No. If someone wants to tell me what they believe, I'll listen. An' I won't call the loon dockers to drag 'em off. I just want the same chance to explain to them what *I* believe. They got a right ta believe whatever they want. But they also got a right ta know the Truth."

Ira shook his head in frustration. "That kind of talk is exactly what I mean when I say intolerant. Just because something is true for you doesn't mean it's true for someone else. Everyone has their own version of the truth. You shouldn't project your truth onto others."

"I don't project *my* truth. I project *the* Truth," Piper said with finality.

"Well, what exactly is the truth?" Ira asked exasperatedly. "If you can show me the truth beyond a shadow of a doubt, maybe I'll believe you."

Piper beamed. "Ok. Sure! He's standing right behind you."

"What?" Ira asked as Piper's face became illuminated by more than just her smile. He turned around slowly.

Standing before him was the most incredible being he had ever seen. He was shining with a brightness as intense as the light Ira had encountered in the windstorm outside the wall, except it wasn't hurting his eyes. Warmth and love emanated from Him; and there was another quality Ira couldn't describe, because he had never before experienced it. He only knew that standing before this Man, he felt completely exposed. The memory of every selfish act he had ever committed suddenly surfaced, the truth of his motives flashing through his mind like a picture collage in a visor. He felt immediately ashamed to be standing before someone Who was so...he grasped for the word, but couldn't find it. Yet even as Ira felt engulfed in his shame, he realized the Man wasn't accusing him of anything, and He was looking tenderly at Ira—as He would look at an old friend, or as a father would look at a son.

"Hello Ira," the Man said gently.

"Hello," Ira gulped. "Piper tried to tell me who you are. Are you…*Truth?*"

"I Am," He said.

As the Man spoke these words, Ira's range of vision narrowed to crystal clear focus. The Man standing in front of him seemed to encompass the universe in its totality. Somewhere, he could hear unearthly voices crying out, *"Holy, holy, holy, Lord God Almighty, which was, and is, and is to come."* Ira suddenly found himself flat on his face. More and more of his life was revealed to him, including the most recent events, when he had tried to justify working for someone with questionable morals in order to save his own skin. Everything was so clear to him now. Truth was not subjective. Truth was a Person. And that Person was now helping him to his feet.

Ira wondered why his face felt wet and realized he had been crying. "I don't understand exactly who or what you are, but I know that you are…*holy,*" Ira recalled the word used by the voices and realized it was the one he had been looking for.

"I am the Way, the Truth, and the Life," the Man was saying. "My name is Jesus. I am the Alpha and the Omega, the beginning and the end, the first and the last."[85] He paused as if to let Ira process the brevity of His words. Somehow Ira sensed that this Man who called Himself Jesus was not only complete in Himself, but He could somehow complete others—could bring wholeness and meaning to those who felt hollow and without purpose. Ira was inexplicably drawn to Him as someone who has been wandering in the desert is drawn to a spring of water. As if reading Ira's thoughts, Jesus continued, "I will give unto him who is thirsty of the fountain of the water of life freely. He that overcomes shall inherit all things; and I will be his God, and he shall be My son."[86] Jesus was smiling gently at him, waiting, Ira realized, for him to say something.

"I don't know *how* to overcome," Ira confessed. "It has become clear to me that most of what I've done through my whole life has been for selfish reasons. I thought I was a good person, but I'm really not. And even if I were, I still don't think that would be good enough. So how can someone like me overcome anything?"

---

[85] Revelation 22:13, KJV
[86] See Revelation 21:6-7

Jesus smiled at Ira. "Take heart," He said warmly. "I have overcome the world.[87] If you will have Me as your Lord and Savior, I will show you how to overcome by My blood and by the word of your testimony."[88]

Ira swallowed hard. "Piper said you brought me here because I can help. I just don't see how I could ever do anything that would make a difference. Especially since I've seen what I'm really like."

"You already helped Piper by accessing a complete version of My Word right before we opened the door for you. And there is so much more you can do. Ira, before I formed you in your mother's womb, I knew you. I know the plans I have for you,"[89] Jesus said. "They are good plans—not just something I threw together on a moment's notice. There is so much I want to give you. Will you accept My gift of forgiveness? Will you accept My gift of life?"

Ira hesitated. He had never been one to make snap decisions. Doubt began to nibble at the edges of his mind. What was he doing? He was supposed to be deciphering a program. How did he know that this Jesus character wasn't something created to throw him off the trail? Suddenly he thought he heard footsteps behind him. The edges of the scene before him seemed to grow fuzzy. Was he losing the connection? Had someone stepped into the room? What would they think if they saw him crying? He looked up into the Man's eyes in time to see a look of sadness flicker across them, and then he was suddenly staring at blackness and lines upon lines of code.

"How's it going in here?" asked a voice at his side.

Ira pulled off the visor and looked up into the face of Dr. Moses. "Uh, I thought I made a breakthrough, but it was a dead end," Ira confessed.

Dr. Moses looked at him strangely and handed him a tissue. "Are you alright?"

"Oh, of course!" Ira said, drying his tears. "The visor just puts a strain on my eyes. Years of using monitors."

"Who were you talking to?"

Ira tried to swallow, choked, and reached for his glass of water. "Sometimes I talk to myself when I'm working," he managed, after he had taken a drink.

---

[87] See John 16:33
[88] See Revelation 12:11
[89] See Jeremiah 1:5 and 29:11

Dr. Moses observed him quietly. "Why did you turn off your visor after you accessed the State Archives?" he asked.

Ira's brow furrowed. "I didn't turn it off. See?" He held up the visor so Moses could see the lines of code.

"Yes, I know it's on now—but you turned it off right after you downloaded a file from the archives into the program. For a moment I thought you were getting somewhere, but then you disconnected. Your visor has been off for almost half an hour. You just now turned it on again," Moses said. "Explain."

"I didn't turn it off." Ira repeated, confused. "I was engaged with the visor during the whole time. And I didn't download anything—at least, not to my knowledge. I thought I found a way in. That's why I referenced the archives."

Dr. Moses seemed to study him for a moment. "Ira, I think you'd better call it a day. I'll forward you the records of the download and the visor usage, so you can see what actually happened. It's possible we've been overworking you too soon after such a stressful event in your life. You may be remembering things incorrectly, or perhaps you fell asleep from exhaustion and were dreaming that you were actually using the visor. Whatever the case, go home for now. We've straightened out your Geeves unit, so it should let you back in, no problem. I'll see you back here tomorrow, 0700 hours."

"Certainly," Ira said, frowning in confusion.

Dr. Moses turned to go and then once again looked back at Ira. "If you do make a habit of talking to yourself while you work, you might consider giving yourself some positive reinforcement. You sounded somewhat discouraged. There's nothing wrong with giving yourself a little pep talk now and then. You can do this, Ira. I have great faith in you." Dr. Moses smiled, and with that, took his leave.

Ira sat very still, going over everything in his mind. He knew he hadn't turned off the visor. There had to be some mistake. A quick look at the placement of the power button confirmed it was in its normal location on this model, so he couldn't have accidentally bumped it. Besides, he had been engaged with the virtual environment the whole time.

Unless…

What if Dr. Moses was right, and everything he had just experienced was some sort of dream—or worse yet—a symptom of neurosis brought on by stress? He carefully unzipped the sensory suit and gingerly climbed out of it. Perhaps JoMo was right. All he needed was a good night's rest. The girl—the incredible man—even the wall—were all probably just part of a dream he had when the stress had become unbearable. He must have had a memory lapse, turned off the visor and had fallen asleep to escape the wretched reality that at any moment, if he failed, he might be back in jail. He smoothed his hair down and straightened his rumpled shirt, attempting to look as normal as possible when he stepped into the hall.

Suddenly, there was a commotion a few doors ahead to the left. Ira paused as the scene unfolded. A nurse was apparently checking on a patient, and the patient had taken her by surprise. "Calm down, now. You're ok. Everything's ok," the nurse said as she attempted to force the patient back into the room.

"I just wanna step out in the hall for a minute," the patient said.

Ira froze. He knew that voice. It was the voice of a young girl. The girl ducked her head underneath the nurse's arm for a brief moment, made eye contact with him, and smiled radiantly. Her hair was mere stubble, but Ira would know that smile and those eyes anywhere. She waved at him before another nurse came to the aid of the first one and the girl was dragged back toward the room. "I don't know how she's even on her feet," one nurse said to the other. "She's so heavily sedated."

Ira stood still in the hallway, his heart pounding. The girl was real. She was the one with whom Dr. Moses had been trying to establish a link. If the visor had been turned off immediately after he accessed the archives, as Moses claimed, how could he have any knowledge of her appearance? There had to be some mistake. "Jeremiah 29:11!" the girl was calling out. "Jeremiah 29:11!"

Ira stayed where he was until the girl was safely returned to her room and his rapid heart rate had returned to normal. He would get to the bottom of this when he got home and could access things privately.

Dr. Moses had kept his word. The Geeves unit for his apartment let him in with no question after he flashed his palm across the digital doorknob. Not that it mattered. Ira could have reprogrammed it himself. The real reason JoMo had "straightened out" the unit had less to do with courtesy and everything to do with monitoring him. He had undoubtedly installed something Ira would find hard to get around—something that would detect if he attempted to deactivate it. He went to the window and stared down at the illuminated form of the Gateway Arch. "Geeves, activate window screen and access the information forwarded to me by Dr. Joseph Moses this afternoon," Ira said. The scenic view suddenly faded as the window became opaque and a log of today's events appeared before him. At 0900 hours, visor use was initiated. At 1429 hours, the State Archives were accessed, and seconds later, there was a download of Archival File 379B5 to an undisclosed location in the building. Visor power connection terminated at 1430 hours, and visor power connection was reestablished at 1452 hours.

It made no sense. If the visor had been off, then none of what he experienced could have happened. But then there was the girl. He knew it was the same person he had seen in the visor. What had she been yelling as she was being dragged away? *Jeremiah 29:11*. If he wasn't certain his Geeves unit had been compromised, he would do a search. His personal visor usage was also undoubtedly being monitored, so that was out of the question as well.

Ira took a deep breath and looked miserably around the room. There was nowhere to escape. There was no privacy. Not that there ever had been, but he had never had to think about it before. Grandfather had been right, as he had been about so many other things. Ira smiled grimly as he remembered the old man. What would he have done in this situation? Ira laughed and headed to the bathroom to draw a bath. That was Grandfather's answer to dealing with things you couldn't change. He would take a long, hot bath in an attempt to relax. Then he would have a cup of hot chocolate and go to bed. Somewhere in the middle of the night, maybe the answer would present itself.

Surprisingly, the bath helped calm his nerves. He reflected on his situation. He knew that he had much to be thankful for. He wasn't in jail. He was working in his preferred field. He had the respect, if not the trust, of the foremost mind in the field of biotech interface. He had a nice, warm bed in a swanky apartment, and as soon as he had a cup of hot chocolate, he would curl up in bed and get a good night's sleep.

Ira dried off and slipped on his pajamas. When he went to the cabinet, he discovered there was no hot chocolate, only coffee and several different varieties of tea. Ira frowned. There wasn't even an herbal tea. It was all highly caffeinated stuff, geared for his long days of monitor watching in the drone readout room. He closed the cabinet and contemplated going to bed. The problem was, he was accustomed to getting exercise after work. It wasn't only today's events that made him restless. Sitting still for nearly seven hours straight made his body crave activity. He sighed and changed into running clothes. It was still early. He could go running before the fog came up from the river, and if he stayed out late enough to encounter any, he could take a shuttle home.

The chilly spring air felt refreshing as he stepped out onto the sidewalk. Ira headed west and then south, slowing a little as his rate of breathing increased and his lungs burned slightly from the pollution. He thought wistfully of the clean air of the Preserve. Running there had been almost transcendent, his legs pumping along the old road beneath the causeway, his lungs uninhibited in their function, sucking in gulps of the oxygen-rich air. Its purity was rivaled only by the world inside the visor. His step faltered as he remembered the desert trail and the green meadow. In his mind, he could clearly see the girl called Piper smiling radiantly at him, her eyes shining. Suddenly his foot caught the edge of something on the sidewalk, and he tripped and nearly fell. "Watch where you're going, eh?" said a man sitting on the sidewalk near a subway entrance. Ira glanced down and realized he had kicked the man's guitar case that was resting beside him.

"I'm sorry," Ira mumbled, wondering internally why on earth he should apologize, since the man was obviously sitting in a highly trafficked area. The man glared at him and went back to strumming his guitar. Ira had been so lost in thought that he hadn't even noticed him before. He decided to keep a closer tab on his surroundings and looked around the area. A few specialty shops and restaurants lined the street, giving the neighborhood an inviting atmosphere. He had taken a good run, but when he thought about his apartment, he realized he wasn't quite ready to head back home. If he walked until the fog rose, he could make a quick exit to the subway and be home in no time.

He hadn't gone very far when he began to smell something delicious. It was being carried out in cups by people who were leaving the shop up ahead, he realized. A signboard was set up on the sidewalk. "Today's special: Comfort Cocoa, made with imported Belgian chocolate and heavy cream." He smiled. Grandfather would have loved that. He opened the ornate, antique wooden door and stepped inside.

"Welcome to Talk-A-Lot Chocolate," said an attractive older woman with long, silvery gray hair. "I'd ask you for your visor, but I see you aren't wearing one," she said.

"My visor?" Ira asked.

"Yes. We ask that people check them in at the door. It encourages people to interact more, rather than just stare at a screen while they sit together."

"I've had enough of staring at screens for one day," Ira said wearily. "I'd like to try your special—the Comfort Cocoa, I think it was."

"I'll put in your order right away. May I show you to a table, or would you like it to go?" the woman asked pleasantly.

Ira was about to decline the offer of a table when something made him stop. There was something unusual about this establishment. Then he realized that it was the sound of conversations taking place all around him. A couple at a corner table were holding hands, talking softly to each other. A group of teenagers was laughing and joking at a booth across the room. Everywhere he looked, people were engaged in some sort of verbal interaction. He looked back at the woman to find her smiling at him knowingly. "Refreshing, isn't it?" she asked.

"It certainly is," Ira admitted. "I'd like a table, please."

"Follow me," the woman said and showed him to a small table by the window. "My name is Luciana. Contessa will be your server. We also have a variety of pastries and paninis," she said, placing a menu in front of his seat.

Ira thanked her and sat down. It was then that he noticed the words carved into the tabletop under the glass table covering. *"For I know the plans I have for you, says the Lord, plans for welfare and not for evil, to give you a future and a hope."*[90] They had a familiar ring to them. It was strikingly similar to what the Man in the meadow had told him.

---

[90] Jeremiah 29:11, RSV

"Excuse me!" he said quickly. The woman turned back to the table. "Can you tell me what this is from—this saying carved in the table here?" Ira asked, tapping the glass.

"Jeremiah 29:11," she replied. "It's a beautiful quote, isn't it?"

Ira's heart began to pound as he remembered the girl calling out those exact words to him in the hallway at Dr. Moses' lab. "Yes, it is. But why do you have it carved into your table?"

"Well, don't you find it encouraging?" Luciana asked.

"I suppose so," Ira said. "Is this carved into all of your tables?"

"No, just this one," Luciana said warmly. "When you walked in, you looked as if you could use a little encouragement. I seated you here for that reason."

Ira was dumbfounded. "That's incredible," he said to himself.

"Isn't it?" Luciana said. "To think the Creator of the universe would have plans in mind for us? There's another place in the book of Jeremiah where God says, 'Before I formed you in the womb, I knew you.'[91] I find both of those quotes to be very encouraging. I wanted to include that one on this table as well, but there wasn't enough room."

"No, I mean, I just encountered this quote earlier today," Ira explained. "Both of them, actually," he added, upon reflection.

"You did? Where?" Luciana asked, genuinely surprised.

"It was…it's difficult to explain," Ira finally said. His brow furrowed as he looked up at the hostess. "You seem to know a lot about the Christian Bible."

"I'm a student of ancient literature," Luciana said carefully.

"What can you tell me about Jesus?" Ira asked.

Luciana smiled as she slid into the chair across from him. "I know a few things," she said.

---

[91] See Jeremiah 1:5

25

JANICE wearily stepped out of the shuttle and began the short trek to her apartment building. She had just finished exercise class, and although she had felt invigorated immediately after it was over, tiredness had crept in during the ride to her neighborhood's shuttle stop. Her muscles were still sore from the previous workout, and she had pushed herself to the limit again today, trying her best to keep up with the aerobics instructor. "Come on, Janice!" the instructor had offered encouragement. Janice had tried to smile, but it was hard to manage when it felt as if her lungs were about to burst into flames. She was relieved when the class was over and her breath finally stopped coming in ragged gasps. "You're doing great!" the instructor said, patting her on the shoulder before she bounced away to teach her next session.

Janice started to pull down her visor to check the time and then remembered she didn't wear one anymore. There was no need. Since she had the chip, she always had access to the correct time. All she needed to do was focus for a moment, and she was linked to the *Local Time, Weather, and Events* page via the internet.

1900 hours. She would have to hurry home to eat supper and finish her meditation so she could be in bed at the prescribed time. Her pace quickened, even though she was tired. She had to adhere to the schedule. If she didn't, the new part of her brain would take over again, like it had the day she had decided she didn't want to continue working out. That had been terrifying, like watching herself from a window. When she fought to regain control, she had blacked out—only to regain consciousness after the workout session, breathing heavily, her lungs screaming for air. After that incident, she determined she wouldn't deviate from the protocol.

At last, she reached her apartment building and headed straight to the elevator. She was tired, and taking the stairs meant she might be late for supper. Janice paused. Her protocol dictated that when faced with the choice of stairs or an elevator, she must always take the stairs. Janice shuffled as quickly as she could to the stairwell door and pushed it open. The first of seven flights stared menacingly down at her. "This is ridiculous," she said to herself. "I simply can't make it in time. I'm not taking the stairs." As she turned back to the elevator, she had a sickeningly familiar feeling. She was momentarily detached from her surroundings as if she were floating. The chip and the new part of her neural network were now in control, carefully calculating the speed at which she would need to ascend the stairs to arrive at her seventh-floor apartment in enough time to complete her tasks before bedtime. Janice watched as her feet pivoted back toward the door to the stairs. She watched her hand reach for the door knob and could feel its coolness under her fingers as she opened it; but otherwise, she was merely a spectator. Her legs strode purposefully toward the stairs and began the ascent, taking one step after another in rapid succession. *This is madness. I can never make it in time!*" she cried silently. As if in response, the new part of her brain quickened her already rapid pace. Janice could feel her heart rate increasing, her breath coming in deep gasps. *"Don't you understand? I can't do this! It's physically impossible!"* she cried desperately to herself. Her heart was banging against her ribcage as if it were attempting to break out of prison. It felt as though her ribs were trying to squeeze her heart into submission, her chest locked in a vice. A pain began to spread up her neck and into her jaw. Blackness feathered the edges of her peripheral vision, and Janice lost consciousness on the fourth flight of stairs in Crystal Riverview Apartment Complex.

She awoke with something cold and rough pressed against her cheek. Upon opening her eyes, she was faced with a foggy, gray, rectangular slab just a few inches away. It was topped by a gray, textured rubbery surface. Janice's eyelids fluttered, brushing the concrete floor of the fifth flight stairwell. She slowly pushed herself up off the floor and scooted to the wall, bracing her back against its steely grayness. "Why is everything gray?" she wondered absently. She was fairly certain she had just had a heart attack, and yet she found herself absurdly preoccupied with the color of the walls. *"What color would you prefer?"* she felt a voice inside her ask. And then she realized. For some reason, her environmental preferences must have been overridden. She was now seeing the world as it actually was, without the help of her chip or a visor—a drab reality most individuals had decided not to face. "I'll take, uh…" Janice faltered as she attempted to make a decision. Even a choice of color seemed like too much of a strain at the moment. Suddenly, she could hear footsteps on the stairs.

"Citizen Druthers? Citizen Druthers, are you okay?" called a voice from a flight below her.

Still dazed, Janice tried to collect her thoughts. She could hear the sound of someone approaching but couldn't focus enough to respond.

A man and a woman in emergency medical uniforms appeared over the top of the stairs below her. "Janice?" said the woman, "We're paramedics. Your chip sent notification that you were under severe cardiac duress, so we came to check on you. Your vitals have returned to normal now, but we were already here, so we thought we'd ask how you're feeling."

Janice squinted. Everything still seemed a little blurry. "I thought maybe I was having a heart attack. My chip wouldn't allow me to take the elevator," she said weakly. "Is my heart okay? Did it do any damage? Maybe I should go in and get it checked out."

"Well, actually, your chip verifies that your heart is in perfect working order. No damage done!" the woman said reassuringly.

"I can take your blood pressure, if it makes you feel better," said the other paramedic, pulling some equipment out of a bag.

"I would appreciate that," Janice said gratefully. "I had forgotten the chip monitored my physical condition and could perform a self-assessment. There was so much to remember at orientation that it's hard to keep it all straight."

The woman patted her shoulder. "It was hard for me at first, too. Then I remembered that all I had to do was focus, and I could access all the information I needed. The chip can alert you as to whether or not your body has a problem that needs medical attention. So the next time this happens—"

"The next time?" Janice cried. "I don't want there to be a next time! It totally took over! I didn't have a choice. I knew I couldn't keep to my schedule if I took the stairs, but instead of letting me take the elevator, it just made me go faster! It almost killed me!"

The paramedics exchanged glances. "The chip wouldn't do anything that would endanger you," the man explained, rubbing the titanium port on the back of his neck thoughtfully. "It's the Great Protector. It watches over you and helps you to watch over yourself when the natural part of you isn't using good judgment. We know you're on the Trimfit program. It can be rigorous, but it gets results."

"Janice, think back to what happened just before this incident. Is there anything you could have done differently that would have given you more time to get to your apartment?" the woman asked as the man took Janice's blood pressure.

Janice thought back to her time at the gym. After working out, she had sat down and rested on a bench beside a monitor that was showing videos of life in a coral reef. Colorful fish darted in and out among the coral. Schools of herring hovered in the water, little shards of silver moving as a single entity in the underwater haven—hundreds of individual fish turning and swirling as if they shared a collective mind. It was beautiful. She had sat there, wondering how tiny life forms with such a simple level of intelligence could coordinate their movements so precisely. There must be a higher intelligence behind it all —something that was helping them react to the changing conditions of their environment.

Perhaps everything they did was somehow tied to their instincts and their ability to react immediately to the movements of their fellows in close proximity. But something had to come up with that idea in the first place. *My Truth* taught that the Source was behind all life. Did the Source come up with this method of evading predators? Did it use evolution or natural selection as its tool, slowly shaping the behavior of the fish by weeding out the ones who didn't react quickly enough, allowing them to be eaten by barracudas, sharks, and dolphins? It seemed a cruel way to make things the way they are. The result was beautiful, but the method was cold and dispassionate. Wouldn't it be wonderful if there really was a better beginning for everything—a better way of forming things into the way they are now?

"Janice?" the woman was saying. "Do you remember now?"

Janice collected her thoughts. "I think maybe I sat down in front of the video screen too long," she admitted. "I was tired after class, and it was showing fish in the ocean. I could have watched them all night, but then I realized it was getting late."

"So you see, you could have avoided all this unpleasantness with a little better planning. The chip is a good educator. It will teach you time management and how to prioritize things," the woman said.

"Your blood pressure checks out within acceptable parameters," the man said as he undid the cuff from Janice's arm.

"Are you sure?" Janice asked worriedly. "Because it just doesn't seem like things are working right. When I woke up, the walls were all gray. In fact, they still are."

"Bryson, hand me the visor," the woman said.

"You still have to use a visor?" Janice asked. "I thought you said you had the chip."

"I do have the chip. But in order to assess you, I'm going to use an external device. Unless, of course, you would prefer to form a link?" the woman asked. "I had assumed you hadn't yet ascended to that level of chip operation, since you've only been implanted within the past month. But under the circumstances, I can form a link with you to gain a better understanding of what's actually going on inside of there." The woman tapped her finger to her temple and raised her eyebrows.

"I've heard about linking. That's one of the things I've really been looking forward to," Janice said eagerly.

"Well, this will just be a link for a health assessment," the woman clarified, "and if you'd like to do that—"

Janice nodded vigorously.

"Then first off, you need to know my name. Etherea Daniels. I'll come and knock on your wall and tell you my name. In order to establish the link, you have to let me in. Then I can perform the assessment."

"This sounds fun." Janice was feeling better already.

"Well, it isn't a social link. It's just a medical assessment," Etherea said firmly. "I'll just pop in and check you out—see how things look from your perspective. After that, I'll be able to advise you as to the best course of action."

"Okay," Janice said breathlessly. She was suddenly strangely aware that she had felt lonely since she took the chip, even though she had been promised she never needed to feel lonely again. The ability to link, she was certain, would put an end to her loneliness. Then she realized she didn't even know what her neural wall looked like. "Uh, I just remembered I've never even seen my wall. How will I know where I am? How will I know where to let you in?"

"Remember the emptying and focusing techniques you've been learning in meditation? Just start with that. If you still can't figure out where you are, you'll hear me knocking. Trust me, you'll know your wall when you come to it," Etherea explained. "Now, focus, Janice. Close your eyes, if it helps. Find your center, and then access the chip. When I knock and give you my name, all you have to do is let me in."

Janice closed her eyes and concentrated on controlling her breathing. Then, she focused all her efforts on accessing the chip. In an instant, she was in that inner world she was beginning to to understand. She had the wealth of humankind's knowledge at her fingertips. She looked around her, bombarded with all the different drop-down menus she could access. It was often overwhelming, but focusing was the key. As she did so, the drop-down menus vanished, and she was confronted with a vast plain, studded with a few memory blips she had learned to avoid. Although they had looked enticing when she first saw them, they led to depressing episodes in her past. Now that she understood what they were, she could avoid them altogether. Each time she centered and avoided them, they became easier to ignore, while the paths that had led her to them repeatedly during her life became overgrown with mental re-routings to new experiences. She was glad to see the old paths disappearing. She didn't need those parts of herself anymore.

Suddenly Janice paused in her musings. A knocking sound could be heard coming from somewhere in the distance. She moved toward the sound and could see a low, crumbling structure ahead, reminiscent of ancient ruins or something one might find in a war-ravaged country. Was this another memory blip she had not yet encountered in her wanderings? Janice hesitantly moved toward the structure, which stretched as far as her eyes could see to the left and right. As she came nearer, a figure became visible standing on the opposite side of the old, broken stones piled haphazardly on top of one another. The figure bent down and knocked on the pile of debris. "Janice," the figure called. "Janice, it's Etherea Daniels. I'm here to form the link."

Janice stopped short just inside the line of rubble. She had been told she would know her wall when she saw it. And the woman on the opposite side looked different than the woman she had met in the outer world. She was more attractive, maybe even a little taller. "Are you really Etherea Daniels? You don't look quite the same," Janice said cautiously.

Etherea laughed. "Well, in here, we project the appearance we have formed of ourselves," she explained.

"I thought you were supposed to meet me at my wall," Janice asked, confused.

Etherea glanced down at the crumbling stonework at her feet. "I did. It's just not much of a wall." She looked back up at Janice. "Are you going to let me in?"

"Oh! Of course. Come on in," Janice said.

Etherea paused, looking up and down the wall as if searching for a door, and then simply stepped over it. Once inside, she looked at Janice carefully. "Janice, you really should have a better opinion of yourself," she said with genuine concern. "You don't look at all like your self-projection."

"I don't?" Janice asked.

"Certainly not," Etherea said, glancing away from her as if she couldn't bear to gaze upon Janice for very long. "But let's get down to business, shall we? We're trying to figure out why everything looks gray to you now."

Janice nodded, and Etherea began accessing Janice's Perception Menu. Once there, she selected a submenu that covered color preferences. "Ahh. Here it is. You haven't selected a predominant color. That's simple enough to fix. Just pick a color, and your chip will project that onto the walls around you, just like your visor did. And remember, if you get tired of that color, you can always choose another one. Once you get good at linking, you can even choose to select your friends' color preferences for your own, so you can see the world through their eyes."

"But what I don't understand is, why did it go back to gray? I already chose a color. It didn't go back to gray until I woke up on the floor just a few minutes ago," Janice explained.

"Well, according to your settings, it's always been gray," Etherea stated.

"That's just not true. The real me may be stupid, but I know *that* much," Janice said, a little perturbed.

Etherea scratched the back of her neck. "Well, let me see here," she said, and after some focus, delved into Janice's programming. "Ah-hah! It appears that the physical difficulty you just underwent caused some of your perception preferences to reset to zero. That explains it."

"So almost having a heart attack reset some of my programming?" Janice asked.

"Apparently so. But it's easily fixed, as I said earlier. All you have to do now is choose what you want."

"Thank you, Etherea!" Janice said as she mentally reset her preferred color to blue.

"That's it. Now, if there's nothing else you need help with, I'll disconnect," Etherea said.

"Wait!" Janice said quickly, unwilling to be alone again just yet. "You, uh, said something about my perception of myself. What did you mean? Can you help me with that?"

Etherea glanced toward the other side of Janice's wall. She was on call, and this wasn't part of the job description in her protocol. "That's really more in the field of psychology. You may need to seek professional counseling for help with that."

"But I just want to know what's wrong with the way I project myself. You said I don't look at all like my projection. I'd like to know how to project the type of image you do. One that people aren't afraid to look at," Janice said pleadingly.

"Well, that really depends on how much you believe in yourself. Someone with a good self image will naturally project a more attractive one than someone who is struggling with their self-perception. When I first got the chip, I didn't have a very good projection, either. But after I learned to work with my programming and submitted to the protocol completely, I began to change, physically and emotionally. Now I'm the me I was always meant to be. If you learn to work with your programming instead of making excuses to deviate from it, in a few months, you'll be more and more your true self. Then you'll feel good enough to project a better image."

Janice's difficulty adapting wasn't news to the State. Although her performance at work had soared above her pre-chip levels, she was still not the poster child of biotech all the newly chipped were supposed to be. The fact that she lacked the bubbly, outgoing personality she had previous to implantation was not lost on her coworkers, and people were starting to talk. Fewer employees had signed up for the procedure since she had returned from orientation, and State liaisons didn't consider this to be coincidence.

"But I wasn't making excuses," Janice insisted. "Please, couldn't you just show me how to change my image in *here* so that I at least look good on the *inside?* Maybe people will come visit me more if I do."

"Janice, this was just a link for medical purposes. You really shouldn't engage in social linking until you've gotten the basics of chip operation under your belt," Etherea cautioned.

"I understand. But don't you think I should be ready when the time comes?"

Etherea sighed and attempted to hide her irritation. It was harder to conceal one's feelings when linked. "Self image *is* a very important part of mental health," Etherea finally said. "But as I said earlier, submitting to the chip is the way to happiness. If you don't feel you can wait for the better mental outlook that will come with the physical improvements you will eventually achieve with the Trimfit program, I can schedule an appointment for you with a chip-tech psychologist who can tweak your emotional programming."

Janice was about to say yes when a sudden realization hit her. "No, that's alright," she said instead. "I'm certain I just need to work harder, and a better self image will come."

"That's the spirit!" Etherea congratulated her. "Now, I'd better be going. Someone else may need our services soon."

"Thank you for coming to check on me," Janice said as Etherea stepped over the dilapidated wall, and then she was alone again. From the outside world, she could faintly hear the departing footsteps of the paramedic team as they descended the stairs. She turned around and faced her inner world. Janice hadn't felt so alone since before she had been chipped, but as miserable as she was, she was encouraged. The fact that she felt alone and sad and anxious was a good thing, because it meant her color preference wasn't the only thing that had been reset. And it meant there was hope she could be in control again.

She would have to be careful not to raise suspicion. If she was caught, there would be repercussions; and she was certain that with a few more tweaks of her programming, the real Janice might be lost forever, completely unconscious —or worse still—watching as her body was controlled by the new part of her neural network. She vividly recalled the chat she had with Ainsley Abbot, the new Employee Interrelations Specialist, on her first day back at work. She had made it clear that Janice needed to remember she was an example to others now. There could be no discussion with her coworkers of how she had changed her mind right before the procedure—in fact, her programming prevented it. She would meet the expectations set for her in her new protocol, or she would be altered in whatever way necessary to make her operation appear a success. It seemed the State was holding all the cards.

But now Janice had a few cards up *her* sleeve; and if she played it right, she figured she could be in control again without anyone being the wiser.

26

"Sᴀᴅɪᴇ, are you doing alright?" Kylie asked. Her daughter had been making a batch of sourdough bread, kneading and punching it with a vengeance for the last fifteen minutes.

"Fine," Sadie answered curtly and gave the dough another turn, crushing it into the breadboard with the heels of her hands.

"Well, you could've fooled me," Kiley said playfully but frowned as the girl continued her vigorous kneading. "If something's wrong, you know I'm always available to listen. You don't have to take it out on the bread!" she laughed.

"I said I'm *fine*," Sadie said rather loudly.

"Yeah Mamma, she *fine!*" piped up Sadie's sister, Denali, who had been standing on a stool beside her and watching the proceedings with great interest.

"What's going on in here?"

Sadie winced as her father stepped into the kitchen.

"Everything's fine, Seth," Kiley said, aware that forcing her daughter into a conversation would be counterproductive.

"So I heard," Seth said in a serious tone. Sadie could feel his eyes boring into the back of her head. "I'll not have you disrespecting your mother and being a bad example to your little sister. Change your attitude and choose the right path."

Sadie had always been compliant. Her brothers and sister were a different story. Each of them knew the sting of a switch, but Sadie usually chose the path of obedience. Even as a small child, she had never been spanked. A verbal reprimand had been enough to send her running to her room in tears.

"Yes, Daddy," Sadie answered calmly, but inside she was boiling.

Seth watched her for a while and then retreated back into his study, where he was working on a sermon for the following day.

"I know how ta pick a good switch, Deedee, if ya need me to," said Denali, who had learned that the thicker ones didn't sting as sharply.

"That's enough, Denali," Kiley said and ushered her youngest child off the stool and out of the room. "Go play with Yancy."

"Yancy workin' in da garden," Denali protested.

"Well, go help him."

"I wanna stay an' help Deedee."

"Go help Yancy, or you can pick out your own switch," Kiley said with raised eyebrows.

Denali stuck out her lips and raised her eyebrows back at her mamma but then grinned mischievously and turned to go.

Kiley went back to shelling peas. It wouldn't do to keep prying when Sadie wasn't in the mood to talk. There had been so much suspicion and division in their community since Garrison left. Everyone had been on edge. Individuals had been singled out for scrutiny, beginning with Genevieve and Selah and then Garrison's parents. Even Payton Hamby had been isolated for a time when the board was concerned his judgment had somehow been compromised. With Selah's recent departure, things had gotten even worse. Kiley feared the community's teens had born the brunt of the suspicion, and parental ties were strained as children began to be seen as potential threats to the community's safety.

But in the weeks following Zack's miraculous healing after he was mauled by a bull, there was a shifting in attitudes and the atmosphere of the valley. No one could deny the spiritual unity that was growing, replacing the suspicion that had hung over them like a suffocating shroud. Now, faith was blossoming in individuals and the church body as a whole. Even Seth noticed it, Kiley had decided, though he had not admitted as much.

Her husband was a complicated individual, committed to God and the protection of the valley's residents. When the board had overruled him and called an open meeting, it had wounded Seth deeply. He would have withdrawn from community life completely had it not been for Payton. The valley's acting pastor had led the meeting, revealing Genevieve's call to be a missionary and the true motive behind Selah's departure. News of it had stirred those present, causing sincere soul-searching among them all. But before the meeting's end, Seth had grasped Kiley's hand firmly and gotten up to leave, staring at each of his children to make certain they followed. "Brother Seth," Payton had called from the front of the room, "We value your input. As your family is the recent recipient of a miracle, would you care to offer God thanks and ask for His wisdom and guidance for us all?"

Seth had hesitated and responded with a short, stiff prayer. "Heavenly Father, You are so gracious to us. You have offered us protection from the outside world for generations, and even though some of us have acted rashly, you have granted us a miracle. Thank You, merciful God. And in Your great mercy, give us wisdom not to behave foolishly in the future. Guide us into the truth of what You would have us do in the days and years to come. Amen."

The room was silent for a minute, and then a few "Amens" were spoken from around the room as people looked up from bowed heads at Seth and at one another cautiously.

"Amen and amen," Brother Payton said warmly, choosing to ignore the insinuation of Seth's words. "Isn't it good to know we can look to God for guidance? He who has begun a good work in us will perform it until the day of Jesus Christ!"[92]

Seth grimaced and turned toward the door, his family close behind him. But Payton was not to be swayed in his efforts to win Seth over. He pushed through the crowd and caught up to him at the edge of the road. "I'm looking forward to your sermon this Sunday night," he said affably.

Seth stopped short and stared at Payton. "I don't expect I'll be preaching. The board went against my recommendations to hold this meeting. Our agendas differ, and those differences cannot be reconciled. We are parting ways."

Payton looked shocked. "But I thought you changed your mind about resigning. Has the board asked you to step down from your position as a senior elder?"

---

[92] See Philippians 1:6

"Well, no, but—"

"Then you are leaving your post, when we so desperately need men of mature faith such as yourself?" Payton asked. "You're a man of the Word, Brother Seth. Search the scriptures. Search your heart. Ask the Lord what He would have you to do in these changing times."

Seth surveyed Payton silently for a moment. "The Lord's messenger told our ancestors what to do. He told us if we would stay here, we would be safe. We could raise our children to know the Lord and resist the onslaught of sin's advancement in the outside world. But now our safety here has been compromised. Our future is threatened. First Garrison left, and now Selah. And you would have us believe it was all part of God's plan—that Gevevieve actually had a calling on her life to leave and be a missionary to the Old Country! It's only by the grace of God that we haven't been discovered and taken into custody already. God is withholding His wrath so that we have a chance to repent. But if you continue pursuing this reckless course of attempting to exonerate Miss Genevieve and Selah by your insistence that their ideas of leaving were the result of a divine calling, I pity you. The downfall of this community will be on your head," Seth said in a low voice.

"But Dad, what if they really were called by God to go?" Sadie began.

Seth whirled around. "Don't contradict me, young lady!" he said sternly.

Sadie ducked her head and went to stand beside her older brother, Zack, who cleared his throat tentatively. "But isn't she right, Dad? Didn't Jesus tell us to go into all the world and preach the gospel to everyone?" he asked sincerely, lifting his eyes to meet his father's startled gaze.

"I don't know what's gotten into you kids. I've taught you the right way, and now you think you can just ignore it because a few people have chosen to go their own way," Seth said in consternation.

"Did they go their own way, or were they just following the way of Christ? He's the one who said to go preach the gospel. Not Selah. Not Genevieve. Not Brother Payton. It was Jesus who gave us that command thousands of years ago. And we've been ignoring it, until now," Zack said, trying to balance respect for his father with the boldness he felt in his spirit.

The color rose in Seth's face as he clenched his jaw, looking at his family quietly. "Kiley," he finally said, "please take the children home. I will be there shortly."

Kiley gave her brood a knowing look and turned to lead the way, her stomach tied in knots. She knew Zack and Sadie were right in this instance. Why couldn't Seth see it? Hadn't he learned anything by seeing the miracle of healing? God wasn't mad at them. He wasn't withholding His blessings or His protection. If anything, the miracle seemed like a stamp of approval— like He was bringing them into a new season of growth and revelation. But she didn't want to contradict her husband in public. She would submit to him and allow the Holy Spirit to be her champion as she prayed for her husband's eyes to be opened.

Kiley remembered the verses Miss Genevieve had taught the girls in the community when they became teenagers: "Likewise you wives, be submissive to your husbands, so that some, though they do not obey the word, may be won without a word by the behavior of their wives, when they see your reverent and chaste behavior."[93] These verses were extremely unpopular with most of the girls. Kiley felt some men used this as an excuse to always get their way. Her friend, Joan, had hated this passage and had always quoted it through gritted teeth.

"I'm as smart as any boy, and I work a lot harder than most of them! Why should I have to submit?" she had complained to Miss Genevieve.

"My dear, you are probably *smarter* than most of them, and I don't doubt you work harder. But submitting is a sign of greatest strength," Miss Genevieve had said.

"How can *that* be? It looks like weakness to me—doing what someone else says when you might have a better idea about how to do things," Joan had argued.

Miss Genevieve leaned back in her rocking chair on the porch and looked at the faces of the young girls gathered there. They were all looking at her expectantly, for Janie was precocious enough to voice the question they had all kept

---

[93] 1 Peter 3:1&2, RSV

to themselves. "So you think if you are stronger and smarter than someone, you shouldn't allow yourself to be controlled by them. And anyone who *does* willingly submit to this kind of treatment isn't acting within their rights?"

"Even if they *aren't* stronger or smarter, I don't think it's fair to push them around," Joan said adamantly.

"Well, you're right. It isn't fair to push them around. 1 Peter 3:7 says a husband should live considerately with his wife, giving honor to her. There's even a warning in there that his prayers might be hindered if he doesn't treat her well.[94] A good marriage is a partnership. Husbands and wives should talk things over when making decisions. But in the end, even if she doesn't agree with him, the wife should submit to the husband's decision."[95] Genevieve paused and raised her index finger to make a point, "Unless, of course, that decision goes against the laws of God."

"I guess God must love men more than women. Or maybe He thinks they're better than women," Joan said, fuming.

"Because He asks women to submit to their husbands?" Genevieve queried.

Joan nodded with a glare, and Genevieve responded with a wry smile. "How do you think God feels about Jesus?"

Joan scowled at the obvious question. "Well, He loves Him! Jesus is His only begotten Son. Maybe it would've been different if Jesus had been a girl."

Some of the girls gasped, but Genevieve chuckled. "Would you all say that Jesus is smart?" she asked, looking around the circle of faces.

"Jesus is smarter than anyone! He's God, in human form! He knows everything!" Joan had sputtered.

"True," Genevieve affirmed. "Would you say that He is strong?"

"He stopped a storm just by speaking to it," said Jannica from her seat on the porch railing. She had been making a daisy chain during the conversation, and no one had thought she was listening.

"That sounds pretty strong to me," Miss Genevieve nodded. "So why did He submit to His Father in obedience and go to the cross? And why did He submit to the torture we humans put Him through?"

---

[94] See 1 Peter 3:7

[95] This scripture is not a license for spousal abuse. Women who are victims of abuse in a marriage need to carefully seek help, not stay and submit to the abuse.

The only sound for a while was the buzzing of the cicadas in the surrounding canopy of oaks.

"Because He loved His Father. He loved us." Kiley had finally said.

Genevieve had looked at her and smiled. "Exactly. Submission out of obedience and love, *especially* when the person submitting is strong and smart, is a sign of greatest strength. Which brings us to the next verses you are going to memorize: Ephesians 5:22-25. Now, the first part of this passage is about wives submitting to their husbands." Genevieve paused as a series of groans arose from the group. She held up her hand for silence. "But listen to the last part. 'Husbands, love your wives, even as Christ also loved the church, and gave Himself for it.'[96] If your husband loves you this much, he will be putting your well-being above his own. You won't be afraid to submit to someone like that."

"But what if he doesn't always make good decisions?" Kiley had asked worriedly.

"That's why I taught you the verses in 1 Peter, chapter 3. When you lovingly submit and pray about the situation instead of fighting with him about it, God will take care of things. He will either change your husband's mind, or will soften your heart and change *your* mind. Just think about it. Who would do a better job of changing someone's mind: you, or the Lord? And if your husband isn't following the Lord as he should, when he sees your kindness to him even when he makes mistakes, this will be a witness to him of the love of Christ within you."

Kiley had practiced what the Bible said about submission, even though it wasn't always easy. But on this occasion, it seemed to her that Seth was not obeying the Word of God, which clearly stated they should try to reach the lost. *"Lord, please give Payton the words to say to Seth,"* she prayed silently as the family made their way home. *"And please help him not to be too hard on Zack and Sadie."*

When Seth came home a while later, nothing more was said about the incident at the community hall, and Kiley wondered if he had a change of heart. In the days that followed, however, Seth's sermons proved otherwise. When

---

[96] Ephesians 5:25, KJV

Payton's Sunday morning message spoke of the missionary journeys of Paul, Seth's message that evening dealt with the the curses of disobedience, found in Deuteronomy 28. When Payton exhorted the parishioners to "be filled with the spirit," as taught in Ephesians 5:18, Seth preached out of 1 Corinthians 14, discouraging the congregation from speaking in tongues, since they couldn't be certain anyone had the gift of interpretation. Although he was using scriptures to try to support his position, his messages were rooted in fear and anger. Besides, Kiley remembered that Miss Genevieve would sometimes speak in tongues, and someone else would give an interpretation. No one had operated in these gifts since Miss Genevieve passed away, but Kiley was convinced that if people were open to hearing from the Holy Spirit and were obedient, He would begin using them in these giftings again. She wondered if Seth even realized he was bending the scriptures' meaning to suit his own purposes. She prayed more fervently for him, keeping her opinions to herself, but reminding God of His promise to her in 1 Peter. Surely if she trusted the Lord and interceded for Seth while honoring him as his wife, God would fulfill the promise in His Word and open Seth's eyes.

Then one day as she was praying, one of the ten commandments popped into her mind: "Thou shalt have no other gods before Me."[97] Kiley suddenly realized she had been holding back in her relationship with the Lord because she was afraid of going against her husband's wishes. Surely she could seek the Lord and put Him first in her life while still honoring her husband. To do otherwise was to put Seth in God's place on the throne of her heart. "God, I want to honor You above all others. Help me to honor my husband, even though I don't agree with him," she prayed. "And if You want to fill me with Your Holy Spirit, I am ready and willing. Let me be Your vessel."

It seemed a burden had been lifted off her shoulders. From that day on, she began earnestly seeking what the Lord might have her do as her community began moving out from under the shadow of fear. And although Seth didn't particularly like it when she went to the women's meetings at the community building, he didn't forbid her from doing it. Kiley's soul yearned for more of God, and she clung to every scrap of Bible teaching like a lifeline.

---

[97] Exodus 20:3, KJV

Her breakthrough came when Addy Hamby led the meeting. Addy had never spoken in public that Kiley could remember. She was a gentle, softspoken woman, given to caring for others in need, but shying away from attention. On this particular night, however, Addy was the speaker. She walked to the front of the room with a page of notes and a Bible and asked everyone to turn to Philippians chapter 2. Addy started reading in verse one. "So if there is any encouragement in Christ, any incentive of love, any participation in the Spirit, any affection and sympathy, complete my joy by being of the same mind, having the same love, being in full accord and of one mind. Do nothing from selfishness or conceit, but in humility count others better than yourselves. Let each of you look not only to his own interests, but also to the interests of others."[98]

Kiley's eyes brimmed with tears. She wished desperately that her husband would be in unity with their pastor and the church body—would be in "full accord" with them.

Addy continued. "Have this mind among yourselves, which you have in Christ Jesus, Who, though He was in the form of God, did not count equality with God a thing to be grasped, but emptied Himself, taking the form of a servant, being born in the likeness of men. And being found in human form He humbled himself and became obedient unto death, even death on a cross."[99] Addy paused and looked up from her Bible. "Jesus left everything, laying aside His omnipotence and all the glory of heaven, submitting His will to the Father and to the treatment He received at the cross."

Kiley remembered the front porch conversation with Genevieve. It was difficult for her to submit to Seth, but surely if Jesus could go to the cross, she could continue to submit in love. But submission to one's husband was not Addy's point, she discovered, as the woman closed her Bible and looked around the room.

"For generations we have lived under God's protective hand in this little valley, cloistered away from the troubles of the outside world. One of our elders, Miss Genevieve, had a calling on her life which she put aside because she wasn't certain how to go forward with it. And I'm sure she was also uneasy about

---

[98] Philippians 2:1-4, RSV
[99] Philippians 2:5-8, RSV

putting us all in danger. But doing God's will isn't always the safe thing to do. It cost Jesus His life. And Jesus told us that in this world we would have tribulation, but to be of good cheer, because He has overcome the world."[100] She looked each woman in the eye for a moment. "I know with all my heart that Selah left for the right reasons. She was obedient to the truth of the gospel and has taken that truth to the Old Country. She gave up her safety, her home, and her family to do this—what most of us wouldn't dream of doing—to be obedient to the call. Now, we have a choice. We can support her in prayer, or we can live in fear and be angry with her for what she did." There was silence in the room as Addy fixed each one of them with her gaze. "It's because of Selah seeking God that I received the baptism of the Holy Spirit," Addy continued. "I don't know why our community hasn't been operating in the gifts of the Spirit, but I think it's time we started seeking God about this again. After all, it was through the gifts of the Spirit that our ancestors were warned to leave the State in the first place. And I think that at the time, this was exactly what we were meant to do. God was preserving a remnant of people. He was also protecting copies of His Word," she said, holding up her Bible to illustrate her point. "But was He doing this because He wanted us to stay here forever, hoarding the riches of His grace to ourselves? *No!*" Addy nearly shouted, slamming her Bible down on the pulpit. Several women on the front row jumped. A few nervous snickers were heard, but all fell quiet under Addy's piercing gaze. "He was doing this so that those people in the State who have been robbed of the Truth for so long would someday have an opportunity to see the Light again. He was preserving a remnant so He could send it out again!"

The women sat in stunned silence. Addy's conclusion seemed so obvious. Why had no one thought of it before? Jannica Breedon raised her hand for permission to speak. "Well, if that's true, what should we do about it now?" she asked.

"Someone already has done something about it," Joan interjected, "whether we like it or not."

"And she's just a child—one of our daughters," Megan Scoffield said, looking sympathetically at Asha, who was sitting beside her.

---

[100] See John 16:33

Suddenly, all eyes turned to Asha, who swallowed and held her head high. "I stand behind my daughter and her decision. What's more, I wish I had the courage to do it, myself!"

Several gasps were heard from around the room, but Megan clasped Asha's hand and squeezed it. "So do I," she said, and looked at Addy, who nodded for her to continue. "Paul has been wondering about it for years—whether it was safe to go back and what is the condition of the churches that were left behind. And then Garrison left. We almost thought about going after him, but we knew the board wouldn't approve, and we could be placing the community in even greater danger. But now, Selah's gone, too. And I keep wondering—shouldn't somebody go help her? Are we leaving this dangerous mission to our children? And even if my son may not have left for the same reasons, shouldn't I go and find him? What would you do, if it was your son or daughter who had left?"

A chorus of excited mutterings could be heard around the room, and finally, Joan spoke up. "I think we all know what we would do," she said. "As mothers, our hearts are tied to our children. We would rather die than see them come to harm, even if the harm is something they may have brought on themselves. I know if my Janie were out there…." She stopped and bit her lip as emotion overwhelmed her, and she looked carefully at Megan and Asha before continuing. "I'm a member of the board. I think you all know where I stood on this matter before. But the scriptures clearly tell us to examine ourselves.[101] And the events of the past month have led to some serious soul-searching on my part. Asha…Megan, I wouldn't blame you one bit if you left to go looking for your kids. In fact, I'm not certain some us shouldn't volunteer to go with you!"

More excited mutterings erupted around the room. Addy stood quietly behind the pulpit until the chattering stopped and people became aware that she was waiting for their attention. "Ladies, I think that as a community, we have misunderstood our purpose and the reason God brought our grandparents out of the Old Country and into this protected valley. I would like to challenge you to begin seeking the Lord as to how He would have us to proceed. Pray for your husbands, that they would receive wisdom and direction. Pray for your families. And pray for lost souls—people who may never have heard about Jesus—

---

[101] See 1 Corinthians 11:28 and Psalm 139:23-24

people who may be just a little ways from here, as the crow flies. What if God really did guide our ancestors to leave so that their children could be missionaries? And what's more, what have we done with the time of seclusion we've had? Have we drifted away, forgetting our roots? Has the fire of the Holy Ghost been smothered under the bushel basket of our fear? I can see that some of you say you're ready to go and reach out to the lost, but are you *really* ready? I don't know that we are *all* called to leave this place. I don't doubt that a few of us are. But how many of us are spiritually ready? How many of us are close enough to God that we can hear the Spirit's call? Ladies, before we reach out to the world around us, we've got to make sure we're right with God, ourselves! We need what the book of Titus referred to as the washing of regeneration and the renewing of the Holy Ghost[102] before we set out and try to save others. Let's seek the Lord. All of you who want to join me in this effort of seeking God, I'd like to ask you to come forward."

Without a moment of hesitation, Asha and Megan made their way to the front. Joan Ferrel followed, and then a steady stream of women came to the altars at the front of the room. Mrs. Cornwright snorted awake when someone bumped her as they scooted between her and the pew in front of her. She hastily got to her feet and came forward with everyone else. "Are we doing a craft?" she asked groggily.

"No, Sister Bella. We're going to go pray," Gracie Ferrel said crossly.

"Pay for what?"

"Pray! We're going to *pray*, Bella," Gracie said in a loud voice.

"Oh, good. I think I'll pray about the dream I just had. You know, I didn't even know I was asleep."

Gracie rolled her eyes. "Well, everyone else did."

"Gracie, that's not very nice," Jannica said under her breath.

"I could barely hear Addy over the snoring," Gracie retorted.

"Gracie, she might hear you!" Jannica reprimanded her friend.

"Not a chance," said Gracie, watching as the elderly woman toddled to the altar. "She's deaf as a post."

---

[102] See Titus 3:5

Jannica looked away, irritated at her friend. Just a few months ago, she would have joined right in with Gracie. But after Selah had stuck up for Genevieve when the two had been gossiping about her elderly friend, Jannica felt convicted in her heart. Selah had shown more love and maturity than she, and the girl was twenty some years her younger. She found an open spot at the altar, knelt down and began to pray. A few minutes later, she felt a hand on her shoulder, and Bella Cornwright was whispering loudly in her ear. "My dear, would you mind listening to this dream and telling me what you think? It's the strangest dream I've ever had, and I can't even concentrate on praying because I keep seeing it again and again in my mind." Jannica looked up at the wizened old face, aware that Gracie was watching with a satisfied smirk.

"Well, I can listen, but I don't know if I can help you with the meaning," she replied patiently. She could see Gracie's look of surprise out of the corner of her eyes, but turned her full attention on Mrs. Cornwright.

"Well, I was on the banks of this river or something. No, no, it wasn't exactly a river...." She stopped for a moment as she struggled to describe the scene. Jannica could see Gracie rolling her eyes, for the woman didn't realize she was speaking loudly enough so that everyone in the room could hear her. "It was a spring pool! That's what it was," she continued, her eyes staring into the distance. "I was standing on the banks of a spring pool. And there was this little boat. It was just big enough for one person, and I thought, 'Well, Bella, that's *your* boat! It was made just for you!' So I climbed into the boat and started floating out into the waters, closer to the source of the spring. And you know, that boat was so little, and it felt kind of tippy—like it might turn over at any moment. I really had to concentrate to keep my balance. And the current!" She paused, her eyes opening wide. "The current didn't look very fast, but when you got out into it, it was so strong! And what's more, I didn't even have a paddle! But even if I had, I don't know if it would have done any good!"

"Uh-huh," Jannica nodded politely, aware that most of the women in the room could not possibly concentrate on praying and were listening in on the conversation. She couldn't blame them. The sweet old woman was so loud, she was impossible to ignore.

"So here I am, swirling around the source of this spring where it bubbles up and all, and I can see that the current is taking me toward a gate, of sorts." She stopped and pantomimed the framework of a gate. "And the water is pouring through this gate. I can't see where it's going, but I'm afraid it's a waterfall, and I don't want to go down *that!* So when the boat gets close to the gate, I just step out of it and grab onto the fence railing around the pool."

"The spring pool had a fence around it?" Jannica asked.

"Yes, it did. And now I know why. It was a spring by a mill. And the gate was where the water left to travel down the channel that took it to the waterwheel."

By this time, the rest of the women had given up the pretense of praying and were watching Mrs. Cornwright grow more animated as she told her tale. "And then I was looking over the railing, but it wasn't around the spring pool anymore, and it wasn't by a mill. It was the railing in the loft of our cabin when I was a little girl. I used to fly paper airplanes off of that thing." She smiled at the memory. "Anyway, I could see Mama and Daddy down there below. Mama was reading her Bible, and Daddy was praying. While I was up there in the loft, I was thinking about all the walks I took by myself out in the woods. I used to like to talk to God a lot when I was a little girl. I would ask Him about how He came up with the ideas for all the things He made—like trees and flowers and chipmunks and butterflies." She stopped again and looked Jannica in the eye. "You know, I don't talk to God like that anymore. We used to have a lot of *fun* together. At least, *I* had fun. But for some reason, I really think maybe God enjoyed it, too. Now all I do is ask for things, and everything has to be so serious all the time."

Jannica sighed and waited patiently for Bella to get back to the point of her story.

"Anyway, after I think about walking around in the woods and spending time with the Lord, I notice that the area below the loft isn't the family room anymore. I can't really tell what it is because it's kind of dark. But there's a fire down there coming from a blacksmith forge. Someone is working on something, and I decide to go down and see what they're working on. So I go down the stairs, and this old blacksmith is hunched over the forge. He has been working there so long that he is all bent over. When he sees me there, he turns and looks at me, and I notice—*my goodness, he only has one eye!* The other one is missing, but with the eye he has left, he stares at me real hard, and his eye is opened really wide, and his face is all dirty and sooty from the fire. He looks kind of scary, but I'm not scared at all. Then he smiles at me and takes off his leather apron and puts down his tools and motions to me to start working at the forge. So I go up to the forge, and he leaves. And I realize I have no idea how to do this kind of work. I pick up the tongs and try to grab what he had been working on, but I'm so clumsy at it, I really make a mess of things. I can't seem to hold onto the hot metal with the tongs, and I'm having trouble getting it to do what I want it to do. I try to hammer on it a few times, but I'm just not very good at it at all. Then I find myself at the top of the balcony again, with my back turned to the workshop below. I'm distracted by something else—you know, dear, I don't even remember what I was looking at—when all of the sudden, someone taps me on the shoulder from behind. I turn around, and there's another worker from the forge. He's all dirty and sweaty, but he smiles at me, and he holds out this piece of metal with the tongs. It's the project I was working on, and I can see it's supposed to be a sword, but it's unfinished. He holds it out to me as if to remind me that I need to finish it. So I pick it up with the tongs and start hammering. And that's the end of the dream."

"That's the end?" Jannica asked.

"Yeah, that's the end of it," Mrs. Cornwright said. "Now, isn't that an interesting dream?"

"But you didn't finish the sword?" Jannica asked.

"No, but I was hammering on it," Mrs. Cornwright said defensively. "Do you think it means something?"

"It means the beans you ate for lunch are fighting with the sauerkraut you had for supper," Gracie said with a dismissive laugh. She looked around the room to see if anyone else found her comment entertaining.

"It does mean something," Kiley said suddenly, her heart pounding, for the meaning of the dream had unfolded to her as clearly as if she were reading the words of an illustrated storybook. "The dream isn't just for you. It's for all of us. The boat is some new work God has asked us to step into. Each of us has something designed specifically for us to do. That was why Sister Bella felt like the boat was made just for her. When God created us, He had this particular destiny in mind. Stepping out in faith might be scary. Getting closer to the spring —or the purpose for our lives—might be scary. The current can get strong, and suddenly we realize we really have little control over our situation. But the good thing is, God is the One in control. He is the underlying current in our lives, and He won't steer us wrong. He will guide us to the work we're supposed to do. We don't need to be afraid to take the plunge—that's the part when the water was about to go over the waterwheel—because He's directing us toward the work we were designed to do. He is the power behind it, and He will use us to perform this work, if we will trust Him. Sister Bella, when you were looking out over the balcony at your parents, God was trying to tell you and all of us once again that He has prepared us for this destiny through our heritage of faith. And when you were remembering your time talking with Him as a child, I think He wants us to remember that in our personal lives, when we began to seek Him with childlike faith and trust, He will be there and we will actually enjoy what He has designed us to do. After all, He designed it with each of us in mind, and He created us with a specific calling in mind. The blacksmith represents the people who have already done their part working for God's kingdom. He only had one eye because that represented singleness of vision—the fact that he was focused on his task. The work of the people gone before us is past, and now it's *our* turn. *We* are the ones who have to finish the sword. We have the job of presenting the sword of the Spirit—*the Word of God*—to the world. Some people may not understand us or may even think we're a scary bunch of people. But we can't let that bother us or keep us from doing our work. I believe this dream is not only talking about the specific work each of us has, but the work of our community as a whole. We each have a part to play, just like the old blacksmith. But he could not finish the project by himself, in his lifetime. We, along with our relatives who came here to begin with, all work together to make it happen, and God is the power behind it all." Kiley stopped talking, her eyes wide in surprise. She had never interpreted a dream before, but she knew this was what it meant. Her heart stopped pounding, and the feeling of God's peace and presence settled over her. The women around the room looked at her in astonishment. Kiley was timid by nature. She didn't often speak forcefully, and her words had come out with such certainty and precision that no one even thought of debating the matter.

"Well, I declare!" Mrs. Cornwright exclaimed.

"That interpretation bears witness with my spirit, Sister Kiley," Addy said, staring at her thoughtfully.

"Mine, too," said Asha softly. Several other women nodded in affirmation.

Jannica, who seemed to be studying Asha even before she spoke, suddenly got up from her place at the altar and went over to her, looking at her searchingly. "Asha, will you please forgive me for the way I behaved toward Selah and your family? I feel like I turned my back on you all because I was scared and angry. I'm sorry. I can see that I was wrong."

Asha's mouth opened slightly in surprise before she could muster a reply. "Oh! Of course," she answered.

Joan Ferrel was the next person in line. "Asha and Megan, I want to offer my sincere apologies for the role I played in this whole thing. I know some of the things I said led to Miss Genevieve being ostracized, and I know your families have probably felt like you were walking on thin ice around here. I can't tell Miss Genevieve I'm sorry. But I can tell you. I hope you can forgive me, too."

Megan grabbed Joan in a bear hug, and the two began to weep. "Of course, I forgive you, Joan!" Megan said.

"And I do, too," Asha said.

Joan looked over at her and reached out her hand tentatively. "I know I caused you such grief, actually preparing a holding cell for your little girl!" she said.

Asha ignored her hand and reached out to embrace her. "All is forgiven, Sis," she said softly, the tears rolling down her cheeks.

One after the other, individuals came forward to voice their apologies to the two women who had felt shunned by their community. The convicting power of the Holy Spirit had fallen on the group, and the result was a powerful time of confession and forgiveness. Finally, only Gracie remained. She stood apart from the rest of the group, her eyes filled with tears, shaking her head in shame. "I'm so sorry," she said over and over. "I know I'm a gossip. I know I hurt you —and you too, Addy!" she sobbed and buried her face in her hands. Asha,

Megan and Addy quickly closed the distance between them and encircled her in a group hug.

"We forgive you, Gracie. And so does the Lord!" Addy said joyously.

"I feel so much love in this room," Kiley said in awe. "I could just burst!"

"That's the Holy Spirit," Addy said, and lifted her hands. She closed her eyes and began to sing a worship chorus. After a few words, the rest of the room joined her. Kiley had never felt such peace and happiness. The stress of the tension at home melted away, and she was able to focus on the Lord. After a few minutes, she felt a hand rest on her forehead, and Addy began to pray over her. "Lord, please give Kiley the desire of her heart. She longs to be close to You. Help her to sense Your presence in a mighty way. Your Word says, 'You will seek Me and find Me; when you seek Me with all your heart.' [103]" When Kiley heard these words, she was overwhelmed. The Lord had heard all her prayers about wanting to be close to Him. As she began to thank Him, she began to speak in another language. Some of the women who were near her stopped singing as they realized what was happening and turned to each other, chattering excitedly.

Mrs. Cornwright toddled over closer to discover what all the fuss was about. "Will you look at that!" she exclaimed. "This is the real deal! Sister Addy, can you lay hands on me too? I need more of God."

Addy grinned from ear to ear and began to pray for the old saint. By the end of the evening, several women had received the baptism of the Holy Spirit. No one wanted to leave because the presence of the Lord was so precious in the room. Kiley looked around at all the faces, glowing with happiness and wet with tears. Revival had started, whether her husband was ready or not.

---

[103] Jeremiah 29:13b, RSV

27

Bryson Wilcox and Etherea Daniels pulled out of the hospital parking lot with lights on and sirens blaring. "So what did dispatch say?" Bryson asked. "I don't want to access while I'm driving. I know the chip can drive for me. I'm just not comfortable letting it do that yet."

"Kind of like you hardly ever let *me* drive?"

"I let you drive," Bryson said as he slowed momentarily at a stoplight to make certain other drivers were yielding.

"Yeah, one day last week. And you coached me the whole time."

"Well, you need it. I thought *we* were going to need an ambulance by the time we got there—if we got there at all."

"What's wrong with the way I drive?"

"Let's just say sometimes I'm surprised your chip doesn't take over for you. And sometimes I wish it would. Can you just tell me what kind of injury we're going to be dealing with? You never know, at a factory." He glanced at Etherea when she didn't respond and then realized she was accessing.

"It's someone who's been chipped," Etherea finally said. "In fact, we responded to the same citizen last week. Janice Druthers. The woman who almost had a heart attack on the flight of stairs. Remember?"

"Oh yeah. She was trying to blame it on the chip. Well, what's she done this time?" Bryson asked as he took a sharp turn.

"She hasn't lost any blood, so I guess she hasn't fallen into an auger or something of that nature. Her body temperature is extremely low, though."

"Is anyone from the factory going to meet us?" Bryson asked as they pulled into the SynthaMeat entrance.

"I'm not even sure they realize there's a problem," Etherea said as a guard waved them down at the station by the gate.

"We didn't send for an ambulance," he stated, looking at the van suspiciously.

"Well, someone did. The call was made remotely—by chip," Etherea explained.

"Is it Janice Druthers?" the guard asked worriedly. "She hasn't been the same since she got the chip. I mean, she's smart now. But she used to always say hello and laugh at my jokes. Now, she just walks around like a zombie. Is she having some sort of trouble with her implant?"

"We can't discuss who it is, but someone *is* in trouble; and if you don't let us in, we won't be able to help her," Etherea said, flinching as she realized she had just revealed the gender of the patient.

"It *is* Janice, isn't it? Well, hurry up!" the guard said, raising the gate and waving them through.

"What an idiot. I should report him for technology discrimination," Etherea muttered as they sped to the main building.

"I'm not certain he went so far as to discriminate," Bryson remarked.

"It could be argued that he did. The time he cost us could mean her life. If he was chipped, he would've instantly known we were telling the truth by a quick observation of our biological indicators or just by accessing the system to see a call had been made. Maybe I should recommend him for reconditioning. In the very least, if we got him fired, he could be replaced with someone who was already implanted."

"You don't always play nice, Etherea."

"No, but I play for the greater good. Bigots like him belong with the Discards."

Bryson shook his head. "I guess pointing out the bigotry of that statement would be pointless."

"You can be snooty with your ethics if you want to, but you know I'm right. Get down off the soap box and let's just do our job. We know Janice isn't a model citizen. But she has the chip, and she's in trouble—and depending on the circumstances, that could look bad for the Chip Implantation Drive," Etherea said as she hopped out of the van. "Her locator beacon is broadcasting from somewhere on the main floor. Let's go."

At the building entrance, the two flashed the palm scanner, which was programmed to open for emergency personnel. When they rolled the cot onto the factory floor, they were met by Tommy Telquat.

"What's going on?" he demanded.

"We received a remote call from someone's chip. They're in trouble, and they're transmitting from that direction," Etherea explained, pointing across the plant through the maze of assembly lines.

"I'm the floor supervisor, and I haven't received reports of any accidents or disruptions today. I'm not aware of anyone becoming ill or collapsing on the line," Telquat said, confused.

"Well, as I said, we got the call. Can you help us find them as quickly as possible?" Etherea asked.

"Certainly. Follow me," Telquat said. "If I only had the chip, I would have probably known about it. I could have met you at the entrance. But I'm still on the waiting list for Level 2," he said apologetically as he led them around a conveyer belt that was plopping fully completed packages of ground SynthaBeef into a hopper.

After following Telquat through several junctions of the line, searching for signs of an accident as they went, the group came to the other side of the floor. "That way," Etherea said, pointing to the right. She took the lead and quickened the pace. After going about forty feet, she stopped. "She's on the other side of this wall. What's the quickest way there?"

"This way," Telquat said, turning back the way they had come. After a few minutes, the group arrived at a large bay door. "This is the door to our freezer section."

"That would explain her core temperature," Etherea remarked. "Open it."

"It's opened by weight sensors on either side. We're not heavy enough to register," he explained, and pulled his visor down. "I need a forklift at the freezer immediately," he announced over the factory communications system.

"We need to hurry," Etherea said when a few minutes had gone by.

"Where's that forklift?" Telquat barked, and waited as he listened to a response. His face reddened. "The operators are all on the other side of the plant, in C Building. We'll have to go to the pedestrian entrance on the south side of the floor if we want to get in. It could be fifteen minutes before they can make it over here," he said and took off at a run down the corridor with Bryson and Etherea close behind. Finally, they reached the door. Telquat jerked it open, ushering in the paramedics.

"Dang, it's cold in here," Bryson said as they rushed through isles of wrapped pallets.

"That's kind of the point of a freezer," Etherea quipped.

"People aren't usually in here without insulated coveralls, and they're usually driving a forklift. But a driver should be here to open the bay door in a few more minutes, so we shouldn't be in here very long," Telquat explained.

"There she is," Etherea said. At the end of a row near the wall, they could see a figure hunched into a ball, leaning against a pallet of SynthaFish.

"Who is it?" Telquat panted, coming to a stop behind them.

"Janice Druthers," Bryson said as Etherea checked her vitals.

"Is she…?" Telquat asked, his voice trailing off.

"She's just unconscious, but we need to get her out of this cold," Etherea said while Bryson lowered the cot.

"Where is that forklift? We could get her out much sooner if they would just open that door," Telquat said anxiously. As if in answer, the bay door suddenly opened. Telquat hurried over to explain the situation to the forklift driver. He was back a few minutes later as they began wheeling Janice out.

"What was she doing in there?" Telquat wondered aloud as they stepped out of the freezer.

"Is there an easier way out of here?" Bryson asked, looking back the way they had come through the factory production floor.

"Oh, of course! This way is shorter," Telquat said. "She's going to be alright, isn't she?" "I think so," Etherea replied, "but if her chip hadn't called us, it could have been a different story."

Telquat shook his head as they made their way to the exit. "If only I had the chip, this whole thing could have been prevented. As a supervisor, I would have been notified of the situation and could have reached her sooner. But I'm still waiting. There are other people in line in front of me." He paused for a moment, pretending to be struck with a sudden epiphany. "I was just thinking, if you could somehow get word of this incident to your supervisors, I might be moved forward on the list. That way, nothing like this would ever happen again."

"I'll see what I can do," Etherea said and then suddenly looked him in the eye. "Your security guard could certainly benefit from the chip. He didn't believe us at first. We didn't think he was going to let us in. And he spoke of the chip in a negative light," she said with an accusatorial tone.

"I'll see to it that he's recommended for reconditioning therapy," Telquat said officiously. When they neared the exit, he hurried ahead to flash the scanner for them. "Oh!" he exclaimed, as the door opened to reveal a striking woman clad in an exquisitely tailored business suit. "Specialist Abbot! I wasn't expecting you today. We have somewhat of an emergency on our hands," he began.

"I know all about it," Ainsley Abbot said brusquely, putting a hand on the cot and directing her gaze to the EMTs. "Take this patient to the address I just sent you," she said in a commanding tone.

"But she needs immediate medical attention," Bryson interjected.

"If you'll access the address I sent, you'll realize it's nothing we can't handle at our facility," Ainsley said firmly.

Etherea and Bryson stood momentarily transfixed as they accessed their chips. Milliseconds later, they were moving the cot into the van. "We'll be there as soon as possible," Bryson said.

Ainsely turned to Telquat, who was looking back and forth from one person to another, trying to grasp what was happening. "Not one word of this goes anywhere," she said.

"Not a word," he promised, and then put his hand to his mouth worriedly. "The forklift operator knows," he added.

"Does he have the chip?" Ainsley asked.

"Why, yes, he does," Telquat answered.

"Get him over here."

Telquat quickly contacted the driver, who was headed back to the other building. "You know, this whole incident could have been handled more efficiently if I wasn't still waiting for the chip," Telquat said remorsefully as they waited for the driver to arrive. "I understand that your people are working hard to roll out the Level 2 version, but as you can see, some delays can result in near tragedies."

Ainsley's eyes darkened. "We'll make certain you receive what you need," she said with a tight-lipped smile.

"Thank you," Telquat said gratefully. "I just feel woefully unprepared at moments like this. I know the chip could make all the difference."

"That it will," Ainsley said softly as she watched a man in a gray driver uniform sauntering down the hall.

"Step it up, Matheson," Telquat snapped.

"I'm coming. But if we're late getting out the 220 pallet Unimart order because of this, it's not *my* fault," he said. "Say, I guess Janice left a forklift back there in the freezer. Looks like she had just stacked a partial pallet in the odds and ends aisle. There's only one big box on it. P.A. never sets foot in the Big Freeze. What the heck was she doing?"

"I don't know. But that's none of your concern," Telquat snapped.

"Well, it kind of is, because she took the key out of the forklift. I had to grab the key out of mine to get it out of there." He stopped for a moment and looked Ainsley up and down appreciatively. "He*llo*, Specialist Abbot. What can I do for *you* today?"

"Ahh. Matheson. *Bradley* Matheson, isn't it?" Ainsley said with a flirtatious smile. "Would you be a dear and grab that partial pallet for us?"

"I'd be delighted," Matheson replied, his eyes glancing over her figure again before he turned to comply.

Telquat glared at Matheson before the two began following him down the wide hall. "There's a freezer in the P.A. Lab, so unless they ran out of storage space, there's no reason she should have been in our freezer section," he prattled on to Ainsley. "But I can't imagine them running out of room. All they use it for is storing the protein samples they're testing."

They reached the bay door, and Matheson drove one of the forklifts back inside to retrieve the box. "Protein Analysis doesn't start their shift until an hour from now. Janice shouldn't even be at work yet. None of it makes any sense," Telquat said.

"Don't worry Tommy. We'll get to the bottom of this," Ainsley said with a sigh. Ten minutes later, Matheson was still inside the freezer.

"What's taking him so long?" Telquat said impatiently.

Suddenly, they could hear the sound of the forklift approaching. Matheson appeared and deposited the pallet with its single box on the floor in the corridor. As he hopped out of the forklift, he was brandishing a key. "Well, I don't know why she was in here, or why she took the key out of the lift, but I think I figured out why she nearly froze to death," he said with a grim smile. "The key had fallen down one of the drains in the floor. I just happened to see it when I was driving over the drain where she had parked the lift."

"Well, how did you get it out?" Telquat asked.

"I took the drain off with a screwdriver," he said, patting his tool belt. "If she had some tools with her and had seen where she dropped it, she could've gotten the key and driven right out, instead of trying to make it back to the pedestrian door on foot. Janice isn't in the best of shape. And she has really short legs."

Ainsley inspected the box, which was marked with an appropriate label: *Protein Analysis: Protein Samples.* "Thank you, Bradley," she said after a moment. "Would you mind terribly if I asked you to take this box and put it in my vehicle? You'd have to lift it off the pallet and put it in my van by hand. Do you think you could do that?"

Bradley gave the box an experimental nudge. "Definitely. That box is too heavy for Janice to tote very far, but I can manage it." To prove his manhood, he picked up the box and set it on his shoulder.

Ainsley gave him a sideways smile. "Are you sure you don't mind? You can always drive it down there."

"It's no trouble," Matheson said, and took off walking down the corridor.

"Thank you, Bradley," Ainsley said when the box was safely inside her van.

"Well if that's all, I really need to go help finish up that order," said Matheson, turning to go back inside.

"There's just one more thing," Ainsley said. "I need to perform a routine update on your hardware."

The driver raised an eyebrow. "My chip isn't due for any updates. And I always have those done at the facility."

"Well, today the facility is coming to you," Ainsley said as she sidled up to Matheson, holding him captive with her long-lashed eyes.

"That's mighty neighborly of you…" Matheson began and then froze as Ainsley suddenly inserted a metal device into his port.

Telquat watched, transfixed, as Ainsley kept her hand on the back of Matheson's neck, seeming to steady his rigid form. In a few seconds Matheson's eyelids fluttered, and Ainsley pulled the device out of the port. "Bradley! How good to see you," Ainsley said with a smirk, slipping the device into her pocket.

Matheson wobbled sideways and looked confusedly from Ainsley to Telquat. "What am I doing here?" he asked. "I was just over in C Building helping load the Unimart order."

"Your chip needed a routine update," Ainsley said. "If you'll access the records, you'll see you neglected to keep your last appointment."

Matheson was quiet for a moment, his eyes staring off into the distance. "So I *did*," he said in surprise. "I'm sorry if I caused you any inconvenience," he added, grinning at Ainsley's close proximity.

Ainsley backed up to stand by Telquat. "Not at all. It's our pleasure to serve the citizens of the State. But next time, don't skip your appointment."

"I won't. Especially not if it means I can see *you* again," he said with a lascivious smile.

"Well, go finish helping with the order," Telquat said sharply, waving his hand in a dismissive gesture. He turned to Ainsley as the driver walked away. "That was remarkable! Is the ability to erase and alter memory available to Level 2?"

"Don't worry, Tommy. You'll be taken care of," Ainsley said, smiling vaguely. "And now, I wonder if you could get me to the Protein Analysis Lab. It's important we get there before their shift starts."

"Of course. Anything I can do to help," Telquat said obsequiously.

"Oh, Tommy, you're always incredibly helpful," Ainsley said, flashing him a smile. Telquat cleared his throat and ran a finger under his tight collar. "I'm honored to be of service," he said and led the way to the lab by the most direct route.

"Where's their freezer?" Ainsley asked when they had reached the lab.

"Right over here," said Telquat, going to a stainless-steel box on the counter and opening the door. "My goodness! It's full to capacity!"

Ainsley's eyes narrowed as she went to a nearby computer terminal and began accessing the previous day's data log. Moments later she returned to the mini freezer and began removing several racks of samples.

"What are you looking for?" Telquat asked.

"Tommy, would you be a pal and grab something to carry these in?" Ainsley asked, ignoring his question.

"Okay," he said compliantly, leaving and returning momentarily with a plastic storage tub. "But I still don't understand what you're doing."

"I'm just removing all the extra samples Janice made. It wouldn't do to arouse suspicion," Ainsley explained.

"No, indeed," Telquat agreed. "Extra samples?"

Ainsley chose to ignore his question once again. "And now, if you'll accompany me to the facility, I have a special project for you," she said with a seductive smile.

"Well, uh, I would love to, but I can't neglect my duties here," Telquat hesitated.

"Oh, don't worry about that. I just notified someone to send a replacement from the facility to cover for you. It's all taken care of. I really need your help with this. You wouldn't disappoint me, would you?" she asked, handing him the tub.

"Oh, most certainly not," Telquat said as a wave of libido swept over him.

"Then, off we go!" Ainsley smiled and led the way with Telquat following, his chest swelled out with pride.

28

JANICE looked around the dismal plain of her neural network. Even though it was chaotic, retreating within her mind was preferable to waiting for the more unpleasant symptoms of hypothermia to take effect. Maybe she would even be able to watch her system reset from here. Even better, perhaps she could have some influence on which preferences were set back to default.

It had taken some time to decide how to carry out her plan, but Janice had finally come up with a way to achieve a state of near death without actually passing over its threshold. The trick was how to proceed without revealing intentionality or rendering permanent damage.

Obvious methods such as an "accidental" overdose of medication might destroy the original part of her brain, but leave the chip and its growing network of biotech intact, so that was out of the question. She considered cruder methods—falling on a pair of scissors, for example—but was certain the chip would somehow prevent it by taking over and throwing the scissors to the side at the last minute. Besides, Janice was squeamish. The idea of pain and blood left her feeling faint. "Tripping" in front of a subway train was even more horrifying, and would probably result in more than a *near* death experience. She had decided the subway idea could work for plan B, for if she couldn't figure out how to be in control of her own life, Janice was convinced that ending her physical existence and coalescing with the Source was a better alternative than being a slave in her own body.

Suicide wasn't discouraged in the State as long as it was conducted under the direction of the proper medical authorities. Unless you were chipped, of course. In that instance, it wasn't an option, because the desire to end one's life after taking the chip wasn't much of a testimonial of its benefits.

Janice wished there were someone she could talk to about her dilemma, but any discussion of the subject would surely be stored in her new memory, giving clues to the authorities that she was intending to bring herself to the brink of death. There didn't seem to be any foolproof way to execute a plan—until one day, when she was retrieving a tray of protein samples from the little freezer in the Protein Analysis Lab. The tray was so cold it hurt her fingers. *"I'm glad I don't have to transport product to the walk-in freezer anymore,"* she thought. It was viciously cold in there. She had always been afraid the sensors for the forklift door might stop working. If her visor stopped working at the same time, she would be trapped inside.

Then the idea struck her: if she were to drive the forklift to one end of the freezer and somehow "lose" the key, she would have to walk all the way back to the door on the other side. If she weren't wearing a coat, that could be enough time to develop hypothermia. The chip would, of course, call an ambulance for her, which would arrive in time to save her life, but hopefully not in enough time to keep the chip from resetting more of its functions to zero.

All she had to do now was to come up with an excuse to be in the freezer. Fortunately, the lab's freezer was tiny, so if she were to ramp up production of new combinations of proteins, they would soon run out of storage space.

Janice waited until Thursday, when she knew all the forklift drivers were busy filling a standing order for Unimart from a freezer on the other side of the plant. Then she went to work a couple of hours early, producing more new protein samples than was humanly possible without the benefit of a chip. Soon she had more than the small lab freezer could handle and thus an excuse to visit the factory's freezer unit. After wheeling the large box of samples on a cart down to the bay where forklifts were parked, she set it on a pallet, hopped into a forklift and headed to the freezer. Ten aisles past the bay door, she located what she was looking for—a section of odds and ends that would seem an appropriate place for a box of protein samples. After neatly stacking the pallet with its single box, she parked the forklift and shut it off. Floor drains were spaced evenly along the center aisle, and as luck would have it, there was one right beside the row of odds and ends. Janice quickly pulled the key out of the lift, climbed out, and dropped it through one of the slots of the drain. She could just see it, glinting in the harsh blue hue of industrial lighting.

The cold was quiet and strangely peaceful, now that her forklift motor wasn't running. Janice tugged the thin lab coat more closely around her plump form and stared at the boxes of SynthaTripe and Synth-Offal. "What is that stuff, anyway?" she asked out loud, delaying as long as she dared before she started the trip back. When she was convinced that she had given hypothermia a head start, she began slowly walking to the other side of the freezer. No one would realize she was here until her chip made the call. At -25° Fahrenheit, wearing no coat, it would not take long for hypothermia to set in—certainly less time than it would take her to walk all the way back to the pedestrian door.

By the time she passed the forklift entrance, she was shivering uncontrollably. Suddenly she panicked. "What am I doing?" she thought. She tried desperately to control the emotions she had recently regained. If the chip sensed she was in distress or was confused, it might take over. Then she remembered her meditation techniques. After some breathing exercises, she calmed down and concentrated on her inner world.

Flashes of light streaked across the horizon of her mind like the lightening of a distant thunderstorm. She wondered if everyone else's neural network looked like this. It had an eerie resemblance to an immense ocean, and she was somehow standing on its surface. Then she remembered her neural boundary, which Etherea had suggested wasn't much of a wall. Perhaps there was a way to make the wall stronger—to build it up a bit. She had no idea how to build up a neural wall, but it wouldn't hurt to try. Janice stared across the windswept vista and gingerly stepped toward what she hoped was the right direction. Twenty minutes later, she located it: the line of broken rubble she had encountered earlier when she and Etherea had formed a link. She knelt down on the ground, which felt a little like sand shifting under the waters of an incoming tide. One by one, she began to pile up the broken bricks and stones which comprised her wall. In a few minutes, she had built up a one foot tall by two feet wide section. Janice stood up to admire her work. "This isn't as hard as I thought it would be," she said, pleased with herself. Then, as she shifted her gaze to the seemingly endless wall of debris on either side of her, she sighed. She had a lot of work to do. Blinking lights back at the core of her neural network were calling her back—calling her to take action and do something to get out of the freezer, but she knew it was too late. Not even the chip could get her out in time to save itself from being reset. Janice hunkered back down by her wall and busied herself with the building project. It was enjoyable to be able to perform a task that stayed done for a while. Unlike factory work or housework, which never ended, this wall could be something she could look back on and take pride in for years to come.

Minutes stretched into an hour. The section of wall was really beginning to take shape. Janice had decided to make a section one foot high around the whole perimeter of her network and then gradually add more height. So far, she only had six feet completed, but it was a start. She began to hum as she worked. She suddenly realized the tune she was humming was one she had frequently heard Viv singing to herself. *"Jesus loves me, this I know! For the Bible tells me so! Little ones to Him belong. They are weak, but He is strong."*[104] Janice frowned thoughtfully. Jesus, indeed. She knew Viv had never meant to hurt her by telling her about the Christian form of the Source. In fact, she knew that Viv really believed what she said. She actually believed that there was only one way to the Source, and Jesus was that way. Janice shook her head. Viv had only been trying to help her, she realized now. It had taken a lot of courage for her to do what she did—revealing that she was monotheistic. After all, it was a crime punishable by reconditioning or even personality reassignment. Janice shuddered. That was exactly what they had done to her. She had gone to the State for help, and they had violated her will. The chip wasn't the answer to everything after all. It was just like every other relationship she had ever had: everything was fine as long as she did everything right for the other person involved. Sometimes even if she *did* do everything right, the other person just got tired of her. They punished her for not being perfect for their desires, or they used her up and left her. Well, not this time. This time, Janice was going to be in control. This time…

"Hello, Janice," said a voice directly in front of her.

---

[104] From the hymn, "Jesus Loves Me, This I Know," words by Anna Bartlett Warner

Janice looked up to see Ainsley Abbot, her commanding form clad in a dark purple cloak that flapped and fluttered in the breeze. She, too, looked different in this inner world. Taller. Menacing.

"Hello?" Janice said meekly, and then remembered she was in control now. She clambered to her feet. "Hello," she said again, clearing her throat and squaring her shoulders. "I'm going to have to ask you to step away from my wall," she said in the most authoritative voice she could muster.

Ainsley smirked darkly and pushed at the sandy ground around the base of Janice's wall with the toe of her black leather boot. Instantly, the sand shifted —and with it, the bottom bricks. In a few seconds, all of Janice's neatly stacked blocks had tumbled to the ground to rejoin their scattered brethren. "What wall?" Ainsley asked with a leer, and stepped over the pile of rubble.

"Hey! You can't do that!" Janice exclaimed. "You're supposed to knock! You can't just come in!"

"We're not certain exactly what you're up to, Janice; but we're going to find out, now that I've established a link," Ainsley said, completely ignoring her protests. "They're accessing your memory through your port even as we speak. I'm just here to make certain you won't interfere with anything."

"Well, I won't let you come any further!" Janice said, her voice rising in pitch.

"Calm down, Janice. Isn't that temperament of yours what earned you that baseline emotion program? But something tells me you found a way around that. Otherwise, you wouldn't be so upset."

Janice clamped her mouth shut and watched Ainsley with wide eyes. *This is my mind! She has no right to be here!* Janice thought to herself. With that thought bolstering her courage, she suddenly ducked her head and charged Ainsley. There were some advantages to being short, after all. But as she threw herself at Ainsley's tall form, the woman lithely stepped to the side. Janice found herself facedown, her legs resting on the scattered bricks, the top half of her body in the misty surface outside of her neural boundary.

"Oh, my! That wasn't very well executed," Ainsley said tauntingly.

Janice felt as if she were sinking in the cold, unstable ground outside her neural network. She attempted to roll over so she could pull herself back inside with her legs, but she couldn't maneuver in the tumultuous waves. "Please help me!" she cried as she floundered helplessly.

"Of course!" Ainsley said, grabbing hold of her feet and shoving her into the misty deep.

"You can't do that!" Janice gasped, groping for the broken bricks of her wall.

"I just did," Ainsley said.

Janice managed to grab hold of one of the bricks to keep herself afloat. She wondered how Ainsley had been able to stand up in the ocean outside of her mind.

As if reading her thoughts, Ainsley smiled. "Not much to hold onto when you're out of your mind, is there, Janice? But at least now you won't get in the way. We'll have you set up in no time. No more interference. No more games. Just the new Janice—smart, witty, and engaging. With the personality you're going to have, you won't even need Trimfit to find a fulfilling relationship. There really is a lot of truth to that old saying, 'It's what's on the *inside* that counts.' Of course, now that you won't be able to interfere anymore, you really *can* have everything—a new body, a sparkling personality, a high IQ. It really is going to be a new start for you. And now, I think I'll go help form you into the person you were always meant to be." Ainsley's eyes narrowed as she turned to go.

"Wait! No!" Janice wailed, as she watched Ainsley moving deeper into her neural network. She tried to pull herself up onto the wall, but as she did so, the brick she was holding onto shifted and seemed to disappear into the depths. Janice grabbed onto another brick, and another, struggling to stay afloat, but all of them sank when she put any weight on them. Her wall had no foundation, and it was only a matter of time, she knew, before she ran out of strength and could no longer tread water—or whatever this was outside the boundary of her mind. She watched as lights within the network flickered and danced. What were they doing to her mind? Would she even be able to recognize herself when they were finished?

A feeling of total helplessness enveloped her. Was this what it was like to be insane? To be completely out of control of your own actions? Janice heard a strange noise, and then realized it was emanating from her own body. She had started moaning in desperation, and was soon sobbing uncontrollably.

"Source!" she cried. "I'm ready to join you, Source!" The waves tossed her around like a tiny bobber. "I want to become one with you, Source!" Janice tried again. There was no answer—just the violent crashing of waves against her crumbling wall. Janice began sobbing again. "It isn't fair! No one loves me! No one has *ever* loved me!" she cried out in anguish. At that exact moment, a tumbleweed from within her neural network came careening toward her wall and stopped to rest on its edge, perched there like an unearthly bird. Janice squinted her eyes through the blustery spray of waves, wondering if her mind was beginning to break apart into little pieces which would soon be joining her. Suddenly, the tumbleweed rolled off the wall into the frigid sea of nothingness, floating there like a piece of flotsam. It was a memory blip, Janice realized. It wasn't one of the nasty ones, either. It was more recent. And she was fairly certain it had something to do with Viv.

Janice paddled toward the memory and grabbed hold of it. It was surprisingly warm and buoyant—not prickly like you would expect a tumbleweed to be. She squeezed it close to her chest and let its essence surround her. There, in the tempestuous ocean outside of her mind, Janice could experience some sense of sanity, and it came in the form of Viv's voice. *"Jesus loves me, this I know, for the Bible tells me so! Little ones to Him belong. They are weak, but He is strong!"*[105] Viv sang. Janice hugged the memory fiercely. If ever she needed someone to love her—someone who was strong—it was now.

"Jesus! I know Viv believed in you. If you're really real, please help me! I need you! I need your help!" Janice cried. She shut her eyes tightly against the waves and buried her face in the memory. As she listened to the song over and over again, she became aware of another voice.

"Peace. Be still!" the voice rang out across the tumult. Instantly, the raging waves were calm. Janice opened her eyes. She was no longer floating in a stormy sea. She was crouched on a giant rock, still clinging desperately to the memory of Viv and her song. Standing before her was a Man in a white robe, stained in places with crimson red. "I'm here, Janice," said the Man.

Janice sat up, still hugging the memory like a security blanket. "Who are you?" she asked.

---

[105] From the hymn, "Jesus Loves Me, This I Know," words by Anna Bartlett Warner

"I am Jesus. You called out to me, and I answered," the Man said gently, and offered His hand to help her to her feet.

"You're *Jesus?*" Janice asked incredulously. "I thought you were on a cross somewhere."

Jesus smiled. "I was. I died there and was buried. But three days later, I rose again so that I could offer you freedom from sin and hope of eternal life."

"Viv told me about that, but I didn't believe her at the time," Janice said apologetically. "It seemed too simple—and too strange. I mean, no offense, but why would you want to die for someone like me?"

"Because I love you. Heaven wouldn't be the same without you," Jesus said with a tender smile.

"Heaven? Is heaven really real?" Janice asked.

"It is. But more importantly, My love for you is real; and My sacrifice for you was real."

Janice's heart jumped. Could this man be telling the truth? And if he was, wouldn't he just end up being disappointed in her, like all the others?

"I'm not disappointed in you, daughter. I love you more than you can imagine. There's nothing you can do to make Me love you any more than I do now, and there's nothing you can do that will make Me stop loving you," Jesus said.

Janice's mouth dropped open. He had read her mind. And somehow, she believed Him. Then her heart sank. She had already rejected this Man so many times. How could He accept her as His own?

"Janice, do you believe in Me?" Jesus asked.

"Yes, I do—I do *now*," Janice said quickly. "I always believed the Source was God. But Viv said there was only one way to the Source of all life, and His name is Jesus. I didn't believe her then. But I believe now. When I called out to the Source, nothing happened. But when I called out to Jesus, You came to rescue me. It's just…" Janice stopped abruptly.

"Go ahead, daughter. I'm listening."

"I've done things the wrong way my whole life," Janice said, tears rolling down her cheeks.

"Are you ready to start doing things the right way?" Jesus asked her.

"I want to. But I don't even *know* the right way," Janice said miserably.

Jesus cupped her chin in His hand. "You do now," He said, and suddenly Janice was filled with more love than she ever knew existed.

"Is it really true, what Viv said? Is it true that if I give my life to You, You'll never leave me?" Janice dared to ask.

"It is true, dear one," Jesus said softly, and Janice could feel He was telling the truth—indeed, that Truth was the only thing this Man was able to speak.

"Where do I start?" Janice asked meekly.

Jesus stared out over the waters surrounding them, toward the direction of Janice's neural wall. "A new life should always start with a good foundation," Jesus said, His voice echoing over the glassy sea. "I'm going to show you how to build your wall on a solid Rock."

Janice marveled as Jesus led her across the ocean. As she held His hand, every step she took was on steady ground. When they reached the wall, He turned to her and smiled. "Starting a new life can be difficult, but it helps when you have a friend who also knows Me. They can be there to teach you more about Me and help you to understand My Word."

"Do You mean a friend like Viv?" Janice asked.

"Yes. But Viv isn't able to come help you where you are right now. I'm going to introduce you to another friend who can help."

"Aren't You going to stay here with me?" Janice asked worriedly.

"I certainly am," Jesus said. "I will never leave you nor forsake you."

Janice stared at her neural network over the wall. "What if they won't let us come back in?" she asked in a timid voice.

"Don't worry, daughter. They have no dominion over you any more," Jesus said, and as He turned toward the flashing lights of the network, His voice took on a tone of authority. "Come out of her!" His command reverberated throughout her mind.

Suddenly, from within the expanse on the other side of the wall came a rumbling and a shaking. The sound of a roaring wind could be heard. A whirlwind appeared on the horizon and began rushing violently toward them. Janice watched in shock as the wind approached. She could see within its walls the tall figure of Ainsley, tumbling 'round and 'round, along with some grotesquely shaped figures she didn't recognize but which somehow seemed familiar. The whirlwind spun to the edge of the wall and violently flung the figures out into the sea, where they sank instantly.

"Is Ainsley going to drown?" Janice asked anxiously.

"No," Jesus explained. "She's just banished from your mind. The link has been severed."

"What were those other things?" Janice asked, shuddering involuntarily.

"Those were evil spirits you unknowingly let into your life when you opened the door for them to come in. They can't stay here anymore because I live here now," Jesus said.

"Are You really going to live here?" Janice asked hopefully. "Like, *live* and not just visit?"

"You betcha," Jesus said, and winked.

Janice giggled. "You're a lot more fun than *My Truth* made You sound."

"Janice, that blog you used to read couldn't be any farther from My Truth— *The* Truth. But as I said, I'm going to introduce you to someone who will help you along in your new life," Jesus said. He steadied Janice as she stepped over her wall and back inside her neural network. "And now, about that foundation we were talking about earlier…" Jesus began.

"That may be a problem," Janice said. "The ground around here is like sinking sand."

"That's where I come in," Jesus said and lay down on the sandy soil. Suddenly, Jesus disappeared and the sand was gone, changed into a solid rock foundation, like the rock where Janice had first encountered Jesus on the ocean. "Jesus, where did You go?" Janice called out fearfully.

"I'm right here," said a voice from within her spirit.

And then Janice understood. Jesus really *was* living inside of her now. He would never leave her alone, and He, *Himself*, would be the solid foundation on which she could build her life. A deep peace settled over her. "I love You, Jesus," she said softly.

"I love you, daughter," she felt His reply.

Janice began humming the tune again, this time with an assurance that the words were true. Each brick she put on her new foundation stayed in place. A warm feeling swept over her. She had a lot of work to do, but she had a firm foundation now. And Jesus had promised He was going to send someone to help her.

"Hi, Janice. Can I come in?"

Janice looked up to see a young girl standing outside of her wall.

"My name's Piper, and Jesus just told me you could use some help!"

Janice looked at the thin figure. She had a smile like sunshine, and even though she was small, Janice could sense an incredible strength coming from within her. She stood up and extended her hand. "Any friend of Jesus' is a friend of mine," she said. "Come on in!"

Piper grabbed her hand and stepped over her wall. "I've brought a lot of building material with me," she said happily.

Janice looked around but couldn't see anything.

"You'll see it as soon as I speak it," she said in answer to Janice's unspoken question. "This is from God's Word in Matthew 7:24 and 25. 'Therefore whosoever heareth these sayings of Mine, and doeth them, I will liken him unto a wise man, which built his house upon a rock: And the rain descended, and the floods came, and the winds blew, and beat upon that house; and it fell not: for it was founded upon a rock.'"[106] As soon as Piper had spoken, a pile of bricks appeared, neatly stacked next to the building site.

"Wow!" Janice exclaimed. "How did you do that?"

"It's not me. It's the Word of God. It's alive, an' it's powerful. It can help ya build good paths to walk in an' build a strong wall against the enemy," Piper explained. "How 'bout we lay some bricks?"

Janice grinned at the diminutive girl. "I'm game," she said.

"All right! Here we go," Piper said joyfully, and handed Janice a brick.

"Hey, have you ever heard the song, *Jesus Loves Me?*" Janice asked tentatively.

"No, can't say I have," Piper said, "but it sounds like a good'n. Maybe ya could teach me?"

Janice's smile broadened and she began to sing. As the two worked together, singing as they went, the wall began to grow. When they ran out of bricks, Piper would teach Janice another scripture, and a new stack of bricks would appear. Janice knew this was going to take a while, but she didn't mind at all. She had

---

[106] Matthew 7:24-25, KJV

met the Love of her life and had made a true friend, all in the same day. She didn't care if it took forever.

29

AINSLEY Abbot's eyes shot open and darted around the room, looking for some sort of external interference that could have caused the link to be severed. The only noise was the steady sound of Janice's heart beat, indicated by old-tech monitors the lab was using during the chip reprogramming process. A digital panel on the warming blanket emitted a cozy orange glow as it displayed Janice's body temperature. Overall, Janice was recovering well from hypothermia. There didn't seem to be any physical trauma that could have caused what Ainsley had just experienced inside Janice's mind. She closed her eyes and sent a message to Dr. Moses to inform him of the situation. In a few moments, she could hear his footsteps in the hall.

"Would you mind relaying that to me again?" Dr. Moses asked as he leaned against the doorframe. "Some things are best described in person."

Ainsley folded her arms and studied Janice's still form as she spoke. "I was making some real progress. Janice was no longer an issue, as I had pushed her out. Everything was going smoothly. I was laying the foundation for Janice's new personality when something picked me up and threw me outside the neural boundary, severing the link. It happened so fast that I couldn't see much of what was going on. But when I looked back, I could swear I saw two figures—Janice and…someone or some*thing* else. Janice was back on her wall, and this figure was standing there beside her; but I couldn't make out exactly who or what it was before I lost contact completely."

Dr. Moses' eyes seemed to darken. "Wait a minute. Go back to what you were saying about pushing Janice out. What do you mean, exactly?"

Ainsley's brow furrowed. "She was interfering. She tried to kick me out, so I took care of the problem by removing her from the situation."

Dr. Moses was quiet for a moment. He had hired Ainsley because of her talent for programming, superior communication skills, and her charisma. But there were other qualities she possessed which he knew would need refining. He cleared his throat. "I realize that in order to achieve our objectives, we often circumvent standard procedures in dealing with patients. However, our ultimate goal is for each individual to willingly submit themselves to the enhanced life they can experience through the chip. When they realize they never have to be alone again, and when they experience the strength that is theirs through linking with others, they won't have to be coerced. When an individual can feel the incredible connection they have with other people and know they are a part of something much bigger than themselves, divisive components of society will become extinct. We will understand each other better. Race and religion will be a thing of the past. We will all simply be part of the human race, linked together into a unified whole. Just think what we will be able to accomplish! But in order for our argument for globally integrated consciousness to be effective, it is essential that the individual retain their right to choose. We can't be dictators. We must simply make them an offer they would be fools to refuse."

"Is that what you told the little Discard girl in 201?" Ainsley said with a sneer.

Dr. Moses' facial expression barely registered her catty remark. "Some sacrifices must be made for the greater good. Even certain religions have pointed out this truth. Piper is a Discard who has committed hate crimes, and she is obviously delusional. We are trying to help her and those she has hurt. Whereas Janice is a citizen who came to us for help. Somewhere along the way, we have failed her. Violating her trust by forcing her to become a mindless robot is a method that does not advance our cause."

"So who's going to know?" Ainsley said with a flippant smile. "By all outward appearances, Janice will be a happy citizen with an ideal life."

"But if we do this the right way, she won't just *appear* to be happy," Moses said in a calm, quiet voice. "She *will* be truly happy and fulfilled. Otherwise, we are no better than those in the past who have forced their agendas upon others. I did not hire you to hijack people's bodies and bend their minds to your will. I hired you because I saw your potential to encourage and convince others to become more than they ever dreamed they could be."

Ainsley rolled her eyes. "Please, Joseph. You knew what I was capable of before you hired me. And I *am* capable, if you'll stop telling me how to do my job and just allow me to *do* it. You're starting to sound like the moralists you're always criticizing for lacking the nerve to do what needs to be done."

"Aside from the fact that your tactics completely ignored the will of the individual and literally drove Janice out of her mind, did it occur to you that anyone attempting a link with her might wonder why there are two Janices: the one they know on the surface who is inhabiting her neural network, and the original one desperately attempting to regain control of her faculties?" Dr. Moses asked without waiting for an answer. "I'll tell you how to do your job as long as I can see you're struggling and need the instruction. Now, go back and attempt the link. And this time, I'm coming with you," Dr. Moses said firmly.

"You really don't trust me anymore, do you?" Ainsley said with her characteristic smirk.

"I'd be lying if I said that I did. But I also want to see this other figure you mentioned for myself," Dr. Moses replied, pulling up a chair beside the one Ainsley had been using.

The two sat in silence, focusing their thoughts.

Suddenly, within the boundaries of Janice's mind, Piper paused as she handed Janice a brick. "What's wrong?" Janice asked.

Piper frowned thoughtfully. "I think someone's comin'," she said.

Janice looked around worriedly. "Who?"

"I don' know."

"My wall's not ready yet. What if they want to come in, and they just bust on over it, like Ainsley did?" Janice fretted.

Piper looked back at Janice and smiled. "They can't come in if ya don't let 'em —if ya don't open the door. They can't come in if ya guard ya mind like I been showin' ya through God's Word."

"But right now, a person could just step over this wall. They wouldn't even need me to open the door." Janice peered anxiously at the horizon.

"Ya know, Janice, you're right. We've managed to build up this wall a whole bunch, but there's only so much we can do. An' right now, it ain't enough," Piper said with a confident smile.

"What are you smiling at?" Janice sputtered. "You just told me that I can't protect myself!"

"Not on ya own, ya can't," Piper said, glaring into the distance and somehow smiling at the same time. "We've done what we can do in the time we had. Now God's gonna do what we can't." She turned to Janice and took hold of her hands, placing them on the wall. "Jesus, we need Ya help. This wall ain't strong enough to keep out the enemy. But *You're* strong enough. We have put ourselves in Ya care, and Ya Word says the angel of the Lord encampeth round about them that fear Him, and delivereth them."[107]

As Piper finished speaking, a brick appeared on the wall in front of them. And then another. And another. They began appearing so quickly that Janice stopped trying to keep track. In a blur, the wall was suddenly above their heads, and it kept growing. Janice looked to the left and right. The wall stretched as far as she could see. As it grew in height, the dismal gray of the area beyond her boundary disappeared, and Piper and Janice were bathed in a golden light that seemed to be coming from the core of Janice's neural network.

Janice stood to her feet and placed her hands against the wall to steady herself as she stared at its towering height. "Thank You, Jesus!" was all she could think to say. "Oh, thank You, thank You!"

"Isn't He somethin'?" Piper beamed. "And now that we got the outside influences of the world in their proper place, it's easy-like to focus on Him." She raised her hands, bathing in the light shining on them. "There ain't nothin' like the peace o' God."

"Is that the glow I see over everything?" Janice asked.

"Yup. Ya see, when Jesus comes, He brings peace. He said, 'Peace I leave with you, My peace I give unto you: not as the world giveth, give I unto you. Let not your heart be troubled, neither let it be afraid.'"[108]

---

[107] See Psalm 34:7
[108] John 14:27, KJV

Janice turned her face toward the glow and closed her eyes, basking in its warmth. "I know I have a lot to learn; and I always hated school, because I couldn't see that any of it really mattered. But everything you're teaching me has really made a difference!"

"Jesus *is* the difference!" Piper exclaimed. "An' ya never stop learnin', far as I can tell. The Holy Spirit is a wonderful teacher."

"The Holy Spirit?" Janice asked, opening her eyes.

Piper smiled. "Yup. Jesus made sure His disciples would have all the help they needed. He explains it all in John 14. He tells 'em He's gonna send 'em a teacher to help 'em understand everything and remind 'em of everything 'e told 'em."[109]

"He thought of everything, didn't He?" Janice said gratefully.

Suddenly, the two could hear a loud banging noise.

"What's that?" Janice whispered.

"That's just someone tryin' ta get in," Piper explained.

"But they can't get in unless I open the door, right?" Janice asked.

"That's right. An' there's lotsa things ya need to guard against, besides just people," Piper said. "What ya need now is the Filter."

"The…*Filter?*"

"Yup. Philippians 4:8. 'Whatsoever things are true, whatsoever things are honest, whatsoever things are just, whatsoever things are pure, whatsoever things are lovely, whatsoever things are of good report; if there be any virtue, if there be any praise, think on these things.'" Piper quoted. "If it ain't under none o' them categories—if it can't pass through the Filter—ya shouldn't let ya mind camp out on it."[110]

Janice smiled. Suddenly, the thudding noise stopped.

Outside the boundary, Ainsley and Dr. Moses watched the massive brick wall they had encountered suddenly blink into blackness and morph into line after line of coding. Dr. Moses opened his eyes and looked at Ainsley, who had

---

[109] See John 14:16-18, 26
[110] Bishop Jerry Haynes applied the term "the Filter" to Philippians 4:8 in many sermons over the years.

also stopped attempting to link. "The wall wasn't like that before," Ainsley said quickly. "There's no way she could have done this on her own."

"No, of course not," Dr. Moses said, looking at the prone figure in the hospital bed. He stood up and walked toward the door. "This is the second patient I've encountered with this malware. Don't make any more attempts to link with her until I assess the situation. We have to stop this before it spreads any further."

30

ZELDA awoke with the stirring of the birds. Even before they started singing, she could hear their soft flutterings as they moved away from their night perches and began to flit from branch to branch. She slowly opened her eyes and gazed through the latticework of leaves at the sky. The lights of the city reflected off the clouds above, creating an endless twilight that could almost convince her dawn could still be hours away. But the birds and her back told her otherwise. She needed to get up and get moving. The more distance she placed between herself and the State, the safer she felt.

It had been ten days since she had made her final passage through the great gray wall that was the boundary of the outer docks. Traveling was proving more difficult than expected. Zelda had grown up walking on pavement. Her earlier excursions into the Preserve had been at a leisurely pace, always with the intent to stay near enough to the wall to be back before nightfall. Now she was walking as much as her broken-down body could manage in a day. The uneven terrain worked against her, surprising her with rocks that rolled under her feet beneath the leaf litter of the forest floor. Green briar and multiflor rose grabbed at her clothes and snagged skin that was thinned from age and years spent in the sun. The cold night air seeped into her bones and left her stiff in the morning. Yet each day, when she raised her head from the lumpy pack she used as a pillow and stretched out her legs that were scratched and bloodied from brambles, she breathed deep and peered into the burgeoning daylight with a snaggletoothed smile. No matter the difficulty of this new life, Zelda was free.

She struggled to her feet and stretched her back. It would be another long day of walking. The old woman pushed her frazzled hair out of her face and hunched over the pack, digging around in it until she found an energy bar from one of the MREs. She had rationed out the meals as much as she could, supplementing them with whatever she could find. Her knowledge of wild edibles was limited to blackberries (which weren't in season) and dandelions, which were never scarce but didn't contain the calories she needed. The bow Selah had given her was always close at hand in case an unsuspecting animal might wander by when she stopped to rest. So far, her main source of calories consisted of slugs she found as she walked. She deposited them into a dented yogurt cup in a pocket of the pack and would cook them over a sparse fire when she stopped for the night. For now, she ate a portion of the precious energy bar, took a swallow of water out of her canteen, and was on her way.

Zelda wasn't certain how much distance she had covered. She had decided to head due south, putting the causeway and its industrial hum at her back. Once in a while, she would come upon one of the old roads and was tempted to follow it to ease her difficulty walking; but it was only a passing thought. The roads were watched closely, and only a fool would follow them. She kept to the wooded areas, her eyes open for rabbits, squirrels, or groundhogs that might be in shooting range. The morning wore into midday and stretched into afternoon. Zelda stopped at every stream she encountered to refill her canteen and look for crawdads. Occasionally, she had found a few big enough to eat. They went into the yogurt cup with the slugs.

She wondered if her absence had been noticed. If Selah had kept her promise not to preach until a week had passed, she might still be in the clear. But once they caught the girl, they were sure to chip her. Then all Zelda's secrets would be known, and *she* would be the hunted. Zelda grunted and shook her head. Selah had kept her promise—she was sure of it. Zelda prided herself on being a good judge of character, and Selah was the promise-keeping type.

"Ri*dick*lous," she said to herself as she thought of Selah's desire to preach about Jesus to the Discards. The girl had everything Zelda had ever dreamed of: freedom, food, land to farm and hunt, no State breathing down her neck. And while Zelda was fleeing the State to pursue what Selah had, Selah was running toward it—throwing her life away for an idea. Zelda scowled. How could she be so blind? Piper was the same way, Zelda reflected as she topped a ridgeline and surveyed the wooded slope below. If she had just kept quiet about Jesus, she could have come with her instead of being caught by the loon dockers. "Fool!" Zelda hissed, but the word caught in her throat. "Pipah. I wished I coulda saved ya. I wished ya was wit' me right now," Zelda said, and to her surprise, her eyes began to well up with tears. She dropped the pack, covered her face in her knobby hands and sat down in the crunchy oak leaves that carpeted the forest floor. Zelda could not remember the last time she had cried. Her sides heaved as she gasped for air. "It ain't right!" she sobbed. "She nevah done nuttin' wrong to nobody, an' dey takes her away!" She pressed her gnarled fingers against her eyelids as if trying to squelch the memory. Years of hardship and suppressed emotion rolled in upon her like river fog after a rain. There was no one to pretend for anymore…no reputation to uphold. She allowed herself the luxury of a good, long cry. Eventually, her sobbing subsided into sniffles that jerked her body at spasmodic intervals. Finally, her emotions spent, she began to breathe regularly.

It was then that she heard it: the crack of a twig, the shifting of leaves right beside her. Zelda froze and held her breath. She opened one gray eye and peeked through her wrinkled fingers. Standing between her spraddled legs was a dog the color of last week's goulash.

"Ahhhhhh!" Zelda yelled, pulling her hands from her face and pouncing to her feet.

"*Rarf-rarf-rarf!*" answered the dog.

The bow, which she kept slung around her shoulder, slid to her wrist. While Zelda fumbled to find an arrow, the animal cautiously approached her and began licking her pants.

"Ackk. Gi' back, dog!" Zelda growled, but instead, the dog started licking her hand. "I'm hungered 'nuf ta eatcha! Back off, so's I kin git a good shot atcha." But the more Zelda tried to fend off the dog's affection, the more affectionate it became. "Stupid dog," Zelda said. She put down the bow and reached for her spear, which she had thrown in the leaves. As if anticipating her next move, the dog grabbed it by the butt end and started down the slope with it, wagging its tail as it tugged the spear in crazy arcs around the tree trunks. "You come back wit' dat!" Zelda yelled, stumbling down the hill after the four-legged thief. After just a few minutes, she had to stop and rest. The dog stopped and looked back at her, its tail still wagging. "Stupid mutt." Zelda said. "I knew I shouldn'a left ma bow back there." She suddenly changed tactics. "Here, poochie pooch. Let's play fetch! Gimme da stick!"

The dog dropped the stick and cocked its head, studying Zelda intently.

"Dat's it! It's my turn wit' da stick. Gimme da stick," Zelda crooned as she slowly approached.

When she was five feet away, the dog suddenly pounced on the spear, grabbing it in its jaws and taking off down the hill again.

Zelda let out a string of cuss words that would have made a river clean-up crew blush. She looked back up the hill at her pack and bow and then downhill at the canine thief. It had nonchalantly settled down into the leaves, placing the butt of the spear between its front paws and gnawing on it like a chew bone. Zelda swore again and decided to make her way back up the hill to retrieve her gear. The dog didn't seem to be in a hurry to run off. Maybe it would lose interest in the spear if she didn't appear to be interested in getting it back.

Going uphill was the bane of Zelda's trekking experiences. She avoided it at all costs, but there was no alternative. She stood at the top of the ridge, waiting for her huffing and puffing to return to normal breathing. For a fleeting instant, she wondered if she was too old to make this journey—if she had overestimated her stamina and resolve. She shoved the thought aside. There was no room for second thoughts, and it was too late to change her mind now. She shouldered the pack and the bow and carefully picked her way down the hill with the dog watching her all the way. She considered shooting it with her bow; but if she missed, she risked wrecking the arrow by hitting the rocky ground. Plus, the dog might run off with her spear again, and she might never get it back. Zelda avoided eye contact with the animal. When she was just a little way up the hill from it, she turned east and began casually walking in a parallel route, as if she were just passing by. Most of the dogs in the outer docks had been eaten, but Zelda remembered when she was a child—before things got so bad—that she had a pet dog named DooDad. She could remember a few things about DooDad's behavior. He was smart, and he liked to play games. Zelda figured if she stopped chasing this dog, it would drop the spear and start following her. After all, it was probably lonely out here. Suddenly Zelda froze in her tracks.

The dog didn't look or act hungry, and it had energy to play. That meant it was either running with a wild pack that hunted together, or it was being fed by humans. She suspected the latter, because this dog wasn't scared of her at all.

"Hmmmph," Zelda grunted. Selah's community must not be that far away. Maybe they were even out looking for her. If they made their way to the outer docks and started asking around, the State would go on high alert. An all-out search would begin. With the information they would glean from chipping their new prisoners, they might learn of other outposts in the Preserve. The woods would be swarming with Pod-Ops. Zelda couldn't let that happen. If these people were looking for Selah, she had to tell them to turn back, or there would be no safe haven left anywhere. She glanced back at the dog, which had dropped the spear and stood up, wagging its tail. "Ok, dum-dum. Take me to ya people," she said over her shoulder. The dog opened its mouth in a lopsided grin, picked up the spear and dragged it over to her, placing it within her reach.

Zelda raised her eyebrows and picked up the offering. The dog wagged its tail and took off in a direction down the hill, stopping to look back to see if she were following. Zelda grinned. Maybe the mutt wasn't so stupid, after all. "I'm comin'" she said, and started after it. Fifteen minutes later, she thought she caught a whiff of wood smoke. The dog stopped and waited for her to catch up. "We gettin' close, ain't we?" Zelda asked. And then she could hear voices.

"Macy! Come here, Macy!" At the sound of the voice, the dog's ears perked up, and it uttered a greeting bark.

"So dat's you, eh? Macy?" Zelda asked softly.

Macy shoved her reddish-brown nose up under Zelda's knobby hand. "Well, I guess I'm glad I didn' eatcha," she said. "Mebbe dese folks'll have sump'n ta eat." She looked in the direction of the voices. "Hello!" she called out in her raspy voice. "Hello out dere."

The voices fell quiet for a moment, and then she heard a tentative, "Hello?"

Zelda made her way in the direction of the voice, with Macy taking the lead. Finally, the underbrush grew thinner, and she could see a group of people— three men and four women—standing around a small fire. The women and two of the men appeared to be close to Selah's age. The other man was several years older and positioned himself between her and the young people. Macy trotted up to one of the younger men and sat down on his feet. Zelda hobbled over to the group, stopping some twenty yards away. "Don't worry. I's peaceable," she said simply. "Yer dog done stole ma spear. But 'e give it back."

"Hello," said the older man, who seemed to be the leader. "My name is Craig, and this is Garrison, Thom, Lydia, Chandra, Lelah, and Dania," he said, gesturing to the individuals as he spoke.

"Hmmmph," Zelda replied. In case these humans were captured, she didn't want to give out her real name. "You'ns can call me…Wisteria."

"It's nice to meet you, Wisteria," said the girl called Chandra. "Do you live out here?"

Zelda eyed her up and down before she answered. "I's just passin' through. What are y'all doin' traipsin' through da woods? Ya goin' somewheres in partic'lar?"

The young people looked at each other as if each were waiting for the other to answer. Finally, Craig cleared his throat and spoke. "We don't necessarily have a destination in mind. We're just looking for other people who may not have heard the good news."

Zelda's eyebrows knotted together in confusion. "What good news?"

Pastor Craig took a deep breath. "The news about a Man named Jesus. We want to make certain everyone has the chance to know Him, personally."

Zelda's mouth dropped open. Now she knew she must have been right. These had to be Selah's bunch. "What is it wit' you *Jesus* people?" she exclaimed. "Don' ya know y'all gonna git killt? No one, no wheres, cares nuttin' 'bout dat Jesus dude. 'Specially not in da direction ya headed. Cuz you'ns is gitt'n close to da State. Da people what's in da State, dey don' care, cuz dey's all got da chip ta help 'em wit' whatevah dey need. An' da people in da outer docks don' care, cuz dey too busy findin' food an' layin' low. Anyone in da outer docks can tell ya what'll happen if'n ya start preachin' 'bout Jesus. Just ast 'em 'bout Pipah. Da loon dockers done dragged 'er off. Purty soon, ya kin ast 'em 'bout Selah, cuz she prob'ly goin' wit' da loon dockers soon enough."

At the mention of Selah's name, Garrison eyes widened, and he stepped forward. "Did you say *Selah?* What did she look like? Can you describe her to me?"

Zelda stared hard at Garrison. "Girl 'bout yer age. Brown hair. Brown eyes. Knows hows ta walk quiet-like in da woods. She give me dis," she said, holding up the bow.

Garrison took a few more steps forward, at which Zelda stepped back, holding the bow behind her. "She give it to me. We made a trade. I taught 'er 'bout da outer docks an' da people in it an' gave 'er a place ta stay. She give me 'er bow and some food ta go on ma journey. 'Cept I's 'bout outta da food," she said, looking toward the fire hopefully. She could see a pot resting on some rocks over the coals.

"I don't want to take your bow. It's just…I wasn't sure you were talking about the same person until now. I left home intending to go to the Old Country— the State—so I could experience modern life. I asked Selah to come with me, but she wanted to stay. But I guess she changed her mind. Now that I see her bow, I know it's her you're talking about!" Garrison said excitedly.

Zelda studied Garrison. "Ya mean you'ns ain't out lookin' for 'er?"

"No, ma'am," Pastor Craig answered. "The rest of us have never even met her, and as far as we all knew, she was back at Garrison's community, further to the south."

Zelda shifted her feet uncomfortably in the leaves. "How many o' dese secret hideyways y'all got back in here? An' how ya keep 'em secret?"

"God shelters our communities from drone detection. That's the only explanation I have," Craig said. "And I don't have any idea how many of them there are. There are only two that I know of, but there may be more."

"I doubt I would've found their community," Garrison said, gesturing to the others. "But Viv found me and took me there. Maybe you know her? Red, white and blue hair—rides a hover bike?" He felt silly asking the question. There may have been hundreds, even thousands of people in the State who had crazy hair and owned a bike like Viv's.

Zelda looked at Garrison askance. "You talkin' 'bout da deserter. She come back once, lookin' for 'er dad. Needed proof she was *his*, so she could git a good factory job."

"How is she?" Chandra asked quickly. "We haven't seen her in a while. Is she ok?"

"I don' talk to deserters. I mean, leavin' da docks to excape into da wilds is one ting. But flippin' to da State is anudder. An' no, I ain't seen her in a while. She sticks Stateside, mostly. But you's tellin' me she come out 'ere in da Preserve, reg'lar like?" Zelda asked incredulously.

"She did, but it's been a while," Pastor Craig said.

"Dey put trackin' bugs in da cars an' da bikes. How she keep hid?" Zelda asked.

"She told us that she's always careful, but she's pretty sure God keeps her hidden," Chandra said.

Zelda shook her head. "Why would she put herself an' all o' yourn at risk? She know dey could follow 'er."

Pastor Craig smiled. "Viv came to know Jesus just a couple of years ago. She discovered our community and kept coming back to hear more about Him."

Zelda's eyes grew round. "You Jesus people is *crazy*," she said exasperatedly. She looked at Garrison. "I s'pose it'll be people from where *you* dock next, comin' to da State like a flock o' rat birds."

"My community doesn't have the same view as the one these folks are from," Garrison began.

"Well, dey sent Selah, didn' dey? Can't believe dey'd send a young girl like dat, ta talk 'bout an' idee what'd git 'er killt," Zelda growled.

"They didn't send her, I'm sure of that," Garrison said. "She sneaked out, just like I did, but for very different reasons. You say Selah was intent on preaching about Jesus. *I* left because I wanted to experience modern ways of life."

Zelda looked up at Garrison and sniffed speculatively. "You jist keep on goin' da direction ya goin', an' you'll see modern ways, sho 'nuff. You'll see 'em wit' a chip in ya head. All o' you'ns. An' den, dey'll find ya secret hideyways, an' all ya famblies. An' den what'll ya tink 'bout dis Jesus dude? He ain't gonna protect ya."

"I believe He will," Pastor Craig said solemnly. "But even if we have to go through some hard things, we'll still go where He asks us to go. And He'll be right there with us, through it all. He said He would be with us in trouble."[111]

---

[111] See Psalm 91:15

Zelda couldn't believe it. There was no way to talk sense to these people. "Ya still wants ta go, even though ya know dey don' keer, an' dey gonna put a chip in ya head an' do all sorts a stuff to ya? People in da State, dey do tings to ya, what ought nought be done. An' it's like dey don' even know dey's doin' wrong. An' if'n y'all go to da State, den dere's gonna be hundreds o' people out here, lookin' for where ya come from. Don' ya keer none what happens to ya homefolk?"

"They knew the risk when they sent us out," Pastor Craig said. Then, changing the subject, he gestured to the fire. "We're just about to have some supper. Would you like to join us? Thom has been experimenting with goat jerky stew."

"I'm adding lamb's-quarter this time to fill it out a bit," Thom added.

"Well, I s'pose I could be persuaded," Zelda said casually, but the hunger in her eyes betrayed her interest. "I's got some slugs I could throw in," she added, pulling out the yogurt cup.

Dania swallowed hard and quickly said, "Oh, that's allright. I think we'll have enough to go around."

"Suit yaself," Zelda said and began sharpening a stick with the knife she wore on her belt. Satisfied with her work, she skewered the slugs and hobbled over to the fire so she could roast them over the coals. "Hope ya don' mind if'n I eats 'em maself. Slugs don't keep so good."

Dania managed a weak smile and nodded politely before hurriedly turning away to gather more wood for the fire.

"I didn't know you could eat those things," Lelah said, sidling up to Zelda with interest.

"Dey don' taste as bad as ya tink," Zelda said. "Dey just looks powerful nasty."

"I guess it's better than starving," Lydia commented.

"Not much better," Dania said under her breath as she threw another stick on the fire.

"Tell me about Selah," Garrison asked anxiously. "How is she? Do you really think she's in danger? When did she show up in the State?"

"She ain't in the State direckly," Zelda said, glancing away from her slugs as they sizzled over a flame. "She's in da outer docks. Dat's da area what surrounds da State. It's full o' ever'one dat don' want nuttin' ta do wit' implants an' chips an' havin' ya life controlled from da minute ya borned." A thought seemed to occur to Zelda, and she straightened up and tilted her head back proudly. "Selah say she come to tell ever'one 'bout Jesus, *too*. But she say she come to tell da Discards *first*."

"Discards?" Lydia asked.

"Yeah. Discards. Dat's all da people dat lives in da outer docks. Dat's me. I use ta live dere. But not no more. I excaped." Zelda grinned and rotated the slugs to make sure the other side was good and toasty.

"How did you escape?" Thom asked as he stirred the pot of stew.

"It's a secret," Zelda said simply, and clamped her mouth shut.

"How did Selah get in without getting caught?" Garrison asked. "There must be a fence or something surrounding the area to keep people in, the way you're describing it."

"Fence!" Zelda snorted. "Dey gots a fence all right. It's a forty-foot-high wall made o' brick dat's too smooth ta climb."

"Well, how did she make it over? Or did she tunnel under it?" Garrison asked.

"She didn' do nuttin' o' da kind," Zelda said, pulling one of the slugs off the stick and popping it into her mouth.

Dania suppressed a gag and shielded her eyes with her hand so she couldn't see Zelda chewing. Lydia and Chandra glanced at each other with wide grins. Lydia elbowed Dania, who was now holding her hand to her stomach.

"Well, how'd she do it, then?" Garrison asked impatiently.

"I helped 'er git in. An' like I said. It's a secret," Zelda replied.

"Is she doing okay? Did she say how long it took to get there? I mean, is it possible Viv could have given her a ride? It's a long way from our valley to here."

"She didn' say nuttin' 'bout da deserter," Zelda said and pulled the remaining slug off the skewer. "Ya sure ya don' want one?" Zelda asked, offering it to Garrison with a smirk.

Without missing a beat, Garrison took the slug and put it in his mouth. A collective gasp was heard from the girls, but Garrison's eyes never left Zelda's as he chewed and swallowed. "Thank you," he said, his expression never changing.

Zelda tilted her head and studied him for a moment. "You's welcome," she said, and picked up a bigger stick so she could poke at the fire while she considered her next words. "I liked Selah," she finally said. "She an' Pipah, I tink dey woulda liked eachudder too. Dey both talked 'bout Jesus like 'e was dey best dockmate. An' Pipah, she tol' nearly ever'one she met 'bout 'im. She had dis little bitty book dat had all sorts o' stories 'bout 'im in it. She used ta read ta me outta it. An' den, when Selah came, *she* had a *bigger* book dat tol' about stuff before Jesus was even borned."

A thought suddenly came to Garrison. "Viv told me about a little girl she met in the outer docks. She was the first person who ever told her about Jesus. She had a little New Testament—that's a Bible—a book about Jesus—and she was wearing this ratty old coat and had the most beautiful smile—"

"Dat's Pipah!" Zelda said excitedly. "What'd Viv say about 'er?"

"She said it was because of her that she gave her heart to Jesus. And when she went back to look for her later, no one knew where she went," Garrison explained.

"Yeah," Zelda said, and poked at the coals. "I tried ta tell 'er ta stop tellin' people. But she wouldn' stop. An' aftah she tells da people in da trash truck, she up an' disappears."

"I'm sorry," Garrison said sincerely.

"Not sorry enough ta turn back an' go da udder way, I bet," Zelda glared. "Like I said, if ya show up at da gate to da outer docks, dey's gonna start lookin' fo' mo' o' you'ns. Da woods'll be crawlin' wit' 'em. An' den, how's *I* gonna stand a chance? Y'all is fools to leave whatcha got. It's what ever'one in da outer docks dreams about dey whole life—havin' a place ta live free—wit' real food what ain't been eat off of yet, an' bein' able ta hunt an' fish an' raise a garden. Y'all's jist throwin' it away, like it don't mean nuttin'. All for a crazy *idee* 'bout religion."

"Jesus is more than just an idea," Pastor Craig said. "Being able to teach our children the truth about Jesus is why our parents and grandparents left the State in the first place. We wanted them to know that Jesus is more than just an old story. He's alive, and He is the only One who can save us from our destructive, selfish ways. He's the only way we can connect with the living God."

"Well, where I come from, Jesus is ya ticket to a ride wit' da loon dockers," Zelda said. Pastor Craig shook his head and smiled. "Well, let's give Him thanks for this food and see if adding the lamb's-quarter to the pot was a good idea."

Zelda watched as the group gathered in a circle and bowed their heads. Craig cleared his throat and began, "Lord, we thank You for this food, and we ask that You bless it to provide nourishment for our bodies. Help us to be good servants to You and to listen to Your voice. Thank You for sending Miss Wisteria here to warn us about what we might be facing and for letting us know that Garrison's friend, Selah, is going forth with Your message of truth. Please give her wisdom and boldness as she preaches Your Word. We ask that You also bless Miss Wisteria in her travels. Keep her safe, and give her a clear view of You and Your love for her. Amen."

Thom dished out the stew into cups each member of the missionary group had brought with them in their backpacks. Zelda held out her cooking pot, which doubled as a serving bowl. She took a bite of the stew and nodded to Thom, smacking her lips. "S'good," she complimented him. "What's da green stuff? Dandelion leaves?"

"No, that's the lamb's-quarter," Thom replied. "It has a milder flavor than dandelions."

Zelda nodded. "I b'lieve ya right."

"The jerky's a little chewy," he apologized.

"Dat don' hurt nuttin," Zelda reassured him.

"I think it's good, Thom," Dania said encouragingly.

"Mighta been better wit' one o' ma slugs," Zelda said. Dania shot a look at Zelda, but then saw the old woman was grinning at her. She smiled back and ate another mouthful of the stew. After the group had scraped the last drop from the pot, Zelda began whittling on a small stick. These were nice people, but they didn't seem to understand they were making a mistake. She honed the end of the stick to a sharp point and set to work picking a piece of stubborn jerky out of her gumline. After a fair amount of sucking and blowing through the gaps in her teeth and running her tongue experimentally around in her mouth, she was finally satisfied and flipped the homemade toothpick into the fire. She surveyed the young faces in the glow of the flickering firelight and leaned back against a log, waiting for a moment of complete silence to lend brevity to her point. "Tootin' ya horn 'bout Jesus is dangerous," she began. "I *did* like hearin' stories 'bout 'im outta dat little book. So long as da State folk don' find out, it don' hurt nuttin' ta give 'em a listen. But if dey ever catch any o' you'ns spreadin' stories outta it like its real, y'all is gonna wish you 'ad stayed home. Cuz like I said, State folk do stuff to ya dat ought nought be done."

Lelah, who was by nature a quiet person, poked at the fire with a long stick, glancing up to make eye contact with Zelda from time to time as she spoke. "That sounds like the people of Ninevah in the Bible. They used to do the most horrible things to their prisoners. Jonah didn't want to tell them about God because they had a terrible reputation for cruelty, so he ran the opposite direction from where God told him to go. That's how he ended up in the belly of a big fish."

Zelda held up her hand for Lelah to stop. "Girl, do ya mean ta make me believe dat dis dude gits swallered by a fish?"

"Not just any fish. It was a fish that God prepared specifically for that purpose,"[112] Chandra chimed in.

"Hah! Well, I guess dat learned 'im," Zelda crowed. She looked at Lelah out of the corner of her eye. "You really 'spect me ta believe dat?"

"It's the Word of God," Lelah stated matter-of-factly.

"It's no harder to accept than the idea of God coming down and being born as a helpless baby so He could show us how to live and become the sacrifice for our sins," Pastor Craig added.

Zelda shook her head. "Dat's da *stupid* trade Selah was talkin' 'bout. It's soundin' stupider ever time I hear tell of it." She turned back to Lelah and gestured for her to continue. "But go on. I do likes a good story."

Lelah coughed nervously and continued poking at the coals. "Well, when Jonah told God he was sorry and agreed to go to Ninevah, the fish spit him out on the shore—" At this, Zelda slapped her leg and let out a guffaw. Lelah smiled slightly and continued, "and then Jonah went to Ninevah and started preaching. He told the people God would destroy their city because of their wicked ways.

---

[112] See Jonah 1:17

And the amazing thing is, they listened! As cruel and wicked of a culture as they were, they listened to what he had to say and repented."

"Well, I declare!" Zelda said, her eyes wide. "Now, what exackly is *repented*?"

"Repenting is when you stop the bad things you've been doing and turn away from your old ways and start doing right," Garrison explained.

"Hmmm," Zelda nodded, waiting for Lelah to continue the story. "So dat's da end?"

"There's a little more," Lelah said.

"Well, say on!" Zelda demanded.

Lelah suppressed a giggle and continued. "When Jonah saw that God wasn't going to destroy Ninevah, he was mad. He knew how wicked they had been, and he thought they deserved it. But God helped Jonah to see that this was the wrong attitude. He told Jonah how the people didn't know their right hand from their left—basically, He meant that they didn't know right from wrong. God wanted to give them a chance to repent, and Jonah was the tool He used to show them they needed to change their ways. I guess we feel the same way about the State. Even if the people there treat us badly, someone has to tell them they are headed the wrong direction. Someone needs to tell them there's a God who loves them, and He will forgive them and accept them as His children if they turn to Him. Even if they don't want to hear it, they *need* to hear it. They need to know there's a better way—that they don't have to live in darkness. And who knows? Maybe it'll be like the people of Ninevah. Maybe they'll change their minds."

Zelda squinted her eyes and raised her eyebrows. "Now if *dat* happened, it really *would* be a miracle," she said. "Say, one o' you'ns wouldn' happen ta have one o' dem Bibles, wouldja? I woudn' mind hearin' dat story again, da way it talks it in dat book."

"Sure!" Lelah said, and went to retrieve her Bible from her pack.

After Zelda had listened to the book of Jonah in its entirety, read by firelight, she shook her head in wonder. "Dat's da best one, yet," she said. She looked at each face around the fire until she met eyes with Craig. "You's in charge, ain't ya?" she asked.

"Yes," Craig nodded.

"Well, if'n ya like, I can take ya where ya wanna go."

"Really?" Lelah asked. "You'd do that for us?"

Garrison shot Craig a look, but Craig was looking at Zelda knowingly. "It's a generous offer, but we wouldn't want to put you in any danger or distract you from your destination."

Zelda shook her head vehemently. "It ain't no trouble a*tall*. And it ain't gonna distract me from my destination."

"That's what we're afraid of," Garrison said.

Zelda glared at him.

"But if she knows the way…" Lelah began.

Lydia put a hand on her friend's shoulder. "Lelah, I think that's the point. She knows the way and she doesn't want us to get there."

Shock registered in Lelah's eyes. "Oh-ohhh," she said. "I understand."

Zelda stood up and stomped her foot. "Y'all is a bunch o' idjuts!" she exclaimed, grabbed her pack, and shuffled off into the darkness.

31

Macy settled herself down on a patch of thick, green moss and rested her head on her paws. The humans had packed up their bedrolls and cooking gear, put out the fire, and were sitting in a circle in preparation for Craig to talk while he held the precious object. Macy didn't understand this morning ritual, but she knew it was very important to the Kind Man, because He was always there, listening very attentively. At times, He would walk around the circle, lightly resting His hand on the shoulders of those present. Macy wasn't certain why He did this, but every time it happened, the human He touched seemed to change somehow.

Sometimes, the humans would ask a question, and Craig would turn over some of the thin, perfectly rectangular leaves in the object he was holding. Then he would stop and say something else while looking at the leaves, and that seemed to satisfy whoever had asked the question. After the time of looking at the precious object and talking about it, the humans would all retreat a short distance away from each other and talk to the Kind Man by themselves. Somehow, He was able to listen to them all at once and was with every one of them as they spoke. It was all very strange and hard for a dog to understand.

Macy used to grow impatient during the morning ritual until one day when the Kind Man showed her some of what was happening. The precious object was like any other thing the humans carried until they looked at the leaves inside it and spoke. When they did this, Macy could sense the humans growing stronger. One day when the group seemed especially tired and discouraged, Craig picked up the object and started talking. The clearing was suddenly flooded with light and filled with powerful winged creatures. Macy jumped up and started barking, running wildly back and forth within the circle. The humans didn't realize they were surrounded! The Kind Man laid His hand on her head to quiet her and let her know everything was all right; the creatures were there by His command. She watched as the humans were somehow strengthened by their presence, and then they vanished from her sight. After that day, Macy waited patiently while her bipedal companions held the precious object and discussed it, because good things happened for them when they used it.

On this particular morning, the Kind Man surprised Macy by sitting down beside her on the carpet of moss. He laid a hand on her head and smiled. She could sense a sadness in Him, and for a moment, she became uneasy. She licked His hand and watched His face, trying to figure out what was wrong. He could communicate with her better than any other person could—but today, the only thing she understood was that He wanted her to trust Him and obey. Macy wagged her tail and whimpered. It was her way of letting Him know that she lived to do this. If only the humans would listen and obey Him as she did! They might be able to avoid some of the hardships they brought upon themselves.

Every morning before he opened the precious object, Craig would close his eyes and talk to the Kind Man. Then he would look inside at the leaves and begin speaking while the others listened. This day was no different, except that the Kind Man went to stand behind Craig and laid both His hands on his shoulders. He seemed to be helping Craig somehow. Macy could sense love and strength flowing from the Kind Man into this human. There was something else, too. It was the same feeling she experienced when she had a full belly and a place to sleep and someone to scratch her ears. If a dog could form words to match feelings, Macy would have called it "peace." The Kind Man stood with Craig the whole time he was speaking, resonating power and life. Macy could still sense the sadness within Him, but she wasn't worried anymore. He had asked her to trust Him, and she would obey.

After the humans were done listening to Craig and each had spent time talking to the Kind Man, they shouldered their packs and started walking. Macy trotted to the front, just behind her Master.

As the day wore on, Macy grew restless. They were moving in the direction from which she had traveled long ago when she had followed the Kind Man from the outer docks to Adullam. She knew it wasn't a good place for dogs *or* humans. But the Kind Man moved resolutely forward, so she would follow. Soon she began to hear a strange humming sound. The humans couldn't hear it at all; but when she whimpered and glanced up at the Kind Man, He was looking at her over His shoulder. He nodded to let her know He was aware of it.

Toward the middle of the afternoon, the humans became aware of the hum. They seemed excited about it. "That must be the sound of civilization!" Garrison said eagerly. The younger humans became very animated and chattered among themselves, but Macy noticed that Craig was quiet. The Kind Man was communicating with him somehow, and Craig was listening.

"Let's set up camp here," he said when they came to a stand of cedars which formed a ring around a small clearing. "We'll get some good rest tonight and have a fresh start in the morning. Who knows? Maybe we'll meet some citizens of the State tomorrow. We'll need to be at our best."

The younger humans seemed a little disappointed to be stopping so early but busied themselves by finding a place to put their bedrolls. Macy watched as Craig stood a little apart from the others. She noticed that he wasn't making a place to sleep. After a while, he turned to the group and said, "I'm going to scout on ahead a little ways. I should be back before dark."

"I can come with you," Garrison suggested.

"No," he said quickly. "I won't go very far. Macy'll come with me, won't you, Mace?" He grinned at the dog. Macy wagged her tail and trotted over to where the Kind Man was standing, right beside Craig. "Don't make a fire," Craig said as he noticed the younger humans gathering stones for a fire ring. "Let's just play it safe. They'll discover us soon enough, but I'd rather them not take us by surprise." He started out of the clearing and then turned back. "If for some reason I don't come back before dark, don't come looking for me. Macy will lead me back if I get lost. And if I'm in some sort of trouble, I have a feeling she'll come get you. I want to know that you will all be here waiting. If you leave and are out wandering around, she may have trouble finding you." With that, he stepped out of the clearing and began walking. Macy was ready to jump in the lead; but this time, Craig seemed to be following the Kind Man on his own. She dropped behind and stayed alert for any unusual sounds or smells.

An hour passed. The human was still carefully picking his way through the forest, and the humming was getting louder. It made Macy nervous because it interfered with her ability to hear things that might be approaching. But the Kind Man was never nervous, and He still led the way.

The shadows began to lengthen, making elongated pantomimes of the surrounding trees. And then Macy noticed an unusual break in the forest ahead. The Kind Man was leading them toward it. Macy froze. She could hear something else above the humming. She couldn't identify it, but she could tell it was moving along the clearing up ahead, and they were headed right for it. Just as Macy was about to bound up to the Kind Man and give Him her warning bark, He turned around and held up His hand in the gesture He used when He wanted her to stay. She sat down in the leaves, whimpering slightly; and He held His finger to His lips, asking her to be silent. Macy watched as the Kind Man stepped into the clearing. Craig climbed up the ditch that ran along the treeline and paused at the edge, looking up and down it. It was all Macy could do to be still. She somehow knew with every ounce of her being that Craig needed to stay hidden—that he was in certain danger. She stood up and looked at her Master, Who once again gestured for her to stay. As she watched, Craig looked skyward, through the trees. Maybe he heard the noise as well. Maybe he was looking for its source. But he didn't *seem* to be looking. Instead, he started speaking to the Kind Man. And then he climbed the shallow ditch and stepped into the clearing.

Suddenly, the air was alive with sound—the sound Macy had heard earlier but had been unable to identify. It was one of the flying machines she had encountered years ago, swooping down to hover over the human. "You are under arrest. You are in violation of State law, which prohibits traveling through the Preserve unless under the jurisdiction of a State-sanctioned expedition. Remain here to be collected by authorities or risk adding further violations to your record."

This was more than Macy could handle. She jumped up and dashed toward the clearing, but one look from her Master froze her in her tracks. She waited as another flying machine arrived. This one was big enough to carry several humans. Before it even touched the ground, its doors opened and humans were jumping out of it. Macy watched as Craig was handcuffed and forced into the flying machine. The Kind Man never left his side. The machine rose into the air and traveled northward. She listened as the sound of its engine faded and all that remained was the constant, low-pitched hum she had heard for most of the day. Macy whined and settled down into the leaves.

32

CRAIG Goforth peered out the window of the helicopter as it rose from the surface of the old road. Once they were above the treetops, he could see the road intersected what appeared to be a suspended bridge or a giant pipeline stretching both directions as far as the eye could see. He would have liked to ask about it, but the noise of the helicopter made casual conversation impossible. Besides, his escorts didn't seem to be keen conversationalists. The only words spoken had come from the drone he had seen before he had climbed up the ditch and stepped onto the crazed, cracked sections of aged asphalt.

He wasn't certain why, but he knew the Holy Spirit had led him to the road. In his private prayer time that morning, he had felt the Lord was going to ask something very difficult of him. But Craig also knew that ultimately, the decision was his, whatever it was.

So when they arrived at the old road and he had seen the drone flying overhead, he was not surprised when the Lord asked him if he was willing to make himself known to the authorities. It didn't make sense to him to leave the youth behind, but there must be a plan. God always had a plan.

However, it was still his choice.

"Please protect the others, and give me the strength to do Your will," Craig prayed just before stepping out of the leafy shadows into the dwindling sunlight. "Please don't let them catch Macy. Send her back to camp," he added. He knew that Macy had proved invaluable to the group, leading them to water and shelter in inexplicable ways. And then he walked into full view of the surveillance drone.

Without being able to explain why, he knew he had done what God wanted him to do. As he waited for the authorities to arrive, he could feel God's presence surrounding him. Being handcuffed and transported in the helicopter all seemed strangely surreal, but God's presence was more real to him than he had ever experienced before. It was as if Jesus was sitting right next to him as they flew over the verdant, wooded hills. Suddenly, Deuteronomy 31:6, the scripture that was the theme of their Bible studies, came to his mind: "Be strong and of a good courage, fear not, nor be afraid of them: for the Lord thy God, He it is that doth go with thee; He will not fail thee, nor forsake thee."[113]

Soon, the lush green of the forest gave way to the steely barrenness of a walled city. Craig watched the rooftops of buildings passing beneath the belly of the chopper. There was no sign of anything green; in fact, the city seemed devoid of any color except gray. He had seen pictures of civilization before and re-membered glimpses of it from his early childhood: the colorful billboards…the lights…the greenspace of public parks. This area seemed dismally drab by com-parison. He glanced at his copassengers. They seemed to be staring into space, oblivious to their surroundings. Of course, he reasoned, this wasn't anything new to them. They probably traveled by helicopter all the time. He looked at their attire. It was skin-tight and seemed almost to blend into the seats, as if it was camoflauged specifically for the inside of a helicopter. *"Why would anyone need camoflauge like that?"* he wondered. As he was staring, one of the sol-dier-like escorts shifted in her seat; and as she moved, so did the pattern of her uniform. "It's like a chameleon," Craig said wonderingly, under his breath.

The woman turned to him and shouted above the engine, "Precisely. Stan-dard uniform for Pod-Operatives."

Craig gulped. How could she have heard him over the roar of the engine and the chopper blades? She hadn't been looking at him when he said it, so he knew she hadn't read his lips.

She fixed him with her green eyes, seeming to assess him. "We were told you were dangerous. You don't appear to be a threat, physically. And you don't even carry a weapon."

"You don't appear to be carrying one, either," Craig said. All the soldiers he had seen from old photos carried guns and knives, but this one wasn't carrying

---

[113] Deuteronomy 31:6, KJV

anything visible. And he didn't see how anything could be hidden in the scant space between this soldier's body and her clothes.

She stared levelly back at him. "I *am* the weapon," she said simply, and then resumed staring straight ahead.

A few minutes later, they began their descent to a landing pad on an otherwise unimpressive building. Upon landing, Craig was escorted from the rooftop to a small, box-like room with sliding metal doors. In the dim recesses of childhood memory, he remembered entering such a room before. *"An elevator, of course!"* Craig thought to himself. After the strange sensation of moving downward and gliding to a halt, the doors opened into a hallway that was the same, depressing hue as the rest of the city. The soldiers, surrounding him in a cluster of gray that mimicked the walls, ushered him forward to a wooden door at the hallway's end. The door was obviously handmade with expert craftsmanship and an eye for meticulous detail. It starkly contrasted with its sterile surroundings. As they approached, it swung open for them automatically, revealing a spacious office. A spartan desk faced the door, flanked by a full panel of windows overlooking the city. Craig gawked at the walls of the office. They were as full of color as the hallway had been devoid of it, covered from floor to ceiling in a mural. His breath caught in his throat. This wasn't just any mural. He recognized it. Landmarks of his childhood filled the walls. Had Adullam been under drone surveillance this whole time?

Suddenly a side door opened, and a dark-haired man of small stature stepped into the office. He seemed familiar somehow. He walked casually up to them, and the female soldier Craig had conversed with earlier positioned herself between him and their captive. "We were told he was dangerous, Dr. Moses," she said.

The man placed his hand reassuringly on the soldier's arm. "Not *physically* dangerous, Jayka… intellectually dangerous. *Spiritually* dangerous."

Craig's mouth dropped open. He knew that voice. "Yosi?" he asked incredulously.

Dr. Moses smiled. "Hello, Craig."

About the Author

Annika Goodwin grew up in the Ozark hills and loves being outside and hearing the voice of God expressed through His creation. She believes in the restoration of broken lives and has seen it first-hand in the lives of those who have participated in the New Life Restoration Center program in Hollister, Missouri. When not working her full-time job, she enjoys gardening, hiking, hunting, drawing, writing, playing with her cat, and spending time with her family and the extended family of her brothers and sisters in Christ.